CW00750545

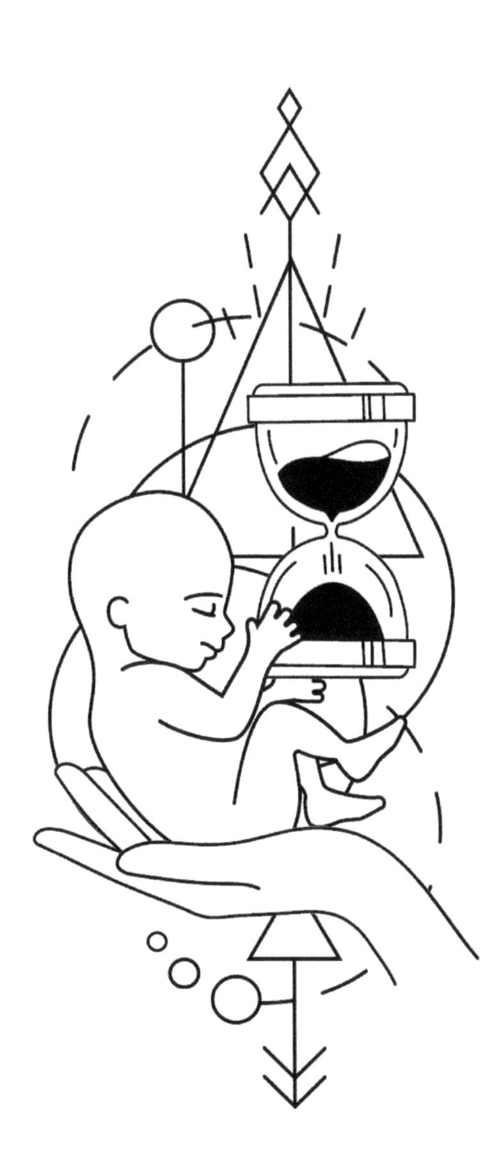

KENDRELL
PUBLISHING

THE BLANCHARD WITCHES

STITCHES IN TIME

MICAH HOUSE

The Blanchard Witches: Stitches In Time

First published 2021

Published by Kendrell Publishing, Birmingham, Alabama

Edited by Crystal Castle

Cover design by Paul Palmer-Edwards

ISBN: 979-8-9887296-2-4

This book is dedicated to a few special fans who are also dear to my life. Their support, friendship, and love mean the world to me. And their passionate enthusiasm for The Blanchards fills me with joy and pride. This book is for you...

Camille, Angela, Chris, Lori, Andrew,
Wendy, Val, and Tess

CONTENTS

Blanchard Family Tree

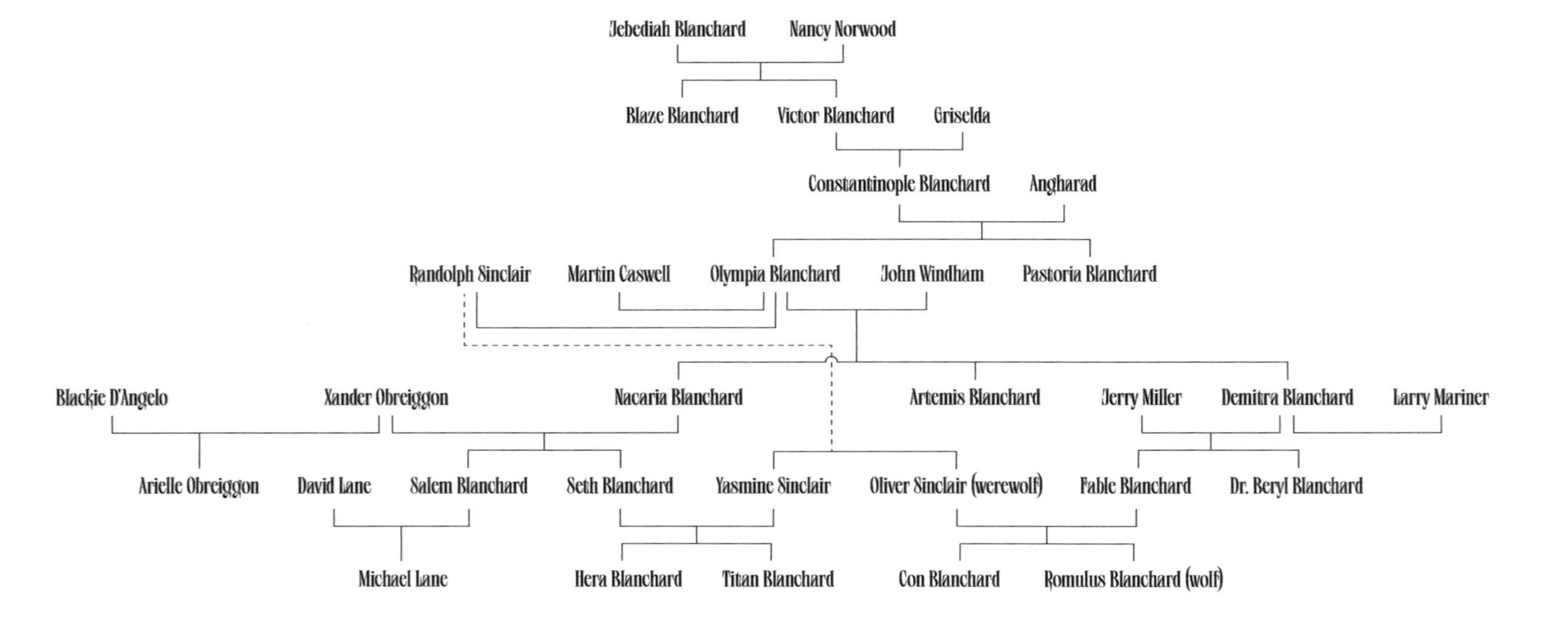

CHAPTER ONE

Blanchards Erased

Artemis surveyed her family with pride. And it truly was *her* family now. She inherited the responsibility of leading her clan of witches two years ago after the death of her mother, Olympia. Olympia had chosen Artemis as the next Hecate, the leader of their coven. Though she knew she would never measure up to the kind of Hecate Olympia had been, Artemis was finally settling in as matriarch of this large and diverse clan.

It was the first time since well before Olympia's death that the entire family and all its close friends were sitting down to a barbeque on the lawn. Artemis sat at the head of the long stretch of picnic tables. She smiled to herself as she admired her brood. The Blanchard family had expanded quite a bit over the years. Her sister Demitra was married now to a man named Jerry Miller. Though the marriage started off unconventionally two years ago, Demitra and Jerry were now very much devoted to each other. Artemis' youngest sister, Nacaria, was also married now—wed to the man she had loved all her life but had been unable to be with for two decades.

Nacaria and Xander shared two adult children, Salem and Seth. Salem was pregnant now, due very soon with a son she had already named Olympus, after her grandmother. Seth had two small children of his own with his wife Yasmine. Hera was four years old and baby Titan was born several months ago. Xander's daughter Cassandra, from his first marriage, was seated with her half siblings, enjoying herself more than she ever thought possible. Raised by her wicked mother to hate her siblings, Cassandra was forging relationships with them now after realizing she had been wrong in the convictions her mother placed in her mind. Xander's youngest daughter, Arielle, had been an honorary member of the Blanchard family for the last several years. Her mother Blackie D'Angelo, Nacaria's best friend, sat happily beside her daughter. Demitra's daughters, Beryl and Fable, were chatting between themselves while Fable's son Con rode on the back of his brother Romulus. The boys, born from a liaison with Yasmine's werewolf brother, were an interesting pair. Con, a boy, and Rom, a wolf, showed no signs of their father's evil. Fate had divided the werewolf strain inside the twins, splitting boy and beast back to their natural stations. The remaining two seats of the table were filled by family friends Zelda and Howard. Zelda, a renowned local psychic, was Olympia Blanchard's lifelong best friend. After Olympia's death, Zelda continued to watch over the family. Howard, the family attorney and financial manager, practically grew up with Artemis and her sisters. In fact, back in the day, Artemis almost married Howard. Her inability to master her magical powers proved a bit dangerous, causing Olympia to insist they end their romantic relationship. Though the embers lingered, they smoldered rather than burned as too many years of mere friendship resigned them to the status of friends.

As Artemis dug into her steak and potato salad, she joined the nonsensical conversations swirling around. She liked meals best when everyone spent the time talking about nothing. Too often her family dealt with more than their share of turmoil, making these times of frivolous chit chat seem golden. After a little while she felt tiny feet climbing the back of her chair. Two little arms wrapped around her neck.

"Hi there, Baby Girl!" she said, pulling Hera into her lap. "Did you finish your lunch?"

"Uh huh," the beautiful little girl said. "Hecate, I think it is time for the cake."

"What cake?" Artemis teased.

"The cake you made this morning, silly," Hera laughed. "Con, don't you think it's time for cake?"

"Yeah!"

"All right, children," Artemis smiled, kissing the top of her young grand-niece's head. "We'll cut the cake in just a minute."

"These kids are sugar-crazy!" Yasmine remarked.

"These kids?" Demitra laughed, gesturing with her fork at her grown daughters, nephew, and nieces. "All of you were at that age, too."

"Same thing with you and your sisters, Demmy," Zelda chuckled. "You an' your sisters were constantly stuffin' your faces with sweets. Kids is kids no matter what generation."

"And there have been quite a few generations on this land," Artemis sighed, looking out over her large family.

Looking around at the massive expanse of meadows, pastures, woods, and orchards around Blanchard House while he chewed his last bite of steak, Jerry nudged his wife next to him and asked, "How long has the Blanchard family lived here?"

Demitra's lavender eyes sparkled under the sunlight, as she wiped her mouth on her napkin and answered, "Oh, a very long time. Even before we were Blanchards."

"It's fun to think about, isn't it?" Salem began. "All the many ancestors who walked these same paths, maybe even sat right here on this same patch of grass. It's nice to belong to a homeplace that spans the generations."

"We are pretty lucky," Seth added. "This was a great place to grow up. I love that our kids get to run through these woods and fields just like we all used to do. And now we also have Oleander. I really do want to spend some more time in Charleston and get to know Dad's side of our family tree."

Oleander was the estate owned by Seth and Salem's father Xander Obreiggon. Though Arielle and Cassandra grew up there, Seth had never seen it before. Salem had only seen it twice since reuniting with their father. Now that their mother and father were married, Seth was eager to visit one day soon and learn about that part of his heritage.

"Nothing would please your mother and I more." Xander grinned.

"Oh do!" Cassandra exclaimed. "If you and Yasmine plan a trip out to see us, I'll show you everything there is to see."

Hera whined again behind Artemis' ear. "The cake, Hecate. The cake."

"I'll go get the cake, Aunt Artemis." Beryl offered.

"Thank you, Beryl." Artemis said. "It's on the counter. A big sheet cake, you can't miss it."

As Beryl stood up, a gentle breeze blew her honey blonde curls over her shoulders. She stood up and gathered the few empty plates from the table. Fable rose to help her, and together they started for the house to put the dishes in the sink and grab dessert.

Everyone went back to their chattering when suddenly the sound of crashing dishes brought everyone to attention. Fable stood alone, horrified as she stared at the empty space on the lawn where Beryl no longer stood. Only a heap of broken dishes in the grass marked where she had been moments before. Fable looked back to the picnic table.

"What happened? Where did she go?"

"Beryl?!" Demitra cried jumping from the table.

Zelda glanced at Artemis. "This is it. I know 'xactly where she is."

Artemis lowered her voice and replied, "Do you mean...."

"Yep," Zelda nodded. "You still got that picture your momma gave you? Everything is 'bout to change."

The picture Zelda was referring to was something Olympia Blanchard had entrusted to Artemis before she died. Upon bestowing the title of new Hecate unto her eldest daughter, Olympia confided something secret she had never shared before. She gave Artemis a photograph. The photo had been taken in Olympia's youth when she, Zelda, and Olympia's sister Pastoria were in their heyday. But there was a fourth woman in the photograph, Beryl. Olympia never gave Artemis an explanation of how a modern-day Beryl Blanchard had managed to be in a photograph taken 60 years ago. She only warned Artemis that Beryl was going to go through something difficult and Artemis would need to be there for her. Olympia also warned everything would change once the event took place. Clearly that event was happening now. Beryl Blanchard just vanished before their eyes. Zelda knew exactly what was going on. She had already lived it.

"Where is Beryl?!" Demitra cried, rushing to the pile of broken dishes on the lawn. She pilfered through the wrecked china as though it would somehow reveal her daughter's whereabouts.

Fable stood flabbergasted. Her sister just disappeared right before her eyes. She opened her mouth to say something but didn't. She felt odd. Like vertigo. She reached out to clasp her mother's arm to steady herself. Her fingers passed through Demitra's wrist. Demitra watched as her youngest child's hand passed through her arm and disappeared. Demitra looked up towards Fable, only Fable was not there. Fable was gone, too.

"What's happening?" Demitra screamed.

Seth jumped up from the table to run to his aunt's side. Dashing across the yard his left foot sprinted forward as his right foot came down. The right foot never touched the ground. Seth disappeared. Yasmine screamed at the sight of her missing husband. Her cry echoed from an empty space at the picnic table...as she vanished too.

"What's happening!" Nacaria exclaimed, grabbing Xander's arm. "Where did they go?"

Arielle lurched forward and swept her arms around her sister Salem. It was instinct. She wasn't sure why she was doing it. But Beryl had vanished. Then Fable. Then Seth. Now Yasmine. It stood to reason Salem would be next. The Blanchard cousins were disappearing right before everyone's eyes. Salem understood her sister's impulse. She clutched tightly to Arielle herself. Everyone remained silent. Baiting their breath, waiting for the next family member to evaporate. Seconds passed. Maybe a whole minute. Salem remained in Arielle's arms. No one else disappeared.

Breaking the stunned silence Artemis said, "Zelda, what just happened? I thought this was specific only to Beryl?"

Zelda's wild eyes told everyone she was just as bewildered as they were. "I ain't got a clue," Zelda gasped. "This is all new to me, too. I just know about Beryl. I remember Beryl. I don't 'member the others at all."

"What about Beryl?!" Demitra demanded, running back to the table to confront her sister and the old woman. "What do you two know about Beryl? About any of this? Where are my children?"

"We know where Beryl is," Artemis announced. "As for the others...I haven't the foggiest notion."

CHAPTER 2

Answers Are Worse Than Questions

From the long winding road leading to Blanchard House, a passerby might be struck with the sheer beauty of the place. The tall, three-story white country manse had a fourth story tower stretching up from the roofline over the wrap-around porch which encased the house (except for the new wing jutting out on the east side). Colorful flowers hung in porch baskets as blue morning glories lined the eaves. It was picturesque to say the least. But a passerby new to Daihmler would not have known that dwelling in the house lived a family of powerful witches—witches who were now gathered inside discussing the latest crisis to befall them.

"I want answers, Artemis!" Demitra shouted, banging her fists on the living room mantle. "Where are the children?"

"Why did only Beryl, Fable, Seth, and Yasmine disappear?" Nacaria asked. "The rest of us are still here."

"Maybe it's the second generation only?" Jerry offered. "The babies are all still here as well."

"But so is Salem," Arielle pointed out. "If something happened to take the second generation away, then why is she still here? Was it because I held onto her?"

"Whatever happened, it clearly only applies to Blanchards and not Obreiggons," Cassandra observed. "Arielle and I are still here."

"But Yasmine isn't a witch or a blood Blanchard?" Howard replied, pacing the living room carpet, more kicking at it than treading across. "Why is she gone?"

Demitra was tired of hearing guesses. She wanted facts, and it sounded as if Artemis and Zelda knew the facts. She settled herself in one of the winged-back chairs by the fireplace then turned to her sister and their old friend.

"You two seem to have answers. I want them."

Artemis turned to Zelda, "Should I start or you?"

"You go. I'll fill in what you don't know."

Artemis took a deep breath as she swept her long, dark hair back over her shoulders and began, "Before Mother died—"

"Mother!" Nacaria cried. "Mother died two years ago. How is she involved in this?"

"Let her finish, please," Demitra said. "We need to know where our children are."

Artemis continued. "The day Mother told me she was appointing me as the new leader of the family and the Coven, she gave me some information I would need to know. One of the things she told me was that Beryl was going to go through something one day. Mother said it would change Beryl's life forever, as well as ours. Then she handed me this." Artemis withdrew a small, framed photograph from a drawer. The Blanchards recognized it right away. It was a familiar piece to all of them.

"That's the picture of Mother, Aunt Pastoria, and Zelda when they were young," Demitra observed. "It sat on Mother's nightstand all our lives."

"Open it," Artemis instructed.

Demitra slid the back off the frame and lifted the piece of cardboard out. Withdrawing the picture, she noticed a portion of the photograph was folded. She lifted the folded end to reveal a fourth person. Beryl. Beryl as she was now, as she had looked a mere half hour ago. Demitra showed it to Nacaria, then the others. She turned back to her sister.

"How?" she asked. "Mother was what? Twenty-five? Thirty? How could Beryl have been there? Beryl wasn't even born. Hell, I wasn't born! Neither were you!"

Nodding in agreement, Artemis explained, "Beryl went to the past. She apparently knew Mother and Aunt Pastoria and Zelda way before any of us were alive."

It was a startling revelation, one no one was prepared to hear. Quiet, stunned faces looked at each other. It all seemed too preposterous to believe.

"How is this just coming out?" Howard asked. "Wouldn't she have said something by now? Was she sworn to secrecy by Olympia?"

"She wouldn't have known," Salem explained. "It hadn't happened yet in the timeline of Beryl's life. She obviously went there today."

"She's there now. Right now," Zelda said. "I 'member the day clearly. She came through that front door over there and had no idea she'd just stepped back in time. Then she saw 'Lympy and me and it sunk in."

Demitra turned her attention to Zelda. "You *knew* about this and never told us?"

"Yep. So did your momma. So does Pastoria. But you know well as I do, you don't tell the future to people."

"You tell the future all the time!" Demitra roared. "You're a psychic for Christ's sake!"

"That's diff'ernt," Zelda said. "That's guidin' people. This thing is sumthin' else." The old woman was unapologetic, almost defiant. She knew they would not understand, but they were young—or, at least, *younger*—there was so much only the very old could fully comprehend.

"I think we deserved to know this, Zelda," Nacaria argued.

"No, you didn't," Zelda replied. "No matter what you think, this is Beryl's story. Not yours. Even Arty has no idea what's gonna happen 'cause of this. Lympy didn't tell her noth'in more than showin' her that picture. She did that for a reason."

"Then you tell us!" Demitra demanded.

"Nope," Zelda said stubbornly. "I love you girls more an anything in this world, but my duty is to your momma. Tellin' the future could undo what's gotta come—what's *gotta* come. 'Sides, ain't a guarantee things'll go the same way this time. I know what happened in my past when I was there livin' this, but if Beryl makes one single diff'rent choice, it might all rearrange. So, there's no need in even talkin' about it till it's done."

"Till what is done?" Demitra asked.

"I'll let you know when it happens."

Xander had remained silent in the background, giving the Blanchard sisters time to ask the questions regarding their children. But he could not remain silent any longer. After all, he had children involved in this as well. He stepped forward and faced Zelda.

"You have explained Beryl's whereabouts. But where is my son and my daughter-in-law? And where is Demitra's other daughter, Fable?"

"I'd actually like to know that myself," Artemis added. "Mother never mentioned them to me at all."

Zelda sighed and shrugged her shoulders. "I got no clue. They weren't in my past with Beryl. I got no idea where the hell they went."

"Could they be there with Beryl now?" Salem asked. "Maybe it's like you said and something changed this time. Maybe for some reason it went differently today, and this time they all went together to Grandmother's past?"

"Naw," Zelda answered. "Cause I'd remember them now." The ancient woman leaned in for emphasis, trying to make them understand. "If the others went back in my younger days, I'd be rememberin' them now. But I don't. My memories are still just of Beryl back then. The others ain't with her."

"Then we have one witch in the past and three others lost to the ether, and we have no idea where they might be," Xander summed up.

"But Yaz isn't a witch," Arielle pointed out. "She doesn't have any powers. Wherever they are, she's the one who doesn't have any way to take care of herself."

Salem wrapped a reassuring arm around her youngest sister's shoulder. "Let's just hope she's with the others, and they will look after her."

CHAPTER THREE

Into the Past

Seth stood in the meadow. A sick feeling filled his gut. Something was definitely wrong. He had just been at home enjoying a wonderful family lunch at Blanchard House when he saw his two cousins vanish before his eyes. Now he himself was somehow transported to some place he had never been. Or had he? There was something very familiar about this ambiguous place. Very familiar. The position of the clump of trees in the distance for example. Three oaks it looked like. They reminded him of the trees in the front yard of Blanchard House. Only the oaks he saw now were a little smaller. Not to mention the fact that there was no house beside them. He could see a house far off in the distance, but it was clearly not the Blanchard home. Blanchard House was huge and crisp white. The house in the distance was little, shabby. It looked to be about the size of a small country farmhouse.

As he stood gathering his bearings, he saw the faint figure of someone walking beyond the trees in the nearby forest. It looked as though they were walking toward him. He kept watching until the figure came more into view as it entered the meadow. It was a woman. Seth walked toward her as she continued coming forward. From what he could see she was quite young, possibly only a few years younger than he, though exposure to weather made her appear older. It was hard to gauge. Despite the color of her sun parched skin, he could see she had many freckles. Her long red hair was tied behind her, and her clothes were very strange—old fashioned. She wore a dingy white blouse, much too loose and ill-fitted, and a faded light blue skirt which hung to her ankles. She marched with a confidence that intrigued him—it was almost an anger. Once they came face to face, he saw it was anger indeed.

"Who are you and what are you doing trespassing on my land?" she asked him. She looked him over and covered her mouth in surprise. "And naked!"

Seth looked down at himself. He was not naked. He was still wearing his yellow polo shirt and khaki shorts. "I'm fully dressed."

"I can see your legs," she gasped. "Men don't tromp around naked in front of women folk."

"I told you I am not naked."

He looked her over more closely, specifically her clothes. Her drab skirt had faint stains in places near her thighs—old dirt she'd wiped over the years which had not come out when washing. Her hemline had frays, probably from years of tromping across fields and being snagged on various limbs and briars. Her dingy blouse covered her from neck to wrist but was worn through at the elbows.

She still did not seem convinced that he was clothed properly but moved on to her more pressing point. "What you doin' on my land?"

Seth wearily replied, "I honestly don't know."

She gave him a stern look and asked, "You been in an accident or something?"

"No," Seth answered. "No accidents. I don't even have my car with me."

"What's a car?"

Seth understood a little better now. This woman in her long skirt and long sleeve shirt. No makeup. Hair tied back. Any other man might have freaked out at the realization that they had somehow been zapped into another time, but Seth had seen and heard much in his lifetime and so this wasn't completely foreign to him.

"May I ask you what year this is?" he asked the woman.

She eyed him suspiciously, squinting her sunburned forehead, "You sure you ain't hurt?" she asked. "You don't know the year?"

Seth placated her, "Maybe I did hit my head or something. Just tell me the year and where we are."

"It's 1876. This is Alabama. My name's Blaze. Blaze Blanchard."

Seth was taken by surprise. "This is Daihmler?"

"No, I said Alabama. I never heard of Daihmler. We are just outside Tuskyloosa. You know it?"

"I know Tuscaloosa very well," Seth answered. He took another bewildered look around at his foreign environment, "At least I used to."

I must be in Daihmler before Daihmler became a town.

Blaze gave him a suspicious look before replying, "I know just about ever'body in these parts, and I ain't never see'd you before."

"No, I am sure you haven't," Seth smiled. "Blaze Blanchard, huh? Any relation to a Jebediah or Nancy Blanchard? Or Victor maybe?"

"Jeb and Nancy was my folks. Dead now. Died a few years back. And Vic's my brother. But he's just 2 years old," Blaze snapped. "How you come to know about my family?"

"Because I'm pretty sure they are my family, too. My name is Seth Blanchard."

"Well, well, well," Blaze laughed, placing her hands on her hips and leaning back a little. "I shoulda know'd another one a you'd show up one day. Guess you a witch, too."

Seth did not expect to hear that reply at all, expecting he would have to expend a great deal of time explaining himself, then proving himself to this stranger. But she did not seem the least bit surprised by his statement.

"Um, yeah," Seth replied. "I am a witch actually. How in the world did you-"

"Met your cousin about ten-twelve years back. Girl called herself Fable. She told me all about your family. I was a little girl then. But I remember."

"Fable is here?"

"Oh no, she disappeared many days later. Some folks came and got her. Guess she went back where she come from. I expect same'll happen to you eventually. Come on back to the house with me and meet Vic. Should be up from his nap now."

. . .

Fable saw the small house in the remote field. She trudged across the muddy meadow toward it. Prickly weeds and cockleburs stung her legs as she moved. Large red fire ant beds spread across the field like minefields to sidestep. As she went she sent out a magical call to alert the ants not to sting her if she failed to miss one of the beds. She also took precaution and sent a similar plea to any rattlesnakes or copperheads that may be hiding in the tall growing grasses.

Closing in on the house, Fable saw a stream of smoke swirling up into the blue sky from the chimney. This seemed strange on such a hot day. Around the ram shackled house lay an array of antiquated farm tools caked with dirt. Behind the house stood a weathered barn. The place looked like one of those broken-down hovels cars pass by while driving long deserted southern highways. Old farm homesteads now the decaying remnants of a lost world. That world was now sitting in front of her, and it appeared to be still in operation.

As Fable neared the house a man came out of the barn. He wore frayed dirty overalls and was wiping sweat from his brow with a grimy handkerchief. He walked with a pronounced limp, and Fable noticed he was using a cane to help distribute his weight. He paused when he saw Fable. With his mouth hanging open, she approached him. Before she got any closer than a couple of yards he cried out.

"Nancy!"

A waif-thin haggard woman opened the door of the squalid house. She looked as if she may have been lovely once, but life here had long etched itself over her. She took one look at Fable and retreated back inside. A few seconds later she returned with a large quilt which she quickly tossed over Fable's shoulders.

"Girl why you comin out here to people's homes with no clothes on!" the man shouted.

"What?" Fable laughed. "I'm in a dress."

"Naw," the woman scolded, swiping her graying wiry hair from her brow to tuck it back in the bun atop her head. "I am in a dress. I don't know what you are in."

"It's a regular sundress," Fable scoffed, looking down at the lovely garment. "I paid $120 for this. There's nothing wrong with what I am wearing."

"And why you tellin' such lies?" the man scoffed. "Ain't nobody got a hundred dollars. And ain't nobody that does gone pay it on clothes."

Fable glanced back down at her lovely dress. She did pay that for it, and it was actually on sale when she did. Of course, how could she expect anyone living in a hovel covered with dirt to know fine taste?

"Honey you're showin your body to ever'body," the woman warned. "You best get in the house with me and let's figure out what you're about."

Inside the house the woman sat Fable down at a rickety table where Fable took stock of her surroundings. The house was rather stark. The table, four chairs, and a couple of wooden shelves stocked with jars, pans, and what looked like metal plates were all that filled the room. Two closed doors stood on the far wall, most likely leading to bedrooms. Beyond the table stood the soot-stained rock fireplace. A large pot hung over the fire in the hearth. The woman was cooking something.

"What happened to you, girl?" the woman asked. "You been attacked or something? Where's your clothes?"

"I told you I am wearing my clothes," Fable insisted. "Can you tell me where I am?"

"You're 'bout 20 miles outside Tuskaloosa. My name is Nancy Blanchard. That's my husband Jeb outside."

"What year is this?"

"You don't know the year?" Nancy exclaimed. "You touched in the head or something?"

"No," Fable replied. "I'm lost."

"Girl you're more than lost if you don't know what year it is. It's 1865."

"Fuck."

"What?"

"Nothing," Fable said.

One of the doors on the far wall opened as a young girl walked out. She had fire red hair and freckles. Fable smiled at her. The girl smiled back. Nancy told the girl to go get a dress for their guest to put on and the girl obeyed. When she returned to hand the scratchy woolen dress to Fable, she introduced herself.

"Hey, I'm Blaze."

...

Beryl knew instantly something was wrong. The dishes she had been carrying into the house had disappeared from her hands. The picnic tables housing her entire family were no longer behind her either. She was alone in the yard. Still, she continued walking toward the house. The house was the only thing remaining she knew. And yet even it was peculiar. Beryl knew the house before her was Blanchard House, but something about it was changed from the house she'd lived in her entire life. When she had still held the dishes in her hands, she was heading toward the backdoor of the kitchen. The door was not there now. And neither was the kitchen. Only a blank, windowless exterior wall stood where the kitchen should have been. Beryl turned around again, just to make sure one last time that her family were not in the yard behind her. The yard was empty. Despite this fact, she still knew she was home. This was unarguably Blanchard House. She wandered around to the front porch since there was no longer a back door to enter. As she made her way, she noticed the pool was gone as well as the wall around it. Her grandmother's rose garden was gone. And all the flowers along the porch were gone too. With the exception being the year after her grandmother's death—when Aunt Artemis was in mourning—flowers had always bloomed in hanging baskets and pots on that porch. Flowers were as much a facet of Blanchard House as the white painted exterior or the four-story tower.

There could be no explanation for the absence of them as well as the kitchen, unless...

I am in the past. Why she would have known this was a mystery to Beryl, but somehow, she knew it to be true. The oak trees, the house, the general size of the yard, the chicken houses in the distance, were all recognizable. But the differences told the story. The driveway was not graveled. The new addition of the east wing was gone. And the absence of the kitchen really cinched it. *Grandfather Windham built the kitchen*, she remembered. *This is Blanchard House before Grandfather came along. But how far before?*

Beryl walked up onto the porch. As she did, she could hear voices inside. She knocked on the front door and waited to see who was going to open it. Her great grandfather? Her great-great grandmother? She hadn't a clue.

The door opened and a beautiful young woman stood before her with long canary blond hair. She wore a peachy colored baby doll dress with a wide plum belt and long dangly plum colored hoop earrings. Beryl's initial thought upon seeing her was *I really need that outfit.*

"Hello?"

"Hi," Beryl nervously said. "I don't really know how to say this, but I have somehow—" she paused herself. How in the world was she supposed to explain this? How could she convey to this person that she had somehow launched herself back in time? She decided to just continue talking and hope for the best. "You must be a Blanchard," Beryl smiled at the blonde woman. "At least I am hoping you are, so maybe you'll understand and believe me..."

Beryl stopped talking and looked more closely at the face standing bewildered before her. There were no wrinkles, no age spots, no signs of the white hair which had been teased into an old lady hairdo all of Beryl's life. But the face...the face was definitely the same. It had been years since she had stared into those tender blue eyes.

"Hecate!" she cried as she pulled the startled woman into her arms and hugged her close.

"Who the hell is this person Lympy?" called a familiar voice from the next room.

Beryl let go of her grandmother and turned to see a sight so familiar it almost made her laugh. Zelda. Zelda looked just as ridiculous younger as she did old. Her mousy brown hair wasn't the magenta of the old woman she knew, but it was definitely still Madam Zelda, dressed in the most colorfully ridiculous attire. She wore an oversized orange and purple tunic wrapped at the waist with a long-braided cord.

Her flowy pants were fuchsia, which matched the scarf tied over the top of her head.

"Zelda!" Beryl cried rushing to hug her friend. Zelda pushed back with a suspicious eye, but Beryl didn't care. She was so relieved to have found people she knew, even if they did not know her. Another woman came into the room from the hallway. Her shoulder length brown hair cut into a bob was almost the exact same style as it would be sixty years later. "Aunt Pastoria!"

"Aunt?"

"Oh my," Olympia Blanchard sighed. "Miss, I think I am afraid to ask this question, but are you by chance from the future?"

Beryl whirled back around, "Yes! Oh, thank God you understand! Yes, Hecate. I am your granddaughter Beryl!"

"Well fuck me," Zelda exclaimed.

...

Yasmine stood at the door of Blanchard House dumbfounded by the sight in front of her. She'd known something was off when she suddenly became aware that everyone in her family was disappearing right before her eyes, leaving her standing alone in the backyard. When she walked around the house to the front porch and opened the door, she was not prepared for what she saw.

"Granddaddy!"

The silver haired businessman before her looked surprised. Before he could thoroughly react, a familiar voice sounded behind him. Yasmine watched as her grandmother, Olympia Blanchard—who had been dead for years—came into view.

"What's going on here?"

"Grandmother!" Yasmine rushed forward to embrace them both, pulling them into her arms. Oh, how she'd missed these two people, two of the dearest people from her life. "You're both here! You're both alive! How did you come back? Where is everyone else?"

"Come back?" Grandfather Sinclair repeated. "Who are you, young lady?"

Yasmine took a step backward from her grandfather. He did not seem to know her. Of course, there was no reason he should have. She had been much younger when he died. But her grandmother should recognize her. Why didn't she? Then behind them Yasmine noticed something she had not seen in a very long time, a shadow flickered across the far wall by the stairs. She recognized it immediately. She grew up with that shadow. Her mother-in-law.

"Oh my God! Nacaria," Yasmine gasped.

"Come in, child," Olympia beckoned, taking Yasmine by the hand and pulling her inside.

They walked into the living room, but it was not the living room as it was today. A different set of furniture and a few different art hangings on the wall filled the space, but it was a living room Yasmine recognized from many years ago. As she gathered her bearings the sounds of feet pounded down the staircase. Four little girls and a boy sprinted past, shouting loudly in play at one another. They disappeared through the doors of the dining room toward the kitchen. Yasmine clutched the stair rail, amazed at the sight of them.

"Which one of them are you, dear?" Olympia asked with a knowing smile.

"Huh?" Yasmine stammered, totally bewildered by the circumstances in which she found herself.

Olympia gave a reassuring squeeze to her hand. "Your hair isn't red enough to be Salem. Or blonde enough to be Beryl. Are you Fable or Yasmine?"

"What's going on, Olympia?" Grandfather Sinclair asked, rubbing his chin between his thumb and forefinger.

"I think this is our granddaughter," Olympia told him. "Aren't you, my Dear?"

Yasmine could only shake her head yes. She found the words after. "I'm Yaz."

Olympia's bright blue eyes sparkled as she embraced Yasmine again, this time of her own volition. She led her into the living room. "You know this happened to me once before. Many many years ago. Beryl showed up at my doorstep. You can imagine my surprise. So, I think I understand what is happening here. Are you aware?"

"I have no idea what's going on," Yasmine admitted.

"Somehow you've been flung backward in time," Olympia explained.

"Olympia, are you telling me that this woman is my little Yazzy?" Sinclair asked.

"Yes, she is."

A befuddled pride glimmered in his eyes. He was still not accustomed to such fantastical events, but he knew Olympia knew what she was talking about. Behind his gray mustache and beard Yasmine could still see the pride in his smile. He approached her with his arms spread wide and wrapped her in a loving embrace. She clung to him and cried. She had not expected to cry, but she did. She cried from fear of what was occurring, and she cried of love for this special man who shaped her life. She had never imagined she would ever have the opportunity to hold him again, and now she had it. The feel of his arms, the smell of the pipe tobacco in his beard and clothes. She never wanted to let go of him.

"Oh Granddaddy, Granddaddy."

Olympia took her arm and gently steered her out of the embrace, placing her on the sofa as she sat beside her. "Be careful not to tell us anything about the future, Yasmine. It is too dangerous for us all."

"I think we already crossed that threshold, Olympia," Sinclair said, wiping a tear from his eye. "This girl is clearly what—thirty? And from her initial reaction it is pretty plain to see that you and I are not alive anymore in her world."

"We do not need to be told anymore," Olympia advised. "Thank Heaven your Uncle Larry is on a work trip and your aunts are representing the family at the Summer Consort. With the exception of the children, it is only you, myself, and your grandfather in the house. No one else will run a risk. I doubt the children would ever remember you being here."

"Is it so terrible her being here?" Sinclair asked his wife.

"Her timeline could be altered if something is changed during her stay. It could undo the future of our family. Lives are at risk. Family history is at risk. We must be vigilant while she is here."

Yasmine had so many questions, but foremost on her mind was, "Why am I here?"

"That I cannot tell you, Yasmine," Olympia said. "I don't even know why Beryl was here 30 years ago. One day, she just disappeared again."

"Where did she go?"

"To where she belonged," Olympia smiled. "As will you, I suspect. Eventually."

"How?" Yasmine asked.

"I have no idea," Olympia admitted. "I assume the others on the other end of your timeline will figure it out and fix it."

"What do I do in the meantime?" Yasmine asked. "Just wait?"

"I am afraid that is all we can do for the moment."

CHAPTER FOUR

Tapestry of a Family

"How the hell can you be her granddaughter?" Zelda bellowed to Beryl. "She ain't even got kids!"

"Apparently she's going to," Pastoria smirked.

Olympia Blanchard directed Beryl into the living room. The living room was like an explosion of the 1960s. Avocado green pod chairs flanked the fireplace where, in Beryl's time, Olympia's more traditional wingback chairs had stood. Thick, high-pile tan shag carpet covered the entire floor and two paisley sofas in psychedelic colors flanked the rather mod coffee table. The white painted plank walls of Beryl's Blanchard House were nowhere to be seen. Swirly wallpaper with huge blue, green, and yellow flowers covered the wood.

"This is crazy," Beryl observed, turning around to see everything. "Are those actually lava lamps?"

"You don't like contemporary decor?" Pastoria snorted.

"Oh, don't be offended," Beryl apologized. "This is spectacular. You just must understand that Blanchard House *does not* look like this in my time."

"No?" Olympia frowned. "This is so very me. I'm shocked I'd change it."

"*Very you*?" Beryl laughed. "Wow. You really were different when you were young."

It was all so overwhelming. Not only to Beryl, but to the other women too. Of course, having been raised by legendary witch Constantinople Blanchard, Olympia and Pastoria had seen their share of fantastic things in their young lives and heard about many more. In the grand scheme of things, this probably was not that outlandish. Nonetheless, it was a remarkable moment. Zelda appeared the most fascinated of all, grabbing Beryl by the arm and pulling her to the vivid sofas.

"What's Lympy like old?" Zelda asked. "And me? You knew who I was so I must still be alive too!"

"I don't think I should say very much," Beryl replied. "I might inadvertently tell you something you might change. That could undo the future as I know it."

"Oh, I doubt that would happen," Olympia scoffed. "Tell us everything!"

Olympia's youthful eyes were gleaming in anticipation. She wanted to know it all. Who would be the next president? What stocks were going to soar? Would the world go to war with Russia? But mostly she wanted to know about herself. And when the utmost important questions she wanted answered was on her appearance in the future, Beryl was beyond shocked. Would she be thin or fat? Would she retain her blonde hair or go gray? Beryl understood at once this Olympia was nothing like her Olympia.

"I think my grandmother would warn me against telling you any of that stuff," Beryl said. "I shouldn't tell you anything about the future which isn't absolutely necessary."

Young Olympia made a pouty face, "Your grandmother sounds like an old fuddy duddy," she snipped, tossing her long hair over her shoulder with an exaggerated huff.

"Aren't you her grandmother?" Pastoria snickered. "Boy, you must change a lot, Olympia!"

"Hell Lympy," Zelda cried as she realized the possibilities. "Does this mean we can just go to the future if we want to? I mean if this girl can go backward, why can't we jump frontward?"

Pastoria appeared to be the only person in the room showing concern about how and why Beryl had come in the first place. Olympia and Zelda were much too concerned with the possibilities time travel might provide them.

"How did you even get here?" Pastoria asked. "What happened to send you to us?"

"I have no idea," Beryl replied. "We were all having a family cookout and I was walking back with Fable to bring the dishes to the kitchen when suddenly I was here in your backyard."

"Fable?" Olympia asked.

"My sister."

"I have two grandchildren?" Olympia's voice was excited at the prospect, which sort of surprised Zelda and Pastoria.

"You have lots of grandchildren," Beryl smiled. She shouldn't have said that, but for some reason she felt the others would find it amusing.

"No," Olympia said, shaking her head. "You are probably right. You really shouldn't tell me." Beryl guessed that her young grandmother had probably not been seized with a sense of propriety but was rather disheartened now at the realization she would one day be someone's old grandma.

"Do I have children?" Pastoria asked excitedly, clutching hands with Beryl.

"What did she just say about telling us about the future!" Olympia scowled.

"Well, you got to know that you do," Pastoria whined. "That's not fair."

Pastoria tapped her fingers on her folded arms staring impatiently at Beryl. She wanted an answer to her question.

Beryl shrugged and looked back to Olympia. "I don't know what to say. Do I tell her?"

Olympia waved her hand to the air in defeat and said, "Just tell her. Otherwise, she's never going to shut up."

"Yes, you have children and grandchildren."

"Yes!" Pastoria exclaimed. "I won't die a virgin."

"Girl, you ain't been a virgin in years," Zelda scoffed.

"Shut up, Zelda!"

"Don't start you two," Olympia warned. "Obviously, we have a problem on our hands here. This woman needs our help. She's family and we don't even know her name."

Beryl laughed at the bickering trio. They reminded her so much of herself, Fable, Salem, Seth, and Yasmine. It was a far cry from the women she had grown up with thinking of them as the pillars of propriety in her life. She outstretched her hand to shake and announced, "I am Dr. Beryl Blanchard."

The three women looked at each other as if Beryl had just said she was the mayor of the moon.

"A doctor?" Pastoria cried. "Like a real bonafide doctor?"

"Yes."

"Wow," Pastoria marveled. "There aren't many lady doctors around, not around here anyway."

Beryl gave a little nod of awareness and replied, "Many things change in the future."

"I knew a lady doctor once," Zelda declared. "Dealt with babies only though. Maybe she was more of a midwife come to think of it." Zelda stared upward to the ceiling as if trying to remember. Then her eyes lit up, and she grasped Beryl's arm excitedly. "You got men patients?"

"Of course," Beryl laughed.

"You ever see em' naked?" The way Zelda said the word *naked* sounded more like *nekkid,* and she had a mischievous glint in her eye as she asked. Beryl ignored the question. Luckily Pastoria broke the awkward second of silence.

"If you are really a Blanchard, then what is your power?"

"I heal people," Beryl replied.

"Like grandfather's brother," Pastoria remarked, nudging Olympia in the side. "Well, I can manipulate molecules, and Olympia can-"

"I'm very familiar with everything you guys can do," Beryl laughed.

"Enough of this idle chit chat," Olympia announced. "We need to figure out how to get this girl back home. And to do that we have to figure out how she came to be here in the first place."

...

Fable had dinner with the Blanchard family. Nancy Blanchard made a vegetable stew and cornbread. Fable ate it gratefully, although she found the meal rather tasteless. Like so many modern-day people, Fable always took flavor for granted. It never occurred to her before just how accustomed she had become in life to the availability of spices. Unseasoned food, straight from the ground to the pot, was not very tasty.

Across the table, the patriarch of this little family was staring daggers into Fable as he slurped down his stew. Fable had seen better table manners from her young son, Con. Finally, Jebediah Blanchard added words to his stare. "How did you manage to come here?"

Fable set her spoon aside and faced the three of them. "I'm just going to spit it out and hope you believe me. I am also a Blanchard. From the future. I think this is the same Blanchard land my family lives on in my time."

Astonishment filled the faces of little Blaze and Nancy while a look of cynicism crossed Jebediah's.

"You're from the what?" he sneered.

"I am—unless I'm mistaken on the gap in generations—your great-great-great granddaughter."

"Girl, I think you hit your head in whatever accident you was in," Jebediah replied. He went back to his stew with a gruff smirk on his face. With every spoonful he jammed into his mouth—spilling most back into the bowl or on his shirt—he eyed Fable as something to distrust.

Taking another bite of the tasteless stew, Fable went on, "Surely you must believe it's possible. After all, we are all witches."

"Stop talking," Jebediah grumbled, pointing his spoon threateningly at Fable.

"You a witch?" Blaze cried. "So is my momma and me."

"Really?" Fable beamed with a hopeful tone. "Then maybe you'll understand what happened and can help me get back."

Banging his fist on the table, Jebediah roared, "I said stop talking about this devil stuff!" From the intense expression tainting his women's faces, it was more than obvious to Fable that this was a frequently-avoided subject. "We are God fearin' round here. I done come from battle and lost just about ever thing I ever owned 'cept this farm. Lost the use of my leg and I seen so much blood shed and death that I don't sleep too good no more. What I need in this house is some peace and some Christian livin'. I done told my wife and my youngen we ain't got nary bit of room in this house for the devil. I done seen enough of his work on the battlefield to last my whole life. Don't be bringing him into this house."

"Mr. Blanchard," Fable said, trying to remain calm—no easy task for her when faced with ignorance. "The devil has nothing to do with witches. If you let me explain to you—"

"Not a word to be said in this house on this matter," he insisted. "You can stay here tonight cause it's getting' dark out. But tomorrow morning you get out of here and don't you come back."

The family finished the meal in silence. It was strange to Fable to witness a Blanchard with an aversion to witches. It never occurred to her that the witchery was not always a part of the Blanchard line. Clearly it was Nancy's family who carried the bloodline.

After dinner was over, Fable tried to help clean up but was told to go to bed. She had no idea what time it was, but she knew it couldn't possibly be later than 8 p.m. She did not know what else to do but obey Jebediah's wishes. She slept with Blaze in her room that night, but the two of them did not go immediately to sleep. They talked at a low whisper to keep Blaze's father from hearing them.

"You're really a witch, too?" Blaze whispered.

"Yes, I am," Fable whispered back. "All Blanchards are. At least my Blanchards are. I guess it is your mother that brought the powers to the Blanchard family name."

"Mama's family was Norwoods. They are the ones with magic. Used to be gypsies," Blaze replied.

Gypsies, Fable thought to herself. *Interesting*.

"Do you have any special ability?" Fable asked.

"Ability?"

"Powers? Can you do anything that only a witch can do?"

"I can make stuff float," Blaze confided. "Heavy stuff. This one time I lifted up Daddy's wagon just by lookin' at it."

"That's a great power," Fable said. "I can talk to animals, and they can talk to me."

"Really?" the girl said excitedly. "That would be nice. I might could get animals to play with me."

Fable immediately felt lonely for the little girl. Blanchard children typically always had built-in playmates in the future. "Do you have any brothers or sisters, Blaze, or is it just you?"

The little girl frowned sadly, "I had a baby brother, but he died when he was a baby. Momma said she had a boy before me too, but he died when he was two."

"That's awful," Fable frowned.

"You got brothers or sisters?"

"I have a sister named Beryl. And cousins I grew up with that are like my brother and sisters. Salem and Seth. Salem can make time stop and Seth can change the weather."

"Both those things would be good to have on the farm."

...

Blaze Blanchard cooked dinner for Seth while he played with her little brother. A few years ago, Seth would not have known how to entertain a three-year-old child, but little Victor was not much younger than his own daughter Hera. A few times it struck him as how incredible it was that this child in his lap was his great-great grandfather.

"I was about 8 when your cousin Fable showed up at our doorstep," Blaze told him. "Boy my Daddy was not happy 'bout that. He never did keep with witches. My momma never told him what she was till way after they was married. Then I came along, and he nearly beat me to death ever time I did anything witchy. Learned to just keep that stuff quiet—even from him."

"Sounds like a mean man, your daddy."

Blaze didn't understand the drawn conclusion. She sort of furrowed her brow and replied, "Naw. He weren't 'specially mean. Just didn't hold with witches. His papa was a preacher. Bible was real important to my daddy. But he weren't mean, really. 'Fact, he did some real good deeds in his day. Helped a lot a slaves get away to up North."

"He did?" Seth gasped. "I did not know that. He worked on the Underground Railroad?"

Blaze gave him a puzzled glance. "Ain't said nothin' 'bout working on a train. He just hid out slaves tryin' to get North. We got a root celler hid under some overgrown bushes out in the yard. He hid a lot of folks there overnight 'till they could rest up and eat and start back runnin."

"How did your parents pass?" Seth asked.

"Pass what?"

"Die?" Seth clarified. "In my time we generally say *passed*."

"Why?" Blaze asked, turning around with the pot and spoon she was stirring it with in hand.

"I don't know," Seth answered. "It sounds nicer, I suppose."

Blaze continued to look at him in consternation. "But they're dead. How can calling it somethin' diff'rent make that be nicer?"

Seth shrugged. It really was an absurd practice.

Blaze went on with her opinion. "My folks died. They didn't pass nothin 'cept into the ground." She returned the pot to her black iron stove and whisked its contents. "People die. That's part a'life. Nuttin' to try and make sound nicer. Happens to ever'body. Daddy died in '73."

"From what?"

"I don't know," Blaze replied very matter of factly. "He just stopped livin'. Died out in the field clearing it."

"And your mother?"

Blaze pointed to little Victor. "Died givin' birth to him. Since then, he's been my responsibility."

Seth looked at the little boy, then back to his older sister. He felt sorry for the young woman—much too young to bear such weighty obligations. "So, you live here and take care of him?"

"Yep. Farm's going to seed for the most part. But I keep enough alive to feed us."

"How old are you?"

"Nineteen. I think," she said.

She looked older than that. Seth felt sympathy for her. It was then he realized he owed her a great deal. This girl gave up her life to raise this baby—her baby brother. Victor Blanchard who would one day become the father of Constantinople Blanchard, who would be the father of Olympia. Blaze Blanchard, whether she knew it or not, was single handedly responsible for keeping the entire Blanchard family line, and land, intact for the future generations. And Seth had never heard of her before. Not being his direct ancestor, she had apparently become lost in the family lineage. He'd heard stories of Constantinople. Even one or two about Victor. But no one had ever told any of the modern day Blanchards about a girl named Blaze. But Seth promised himself that would no longer be the case. He'd make sure his daughter and son, and his nephews, all knew the name Blaze Blanchard—the ancestral aunt whom they all owed their lives to.

"Is this the Civil War times?" Seth asked, suddenly realizing where in the past he had landed.

"The what?"

"The war!" Seth repeated. "The Civil War. The War Between the States?"

"Oh! That ended years back even before Daddy died."

"Did he fight in the war?"

"Course he did!" Blaze exclaimed. "'Bout all the men did."

"Which side was he on?"

"The Confederacy a'course!"

"But if he didn't have slaves, why would he have fought for slavery?"

"Cause that was the way we lived. If'n he'd fought for the North, men round here woulda burned this farm to the ground." Blaze leaned a little closer as if confiding something secret. "But he didn't hold with keepin slaves. That's why he helped 'em if they came by here runnin' away. Said God was the only true Master of man."

"That's good to know," Seth replied. "Slavery was a terrible institution."

"What you people do with negroes where you come from?"

Seth was aghast to hear the word. It was almost as jarring as the other N word. "First of all, we do not call them that. It's offensive."

"Offensive?"

"An insult," Seth clarified. "Where I come from Black people are doctors, lawyers, mayors, governors, even presidents."

"You crazy boy!" Blaze laughed. "Ain't no black ever gone be president."

"His name is Barack Obama, and he certainly was the president...for two terms."

"Well, I'll be..." Blaze was flummoxed. "What a future."

"I think you'd be very surprised at how much changes in a couple hundred years," Seth smiled. "Women get to vote. Black and white people live alongside each other as friends and neighbors. Women have babies without husbands. Gays can marry!"

Blaze whirled back around in complete confusion. "Women folk have babies and ain't married?"

"And nobody thinks anything about it," Seth smiled. He was rather enjoying teaching about the future.

"But what are gays?"

Seth laughed as he began riding little Vic up and down on his knee. "People who love their own sex...homosexuals."

"Huh?"

Damn the world comes a long way, he thought to himself as he leaned back in his chair to try to explain to Blaze. "Gays are men who fall in love with men and women who fall in love with women."

"What are you talkin' 'bout? You talkin' about *sodomites*?" Blaze asked. There appeared to be an indignant tone to her voice. Clearly she did not approve of such goings on. "Sodomites, like in the Bible when God wiped out the city?"

"I guess," Seth continued, not quite certain if they were referring to the same things. He wasn't all that familiar with the Bible. "Men who find themselves attracted to other men and women to other women. In my world they are free to be together. They won the right to get married several years ago."

Blaze was never so confused in her life. She leaned in on her scuffed elbows and asked for clarification. "You tellin' me men get married to other men where you come from?"

"Some do. Yes."

"And don't nobody kill 'em?"

Seth frowned. Blaze did have at least a minimal understanding—obviously her frame of reference leaned more toward this sort of love being an abomination. "Well, sadly there are always some idiot backward people around, but for the most part it's widely accepted. People have the right to marry whoever they want."

Blaze pulled a chair to the table and stared into her descendant's eyes. "How they have kids?"

"Adopt. Or surrogacy usually."

"What's that?"

"Where you pay a woman to have a baby for you."

Blaze's astonishment was growing in leaps and bounds as Seth' descriptions of the future blew her mind. "I don't understand at all. You can pay for somethin' like that? And these people...these gays...they want to be like this? They want to be together?"

"Yes," Seth smiled. "Two men or two women can love each other just as deeply as I love my wife or you might love your future husband."

Blaze made a face. "Well, I don't got no use for a husband. Never met a man I took to. So, you're tellin' me in your world girls can get married to other girls?"

It suddenly occurred to Seth as to why Blaze Blanchard never married or had children of her own and had become lost to the Blanchard family history. He left her statement where it was, but now he had a clearer understanding.

...

It was a surreal experience to sit under the oak tree and watch herself as a child playing with her cousins in the yard. Yasmine felt as if she were being provided some sort of gift to reconnect with that lost part of herself which time and experience had dulled in her memory. Watching little Yasmine run around was giving her a fresh perspective she hoped would come in handy with her own children—when and if she ever returned to her own time. Yasmine supposed she should have felt a little frightened being trapped in the past, but with the exception of missing her husband and children, she felt immensely happy. These had been golden days in her childhood. She missed these young faces—missed her grandfather and grandmother so much. Being back was something she found herself treasuring. She savored every moment.

Many thoughts rolled through her mind. Mostly about how fortunate she was to have had this childhood. Fortunate to be part of such a close knit and wonderful family. Though she wished she could see the aunts and Uncle Larry again, she understood the danger involved. It was lucky they were away for a few days. Her thoughts were disrupted suddenly as her younger self rushed over to her. Yasmine felt it was vain to consider her younger self pretty, but she also had to admit little Yasmine was truly adorable. Soft brown hair. Bright rosy cheeks. And the most glisten innocent eyes.

"Hi," the little girl said, plopping down beside her on the soft grass under the shade tree. "What's your name?"

"My name is Yasmine."

The girl looked surprised. "Mine is too!"

"I know. You are named after me."

"I am?"

"Yes. I'm your cousin."

"You are?"

"I am."

"I didn't know I had any cousins," the little girl smiled. "Did you know my mother and father?"

"I did. They were very nice."

"They died," the little girl frowned. "My brother too. His name was Olley."

Yasmine felt her tears swelling. They matched the eyes of her younger version. That sweet little girl was still in such pain. It was a pain she hid from everyone else. Big Yaz had nearly forgotten how long she'd wrestled her anguish when she was a child. It could only have been a few months since the accident that took that precious girl's family away from her. Yasmine held Little Yaz in her arms. Comforting herself was perhaps the strangest sensation she had ever experienced.

"You do have cousins though," adult Yasmine sighed, gesturing toward the grass where the Blanchard children were playing tag. "You have Beryl and Salem and Fable and Seth."

"Yes, but they aren't my real cousins."

"Oh, but they are," Yasmine told her. "Or at least they will be in your heart as you grow up. They love you very, very much."

"Seth doesn't!" little Yaz huffed, shooting him a perturbed look across the yard. "He calls me Yaz the Spaz and puts gum in my hair."

Yasmine couldn't help but chuckle. *Yaz the Spaz*, she had forgotten about that. She watched Seth running around several yards away. She had forgotten how mean he used to be to her when they were little. She knew now why he had been. She hugged the little girl closer to her and smiled.

"You know he's only mean to you because he likes you, and he doesn't know what to do with those feelings. Believe me. I know what I'm talking about. I used to know a boy very much like him when I was your age. It'll all work out the way it's supposed to. I promise."

"I miss my brother," little Yaz confided. "Seth says he's my brother now. Sometimes he sleeps in my room on the floor when I'm scared. I guess he's nice sometimes."

Her brother. Olley. Patric. Patric the werewolf. Yasmine shuddered when she thought of what all was to come many years from now. It then occurred to her that Olley was still alive. That sweet innocent girl may not be aware of that, but he was. Somewhere up north being taken care of by a man named Teague—the werewolf who turned him while trying to save him from the car accident. For a moment, Yasmine wanted to leave Daihmler and travel north to find Olley. Perhaps if she did, she might alter the outcome of his life. But then the better part of herself remembered the importance of what Grandmother had said. Yasmine must not change anything in the past otherwise she would risk dissolving the future as she knew it. Any little alteration might undo her marriage to Seth, the birth of her children, perhaps end lives. Certainly, it would end lives. If Yasmine found Olley now and stopped him from becoming Patric, Fable would have never had Con and Rom. And those boys were Yasmine's nephews. She loved them both very much. It didn't even matter that Rom was a wolf. He was her blood, and she would never want to live in a world without either of them. She swallowed the desire to save Olley. It was too late anyway.

"I was hoping you'd follow that line of logic," came a voice behind her. It was Olympia. Yasmine had almost forgotten how adept her grandmother used to be at reading thoughts. "Yasmine, dear, run along and play while I speak with big Yasmine."

The little girl ran off to join the others who were now running off to the apple orchard. Olympia sat down on the grass beneath the tree beside Yasmine. Even that was strange to Yasmine's eyes. She had not seen her grandmother able to sit on the ground—well, since she was little.

"I have no idea who this Patric person is, but it's best if you keep everything you know to yourself. And thank you for explaining your existence to your younger self as being a cousin. I doubt she will remember you when she's older, but it could be a problem if she does."

"Maybe I should go to a hotel or something?" Yasmine suggested. "Especially if the aunts and Uncle Larry are coming back soon."

Olympia stared out across the yard, watching the breeze blow through the flowers and grasses. She wasn't exactly sure herself what they should do, but they didn't have to make that decision now.

"We have time to consider that later," Olympia replied. "The Consort is in Miami this year. Artemis and Demitra will be away for several days. Larry will be gone a week. I don't think you'll be here that long."

Yasmine looked into her eyes and asked, "How long was Beryl here when she popped into your past?"

"A long time," Olympia said. For a moment she appeared to be reflecting, but on what she never divulged. "But there were other circumstances involved. If memory serves me, whatever spell brought you here faded after about a week."

"But Beryl didn't go back home?"

"No, she didn't," Olympia answered.

"Can you tell me why?"

"I'd rather not," Olympia admitted. "It wouldn't change anything in your time, but your knowing might alter something in my time. I cannot risk that. I do not think you fully understand how precarious all this is. Just trust me, my dear, even though you don't know me very well."

"Know you?" Yasmine laughed. "Grandmother, I know you far better than you probably realize. You remain the most important figure of my life, except perhaps Seth and our children."

"You see, Yasmine," Olympia cautioned. "I shouldn't know that. Now for the rest of my days I have the knowledge that you are ultimately supposed to end up with my grandson."

"I'm sorry!" Yasmine cried. "Have I messed it all up now? Will things change now?! I can't live without Seth in my life! What if I just undid our family?"

"Relax, child," Olympia said, patting her hand. "I am a wise and seasoned witch. I assure you I can continue onward without endangering your family with my knowledge. However, you see what I am talking about. Please do not tell me anything more, ever. But between you, me, and this old oak tree, I think I am thrilled to know Seth ends up with you. He has looked after you ever since you came here. Oh, he picks on you quite a bit too. But I've had my suspicions that he has a little youthful crush."

Yasmine looked off into the distance, lost in a memory. She gave off a soft chuckle—not one of amusement, more one of realization. She ran her hand through her long brown hair and turned to her grandmother. "I really should have known that you knew."

Olympia eyed her quizzically, "I don't quite follow, dear."

"That day," Yasmine began. "That day we announced to the family that Seth and I were in love. It took everyone by surprise...everyone except you. Looking back, you were the only person who immediately accepted and celebrated the turn of events. *You already knew.* And you knew because you and I sat right here, right now and I told you."

Olympia patted her hand. "The circle of time is an extraordinarily interesting thing, isn't it?"

Yasmine laid her head upon Olympia's shoulder. They remained like that for a long time. No words were spoken, but Olympia knew. This young woman had missed her very much. As long as Yasmine needed to sit there holding her hand with her head against Olympia's arm, Olympia would stay under the tree with her. Once this lady went back to her own time, these would be memories Yasmine would hold onto the rest of her life. And it comforted Olympia to see firsthand what kind of loving, caring young woman that little lonely girl playing in the yard would turn out to be.

CHAPTER FIVE

The Hecate's Vault

Jerry Miller was in the middle of making a row of giant sandwiches from the leftovers in the fridge when Howard Caldwell came into the kitchen. The counter was covered with a smorgasbord of lettuce, ham, turkey, cold chicken, pickles, tomatoes, and sliced cheese. Howard marveled at the spread.

"Only way I can help I guess," Jerry told his friend. "You want one? I'm making lunch for the girls while they're all in the living room trying to figure this shit out."

"And boy is it a lot to figure out," Howard chuckled.

Jerry liked Howard. He liked having another every-man around amidst this world of magic and mystery. Howard helped ground him in a landscape where he felt he had no footing. "I know I'm new to the family, but is this kind of thing normal around here?" Jerry asked.

"Well, I wouldn't say *normal*, but then again it isn't sending anybody into shock," Howard replied as he tossed a rolled-up piece of ham into his mouth. "I mean, Nacaria was a shadow on the wall for more than twenty years, and once Salem sent herself back in time and Olympia had to rescue her. Then there was that time that werewolf tried to kill everybody. So, I guess it's just the life of a Blanchard."

Jerry looked a little surprised as he popped a slice of pickle into his own mouth. "You seem to be pretty calm about it all, Howard."

"Well Jerry, I have been around this family all of my life. I guess I am used to it. Gotta admit though I am pretty worried for Yaz. That girl is like a daughter to me, and she's out there with no powers to protect her. I sure do hope she's with the others."

"Xander seems to be more at ease than I'd expect," Jerry said of his brother-in-law.

"You have to remember, Xander's a witch too. So, this kind of stuff isn't weird to him the way it is to us."

In the living room, the ladies of the family were discussing scenarios and possible ideas to rescue the missing Blanchards. Cassandra, Xander, and Arielle were listening, but keeping a respectful distance and staying out of the planning for the most part.

"I know for a fact Beryl is by herself in the past," Zelda said. "From that we can assume the others went somewhere else. What we gotta figure is where?"

"And why?" Salem offered. "Why did any of this happen?"

Demitra beseeched Zelda once more for clarification, "Zelda, did any of you ever know the reason why Beryl showed up back when you were young?"

"Naw," Zelda answered. "We never did get a reason. She was just there all the sudden. Then she wasn't."

"She simply disappeared again?' Fable asked.

"Don't rightly know," Zelda explained. "I what'nt there when she left. I had my own apartment back then. I was out here to the house a lot, but not all the time."

"And Mother never told you anything about how she left?" Nacaria asked.

Zelda rested her chin on the edge of her palm which was propped up at the elbow upon her knee. She zoned out momentarily, reflecting on the past before she spoke again, "Your momma didn't talk 'bout it much. Figure'd it was some'thin she didn't think I needed to know or else maybe it was painful to her. You see, we all got kindly close to Beryl back then. Losin' her was hard."

"I had no idea you felt such a connection to her." Demitra commented.

Zelda lifted the folds of her skirt and refolded them over her legs, fidgeting as she revealed a secret emotion. "You all know how close your momma, me and Pastoria were. The three amigos. Well, for a time we was four. But we had to forget all that when Beryl left. And then when she was born and growin' up; Well, it weren't the same cause she didn't know us like that then."

Artemis was sitting on the sofa, pensively in thought. She was auditioning many theories in her mind of why any of her nieces and nephew might have disappeared from this plane of existence. Several ideas occurred to her but none which really gave her a satisfactory feeling. But suddenly one did.

"Something just occurred to me," she said, raising her head as if having an epiphany. "Remember when we fought Atheidrelle? Remember how she hurled that chandelier at Beryl and Beryl caught it in one hand? She caught that heavy iron fixture like it was a tennis ball. Also, Atheidrelle threw that spell at her which was meant to tear Beryl apart—the same one she used to kill poor Forest—"

"And it did nothing to Beryl!" Nacaria chimed in. "Beryl sort of shook for a second and nothing more. It had no effect on her."

Artemis pointed her index finger at Nacaria in registered agreement. "Exactly. And before Mother died that night," Artemis reflected, "she confided in me something else about Beryl. She told me 'It's called the God Strain.'"

Xander suddenly snapped to attention. "What did you say?"

The Blanchards turned toward him, surprised by his sudden interest. Demitra walked closer to her brother-in-law, anticipating that perhaps he knew something now.

Artemis approached Xander as well, continuing with her thought, "Mother told me Beryl was changing. She called it The God Strain."

Xander peered intently into Artemis' eyes. "Are you certain Olympia used those words specifically?"

Nacaria placed her hand on her husband's shoulder. "Darling, what do you know about it? What is The God Strain?"

With his wife and two sisters-in-law surrounding him, Xander felt pressure to answer but wasn't sure he had any information to impart. His brow furrowed as he struggled to find the words to explain what little he knew. "I have never known anyone who has known one. I didn't even know it was real."

"What is it?" Demitra cried impatiently.

"My father talked about it once, and once I heard Atheidrelle speaking with her brother Thaddeuss. She flippantly remarked how she wished she had the God Strain so that she could rule over all the witching world."

Artemis was losing patience, resorting to her trademark wringing of her long raven hair whenever she was frustrated--a quirky characteristic Salem, who was doing the same thing now, shared. "Xander you still are not telling us anything. What exactly is The God Strain?"

"I really don't know," Xander admitted. "It's not a part of our world. It is something else altogether. Something powerful. More powerful than any witch can ascend to."

"How do we find out more about it?" Salem asked her father.

"I don't know if you can," Xander said. "I don't know if there are any witches around today who know much more than I do. It is a term steeped in legend; its origin and its connotation has been lost over the generations. In all my years on the Witches Council, that phrase never came up. I think it is beyond our sphere."

Salem looked at Artemis. "Maybe there's a book in the vault that mentions it."

The vault was the secret room under the kitchen stairs where all the Blanchard family spell books, records, and potions were stored.

Artemis turned abruptly to her sisters but said nothing—still turning her thoughts over in her head. Demitra and Nacaria noticed the change in her demeanor as they waited, watching her turning something over and over in her head, yet saying nothing aloud. Demitra exchanged puzzled looks with Nacaria--Artemis knew something no one else did, and she was not very good at concealing it.

"What is it, Artemis?" Nacaria asked.

Artemis remained silent. Pondering. She shouldn't tell them the final secret her mother had imparted to her. It might be too dangerous. Too much to bestow upon a lesser witch. Artemis only knew because she was the guardian of the family now. The coven leader.

"Artemis!" Demitra exclaimed. "The look on your face. What do you know?"

Artemis snapped back to reality and addressed her sisters. "I am not certain that I actually know anything. But there is a chance I might. I must investigate. I need everyone to leave the house for a while."

Nacaria took an indignant step back and raised her voice to her sister. "What? Leave the house? Why?"

Artemis opened her mouth to say something, then hesitated.

"My children are missing!" Demitra shouted. "If you know something, you owe it to me to tell me."

"Me too!" Nacaria cried.

Artemis couldn't. There was nothing more she wanted than to share what she knew with her sisters. She had always shared everything with her sisters. But her new role complicated things now. She was not a sister any longer. She was Hecate, the coven leader of the Blanchard witches, and that responsibility carried great discretion. Her mother cautioned her on that subject before she died. There would be things Artemis would always have to carry alone for the protection of the family... and sometimes the world.

Taking one last wring of her hair in both hands she flipped it back behind her and declared, "Everyone must leave. Go eat your lunch in the kitchen, and then I need for everyone to go away from Blanchard House for a few hours."

Demitra was defiant. "No," she said. "This concerns us all."

The air in the room was tense. Everyone was on edge. Everyone was concerned with their lost loved ones, and no one felt this was a time for secrets. Only Artemis understood why, that even in the most pivotal of times, some confidences cannot be betrayed.

Zelda understood. Perhaps she was the only one who could. She stepped in to aid Artemis. "I don't know what this is about. But Arty sure looks like it's purty serious. I think y'all need to just do what she says. Let's all go and come back this afternoon."

"I refuse," Demitra announced with exaggerated hand motions. "This is my house too, and both my daughters are missing. I'm not going anywhere."

Having had enough of the argument, Artemis whirled around with a furor, "I am the head of this family! I am the head of this coven. As your coven leader I command everyone to leave this house for the next three hours. Anyone who disobeys my order will have their powers bound!"

No one spoke to Artemis as they resentfully filed out of the door. Zelda gave her a supportive wink as she ushered out the hostile hoard. Artemis' sisters were furious with her, but everyone complied with her orders. Once the final car had driven away, Artemis began her trek up the three flights of stairs to the Blanchard tower, known as the magic room. As she went, her mother's words echoed in her mind:

"*There is another vault in Blanchard House. It can only be accessed in the magic room. Under the floor. It is the place where the most powerful things are kept. The things in the coven leader's vault should never be messed with unless there is no other way.*"

Artemis opened the door to the magic room. The early afternoon light shone through the windows on all three walls before her. The only door to the room was the one she walked through. She carefully moved the various tables and workstations out of the center of the floor. This was where the family practiced their magic. This was where little Hera, Con, Olympus, Titan, and possibly even Rom would one day learn how to cultivate their powers—just like the generations before them. Artemis knew something no other Blanchard knew. There was a door under those floorboards.

It was her own divine luck that Artemis carried the power to manifest things to happen merely by thinking about them. Standing with her back against the windows, she envisioned the plank boards of the floor lifting free of their hold and stacking neatly next to her. After the first five boards lifted away, the borders of a door came into view beneath. Artemis continued removing planks until the entirety of the door was uncovered. She opened the door and saw the stairs.

Cobwebs covered the hole in the floor which she wiped away with her hands upon descending the stairs. The staircase was very narrow, being that it secretly rested between the wall of Seth's bathroom and the wall to Fable's bedroom. Running right through the center of Blanchard House, the stairs led to the second vault. It grew darker and darker with each step down as the light from the tower could only stretch so far. Artemis envisioned the candles in the magic room above her lighting and floating behind her down the stairs to light the way. The candles obeyed.

She descended all four stories of the house back down to beneath the first floor. The second vault lay somewhere underneath the house, but she had no idea just how far under it went. It seemed to take forever to reach the door at the end of the stairs, but in truth Artemis assumed she must be about two stories underneath Blanchard House. She opened the door.

The candles followed her inside and set themselves atop several sets of shelves lining the room. From the faint light emitted by the candles, Artemis could see that there were lanterns placed in brackets all around the walls. She imagined them lighting and they did. Her jaw dropped. The room was enormous. Much larger than the vault under the kitchen. This one appeared to be perhaps even larger than the entire first floor of the house. Many closed doors led to other rooms, and a set of stairs led down to another level about six feet lower than the place she stood. It was almost like a library of magic. Strange objects covered even stranger tables. A glowing orb encased in glass shined on top of a dusty desk. There were two maroon velvet couches covered in thick layers of dust positioned in front of the desk. Parchment scrolls rolled upon themselves piled high atop a table against the wall. And the shelves all seemed to house some strange object or another, the likes of which Artemis had never seen before.

"This is the secret vault of the Blanchard coven leaders," Artemis said to herself. "A place even my mother never entered in her lifetime."

It occurred to Artemis then that she herself should not even be in this place now. The problems facing her family were not grave enough to warrant the power in this room. Her mother Olympia even warned her of that. When Artemis asked her how it was that Olympia had never even been down into this vault before, Olympia's answer was that the family had never faced a danger so great as to justify the usage of this room. The disappearance of Beryl, Fable, Seth, and Yasmine did not warrant such a visit either, and Artemis knew this. In the large scheme of magical things, they had only been zapped to another plane. The known magical world could eventually figure out a solution to that problem. Zelda even said eventually Beryl went back to where she came from. The disappearance of the four Blanchards was not the reason Artemis had dismissed the family and ventured down here today. No, Artemis was here for Beryl. She needed to understand what this God Strain was. It sounded too ominous and important to remain ignorant upon the subject.

Artemis was careful not to touch anything in the room, no matter how curious she found herself. Her mother had warned her that using the objects in this place came with a great price. Artemis left it all alone, which was extremely hard for her since everything around her seemed so strange and curious. But she held herself steadfast to her mission and the one thing she sought from that place. She assumed the knowledge she was seeking would be in book form, but she was apprehensive to explore any of the books in sight. Artemis knew it was dangerous to learn knowledge you may not be prepared to learn, and this place was a treasure trove of things she was certain she had never heard of. She just needed the one book which would explain what she needed to know. Closing her eyes, she focused her mind on information. What is *The God Strain*? She envisioned the book propelling forward, open to its page, spilling forth the answers. But it was not a book which came to her.

Artemis Blanchard stood in the secret magic room, astounded as a single bottle floated across the room. She had no idea from where it had come. She had not noticed it at first until it was just a few yards from her. Her face contorted to one of confusion as she grabbed it midair as it approached.

"Pepsi?"

She stared down at the vintage bottle in her hand. It was definitely a Pepsi bottle. It must have been one of the first the company ever made. Very retro. As she looked it over, she noticed the cap was missing and in its place was a cork stopper. It was then she saw the bottle was not filled with the liquid of a decades old soft drink, but rather granules of dark, almost black sand.

"Mother, I don't understand any of this," she said out loud. "Why would you have this? Where is this sand from?"

It then occurred to her that even her mother was not as old as this bottle. Her mother had never been down here. This had to be something from her grandfather Constantinople Blanchard's time. That realization did not provide any new insights. Artemis uncorked the bottle and poured a few granules into her palm. It was only dark sand. Nothing more. *Maybe there is something hidden in the sand?* Walking over to the large table, she gingerly scooted the objects on top out of the way. Nearby was an old map rolled up with twine tied around it. She gently untied the twine to unroll the map. It was an ancient map of Istanbul. She turned it face down atop the desk. Just in case this sand bore more importance than it appeared, she needed to keep it preserved. She would be able to roll the map into a funnel and put the sand back in the Pepsi bottle. Slowly she began to empty the bottle's contents onto the map on the table. Nothing lay inside the bottle. No hidden device or trinket. Yet something did begin to happen. Something peculiar.

Slowly the sand took life of its own and began to swirl across the parchment back of the map. The sand was writing something. The granules began to align in formation across the paper, like ink from a pen. Words began taking shape from the dark sand. Sentences. Explanations. She had to read quickly as the moment all of the sand completed its message, the beginning sentences began to dissipate and pile back into the original mound. Artemis read fast and understood enough, if not all. After she read the final words, she laid the bottle on its side beside the sand. She watched with mild shock as the sand returned itself to the bottle of Pepsi. She returned the cork and released the bottle as it obediently floated back from whence it came, somewhere off into the darkness of the many shelves across the room.

Artemis had her answer. She knew what The God Strain was, and nothing was ever going to be the same again for her family.

CHAPTER SIX

A Defiant Woman

Jebediah Blanchard was not joking when he told Fable she must leave the following morning. She had no sooner finished eating the eggs his wife, Nancy, prepared before he informed her it was time for her to go.

"Ain't got no room round here for witches. You best be on your way."

"I'm afraid I can't do that," Fable contradicted. She watched with a slight bit of amusement as the eyebrows of Jebediah's wife and daughter raised. It was more than obvious they had never defied him before.

"You will do what I say you'll do, girl!" he barked. "This is my house, and I say you're leaving now."

Fable locked eyes with the irritated man and did not break contact, something he was clearly not accustomed to with women folk. "You know you are extraordinarily rude," Fable commented. "Has anyone ever taught you proper manners or how to treat a guest in your home?"

Nancy inadvertently gasped out loud. Her husband dared her with his eyes to make another sound. Quickly, she covered her open mouth with her hand and clutched young Blaze close with the other.

Fable continued speaking. "I have no place to go and until I figure out why I came here and how to get back home again, I have no other alternative than to remain here."

Jebediah hobbled menacingly close and groused. "I done told you you ain't welcome! No devilry in this house! 'Sides I got bis'ness I gotta see after."

Fable simply stared at him in her defiant Fable manner. The audacity she displayed was infuriating him. He shouted at her, reiterating that she was not welcome in his home. Fable simply rolled her eyes at the man and said, "You really need to lower your voice and calm down. You look ridiculous right now. Besides, we are family. You might grow to like me if you try."

His face reddened and the grave crevices of his leathery skin deepened even further. He was not backing down from his refusal to let her stay. "You get out of this house this minute or you're gonna be one sorry woman! I will knock you through that door or you can walk out it on your own!"

She didn't flinch. She seemed amused. Almost about to laugh.

Jebediah Blanchard bounded forward on his good leg, dragging the bad one along. He meant to scare her into retreat, but Jebediah was not prepared for a woman like Fable. He was about to learn firsthand how a woman of the future reacts to being yelled at by a man.

"Don't you raise your voice to me or threaten me!" she shouted. "I am a guest in your home! I am also a woman in need of assistance and a little understanding. And, as I said before, I am also a relative. In my time, that means something."

Jebediah knocked the chair next to him backward with his hand. It tumbled across the floor as he charged another step closer to Fable. He reared his hand back to strike her. "How dare you talk back to me and yell at me in my own house!" He swung forward aiming his fist at her cheek. Like lightning, Fable dodged his attack and leapt to her feet, swiping his legs out from under him with her right foot. Jebediah fell forward smashing his chin into the edge of the table. Blaze screamed!

"Please Jebediah," Nancy cried. "Please don't hurt her. She does not know what she's doing. She's sorry."

"The hell I am!" Fable Blanchard shouted as she brought her own fist down across his cheek and smashed him into the floor. "You wanna fight, dude! Bring it on!"

Jebediah stood up and charged her, sweeping her up in a barrel grip and ramming her against the wall of the cabin. Fable jabbed her elbow into his jaw and kneed him in the groin. He doubled over in excruciating pain. She could tell from the look on his face no woman had ever done anything like this to him before.

"Get up," she chided. "You're a big, strong manly man. You gonna let some girl take you down? I don't even have to use my powers to knock you on your ass. Get up little boy and fight like a man."

Jebediah righted himself and snatched his cane from the table. He swung hard at her face, but Fable ducked it and upon rising she kicked her foot forward and buried it into the pit of the man's stomach. He doubled over.

His wife cried out and his little girl stood with what resembled a thoroughly entertained smile on her face. Fable gave little Blaze a slight wink and reached her hand out to help the girl's father. "Had enough?" Fable asked him. "Let's call a truce and be friends."

Jebediah Blanchard slapped her hand away and punched her squarely in the chin. The blow sent Fable stumbling backward over the chair. She jumped up from the ground with ninja dexterity, smirking in delight. The fact that she was laughing seemed to startle Nancy more than anything else.

"Oh, so we're still doing this then?" Fable nodded to her adversary. She rubbed her chin and spit on the floor. "Good shot. Needs more power to it, though. Does that one usually do the trick for you? Cause I gotta tell you, my sister used to hit harder than you do when we were children." She glanced over at Nancy. "Are you afraid of *that*? Getting hit like that?" Fable asked her. "Because it really doesn't hurt at all. I'd say your husband hits like a girl, but that insults girls. All the girls I know are tougher than he is."

Jebediah came at her again, swinging harder this time. Fable sidestepped the blow and unleashed a torrent of strikes his way. After a succession of jabs to his face, she landed an uppercut to his chin. Jebediah, stunned by the onslaught of punches, stood shakily as Fable pulled one last item from the arsenal of her old high school boxing lessons. A quick left jab to the side of Jebediah's face busted his nose before she right hooked him, sending him sliding over the table. He rolled off the side onto the floor, a pile of crushed pride and bloodied arrogance.

"Does he hit you often?" Fable asked a stunned Nancy. Nancy nervously nodded.

"When he does, hit the mother fucker back!" Fable cried. "You are not helpless just because you are a woman. He does not have the right to hurt you." Fable looked over at the astonished face of young Blaze. "Don't you ever let any man rule over you. You are a female. You work your hands to the bone. You are the giver of life to mankind. You are as strong as any man. No one rules you. No one!"

"Filthy witch," Jebediah coughed, spitting blood onto the floor.

"Well, this filthy witch just kicked your ass," Fable scoffed. Then she did something unexpected. She extended her hand once more to help him up—a second chance for peace. Jebediah stared at her from the floor.

"Take her hand," Nancy said. She wasn't even sure why she said it. Perhaps because she understood Fable was trying now to be kind. Or maybe because it felt satisfying to extend a command to her husband for a change.

Jebediah reached out and took Fable's hand as he rose to his feet.

"I am sorry if I hurt you or embarrassed you," she said. "But where I come from, men do not hit their women. Not good men, anyway. Your woman is your partner. Your equal. She is not a child to be disciplined. Your wife does too much around here for you to treat her with disrespect. If a man attacks me, I attack back. Isn't that what you would want little Blaze to do? Or would you rather some man beat on her all of her life?'

"God's word says the woman should obey the man," Jebediah stuttered.

"God's word says a lot of things," Fable smiled. "A lot of it is bullshit. Written by men who knew how to use fear and propaganda to rule over idiots desperate for something to believe in. People who use it to make themselves feel powerful all at the expense of someone else they deem lesser. You are one of those people, Jebediah Blanchard. You use your Bible to justify the way your black heart treats people.

What you need to know is that treating people with kindness and respect is always the best way. And if you need to turn to your Bible to tell you how to live, look a little closer at it. I think you'll find that Jesus basically said the most important thing to do is show love, kindness, and understanding. Worry a little less about maintaining control of people and focus a little more on living like Jesus."

"I don't take religious advice from witches," Jebediah replied. "I am a God fearin' man."

"Then if fear is what it takes to teach you, follow me."

Fable walked outside into the yard. Jebediah stumbled after her with Nancy and Blaze behind him. Fable stood silently for a moment with her eyes closed. The others had no idea what she was doing. Suddenly the bright sky grew a little darker. Jebediah and his family looked up. Hovering above the fields around the little house were hundreds of birds. Hawks, crows, blackbirds, red birds, blue jays, robins, owls—every type of bird any of them had ever seen covered the sky above them. Slowly Jebediah looked down and around to the edges of the yard. Standing in square formation around his house stood all the beasts of the earth. Deer, wolves, coyotes, squirrels, rats, skunks, beavers, gophers, possums—even Jebediah's horses, cows, and pigs had aligned in formation. All of them under Fable's control. All of them acknowledging her as their master.

Jebediah stumbled backward, reaching his hands back to find the doorframe of the house in case he needed to take shelter. His wife and daughter stood amazed, unafraid, as they watched the animals of the woods and farm fall into sentry. Across the grass, snakes slithered forward, frogs hopped closer, bees, hornets, ants, butterflies, dragon flies all joined the ranks.

"If fear is what you bow to, let this be the example of what I can do," Fable smiled. She looked at his daughter. "Show him what you can do, Blaze."

Nervously, but excitedly, Blaze walked to where Fable stood and stretched out her arms. All at once the pile of chopped wood by the barn rose into the air a few feet. The loose farm equipment scattered around the house and yard followed suit. The wagon lifted up. The child held it all suspended in the air as she smirked proudly over her shoulder at her father. Blaze never felt so empowered as she did now standing beside this magnificent woman who had come into their lives.

"This is what your child can do," Fable grinned. "Nancy, show your husband your strength. Show him what you are made of."

With a defiance she had never once in her life mustered, Nancy Norwood Blanchard stepped forward. She leaned to the ground and snatched up loose stones from the ground along with a clump of weedy wildflowers growing haphazardly in the yard beside them. Tossing it all into the air, she waved her hand in their general direction. The flowers and stones froze in place, midair—still as a photograph. It was at that moment when Fable realized Nancy was where Salem got her powers. The three Blanchard witches turned to face Jebediah, now trembling in the doorway.

"If I were you, I would be careful not to try to rule over my wife and daughter so much in the future," Fable advised. "Now that you know how truly remarkable they are. Witches are here to protect the earth, not corrupt it. We are not of the Devil. We are higher than you are in the grand scheme of things. But if fear is what it takes to gain your respect…you might want to fear these women."

…

Seth gave Victor his bath while Blaze Blanchard made supper. Blaze's shack had no bathroom—something Seth learned firsthand when he was searching for one and Blaze directed him to the weathered, splintery, outhouse around back. It was an experience he hoped he would not carry with him through life. Seth washed the boy in a large tin bucket. Seth had never seen one of these used before in any other capacity than icing large quantities of beer down at parties. Hauling buckets of water from the well pump outside and heating them on the iron wood burning stove took time, but Seth figured it out quickly enough. Little Vic was enjoying his warm, playful bath.

Outside the sound of thunder clapped overhead as the tiny taps of rainfall began to echo over the tin roof. The ominous sound didn't disturb the child at all, or Blaze who was dredging slices of tomato in a cornmeal batter before frying them in hot lard.

"You don't gotta bathe him for me," she said. "You done enough today. Helping me plant that field was a big chore. 'Specially for a man that ain't got any calluses on his hands."

Seth chuckled. "I was happy to help. And that rainstorm I just conjured should soak the fields pretty well. Besides, I like getting to know this little guy here."

"Vic is a right good boy," Blaze smiled.

"I miss my own son," Seth said. "Taking care of this little man makes me feel better. Plus who else in the world can say they gave their two-year-old great-great-grandfather a bath?"

"I wonder if any more a you folks are gonna show up later on in my life?" Blaze commented. "I'll never forget Fable. Boy, she sure turned things upside down when she was here."

"Fable turns things upside down everywhere," Seth laughed. "I miss her, too. I miss my whole family."

"Y'all are pretty close, huh?"

"Definitely," Seth replied as he made exaggerated faces at the laughing little boy. "It makes me sad to think of you and Vic here all alone. I have a tremendous family. It makes life so much nicer."

"How many of y'all are they?" Blaze asked, flipping the tomatoes to fry on the other side.

"My mom, two aunts, an uncle—though he's fairly new—I have two sisters, and two cousins. Actually, I have three sisters." Seth corrected. "One of those is sort of new too. Then there are the babies. Two nephews, two kids of my own, and a nephew on the way."

"All because of little Vic there?"

"Yep. All thanks to this little man."

Blaze stared off to the wall for a moment, lost in some inner satisfaction. "Kinda makes me feel good," she said thoughtfully. "Everything I go through to keep this farm up and taking care of that rascal. Makes it all worth it knowin' all you are gonna be borned one day."

Seth smiled at his distant relation. "I appreciate everything you do and will do, Blaze. I promise you, you will be remembered by all future Blanchards."

She presented a triumphant grin, then began laughing.

"What's so funny?" Seth asked.

"Just thinkin' about my Daddy. Boy he'd roll over in his grave if he knew the amount of witches he made jus' by havin' Vic."

"And powerful witches they are, too!" Seth replied. "Powerful enough to send me back to my own time if they only knew where I was."

"Yeah," Blaze contemplated. "It's not like you can write 'em a letter." Suddenly she stopped what she was doing and turned to Seth. "Reckon you can?"

"Huh?"

"You could write 'em a letter and I could keep it and give to Vic when he's growed up. He could give it to his youngens, and so on until finally it gets to your people!"

"But Blaze, that would still mean I'd be here till I died. You're talking about them getting the letter 200 years from now."

"Oh, I see what you're sayin'. It's all so confusin'."

Still, maybe Blaze was on to something after all. Seth couldn't help but consider that she might have a solution somewhere within her idea. Surely there was a way to reach the future. After all, he was on Blanchard land. Suddenly an idea came to him.

"Blaze, do you have a metal box or even a glass jar or something? One with a tight lid?"

"Sure," she said. "In the cupboard I got some preservin' jars. Why?"

"Because I think I know a way to send my family a message!"

. . .

Olympia Blanchard was impressed to see her adult granddaughter's skill in the kitchen. Yasmine fried the chicken for the family dinner while Olympia was able to relax at the kitchen table. Not that she was doing much relaxing. The intrepid woman was mulling over some legal documents which seemed to be agitating her a bit. Every so often, she would glance up from her read and comment to Yasmine on how delicious everything was smelling.

"Aunt Artemis taught me to cook. I still mess up sometimes, but I have mastered her chicken."

Olympia went back to her folders and began to furiously scribble notes on a legal pad. Yasmine wanted to ask what she was doing but felt it might be impertinent. She did not have to wait long to find out, however, because when Grandfather Sinclair came into the kitchen after a day of business meetings, Olympia bounded up from the chair and confronted her husband.

"Listen to me, Randolph Sinclair," whenever Olympia used her husband's first name, he knew he was in for it. "What is all this about developing the Brockner Preserve in Oneonta?"

Sinclair hung his head and gave a frustrated sigh. He slung his briefcase down on the counter and gave Yasmine a peck on the cheek. He then faced his wife. "Olympia, would you for once stay out of the study and stop rummaging through my private business affairs?"

"Absolutely not," Olympia answered. "Someone has to keep you on the straight and narrow."

Sinclair gave an exaggerated laugh of sarcasm, "*Straight and narrow*? I'm not building an illegal casino! I am taking a parcel of forest and streams and turning it into a series of lovely residential estates so that other people can enjoy the natural beauty of the area."

Olympia's pursed lips and fiery eyes practically jumped across the table. "You mean other people can *own* the natural beauty of the area," Olympia corrected, then added imperiously, "I will not stand for it. I will fight you in court myself over this. If you'll recall the last time I battled you in court over pillaging the land, I won."

Sinclair produced a genuine laugh this time as he walked over to his impetuous wife and attempted to kiss her cheek, a kiss she dodged. "You won nothing, Olympia. I gave in and withdrew the project."

"Same thing."

"It is not the same thing," Sinclair argued. "I withdrew from the project because I was in love with you and wanted to marry you. Well, I am already married to you now. I have no incentive to cancel this deal."

Yasmine had forgotten how passionately her grandparents could fight. But they always made up, typically because Grandfather Sinclair always eventually gave in. She wondered if he would this time. The argument continued in private, in the living room, while Yasmine finished dinner--but the elevated voices rang through the walls. As she set the table and heard Olympia call the children in to eat, she wondered if her grandparents had settled the matter amicably. But the moment Olympia joined the family at the table and removed her place setting from its normal location beside her husband to move down to the other end of the table, Yasmine knew the fight was still going strong.

The kids chattered away as they ate. Beryl and Salem were prattling on about a boy at school they both thought was the best baseball player on the team (Salem would eventually date that boy for a couple of months when she was older). Fable and little Yaz were not-so-slyly passing their broccoli sprouts under the table to Seth who was leaning back to hide in the potted plant behind him when his grandparents were not looking. Olympia and Sinclair were much too busy glaring at one another to notice much of anything.

Finally, Sinclair broke the stalemate with a suggestion. "Look, Olympia, I thought this development would be a great investment as well as a way to protect the landscape. I have no intention of upsetting the environment out there. I was planning to include a bird sanctuary and strict guidelines on where homes could be located to not have to remove much of the landscape. It was going to be beautiful and natural. Someone else will just come along and clear the whole thing for a shopping center. My way at least respects the area."

Olympia did not say anything at first. She was considering her husband's point of view. If truth be told she was realizing he was right and the best chance the area had to remain as natural and untouched as possible would be to allow Sinclair to develop it. But she did not want to back down. She was never very good at backing down.

"Well?" he asked his wife, knowing he had just won the argument even though she would never admit it.

Olympia softened her grimaced face just enough to ease his agitation, winning herself a few seconds of silence to gracefully cultivate an answer. "If I allow this," she began, "I get final approval on all of the plans."

"If you allow this?" Sinclair scoffed. "Woman, I don't need your permission! However, because I am a generous man, I will allow you to look at the plans and offer suggestions, which I will have final say over."

Olympia begrudgingly nodded. It was a surrender on her part. She rarely surrendered. Because of this, she needed, for her own stubborn will, to reassert her one stipulation. "But I do get final plan approval." The fire in her eyes transitioned to a twinkle of playful flirtation. It always worked with him.

Sinclair knew this game well by now but was still miffed about her interference.

He decided to use this moment to his advantage and quietly come out the winner of this one. "And I get to finally build a pool in the side yard."

Olympia shot forward in her chair, hands smashing onto the table. "No pool!"

It was too late; the children were now interested in this conversation and were cheering their grandfather on. Olympia's face said it all, she was both furious and impressed at how Sinclair routed her. Adult Yasmine could not help but smile as she witnessed the scene. *So that's how we managed to get a pool.*

After another ten minutes of fighting ensued, Sinclair got his way on everything, and Olympia backed down from her imperiousness. Yasmine wasn't certain what had been won or lost by this argument. She just assumed that this was how her grandparents kept their love as passionate as it was. And the children were overjoyed that they would now have a swimming pool in the yard.

As dinner wrapped up and the children had full bellies and sleepy eyes, Yasmine began clearing away the dishes. Young Beryl and Salem helped her while Fable, Seth, and Yasmine wiped the chairs and table down with moist cloths. This was their regular nightly chore which adult Yasmine had forgotten about. As she turned on the water in the sink to rinse the frying pan, she suddenly felt woozy. She staggered a moment but was steadied by young Beryl and Salem, who each grabbed an elbow.

Olympia caught sight of this as she was rushing to the kitchen in a panic. She stood in the doorway between the kitchen and dining room, turning her head back and forth, looking at something occurring in both rooms. At the sink, adult Yasmine was feeling faint, and in the dining room, young Yasmine had experienced quite the same sensation and was now being held by her grandfather as she tried to steady herself.

"The both of them," Olympia said mostly to herself. "This is bad."

CHAPTER SEVEN

The God Strain

The family returned to Blanchard House to find Artemis sitting at the table awaiting them. Demitra was still angry over having been expelled from the house in the first place, but that anger had dissipated somewhat as she took a seat at the table with Nacaria. Salem, Arielle, Cassandra, Xander and Zelda took seats as well while Artemis addressed the group.

"I still have no answers as to why Beryl, Seth, Fable, and Yaz disappeared. However, I do have some answers on what is happening to Beryl."

"Do you know what this God Strain thing is?" Salem asked.

"I do."

"Wait," Demitra interrupted. "Before you go any further, I want to know why we had to leave? What did you do that none of us could see?"

"Dee, I am sorry," Artemis replied. "You and I have always shared everything. But I am understanding more and more as time goes by exactly how difficult it was for Mother. We never fully appreciated everything she had to balance and carry. I can only tell you that I know the answer. I cannot tell you how I found it. Chalk it up to one of the burdens and responsibilities of being the matriarch of the Blanchard family. I cannot reveal certain things. But I do know them."

"Tell us!" Nacaria pleaded. "What did you discover?"

Artemis addressed the table as she stood at the head of it. The seated faces looked on in eager anticipation, waiting for questions to be answered.

"The God Strain is complicated," she began. "I must confess I do not understand very much of what I saw, and it is no longer something I can revisit and see again. But to put things in a concise, easy to understand term…Beryl is becoming God."

The silent befuddled faces around the table stared blankly at Artemis.

"What?" Nacaria finally asked.

"Beryl is on a path of trials and tribulations that will ultimately make her into God."

Demitra was as unenlightened by her sister's statement as she had been before Artemis said anything. She looked to the others to see if any of them understood and might be able to explain to her. No one looked as if they understood anything. Finally, Salem spoke.

"Are you saying Beryl is developing stronger powers that will make her seem almost god-like?"

"No," Artemis replied matter-of-factly. "Beryl is God."

Xander and Cassandra exchanged perplexed glances. Arielle was as lost as they were. Everyone was. Zelda was the only one with gumption enough to speak up and demand more information.

"Arty, you gonna have to do better 'an that for explain'in," Zelda said. "None of us have any idea what the hell you're talk'in about."

Artemis paced toward the kitchen counter and placed both hands on the tile. She gave a half push up against it before facing them again, stopping for some bizarre reason, to adjust the potted plant in the kitchen window so that the sunlight streaming in hit the center.

"I am as confused as the rest of you," she declared, returning to the head of the table. "I saw words write themselves out giving me a kind of history. From what I could comprehend, there are a select few people who have existed since the beginning of whatever the beginning is. These people transform, they advance, they evolve so to speak...into gods. But not just gods, God. Like *the* God. The God Strain is inside them. It is their destiny to become something there are no words to describe. Beryl is one of those people."

"This is crazy!" Demitra exclaimed. "My daughter is a remarkable woman with a sincere and giving heart, but God? You are telling me my daughter is God? The one and only?"

"No," Artemis said, trying her best to convey the most confusing information she had ever been so clumsily imbued with. "There is no one and only. Or maybe there is, and He has shared pieces of Himself with those He has deemed Holy enough to carry the mantle. I have no idea how this works or why it exists. I'm simply trying to impart the extremely vague information I was handed."

"I don't understand any of this," Salem said. "Beryl is good. I've never spent much time thinking about it but she's probably the best person I have ever known, outside of Olympia Blanchard. But is she Holy?"

"She's no Jesus," Arielle noted. "But if you think about it, she heals people. She is always kind. I've never known her to lie or ever do anything malicious."

"And when Atheidrelle tried to kill her the night we lost Grandmother," Salem recalled. "Atheidrelle's blow had no effect on her. It shredded poor Forest into pieces. But Beryl barely flinched."

The assembled group thought a few moments to themselves, each person rolling over personal examples of Beryl's life, her choices, and her morality in which they'd been witness to. The more they individually examined Beryl's character in their minds, the more sense things began to make.

"When I brought Larry back to life, even though he was her father, she was vocally opposed to what I had done," Demitra remembered. "It was a morality issue for her. Instead of celebrating her father's return, she was defending Jerry and his right to life even though he was a total stranger to her. I never understood why she was so adamantly against Larry's return, but maybe it was because she has something pure inside her the rest of us don't possess."

"When you really think about it," Salem added. "Beryl is actually the best of us."

"But is there truly a God?" Cassandra asked. "I have never believed there to be. That is a concept frightened and uncertain people created at the earliest stages of civilization in hopes to give themselves a little peace and comfort. It isn't real."

"Or perhaps it is?" Nacaria offered. "No one really knows."

"But this world has existed for billions of years," Cassandra continued. "Humans haven't been here a fraction of that. Mankind did not begin in a garden with just two people. That's for children or the desperately naive."

"Or is it?" Nacaria offered. "We don't actually know anything for certain. And I am not saying that Beryl is the kind of god who can create a solar system out of thin air. Truth is no one knows how any of us or the universe came to be. The Bible is full of inconsistencies and contradictions."

"Still, things written about in the Bible—floods, eruptions, origin stories, specific individuals—all appear in other cultures who knew nothing about the Bible or what it said," Arielle noted.

Nacaria knew her stepdaughter had a point, but also remained skeptical. "But all of those legends and natural events happened at a time in history when no one understood science or magic."

"And Beryl understands both," Demitra replied. "It's funny. This is all so unbelievable and difficult to follow, but the more I think about it, the more sense it makes. Beryl is a witch. She understands power which most mortals could never comprehend. Yet she has a scientific mind. Educated. Rational. She has one foot in each world."

Xander cleared his throat and spoke up. "If I may offer up an opinion here, I think you all might be attributing our culture's known ideologies of religion and Biblical Deities to a situation we aren't equipped to understand."

"Meaning?" Artemis asked.

"Meaning that we are doing our best to fit Beryl into the constructs of the Divine world as mankind has designed it to be. However, if God exists, we only know Him, or Them if you will, by definitions man has scripted. It is extremely possible that God exists and no one on earth has the slightest concept of what He is or how He operates."

"Until now," Arielle smiled. "Beryl is going to know."

The room fell silent as everyone took in all the new information. The ramifications of this were too endless to comprehend. Everyone wanted an explanation which was unattainable since there was so much uncertainty about what was fact and fiction regarding the Divine.

Demitra wasn't terribly interested in debating theology. All she wanted to know was what was happening to her daughter. "Explain what exactly is happening to Beryl," she urged Artemis. "Is this why she is in the past? Does she know what she is becoming?"

Artemis shrugged. "I have no idea. I do know this is not why she went back in time—at least I don't think it is. Who knows? Maybe the powers that be, so to speak, did this to her as part of her journey to becoming her destiny. Nothing I read mentioned time travel."

"Was there more to what you were told?" Xander asked.

"No," Artemis answered. "I only learned that the God Strain exists. Beryl is not the first. Probably not the last. I have no idea what happens to them after they achieve whatever level of enlightenment they go to. I don't know if she will remain here with us on Earth, or will she disappear to some type of Heaven? I only know Beryl is on a path and it will change her forever. Mother told me something was going to happen to Beryl. I had no inclination it would be something like this."

Suddenly Arielle laughed. It startled everyone at the table, all of them so lost in the seriousness of the matter that her laughter took them by surprise. "Can you guys imagine what's going to happen whenever we find a way to get everyone back and we tell Fable—militantly atheist Fable—that there is a God, and it's her big sister!"

With that remark, the heaviness of the room lightened and those in the room who knew Fable well, all got quite a chuckle out of the idea.

CHAPTER EIGHT

Happy Meals and Unhappy Sisters

Sinclair was watching Yasmine through the large window of the McDonald's while she stood at the payphone outside. The glare from the sun reflecting off the glass obscured his ability to see inside, but twice he pressed his forehead against the pane, shielding the light with his hands to see her munching on fries and laughing with the children. They were all, big Yasmine included, enjoying a Happy Meal lunch. Sinclair listened closely to his wife on the other end of the line as he kept an eye on his grandchildren.

"Everything seems fine," Sinclair told his Olympia over the telephone. "She was a little lightheaded when we first got here but that could have simply been hunger."

"She felt slightly dizzy this morning," Olympia told her husband. "I believe it is beginning to happen."

"What do we do?" Sinclair asked. "Do I tell the girl what's going on?"

"No," Olympia warned. "There is no reason to frighten her unnecessarily. But I do think it is a good idea to remove her from the house. Perhaps to a hotel. Artemis and Demitra will be home tomorrow anyway. It's better if they never know anything about adult Yasmine's visit. Explain things to her. Tell her I will come to see her every day. But it is best that she not come back to Blanchard House with the children."

"I have enjoyed her being there," Sinclair frowned. "And I believe she has enjoyed getting to know her younger self."

"That's just the problem," Olympia forewarned. "We need to keep as much distance between little Yasmine and big Yasmine as possible. For both their sakes. Explain it to her, Sinclair."

With the buzz of traffic from Skyland Boulevard assaulting his ears, Sinclair replaced the phone receiver and looked again through the glass. The kids had barely eaten theirs, instead rushing off to play in the ball pit of the miniature McDonald's playground. Yasmine was devouring her fast-food meal. Adulthood had not rid her of her endearing childlike qualities. He stepped back inside, seizing the opportunity to speak with her while the children were playing.

Yasmine had been back in the past for a few days now. She missed her husband. She missed her children. But she could not help but cherish this opportunity of being able to step backward in time and revisit her golden memories. Sitting at the table and having a meal with her grandfather after all these years was a dream come to life. It had been she who suggested coming to McDonald's for lunch with the children. Some of her favorite memories of childhood consisted of stolen lunches away with Grandfather Sinclair and her cousins to have a Happy Meal. Olympia Blanchard did not approve of such meals for the children, but Grandfather Sinclair indulged them whenever he could. The kids loved him for that.

Watching the children playing outside on the big slide and in the pit of plastic balls, Sinclair smiled at his lunch companion and said, "I'm so happy to have some time alone with you Yasmine." He tossed a French fry into his mouth. "Being able to see what you'll turn out like is a real gift to me."

"Granddaddy, I can't tell you what this means to me." She smiled and looked around. "Do you know how many times you brought me here when I was little? Oh, of course you do. Well, it was always special for me, and now that I'm an adult I think back to those days so often."

She reached over to the abandoned Happy Meal box her younger self had left behind when she went out to play. Yasmine lifted out the toy inside. It was a Looney Tunes character—Petunia Pig—dressed in a Wonder Woman costume.

"I remember the day I got this," she began. "I had totally forgotten that we'd been joined that day by an older cousin passing through town. And now I know that cousin was me."

"You never realized you look just like that cousin?" Sinclair asked.

"I never even thought about it, or her actually. I guess being so many years ago I didn't remember what she looked like. Nice to know that I haven't made much of an impression on myself. That little girl out there won't even remember me."

"I will remember you," he smiled, squeezing her hand gently.

"I do remember this toy, though," she laughed. "I lost it the same day I got it. Or more likely Seth stole it to add to his Bugs Bunny Superman and Daffy Duck Batman. I'll have to ask him when I get back."

"Are you happy in your life, Yasmine?" Sinclair asked. "Seth treats you well?"

Yasmine beamed as she responded. "Oh Granddaddy, I am deliriously happy. Seth is a wonderful husband. He's my best friend. I have never felt so loved. I know you can't see it now, but he grows up to be a pretty standup guy. They all do. You'd be so proud of every one of those kids out there."

Sinclair started to say something but stopped himself. Then he gave one of his devious grins which usually meant he had amused himself with whatever was in his mind. He gave himself permission to ask. "I already know from your reaction when you first saw me that I don't live a very long time. Will you tell me something if I ask you?"

Yasmine was worried, unsure what to say. "Grandmother told us I mustn't reveal anything that could change the future's outcome."

"I know," he replied. "But I think this is benign enough. And I swear I will never tell that you told me. But just between you and me, a Sinclair to a Sinclair, after I'm gone...does Olympia get married again?"

Yasmine did not mean to laugh but she could not help herself. It was exactly the kind of question she would be asking her own offspring if this type of situation presented itself. She squeezed both his hands in her own and replied, "No. No Granddaddy, she never does. She loves you way too much to ever consider anyone else. She never even dates. You are the love of her life, and she readily admits it anytime the subject of you comes up."

Sinclair smiled and nodded. "You know I always figured I was the love of her life. Stubborn mule won't ever say that to me, but I figured as much."

Yasmine winked at him and turned her attentions to the children outside. "I've really cherished seeing them, too. I forgot how special they made my childhood."

"Speaking of the children," Sinclair began, clearing his throat. "After we drop them off back at the house, I think it is a good idea if you and I move into a hotel for a few days."

"A hotel?"

"Yes," he said. "I was speaking with Olympia just now, and it seems your aunts are returning tomorrow. It is best if we keep them in the dark about you. Your grandmother believes you will soon be returning to your own time, so there is no need to bring them into this little matter. I also thought you and I might enjoy some time alone together before you leave. Olympia must stay at the house with the children, but I can sneak away on a "business trip" and remain with you. Your grandmother says she will come see you every day."

Yasmine looked disappointed. But his words made sense. She really did have to get out of that house before Larry and the aunts came back. Still, she had a distinct feeling her grandfather was leaving something important out.

. . .

Downtown Daihmler was not as extensive as it was in Beryl's normal timeline, but she was enjoying seeing what it looked like in her grandmother's youth. The stores were so *vintage* in her perspective. Seeing her hometown at its first stage of growth was perhaps one of the most interesting things about this leap backwards in time. She and Pastoria had spent the last two hours shopping and Beryl hoped that whenever she made it back to her own timeline, she might be able to find a way to bring the outfits she had just purchased with her.

"Let's stop at Shackleford Drug's for a bite," Pastoria suggested, tugging her newfound relative inside.

"Oh my God," Beryl gasped. "This is the CVS drug store."

"No, it's Shackleford's."

"No, I mean where I come from this becomes a CVS drug store—only it's not this same building. They must have torn down this beautiful old building to construct it. Why do people do that where I come from? All these lovely old places they demolish to build something cheap looking."

"I couldn't say," Pastoria replied. "This is new, too. They tore down the old five and dime to build this. Now that was a lovely structure back when it was the old post office—before they built the new one and put the dime store there."

Beryl mused a moment and smiled, "I guess nothing is really all that historic after all. Every generation paves over the last."

Beryl had never in her life eaten at one of the old lunch counters she had so often heard her grandmother reminisce about. She and Pastoria sat down on two chrome plated stools with turquoise vinyl seats. The counter was Formica with shiny chrome edges. Beryl was in retro heaven!

"Would you please stop rubbing the counter?" Pastoria whispered. "You look weird."

"Sorry," Beryl said. "It's just that people pay a fortune to recreate this style."

"The future sounds like its full of stupid rich people," Pastoria remarked as she perused the menu board on the wall. "The burgers here are really good."

"I'm craving a tuna melt," Beryl replied. "I wonder if they have one here?"

"I have no idea what that even is," Pastoria answered.

They both had burgers and fries, and Beryl was glad of the choice because she had never had a burger so delicious that hadn't been prepared by her Aunt Artemis. She ate with gusto and savored every bite.

"That was real meat!" Beryl exclaimed. "Like someone in the back made the patty from scratch with ground beef."

"Of course, they did," Pastoria replied. "What the hell are burgers made out of where you come from?"

"And these fries!" Beryl was shoving the last three from her empty plate into her mouth. "I haven't tasted fries like this in years and years."

"So are fries made from carrots in your time?"

"No, it's the oil. In my time they stopped using oils with saturated fats and other additives because they are grossly unhealthy. But they sure do make fries taste delicious!"

A man approached the counter beside Pastoria and patted her on the shoulder. Beryl caught sight of him in the mirror. He was very handsome, wearing a business suit complete with tie. Though he was addressing Pastoria, his image in the mirror was smiling towards Beryl.

"Pastoria Blanchard, I thought I knew everybody you know. Who is your lovely friend?"

Pastoria turned to the man and replied, "This is Beryl. She is a distant relation who has come to visit. Beryl, this is Nate, a good friend of ours and sometimes Olympia's boyfriend. Are y'all on again or off again these days Nate?"

"Mostly off," Nate chuckled. "I think we learned we are better as friends. Besides, I've seen her head turning more toward John Windham lately."

"John Windham!" Pastoria scoffed. "That jerk? She hasn't said anything to me about it."

"I've seen them out a couple of times," Nate said, never removing his eyes from the mirror where he was watching Beryl. "Maybe it is supposed to be a secret."

Pastoria did not seem pleased. Not one bit. "She would keep that quiet," she huffed. "She knows I can't stand John Windham."

Nate ignored his friend's outrage—too enamored of her visiting relative. "Beryl, is it?" he said, finally addressing her personally. "Where are you visiting from?"

Beryl stammered a moment, trying to think of what to say. The only place that popped into her mind was Mobile, the place Pastoria would eventually move to. "Mobile."

"I love Mobile," Nate smiled. "I'm coming out to Blanchard House tomorrow afternoon to see Olympia. On business. Would it be agreeable to you if I were to call on you as well while I am there? Perhaps we might have dinner?"

"Well…I. I'm not sure if that would be all right," Beryl said.

"Go on and go out with him," Pastoria interjected. "It's clear to see he's mooning all over you."

Beryl wanted to say yes regardless of her aunt's permission. She liked Nate. There was something about his demeanor, and those eyes, that she liked very much. But what would her grandmother say? Beryl already knew the answer to that question. Olympia Blanchard would vehemently discourage any interaction with the world at large while Beryl was trapped there.

"Oh, you should totally go out with him!" Olympia declared an hour later when Pastoria and Beryl returned home and told her about running into Nate. "Nate's the best. And he is a gentleman. You'll have a great time."

Beryl was stunned. This was not the reaction she expected. Young Olympia certainly had a more reckless side to her than Old Olympia did. "Are you sure? What if I do something that messes up the future?"

"Well, damn girl what do you think will happen?" Olympia scoffed. "It's only dinner. As long as you avoid telling him who won the super bowl or who gets elected President of the United States next year, I think you'll be okay. Just go out, have a few laughs, enjoy his company."

I wish Fable was here to see this version of our grandmother.

Pastoria cut off the conversation to address the other tidbit which had come out over lunch. "So, were you ever going to tell me you are dating John Windham?"

Olympia's face fell. She looked almost ashamed. Beryl had never seen her grandmother look ashamed in her life. "I am not *dating* John. We have been out a few times is all."

"That's called dating, Olympia!" Pastoria yelled. "I cannot believe this. You know I can't stand that man."

Beryl listened intently. The man in question—although only she knew it—was her future grandfather. She had never met John Windham. He was dead well before she was born. Randolph Sinclair was the only grandfather she had ever known. But hearing her biological grandfather's name bandied around intrigued her.

"Why don't you like John Windham?" Beryl asked Pastoria.

"Oh, she's just being ridiculous!" Olympia exclaimed. "She hates John because he was the lawyer who sued her friend's father."

"Because of John Windham, Perry had to move away from Daihmler! And he was not only my friend—we were practically engaged to be married!"

"You went out with him for one month!" Olympia scoffed. She turned to Beryl and elaborated. "Perry was a guy she went out with a few times when he was in college. It was not serious."

"It was serious!"

Olympia shook her head at Beryl, "It was not serious. Pastoria had it bad for him is all, but he was going out with several girls. His father defaulted on a loan and was evicted from the house. John is a lawyer for Daihmler Trust Bank, and *it was his job* to represent the bank. Perry's family had to move to Memphis to live with his grandparents. Pastoria just likes to hold grudges."

"I don't care what you say, Olympia! I blame John for Perry having to leave, and I cannot believe you have the audacity to go out with him!"

"I like John," Olympia said. "He's witty and kind and has a very nice, round bottom."

Beryl nearly fainted. Did her grandmother really just say that?

"Perry and I were in love!" Pastoria insisted.

"*You* were in love," Olympia clarified. "Perry just thought he could get some from you—which I hope he didn't manage!"

"That's vulgar!" Pastoria replied. "You're the one who goes out with any man that asks!"

The sight of the bickering sisters reminded Beryl very much of Fable and herself in their early days. However, it was very foreign to her to see Olympia and Pastoria Blanchard fighting because in Beryl's lifetime they had been loving supporters of one another in all things.

"I do not go out with any man who asks!" Olympia shot back. "I am very discerning. I have had a few boyfriends, true, but I do not disgrace myself. Perry was a buffoon. I wouldn't have allowed you to marry him anyway." Olympia's tone was imperious and a little haughty. Two personality traits Beryl never thought she possessed. Olympia went on, "It is my job to make sure you marry someone worthy of you, and that was not Perry Wilson."

"And I suppose John Windham is the worthy type?" Pastoria chided.

"Maybe," Olympia answered. "But I will tell you one thing, when I get married it will be the right man and it will be forever. That is why I date so much, to find Mr. Right, and then it's he and I for the rest of our lives."

Beryl wanted so badly to tell Olympia, in all her arrogance, that she would end up married to three different men. But she didn't.

CHAPTER NINE

A Little Romance

While some people's lives are a whirlwind of adventure or social interaction or romance, Beryl Blanchard's life had always been on a trajectory to achieve her goals. She spent her high school years focused on building her college success through AP classes and multiple extracurriculars. College was no different. No time for parties or keggers or sororities. Her focus was medical school and how to get there the fastest. Med school occupied her every waking moment, and her internship was grueling. She never minded. It was all part of the lifelong vision, and she had achieved it. Throughout her young life, her determination and dedication to her career left little time for dating. Her experience in that department was woefully lacking, so when Nate showed up to the house dressed more dapper than she'd ever had a man dress for her, she was thankful she'd put on one of Pastoria's better dresses and Olympia's most dazzling pair of heels.

His meeting with Olympia did not take long. Olympia displayed little interest in whatever it was he had to show her. Financial matters bored her. She half listened to whatever it was he was saying and then blindly signed whatever it was he put in front of her. Beryl was not in on the meeting. That took place behind the closed doors of the study. But as Nate escorted Beryl to the car and opened the door to his chrome adorned, cream striped, mauve Studebaker President, she caught a glimpse of some paperwork inside an open briefcase as she slid onto the creamy white seat. It was a mortgage document. *Nate must be a loan officer or a banker.*

As Nate shut the driver side door behind him, Beryl closed the lid to his case for him. "You wouldn't want these to fall out."

"No, I wouldn't. Thank you."

"So, is Olympia mortgaging the house?"

He eyed her with slight suspicion but then figured that since she was family it was probably no big secret. "Not at all. Paying it off, actually. Her father mortgaged the property some years ago when the farm stopped being a farm and Mr. Blanchard's attentions turned elsewhere. He was gone a lot on some kind of secretive business. When he died last year, he left some insurance for the girls and a policy to cover the house. Olympia just needed to sign the papers to clear up the deed."

"I see," Beryl nodded. "So, she has plenty to live on, I hope? I'd hate to think I'm a burden being here."

"I couldn't imagine you being a burden to anyone," Nate smiled. "However, Olympia and Pastoria only have enough for a few years. They really need to get jobs or marry soon if they are going to keep the house."

It was strange to hear this information. All of Beryl's life, Olympia Blanchard had been enormously wealthy. Money was never an issue to the Blanchard family. It never occurred to Beryl that she had zapped back to a time in her grandmother's life when money was a consideration. The Blanchards had not always been rich. In fact, when Beryl really stopped to think about it, the Blanchards were not rich at all. John Windham had been reasonably comfortable, and he had left his wife and three daughters moderately provided for. Olympia's second husband, Martin Caswell, had been rather wealthy and split his fortune between Olympia and his only son upon his death. But it was Grandfather Sinclair who came in the door with the multi-millions, setting the Blanchards up with lifetime security. Of course, with Olympia gone, the majority of that fortune belonged to Yasmine, although Yasmine never thought of it as anything but *everyone's money*.

Beryl was lost in thought on the subject when she realized Nate was already cranking the car and peeling off down the Blanchard driveway with a trail of dust swirling behind them. She reached to her right side to grab the seatbelt clasp but could not find it. She turned to see if it was wedged down between the seat and the door, but it wasn't there. She glanced above her where the strap should have been connected to the wall panel...nothing.

"Have you lost something, my dear?" Nate asked.

"The seatbelt," Beryl said. "I can't find it."

"The what?"

Beryl paused. "Seatbelt?" she asked timidly. "Does your car have one?"

"I am not sure what you are referring to," Nate replied. "There's a fan belt under the hood, but I have never heard of anything called a seat belt. Do you need me to move the seat closer to the dashboard, or further back? Is it the seat handle you mean?"

Cars didn't have seatbelts in the 60s, Beryl thought. *Didn't think of that.* When she had ridden downtown with Pastoria the day before in Olympia's old jalopy Packard, she hadn't found one there either. *When did seatbelts become a standard thing?*

"Don't worry about it," Beryl said, dismissing the question. "Just drive safely, please."

"Oh, don't worry, Beryl," Nate smiled. "Traffic in Daihmler is probably much less populated than you are used to in Mobile. Half the residents live in town and don't even own a car, and the other half are country farmers who'd make do driving their tractor and wagon into town when they need supplies."

Nate drove along the backroads for a while without a single car passing them. Beryl thought she noticed the spot on the road where the highway should connect, but there was no onramp. The little lake was there, just as it always had been in her time, but the highway behind it had obviously not been built yet. Nate drove them to a little log cabin roadhouse restaurant on the back side of downtown. She had never seen it before. She could not be sure with no recognizable landmarks around but from the distance they'd traveled from town, Beryl figured this was probably the general area where the Daihmler Walmart would one day be built.

The restaurant's name was Gracie's, and judging from the number of cars parked in the field behind it, it was a popular place. Walking inside, Beryl was struck with how atmospheric it all was. Blue gingham tablecloths, red glass candle holders with that retro plastic mesh lining on the outside were placed on every table and along the large wooden bar in back. The smells were terrific. Steaks, hamburgers, fresh baked bread floated across the air. Beryl was just about to remark on how much she liked the place when one of the waitresses approached to seat them. The waitress, as well as every waitress in sight, were all dressed in flowy tan skirts, white blouses, and red checkered head scarves tied in back making them appear as if they were old southern plantation Mammies. It was only then when Beryl noticed for the first time that every waitress was African American.

"Are these people for real?" Beryl exclaimed.

"I beg your pardon?" Nate asked her.

"They are all dressed like Mammy from *Gone with the Wind*?"

"Yeah," Nate nodded. "It really makes you feel like you've stepped back in time."

"I know a little something about stepping back in time, and this is not appropriate," Beryl replied indignantly.

As they took their seat at the table, Nate looked puzzlingly at Beryl. She was noticeably bothered by the place and most particularly the waitress. He began to become a little alarmed by the look on his date's face. Once the waitress walked away to bring them glasses of water, he asked Beryl if she was disturbed by something.

"Don't you find this offensive?" she asked her companion. "These black women dressed this way serving us?"

Nate's expression changed from one of frivolous casual fun to quite serious. There was a sternness in his eyes when he asked, "Beryl, I should probably tell you right off that I am an advocate for the better treatment of Coloreds. I know that many people want to keep segregation intact, but I fall on the side of giving colored people more opportunities. These women are hard workers. Many of them are supporting their whole family by the wages they earn here. They are good women who deserve employment. If you have a problem being served food by a colored woman, I don't think you and I are going to work out."

Beryl was astounded. She felt simultaneously admonished and impressed by the man before her. Quickly, she clarified her feelings. "No, no, no, you misunderstand me, Nate. I agree with you wholeheartedly. I was reacting to the fact that these women are forced to dress like slaves while they are serving white people. I find that reprehensible."

Nate's eyes still flashed a little confusion, but he felt relieved by what Beryl said. "Their costumes are just a part of the experience. Frankly, I have never even given much thought to it. But I guess I see your point. They do look a little like Mammy. However, it is exceedingly difficult for colored women to find jobs outside of being a housemaid or working on the farms around here. To these women, this job is a way to raise themselves up and make a good living for their families. I'm sorry if the way they dress offends you."

Beryl sighed and shook her head. "Please forget what I said. I should not have judged you or them. I forget I am in a different place than I am used to."

"Mobile isn't that far away," Nate countered.

Beryl gave her date a playful, mischievous wink and said, "Let's just say I am a woman ahead of her time."

Gently, Nate touched her hand with two of his fingertips. "I'm glad you are here, wherever you come from."

"I am too actually," she grinned. "I find that I am really enjoying my visit here."
"And maybe enjoying the company you are keeping a little too I hope?"
"Definitely," Beryl smiled. now stroking the back of Nate's hand.

CHAPTER TEN

Little Witches

The door creaked slightly as she reached a little above her head to gently twist the brass knob and go inside. Hera heard the voices downstairs talking. They talked a lot lately—ever since her Momma and Daddy went away. Aunt Artemis explained to her, and to Con, that their parents had gone away on a trip for a little while, but it didn't make much sense. Hera was only four years old but even she knew something was wrong. Her Momma was always there. So was her Daddy. Then they just weren't. No matter what Aunt Artemis said about a "trip", Hera saw them disappear with her own eyes. She didn't understand how it happened, but since it had, she was making sure to make regular checks on her baby brother in his room, to make sure he didn't go anywhere.

It was hard for her to reach the doorknob but getting on her tippy toes helped. Once she did make it into his quiet little room, she could only stand next to his crib and hope she might see a glimpse of a hand or foot through the slats on the side. Tonight she wasn't able to tell if Titan was in there or not. He didn't have an arm or leg flopped out close to the rails for her to see. He also was sleeping very quietly, if he was in that bed at all. He wasn't making sounds like he sometimes did. Hera Blanchard didn't know what to do. Maybe try to climb?

A noise sounded from behind her, and she whirled around to see what it was. Her cousin Romulus was slinking in, nose down, back arched, paws extending forward in full creeping mode. He had the same idea. Often Hera and he caught each other checking on the baby, making sure he was safe. Rom gave a slight nod to his cousin as he entered. Hera, being only four, did not have the maturity or intellectual development yet to fully comprehend the thought processes of her wolf cousin. Though Romulus Blanchard was also four years old, that was fully grown in wolf time. His intellect was superior even by canine standards being that his brain was more human than animal. He understood Hera's plight without the need of vocal communication. She was worried about her baby brother, as was he. Rom sprang forward from his haunches to leap through the air, landing stealthily on the top of the dresser without knocking over a single thing. Peering down into the crib, he gave a low whimper to Hera and bowed his head, acknowledging that Titan was fitfully sleeping safely in his bed.

"Thank you, Rommy," she squeaked out in her tiny voice.

Romulus jumped back down, giving her a lick to the cheek as he passed back out of the room into the empty hallway. Wandering across the hall to the room he shared with his own brother, Con, Romulus poked his head through the plastic flap of the large cutout in the door bottom—his entrance. With two quick sniffs, he knew Con was also sleeping. With his hourly checks on his cousins and brother completed, Romulus Blanchard continued on his nightly quest to locate his mother.

During the daytime he would wander the Blanchard property, looking everywhere for Fable. Since the day she vanished, he'd searched when none of the adults were looking. But at night he could really prowl. At night he was free from the constraints of his grandmother and his great aunt who were always attempting to soothe him and assure him that his mother would be all right. He wasn't sure he believed them. It wasn't that he couldn't trust in what they said. His grandmother and his aunt were the best people he knew besides his mom. But they didn't know everything. They didn't even know what he knew. Romulus knew where Fable was because he could smell her. He could smell them all.

Aunt Beryl was in this very house. Not the wing he was in currently—the wing housing his and Con and Hera and Titan's bedrooms. But the main part of the house, where the adults were gathered in the living room right now. Beryl was there, only she wasn't. He could catch her scent from time to time in the main part of the house, though it was so faint he sometimes lost it. It was as if there were layers of something covering it. The only way he could frame it in his mind was when Granddaddy Jerry read them bedtime stories. Beryl's scent was like it belonged to one of the early pages of a book, while they were all turned to the end. Somewhere in the pages of Blanchard House, Aunt Beryl was still there. Aunt Yasmine was there as well, lost in pages closer than Beryl, but still too far away to find.

Romulus crept down the switchback staircase at the end of the new wing of the house and walked slowly down the long corridor. His mother's bedroom was on this hall, but she wasn't there. She wasn't in her old bedroom either on the third floor of the main part of the house, although Rom could always smell the time she'd lived in that room. He had been born in that room.

He slinked past Arielle's bedroom as he traversed the first-floor hallway of the newer wing to Blanchard House. He ventured past the guest rooms, one of which Cassandra temporarily occupied during her visit. Soon he made his way into the long glass corridor that stretched between the oaks outside. He could see the bright moon overhead as he continued toward the main house.

He slipped out of the large doggy door in the kitchen without anyone noticing. Once he made it down the back steps into the yard he took off. In broad hurdles forward, Romulus raced across Blanchard land, far into the distance and stopped inside a meadow--long grown wild. This was where his mother was. When the wind was still and the grasses did not sway, he could get a whiff of his mother's scent. Fable Blanchard was here, somewhere, deep behind turned pages. She was alive and he felt her. The full moon above intensified his ability to locate her essence. Though he could not see, hear, or touch her he felt comforted by her presence. He curled up in a ball within the overgrown grass and could sleep.

It was very late in the night when Romulus felt a tap on his back. Con Blanchard stood over him, rubbing his sleepy eyes. The brothers were not inhibited by Rom's inability to speak, for the twins could talk to one another without words. Con laid down beside his brother and rested his small head against Rom's warm fur.

You feel Mama again?

Yes, Rom told him. *She is here.*

Can she feel us?

Rom curled his paw around Con's leg and patted it gently. *I don't think so. But she is here.*

Will they come back?

I don't know. But we will wait for them until they do.

Con was unaware of someone else's presence in the meadow, although Rom knew. He smelled him as well. A hundred yards away, leaning back to sleep quite uncomfortably in a folding lawn chair was Granddaddy Jerry. It wasn't the first time he'd spied little Con wandering outside at night and followed him. The first couple of times when he found the boys in the field, he'd made them come back to the house. Now he didn't. Now he understood that whatever they were doing was of some private importance to them. Jerry now just came equipped with chair and blanket, and spent the night guarding them from a respectful distance. Before sunrise he would awaken and go back to the house before grandma woke up. The boys would follow after.

CHAPTER ELEVEN

Resuming Normalcy

Life had to continue moving forward, even though the Blanchards were mid-crisis. The disappearance of Beryl, Seth, Fable, and Yasmine left its toll on everyone. But no longer could they simply sit around Blanchard House waiting for a solution to present itself. Though no one was giving up the mission to locate and return their missing family members, day to day activities had to begin again.

Howard and Arielle were back at work in Howard's office, Howard now acting in Yasmine's stead handling Sinclair Industries business while Arielle handled office clients, as well as frequently checking the voicemail at Fable's veterinary office, canceling appointments and making up excuses as to why Fable would be away from Daihmler for the unforeseen future. Arielle and Howard had little time to say much to each other as they plugged away at their desks. Arielle's list of client return calls was lengthy, and their requests would take even more time to perform. But she was not complaining. She wouldn't have wanted to switch jobs with Howard for anything in the world.

The executive officers at Sinclair Industries had taken a long time to warm up to the idea of answering to young Yasmine Blanchard. In actuality, it was only the fact that she was the granddaughter of founder Randolph Sinclair—as well as the sole owner of controlling stock—that had provided her the leverage and respect of the board. Largely Yasmine stayed out of day-to-day business operations. She trusted the executives in place to run their offices and steer the company in the directions they envisioned. Yasmine's only real interactions with the behemoth corporation her grandfather started was ensuring it inflicted no lasting damage to the earth. This was the legacy of Olympia which she fiercely defended. Eventually the board got used to running projects past Yasmine for approval. However, with her out of pocket, Howard was the person the board had to answer to. Something they did not appreciate. It wasn't only that he was an outsider with no real familiar connection to the company, it was also that he had a brilliant head for business and was not afraid to challenge them on deals he found less than ideal. Howard had his hands full, and Arielle was glad it wasn't her.

Demitra had been called by her friend Charlie Bennet, Chief of Police of Daihmler, in need of help with a minor robbery case. He'd uncovered nothing in the form of clues to the whereabouts of the thieves and resorted to his ace-in-the-hole, his secret psychic associate, for assistance. But Demitra declined the case, unable to focus on anything else besides her missing daughters and the care of her grandchildren and great niece and nephew. Charlie was disappointed. Demitra never refused to help. However, the second she confided that it was family witch affairs keeping her occupied, he didn't force the issue. The key to Charlie and Demitra's successful relationship was that he asked no questions, and she didn't have to come up with lies. He let it go and was determined to find another method to catch his thief. Demitra used her time co-parenting the children with Salem, when Salem wasn't locked in the study handling her own client accounts from the Atlanta advertising agency she ran. The small Blanchard children were all still very much shaken by the absence of their parents. Demitra and Salem did their best to comfort them and ease their anxieties.

Zelda was at her own home resuming the many appointments she'd postponed when the Blanchard cousins vanished. Her many clients had grown impatient waiting to seek her spiritual and psychic advice. Zelda's day was brimming over with suspicious wives, mournful widows, panicky businessmen, and a mayor worried about reelection. When she wasn't guiding the citizens of Daihmler with her all-seeing eye, she was counseling her two daughters, Melinda and Sarah, on the absolute disasters their dating lives were presenting.

And Artemis went back to her restaurant, The Cobblestone, to attend to the many duties being the owner required. Her beer vendor had overcharged her, citing accidental oversight, although she knew it was purposeful retaliation for having added selections from several Birmingham microbreweries to the bar menu. The fruit delivery was late. And the fish delivery that morning still had her nose in chaos from the nasty, pungent smell of spoiled product after the refrigerated van had arrived malfunctioning. It was one of those days.

Her head cook, Dudley Thrasher—lovingly known by staff as "Skillet"—was celebrating 30 years with the restaurant. Artemis also had the secret task of planning a surprise party for him in the coming weeks. She did not mind that task though. Skillet was special to everyone. Though the place had changed ownership and names several years ago when Artemis took over, Skillet was a fixture then, and now. He was 65 years old but still as active in the kitchen as when he'd been in his 40s. No one could recreate Artemis' recipes like Skillet. Sometimes she even admitted to herself, but to no one else, that he made some of her dishes even better than she did.

Skillet was considered the grandfather of The Cobblestone. All the staff cherished him. Always kind, always concerned with their lives, Skillet doled out parental advice as readily as he plated entrees. It did not take much for him to see something weighing on Artemis' heart as he observed her meandering through the restaurant without purpose to her actions. Taking a break from afternoon food prep and setup, Skillet handed off trimming the steaks to his second in command and followed Artemis into the empty dining room.

He sat down at the large, round eight-top table where she had scattered kitchen invoices along with her notepad and calculator. He plopped down in a seat, clearing his throat to fetch her attention.

"Yes?" she asked, barely looking up.

"You have some kind of dilemma. Not real good at hiding it either, Missy."

Artemis gave a half grateful, half irritated smile and answered, "Just some family troubles at home. It will be alright."

"Maybe you're better off at home handling them if they're that serious," Skillet suggested. "Or were you in need of a distraction today?"

Artemis met his gaze and sighed. "Pretty much."

The older man stared at her with his almost clear light blue eyes—eyes that reminded Artemis of her mother's own. His crackled skin and red complexion were evidence of a lifetime spent over a stove. When Skillet looked at her, or anyone at all, his eyes were like truth serum, forcing down defenses and permitting them to spill their problems forth.

"Distractions are just another way to keep from dealing with things we're not ready to process."

Artemis listened, suppressing a smile. One of Skillet's leading characteristics was his skillful way of restating the obvious without ever actually imparting anything useful to the situation. A kindly man, Skillet considered himself an insightful old sage. And everyone else let him. His wife died years ago, and they never had been blessed with children. For this reason, Skillet considered everyone his child, and his duty—in his mind—was to impart wisdom to anyone in need. But rarely did anything he say make much sense to anyone other than himself. Artemis humored him and continued listening.

"What's on your mind, Missy?" Skillet asked. "What is going on at home?"

Artemis did not want to talk. But she would never have hurt Skillet's feelings for anything. Unable to really tell him the family trouble, she abbreviated it for non-magical purposes. "Some of the kids, the ones I raised, have left for a little while. Their absence has caused some problems. We are hopeful they'll come back soon."

"Ah, I see," he replied as if some brilliant light had shone down on the issue. "Well, I'll tell you Artemis, sometimes kids have to find their own way. Sometimes that way is over here, sometimes it's over there. Sometimes it's across the tracks, and sometimes it's sailing through the air. You just get yourself a net and be ready to catch them. Kids always fall back down."

Artemis generously smiled and gave him a nod to impress upon him that he had been of great help. Satisfied that his pearls of wisdom did the trick, he rose from his chair and started back to the kitchen. Just before passing through the swinging wooden doors, he turned back to his employer and added an addendum. "And Missy, just you remember that when the sky gets its darkest, you can bet a porch light will turn on...providing somebody paid the electric bill."

As the kitchen doors swung shut behind the aging man, Artemis thought to herself *If Skillet were twenty years older, I'd set him up with Zelda.*

CHAPTER TWELVE

A Letter from Beyond

It had been nearly eight days since the four Blanchards disappeared. As the remaining family members gathered around the morning breakfast table, their vacant chairs stood out boldly. Every meal without Beryl, Seth, Fable, and Yasmine was significantly difficult to get through as the banter and commotion they typically added to the dining experience was sorely missed. No one had figured out what could or should be done to try and pull them back to their current timeline. Artemis' newfound knowledge of Beryl's future was providing nothing in means of how to solve the problem. It was someone else who offered solutions and a surprise for the family on that eighth morning. A revelation she could now share.

"I got something to tell y'all this morning," Zelda announced coming through the kitchen door.

"A clue as to where everyone went?" Demitra asked.

"Could be," Zelda said, withdrawing a glass canning jar from her oversized purse. The jar was dirty, aged, and from its design, an antique. The lid was fastened by a rusty hinge—not the screw-on kind found today.

"What is that?" Nacaria asked.

"I'm hopin' it's a little help."

Artemis took the filthy jar and unfastened the rusty hinge. Inside was an envelope. The paper was strange, not smooth and crisp like modern paper. There was a roughness to it, almost a parchment texture. Antique paper. Artemis read the writing on the front and then showed it to the family:

FOR ARTEMIS ONLY. DO NOT OPEN UNTIL A WEEK AFTER EVERYONE VANISHES.

"Where did this come from?" Demitra gasped.

"Your Momma gave it to me before she died," Zelda said. "When that new addition to the house was bein' built, the work crew found this jar buried a few feet down right under where Lympy put that new wing a few years ago."

Demitra was incredulous. This was vital information they should have had in the beginning. She yelled at the old woman, "You have known about this jar for these last several days and you said nothing to us!?"

"Your momma entrusted me with a task, and I followed it." Zelda replied sternly. "Don't know why it had to wait till a week later, but it ain't my job to question the orders of other people. I figure they got their reasons. I'm doin' what I was told to do. Now y'all can open it."

Artemis shot Zelda a look of frustration before snatching the letter from her. Carefully, she unsealed the envelope and withdrew the fragile piece of old paper. She read it aloud to the eager ears at the Blanchard breakfast table.

Aunt Artemis,

I hope you and everyone else are all right and safe at home. We were all together that day in the yard when Beryl disappeared right before our eyes. Then I saw Fable vanish, too. Then suddenly I was gone and transported to another place in time. I hope it stopped with the three of us and the rest of you are safe. Please tell Yaz I love her, and I am okay. In fact, I have enjoyed this crazy adventure. I am in 1876. I am on Blanchard land living with our ancestor Blaze Blanchard and our great-great grandfather Victor Blanchard who is three years old!

I remembered about the new wing to the house and found the location using the oak trees that sit around the house of our time. Hopefully, this jar was recovered and is in your hands Artemis. I know you'll give me hell for making you wait a week to open it, but I wasn't sure how this works. Can you actually come to me before I've even buried the jar? Or would that throw everything into chaos as the past changes before the future can instruct it to? Blaze and I sat up all night trying to figure it out. It was just best you waited until the day I buried the jar.

You guys would be amazed by Blaze. None of us at home have ever even heard of her, and it's because of her that our ancestor Victor was able to

live and grow and remain on Blanchard land. She works the whole farm herself. She has no money to hire help. I've been helping her plant the fields! I know you won't believe that I'd work that hard, but I have been. I've had an awakening experience, but it's time to come home. I have no idea how I got here. I hope you do. Can you come get me and bring me home? My love to you and Yaz, the kids, and everybody at home.
Seth

"Seth is in 1876?!" Nacaria said, astounded.

"And if Beryl is back in the 60s, then that means Fable and Yasmine are probably in some other timeline, too," Zelda deduced.

"Beryl and Seth are both on Blanchard land," Salem noted. "Doesn't that make it seem likely that Fable and Yaz are as well, just in different time periods? Everyone is technically still here at Blanchard House, only spread out over history."

"So, we just have to go and get them," Nacaria smiled.

"Why does that sound easier than it's probably going to be?" Arielle said.

Xander began pacing. He was thinking out the entire situation but continued falling short of any reasonable answers. He looked once or twice in his wife's direction, pleading with his eyes for help. Nacaria was visibly shaken by Seth and Yasmine's disappearances. Every one of the Blanchards was upset by the situation. But Xander was new to this family. New even to his own children's lives. While everyone else was frantic with worry about never finding the lost cousins, Xander was consumed with how little time he'd had with his son and daughter-in-law. He needed more time with them and their children. He finally had his entire family intact. He just had to find a way to bring his missing children home.

"If we only knew how they got there," Xander said. "Nacaria knows enough about spells and potions to go back in time, but that doesn't mean she can bring someone back with her."

"I can try," Nacaria replied. "I can go down to the vault and see what I can do with our stores of ingredients. I will see what I'm able to come up with. Now that I know where to go, that's half the battle."

Artemis was not so certain. She could not shake the idea that it was some kind of spell which propelled the others back in the first place. "There had to be something that happened which caused all this. Some type of inadvertent spell."

"Does it really matter if Nacaria is able to go back and get them?" Demitra pointed out.

"It does matter, I'm afraid," Artemis said. "If a spell propelled them back, Nacaria's magic won't be able to overpower that spell. She could send herself back to where they are, but she won't be able to rescue them and bring them home until that other spell is broken."

"But no one cast any spells. No one was doing anything," Arielle noted. "We were just sitting around eating. Except Hera wanted cake. Do you think the kids could have cast some sort of accidental spell?"

Demitra considered the idea a second and then replied, "Hera was with us, and we didn't hear her recite anything. Rom is a wolf—so far, he hasn't displayed any kind of powers. Con was at the table too, but he did not cast a spell. Titan isn't big enough for something so powerful."

"No one was speaking about anything magical," Cassandra added. "No one at all."

Jerry wanted to help—wanted to be of some kind of use during this trial—but he was not like them. He was a novice at stuff like this. His only use at the moment was to go into work. He still had a job, and his boss wouldn't understand another missed workday. He was dressed in his suit now and rummaging behind the foyer table for his briefcase which had fallen and wedged itself behind the potted palm. He freed it and went back into the living room to kiss his wife goodbye. As he leaned in to Demitra, he stopped short and pulled back. She gave him a quizzical look because he never withdrew his kisses before he'd supplied them. His eyes were pointing upward to that elusive space we all look towards when deep in thought.

Jerry looked back into Demitra's eyes with a look of epiphany. He sidestepped her and addressed the room, most pointedly Artemis. "You know...I'm still relatively new to all of this, but something strikes me as possibly significant. But it just might be a coincidence."

"Tell us what you're thinking Jerry," Artemis prompted. "You never know, it could be relevant."

"Well, I was just remembering—as you read that letter and figured out Seth is off somewhere in Blanchard history, just as Beryl is...it made me think. That day they all disappeared...wasn't Salem saying something at the time about all the people who used to live on this land over the years? I don't remember exactly what she was saying but it was right after she said it when everyone disappeared."

Suddenly the conversation from that day over the picnic table rushed back into Artemis' mind. He was correct. They had all been rather nostalgic, and Salem had, in fact, made a comment about all the Blanchards that had walked these lands before them. Artemis' eyes widened and sparkled with a feeling of hope she had not felt in eight days. She jumped from her chair to rush to her brother-in-law whereupon she kissed him on the cheek. "Jerry Miller, I believe you just saved the day! That is exactly what happened!"

Jerry smiled bashfully and went out the door to his workday.

"Are you saying I did this?" Salem gasped. She felt a little offended. Accused.

Demitra understood her husband's comment now as well as the look of hope on her sister's face. It was so clear now. "Don't you remember?" Demitra exclaimed to Salem. "We were all sitting at the picnic tables when you began talking about all the different generations of Blanchards that have lived here. It wasn't only you—we were all talking about it. That is when everyone disappeared. And it explains why you did not! You cast the spell!"

"I cast no spells that day!" Salem cried. "Besides, I don't even have that power. I freeze time, remember?"

With a smile emerging upon her face, Arielle reached forward and patted Salem's belly. "But maybe little Olympus here has that kind of power. And you were the one talking about it. Maybe he made it happen."

Salem was aghast. "Unborn babies do not have that kind of power. Even witch ones."

"You weren't here much when Yasmine was pregnant with Hera," Artemis pointed out. "Hera's power to levitate things came out in Yasmine. For a short time, Yasmine possessed unborn Hera's powers."

Salem placed her hands gently on her protruding belly and said, "Do you mean my baby..."

"You have the power to halt time," Artemis stated. "And it appears your baby has the power to jump time."

"That's unprecedented!" Xander exclaimed.

"I find this very hard to wrap my head around," Salem admitted, shaking her head in refusal.

"It's not that difficult to believe if you stop and think about it," Cassandra told her sister. "Your ability is to stop time in place, and our father's ability is to travel great distances in the blink of an eye. It is not far-fetched to imagine your baby has taken all that to a whole new level. You are the daughter of a Blanchard and an Obreiggon—two of the most powerful witching families around. I have a feeling that is one unusually powerful baby you have inside you."

CHAPTER THIRTEEN

Nacaria to the Rescue

Nate and Beryl saw a lot of each other over the next few days. It was now the weekend and Nate did not have to work, so he filled the days with picnics by the river and rowboat rides down the stream. Beryl found herself enjoying leisure time for the first time in her life. She had never had much time for leisure and now admitted to herself it was kind of nice. Or perhaps it was Nate's company. He was such a kind man, and it did not hurt matters that he was rather good looking as well. She would have preferred him without the hair grease, but it was the 60s after all and the men around had not yet segued from their 50s styles.

As he steered the rowboat across the pond toward the little island, he watched Beryl shining under the sunlight. "You are extraordinarily beautiful, Beryl Blanchard."

She blushed. "Thank you."

"Do you know how much longer your visit here will last?"

"Trying to get rid of me?" she smiled. She made a clumsy attempt at a flirtatious hair toss but it didn't land well. Her hair was shoulder length and curly and didn't have quite the same toss effect Salem's would have in this situation. Nate didn't appear to notice; he was too busy smiling at the beautiful woman in his presence.

"On the contrary," he said. "I'm hoping it'll be a while before you go back to Mobile."

"I really have no idea how long my visit will be," Beryl said. "I'm taking things day by day."

They reached the small island and Nate helped Beryl step out of the boat without getting her shoes wet. He carried a picnic basket to a little patch of grass and spread out the blanket. Overhead the wispy tendrils of a willow tree danced in the wind. A small patch of wildflowers waved their yellows, whites, and oranges in the breeze at the edge of the tiny island. Nate opened a bottle of wine and poured them both a glass. They raised their glasses to toast each other but Nate stopped, staring into her eyes.

"I think I'm falling for you Beryl."

"Don't say that Nate," she whispered. "I cannot stay here. In fact, I think it may be a mistake even seeing you because I am starting to have feelings as well."

"What's so wrong about that?" Nate replied. "We like each other a great deal. There is no law saying you must go back home. You could stay here with me."

"I can't explain," Beryl said. "But trust me. It isn't possible."

"Is there another man at home?"

Beryl laughed. "No. Definitely not. There have never really been any other men. You are the first I have ever cared for. I mean that."

"Then stay with me, Beryl. Let us see where this could go. I can see a beautiful life with you." He leaned in to kiss her. She returned the kiss passionately. He laid her down gently on the blanket, tossing the glasses of wine aside.

...

"Oh my God! It worked!" Nacaria exclaimed to herself looking around at the vast empty field before her. It was an amazing sight to behold. The journey was such a fast blur that she wasn't certain her potion worked until she looked out into the field. One moment she was standing in the middle of the Blanchard living room with the family all around watching as she smashed the potion she'd made to the floor. Now she was in the past, most likely standing in the same exact spot where Blanchard House would one day be built.

Of course, this rescue mission was still untested. Nacaria was confident of her ability to enter the past. She had done it once before after all, many years ago when she had tried to stop the birth of Atheidrelle D'Angelo Obreiggon. Going to the past was not the hard part for her. Being able to remove her son and nieces from it was another thing entirely. It all hinged on Salem's ability back home to successively reverse the spell her unborn baby cast. If she was not able to do that, then Nacaria was not going to succeed in rescuing anyone. It was a long shot, but the only shot they had.

As Nacaria got her bearings, she saw a tiny house in the distance. It looked about like the sort of house someone in rural Alabama might have in 1876. She was so thankful for that letter from Seth telling them the exact place in time he was trapped in. Otherwise, she might have had to jump around all through the year of 1876 until she found him.

Blaze Blanchard was scrubbing the wash on a metal scrub board when she saw the figure of a woman approaching in the distance. The closer the woman came the more peculiar she appeared. Her clothes were like something Blaze had never laid eyes on before...or perhaps she had, a long time ago.

As the strangely dressed blonde woman in the tight pale-yellow dress approached, Blaze shouted out, "You related to Fable and Seth?"

Nacaria was astonished. This might be easier than she thought. "Well, yes. Actually, I am his mother."

"His momma!" Blaze exclaimed, rising up to dry her hand on her skirt. She extended it forward and shook Nacaria's. "Seth is one good feller. Really been a help to me these last few days."

Blaze inspected the woman before her. The blonde woman's skin was so white and smooth. Blaze wondered if she had ever been outside before. And her hair! It was so long and fresh and clean. It bounced behind her when she walked. Blaze had never seen hair that color before. It was almost the color of apricot juice if you squeezed in some lemon. She wondered how anyone could get any practical work done with hair that long getting in the way. One stretch at a washboard and that hair would get snatched out by the root.

Nacaria noticed the woman looking her over peculiarly but smiled with a sigh of relief as she took in the strange ancestor before her. "Are you by chance Blaze Blanchard?"

"Yeah. That's me."

"I am your great grandniece Nacaria."

"So that preserve jar worked!" Blaze bellowed. She turned her head and shouted behind her toward the house. "Hey Seth! Your trick worked! You got some kinfolk out here. It's your momma!"

The door to the ramshackle house swung open, and Seth emerged holding a small boy on his hip. He stopped in his tracks and stared at the sight of his mother standing in the dusty yard. He beamed a smile and rushed toward her.

"Mom!"

Nacaria grabbed her son in her arms and hugged him tightly, careful not to squish the toddler he was holding. "Oh son, we were so afraid we'd lost you forever. That jar was a brilliant idea!"

She gave her son the once-over and was not sure to make of what she saw. Seth Blanchard, who normally wore nothing but tank tops and workout apparel, was dressed in old denim overalls and a musty faded shirt. Obviously, leftover clothes from some long-gone ancestor. Before she had time to comment on his change, he was eager to have questions of his own answered.

"Where's Yazzy?" Seth asked, looking around. "Did she stay home with the kids?"

"Yasmine is missing, too," Nacaria explained, hating to disappoint him. "You, Beryl, Yaz, and Fable all disappeared."

"Why only us?"

"It's a long story," Nacaria replied. "Basically, your unborn nephew has an immense power and sent you back in time. But we have figured it out, and if Salem was able to tap into it again and reverse her accidental spell, I should be able to take you home."

"Did she come with you?"

Nacaria shook her head. "No, she is at home concentrating on diffusing the spell. She can't travel these distances anyway in her condition."

Seth shifted the little boy to his other hip and wiped the child's runny nose with his sleeve before asking his mother his next question, "Am I the first you've rescued?"

Nacaria nodded as she tickled the underside of the little boy's chin with her slender finger. "Yes. We know where you and Beryl are. I figured you and I would go get her next. But Fable and Yasmine are a different story. We have no clue where they went."

Seth grinned. "I know where Fable is."

...

Blaze Blanchard cooked a final meal for her distant relatives. Nacaria was grateful for the nourishment, but it did take her a minute to choke down the milk. Both Blaze and Seth noticed and laughed at her reaction. Blaze said Seth went through the same thing when he first arrived. Milk fresh from a cow tasted very different from the pasteurized, store-bought milk Nacaria was accustomed to.

Nacaria and Seth spent some time playing with baby Victor. It was surreal for Nacaria, He was their direct ancestor, and she had the opportunity to hold him and listen to him jabber away with the few words he knew. When dinner was finished, it was time for the future Blanchards to depart. Seth walked over to Blaze and gave her a loving hug.

"I will never forget you, Blaze. Everything you did for me while I was here. Everything you've done and will do for Victor. Our entire family owes you a debt.

Thank you. Thank you for keeping the Blanchard family alive. For keeping this farmland intact for the future generations. What you are doing is important and it lasts for generations to come."

The young woman, aged beyond her years from sun and hard work, grinned bashfully and returned Seth's embrace. "It's been a real treat meetin' you, Seth Blanchard. Knowin this family goes on as long as it does is gonna keep me on track the rest of my life. Be sure to say hey to Fable for me. Tell her I never forgot her."

Seth lifted little Vic in his arms and kissed his fat cheek. "I love you, little man. Live a good life. I'll do my best to make you proud." He passed Vic off to Blaze.

Nacaria took hold of her son's hand and focused her mind on Fable's place in time. Withdrawing a potion from her pocket, she smashed it to the floor and in a cloud of mist and vapor, she and Seth vanished from Blaze's cabin. Blaze Blanchard watched smiling as her kinfolk evaporated before her very eyes. Suddenly a new memory from her childhood entered her mind. One which was only now being created.

. . .

Little Blaze Blanchard stood with Fable in the yard watching in astonishment as the figures of two people suddenly appeared a few feet from them. Blaze turned her astonished face to Fable and saw the expression of relief on her distant relative's face. Fable shrieked and ran into the arms of the two people.

"Aunt Nacaria! Seth!" Fable cried. "You came for me!" She pushed back a brief second and cried, "What took you so long?"

"You have no idea what all we've been through to get here," Nacaria told her niece. "Just be glad Seth knew where to find you."

The little redheaded girl was staring at these strangely dressed people. Seth approached the child and gave her a friendly smile. She smiled back.

"It's all right," he told Blaze. "We are relatives. You will see us again when you are older. But we have to go now."

"Wait," Fable demanded. "Not yet." She marched into the house and returned after a few seconds with a woman and a man in tow. The man looked angry and the woman perplexed.

"What's all this?" the man said. "Who are these folks?"

"Jebediah Blanchard, Nancy Blanchard, these are your offspring. My family, come to take me home."

"Good riddance," Jebediah snarled. "Glad to have you off our hands."

Fable gave him a stern look and said, "You just remember what I told you. Be kind to Nancy and Blaze. They are great women with great power. And if you cannot respect them, fear them. Or I will come back here again and whoop your ass."

Nacaria and Seth looked puzzlingly at one another.

"Now let's go home!" Fable cried to her family.

"First we need to find Yaz," Seth explained. "You don't know where she is, do you?"

"Yazzy disappeared too?" Fable asked.

"Yes," Nacaria told her niece. "Beryl went first, then you, then Seth, then Yasmine. Let's go to Beryl, perhaps she has an idea where Yasmine was sent. And we know where Beryl is."

"We do?" Fable asked, exchanging confused glances with Seth. He shrugged in equal confusion.

Nacaria placed her hands on her son and niece's shoulders and chuckled, "Are you guys ready to meet Olympia Blanchard? Olympia Blanchard in her 20s that is!"

. . .

Blanchard House looked almost like it had most of their lives in their own time, minus the impressive array of colorful flowers and shrubs Olympia had always prided herself upon. The starkness of the 1960s Blanchard House was a little startling to Nacaria, Seth, and Fable, but it was still home.

"I forgot how much smaller the place looked without the new wing," Fable pointed out. "And the back looks shorter somehow."

"My father built the kitchen addition when he moved in," Nacaria explained. "That added not only the kitchen, but the vault and two more second story bedrooms. Blanchard House wasn't always as big as you're used to."

Seth stared at the front door, a little unsure what to do. This was technically his home after all, but did that count when in another time period? "Do we just walk in?" Seth asked. "Or knock?"

"I have no idea," Nacaria told her son.

She walked gingerly up the porch steps and to the front door. The porch was noticeably empty of the old familiar rocker and porch swing. This was certainly the home of a different Olympia Blanchard. Nacaria rapped at the door firmly twice and waited. Footsteps sounded in the foyer before the doorknob turned. As the door opened, Nacaria looked at a woman who resembled herself more greatly than she had ever imagined. Long blonde hair, deep blue eyes, and a beauty that distracted from anything else.

"Yes?" the young woman said.

Nacaria was suddenly struck with the fact that the woman standing before her was her very own mother, yet she was young enough to be her daughter. Nacaria swallowed hard and muttered, "Hello, Olympia. My name is Nacaria."

"Well, I'll be damned," Olympia gasped. Nacaria and the others were more than a little shocked at her language. Older Olympia did not cuss like that. Young Olympia continued, "You look just like me, except old."

"I am not old!" Nacaria snapped indignantly.

"Uh, yeah you kind of are," Olympia smiled. "What are you, like 60?"

"I am in my late 40s!" Nacaria exclaimed.

"Same thing," young Olympia replied as she stepped back to allow them inside.

Fable was shocked at what the inside of her childhood home looked like. Crazy psychedelic wallpaper and loud furnishings filled the room where normally more sedate and refined traditional furniture would have stood. *Is that shag carpet?* Fable asked Seth with her mind. Seth replied back, *This is bizarre.* Fable spotted a peculiar, beaded box sitting on the coffee table. She had never seen it before. Without thinking of the impertinence of her action, she reached down to inspect it.

Olympia suddenly took notice and called out, "Hey! Don't touch that."

It was too late. Fable had lifted the lid a few inches before Olympia's warning caused her to lower it.

Oh my God Seth, she told her cousin with her mind. *It's weed.*

"So, you are my daughter?" Olympia asked, returning her attention to Nacaria. "Beryl told me about you guys."

"Do you know who we are?" Seth asked, gesturing to himself and Fable.

Olympia twirled a bit of her long hair around an index finger as she shifted slightly to one side. All his life Olympia Blanchard had been a matronly old woman, to see her now...youthful...beautiful actually, was almost more than he could comprehend.

"Well, I guess so. You're the boy so you must be Seth. Which one are you ma'am?" Olympia asked Fable.

"Ma'am?" Fable sneered. She turned to Seth, "Hecate just ma'amed me."

"I was taught to have respect for my elders," Olympia smiled.

"I am your granddaughter! My name is Fable."

Flippantly, Olympia raised one of her brows and replied, "Well, you're older than me regardless."

Fable turned her back towards Olympia and whispered into Seth's ear, "Why did no one ever tell us our grandmother was a bitch when she was young?" Seth sniggered against her shoulder.

"Mother," Nacaria began. "We are here to rescue Beryl."

"Please do not call me Mother," Olympia sneered. "It's a little crazy. I am not even sure I ever plan to have any children. I really dislike children."

"Dear Lord," Fable sighed again to Seth. "I don't think I am ever going to be the same again after this."

Olympia settled them into the living room and offered them some iced tea while they waited for Beryl to return home. She explained that Beryl was on a date and would be home sometime that afternoon.

Fable, who was swirling back and forth in the avocado green pod chair by the fireplace, did a double take towards Seth before exclaiming, "Wait a minute! Beryl is dating? Beryl never dates."

Seth grinned, "Maybe the men in our time aren't her style. I guess she likes older sensibilities."

"He's a great guy," Olympia replied. "He used to be a beau of mine, but that was never very serious. I'm happy he and Beryl sparked because they are really cute together."

While they passed the time waiting for Beryl to return, Olympia tried to pry information out of her descendants, but Nacaria remained adamant that they tell her nothing about the future.

"All I want to know is what stocks to buy," Olympia cried. "If I get rich it can only benefit you all later too. Nate says I have to get a job if we are going to make it much longer. But can you see me working? I am much too pretty to work. Unless it was modeling. I could do that."

Fable nearly spit her iced tea back into the glass. Of all people in the world she had ever known through her life, she would have never pegged her wise, matronly grandmother--so full of integrity-- to have been such a vain, vapid brat in her youth.

Olympia continued to pester Nacaria to divulge future information she might profit by, but Nacaria refused to say anything. It was rather shocking to Nacaria—the one who always made the most egregious life mistakes—to find out that her mother herself was so carelessly inquisitive with no concern for upsetting the time continuum. Although somewhere inside her heart it was giving her a bit of solace knowing that even the illustrious Olympia Blanchard was reckless in youth, still Nacaria wished for a little more wisdom and guidance in the Olympia Blanchard before them.

Pastoria came in from wherever she had been and displayed little interest in meeting the new arrivals. There seemed to be tension between her and Olympia that the others did not understand. She barked something to Olympia about the power bill being due, grabbed the pearl covered box, and then started for the stairs.

"Are you even the least bit curious who our guests are?" Olympia called after her.

Pastoria stopped mid-tread on the stairs and stomped back into the foyer. "Why should you tell me anything? You seem to like keeping secrets from me. Had any more dates with John lately?"

"He's actually on his way over to take me out now," Olympia snarled. "And I'll thank you to be nice to him when he gets here."

Pastoria stomped her foot on the wooden floor and barked, "Oh, that will never happen. But the sooner he arrives and takes my traitor sister out for the day, the happier I'll be."

Nacaria, not wanting to enter into this sisterly fracas, couldn't help herself. She had to ask. "John Windham?"

"Do you hate him, too?" Pastoria asked, coming closer, as if perhaps she had an ally amongst the strangers.

"No," Nacaria replied. "I wouldn't say that."

Pastoria stared at Nacaria. Her eyes moved quickly to Olympia, then back to Nacaria again. Next she eyed Fable and Seth. She scanned their faces, then their clothes, then she looked back at Nacaria and Olympia again--as if finally noticing the similarities. "Who are you people anyway?" she finally asked.

"Apparently they are more relatives from the future," Olympia answered, almost beleaguered. It was obvious she was bored of them by now, especially since they wouldn't give her any useful information. "They are Beryl's family, and they've come to get her. Meet my daughter and more of my grandchildren."

"I'll meet them when they're born," Pastoria said dismissively. "It's hard enough keeping up with my own life, much less all your future offspring coming and going. But I am going to miss Beryl. I've really come to care a lot about her. Why don't you take my sister with you when you go and leave Beryl? I could use the peace."

"You're as funny as a rattlesnake in a sleeping bag," Olympia scoffed at her sister.

"You know a little something about rattlesnakes," Pastoria retorted. "You are dating one after all. Traitor."

"At least there is someone who wants to date me," Olympia quipped. "I don't see any men lining up on the porch for you much these days."

"There aren't any left," Pastoria smiled viciously. "You dated them all and they are now all at the clinic getting a shot."

"Bitch."

"Slut!"

"Traitor!"

"You already said *traitor*," Olympia sneered imperiously. "But you have the intelligence of a dead skunk so I shouldn't expect a deeper vocabulary."

Nacaria, Seth, and Fable eyed each other and tried not to laugh at the ridiculous immaturity of the two women they had always held in such high esteem. Suddenly a familiar voice rang out from the front door.

"Are you two at it again? I swear I am going to have to stay home around the clock to referee." Beryl came into the foyer with a man behind her. As she plopped her purse down on the front table, she looked into the room ready to intercede in today's sisterly quarrel. Locking eyes on her aunt, sister, and cousin, she let out a howl of joy and rushed into their arms. Nate stood in confusion watching this sudden reunion.

"Beryl?" he asked. "Who are these people?"

"Oh, I'm so sorry Nate!" she exclaimed, dragging him forward by the arm. "Nate this is my family: my sister, Fable; my cousin, Seth; and my aunt. Nacaria."

"Nice to meet you," he replied. "Are you going to be visiting for a while as well?"

Fable gave him a suspicious eye and said, "Actually we've come to take Beryl home."

Nate looked shaken. "No, you can't do that. Beryl and I—well we, we've been making plans."

"Plans?" Seth repeated. Olympia stepped forward just as concerned as her future grandson appeared to be.

"Is that wise, Beryl?" she said.

"Not plans," Beryl corrected. "Nate wants me to stay in Daihmler and not go *back to Mobile.* But I've told him I don't think that's possible."

"Don't *think*?" Fable cried. "It is not remotely possible! You are going back, and you are going back right now."

"No, you can't!" Nate pleaded. Suddenly he fell on his knees and grabbed her wrists. "Beryl, I am begging you to stay. I know we have only known each other a short time, but something special is happening. I know this is crazy, but if it'll get you to stay, I'll marry you."

"What?" Beryl gasped. Her mouth fell open and her eyes broadened. No one had ever asked her to marry them before. Despite the absurdity of her reality and the very fact that she was living in the wrong timeline, she could not help but feel elated as someone was actually proposing marriage to her.

"Yes!" Nate cried. "I will marry you. Marry me, Beryl Blanchard. Stay with me here in Daihmler. We'll have a fantastic life together."

"Well, this is just weird," Olympia remarked.

"They are *your* relatives," Pastoria said sarcastically as she elbowed her sister.

"This is insanity!" Fable exclaimed. "Beryl, you just met this guy! You haven't been here long enough to develop feelings. You two know nothing about each other. He certainly doesn't know about you."

"I know all I need to know about this spectacular lady." Nate smiled.

Beryl patted his cheek gently. "And I know Nate is the kindest, most decent man I've ever known. Not only is he a successful banker, but he is also an advocate for civil rights. Here in Alabama at this time in history, that's really something."

Nate made a peculiar face, "Honey, I'm not a banker."

Beryl blushed a little in embarrassment. "You aren't? I saw the loan papers—"

"Yes, but I don't represent the bank," Nate explained. "I represent the Blanchard family."

Beryl did not say anything as she looked on towards her new boyfriend. She didn't suppose it mattered much that she had misunderstood his occupation—that changed nothing in the way they felt about one another. But she did feel slightly ashamed that she had not previously known that piece of information about him.

"It doesn't make a damn whether you know what he does for a living or not," Fable argued. "This relationship is over. You have to come home now, and you know why Beryl."

"Beryl is staying here." Nate announced.

Beryl looked into his azure blue eyes, her own honey brown eyes were welling with tears now. She knew Fable was right. She did have to go. "Oh Nate," Beryl wept. "There is nothing more I would love than to stay here and build a life with you. But I can't. We are from different worlds. Different in ways I am not able to explain. I do have to go back with them."

Nate was about to say something else, but Nacaria cut him off. This had to end immediately before anything happened to change the future. Nacaria knew something no one else knew and she was hesitant to reveal it. And she would not have to if they could just leave. "We have to go. Now."

She took Beryl by the hand and motioned for Seth and Fable to join her. Nacaria said nothing to anyone as she led her companions to the dining room—or what was supposed to be the dining room. It was not, as it turned out, the dining room. It was a tiny kitchen with a small round table against the window. Shrugging the small surprise off, Nacaria shut the door and linked hands with everyone. There was no time to waste. They had to get out of there. They needed to return home. Nate's heart would hurt a while, but eventually he'd meet the woman he was supposed to marry and be fine. Besides, there were more pressing matters before them. They still needed to find Yasmine. Beryl struggled to loosen her aunt's grip, but Nacaria, Seth and Fable held her tightly as Nacaria focused her mind on the spell to whisk them away. Tossing the glass potion to the floor they readied themselves to sail through time back home again. Nacaria was caught off guard when nothing happened.

"Uh, aren't we now supposed to zap away?" Seth asked his mother.

"Yes, we are."

"Why didn't we?" Fable asked.

"I have no idea," Nacaria replied. "It worked for the two of you."

"Try harder," Seth urged. "I can hear Nate and the others coming."

Nacaria withdrew another vial and tried again with the same disappointing result. She did not understand. This potion was the exact same concoction she'd used to get Seth out of 1876 and Fable out of 1853. Why was it not working now?

CHAPTER FOURTEEN

Zelda's Second Bomb

Zelda came into Blanchard House in the early morning hoping to hear that Nacaria had successfully returned with some of the others. Finding Artemis alone in the kitchen making coffee, Zelda discovered no one had heard from or seen Nacaria in two days. She had not yet returned anyone to their proper timeline.

"Nacaria's first stop was Seth since we know where he was—thanks to you," Artemis said. "I guess from there they are having to time jump around to find Yasmine and Fable. I would assume they went back to your past to retrieve Beryl already."

"Well, that ain't exactly gone happen," Zelda said with a beleaguered wince.

Artemis made a face. "Zelda, if you have any more secret information regarding this mess, I need for you to tell me now."

"I reckon it's safe now," Zelda said, mostly to herself. "I couldn't say nothing 'till something had time to happen. It's happened now."

"Zelda," Artemis grimaced. "I want all the information you have, all at one time."

"You best call Demmy in here. Actually, get ever'body. They all gotta know eventually."

Within the hour everyone left in the family were gathered back in the Blanchard House living room. Zelda faced the crowd which included Artemis, Demitra, Salem, Xander, Arielle, and Cassandra. Demitra demanded she begin, but Zelda said she had one more person they needed to wait for. After several minutes of Zelda being berated by the eager and impatient audience, Jerry and Howard walked through the door, summoned from their jobs for an emergency family meeting. Zelda instructed them to sit down. Howard seemed very confused as to why he was summoned, but he did as he was told.

Zelda began. "The reason I figure y'all ain't heard hide nor hair from the others is because they ain't able to get back."

"What?!" Xander shouted. "My wife is stuck in the past?"

"Naw, she ain't stuck. Neither is Seth, Yazzy, or Fable. But Beryl is. I 'spect Nikky ain't figured that out yet, but she's about to."

"Explain," Artemis said sternly. "Thoroughly, this time."

...

She'd carried this secret with her for over fifty years. Always knowing this day would arrive when it would come out. Of course, she always hoped it would be Olympia spilling the secret and she would merely be the backup. But life didn't play things out that way and now Zelda was going to single handedly be the heavy.

Zelda began, "I came in one afternoon while there were some strangers in the house. As I come in the door, I saw Beryl bein' shoved into the kitchen by three people I'd never laid eyes on before. People I now know to be Nikki, Fable, and Seth. Olympia, Pastoria, and our friend Nate was running to the kitchen after them. Well not this kitchen, the old house's kitchen. Did y'all know the dining room used to be the kitchen? It was so small, y'all wouldn't have been able to all fit in there—"

"Old woman, get to the point!" Demitra roared.

"Settle down," Zelda continued. "Anyway, as I come in that day, I found Lympy and Pastoria, and Nate runnin' into the kitchen. Nate was real upset cause some people had come to take Beryl home. He liked her, you see. I followed them all to the kitchen where Nikki, Seth, and Fable all holdin' hands with Beryl trying to cast a spell to get home."

"Where was Yasmine?" Arielle asked.

"I don't know," Zelda replied. "She what'nt there. Guess they hadn't got her yet."

"Go on," Artemis urged.

"Well, Nikki's spell wasn't workin'. They didn't know why. But I did."

Nacaria could not understand why her spell wasn't working. The fact that Fable and Seth had been able to be rescued meant that Salem's original spell must have been broken. There was no reason Nacaria could think of as to why she was not capable of getting them all out of this specific reality. Everyone looked at her as she grabbed another vial from her pocket and attempted it again. It produced the same result. No one departed the past timeline. With only one final potion left in her pocket, she could not risk using it until she had figured out what was going wrong. It was the only path back home.

"Mother, why is this not working?' Seth asked.

"I'm glad it isn't!" Beryl exclaimed. "You just dragged me in here. I have been living with Olympia and Pastoria for weeks, and I care a great deal about Nate. I do not want to simply pop back home without a proper farewell to them."

Olympia, Pastoria, Nate and a young Zelda rushed into the small kitchen. "Just like that, you were going to leave?" Olympia scolded. "Beryl is like family to us. That was pretty low-down ma'am."

Nacaria rolled her eyes, "Would you please stop calling me ma'am when I am your very own daughter?"

"Daughter?" Nate gasped. "What in the world is going on here? Beryl, are your relatives a little crazy?"

Beryl rushed into Nate's arms and kissed his cheek. "There is a great deal you don't know about the Blanchard family. I am so sorry I didn't tell you about us, but that's really up to Olympia and Pastoria."

Nate was lost. He had no idea what anyone was talking about, but he didn't care. As Beryl clung to him with his arms around her, the only thing that mattered was that the woman he loved seemed to be in emotional distress. Even if her entire family were insane—even if she herself was as well—her wellbeing was all that mattered to him. He kissed the top of her head. Her fuzzy blonde curls tickled his nose.

Seeing this interaction and knowing that things had already progressed too far with her sister and this man, Fable needed to take control of the situation. "Look, I don't care if you two think you're in love, or if grandmother here thinks we are rude to just go without saying goodbye. All I care to know right now is why Aunt Nacaria's spell did not take the four of us home?"

"I can tell you," Young Zelda announced.

Everyone looked over to Zelda.

"Oh my God that's Zelda!" Seth cried. "I'd know her anywhere!"

Olympia took hold of her best friend's hand and pulled her forward. "Zelda is the most powerful psychic I've ever known. If she says she knows what is wrong with your spell, then she does."

"Spell?" Nate gasped. "Psychic? What is happening around this house Olympia?"

Pastoria was never one for beating around a bush. She also had never agreed with her big sister's insistence that they always keep their secret from those closest to them. Normally she always acquiesced to Olympia's wishes. Only now that Olympia cared so little about her own feelings regarding John Windham, Pastoria took a little pleasure in blowing the roof off and revealing the truth. She grinned mischievously as she patted their lifelong friend's hand and, in a calm, matter-of-fact tone, Pastoria spilled the beans. "Nate, we are witches. These people are our relatives from the future. That is where Beryl comes from. The future. She's a witch too. There. Now you're all caught up."

Olympia jabbed her sister in the shoulder, furious at how cruelly blunt Pastoria could be. Still, when Nate turned to Olympia for a sign that this was all a big joke, Olympia simply nodded, letting him know Pastoria was not kidding.

"This is madness," Nate replied. "I think I need some air."

He turned to walk away but Beryl didn't let go of his arm, "Please Nate. Let me have a chance to explain everything to you in a more tactful way than Pastoria possesses the ability to."

"I wouldn't go nowhere," Zelda advised. "This concerns you too, Nate."

"Zelda," Olympia said. "Please use your power to tell us why our future relatives are unable to depart."

"Yes," Nacaria cried. "What did I do wrong?"

"You ain't done nuthin' wrong," Zelda said. "If y'all had all let go of Beryl's hand your spell woulda worked. It's Beryl stoppin' it."

"Because she thinks she's in love and wants to stay!" Fable shouted angrily in her sister's face.

"Nope," Zelda said. "Cause there ain't just four of y'all trying to leave. There's five."

"What?" Olympia exclaimed. "What are you talking about, Zel?"

Folding her plump arms over her chest, Zelda lowered her eyes to give a stern look of complete seriousness. "Beryl's got his baby in her."

A silence fell over the tiny Blanchard kitchen. Eyes widened, bulged. Heads hung in desperation. This was not what anyone expected Zelda to say. Least of all Beryl or Nate. As Nate stared at the floor digesting Zelda's proclamation, Beryl looked towards Fable, astounded herself. Fable's eyes slightly teared. Nacaria looked to her son, but Seth was as oblivious as everyone else. No one said a word for a long time as they all stood tightly crowded in the small kitchen. The only sound to be heard for several seconds was that of a tacky owl clock hanging on the wall by the stove. The eyes of the owl moved left to right as the seconds ticked off. The sound of the clock unnerved Nacaria. It was as if it were mocking her—mocking the dreaded situation. For the thing Nacaria had feared from the start was proving true. From that very first moment when Olympia revealed Beryl was seeing a man named Nate, Nacaria understood the possible ramifications.

Finally finding words to break everyone's silence, Nate stuttered, "Say that again?"

Beryl looked pale and frightened. "I haven't been here that long."

"Only takes once to make a baby," Zelda announced. "And you are as pregnant as it gets. You got two auras."

Seth recognized the gravity of the situation for Beryl, but the witch inside him still didn't understand why that would inhibit Beryl's returning home. As if Zelda had read his mind, she explained. "That baby is from this time, not yours. It ain't goin' nowhere 'till it's born. I'm afraid Beryl's gonna be here for the next nine months."

Nate was shaken. Too much information—unbelievable information—had been flung at him all at once. Still, as he looked into Beryl's teary eyes all he felt was love. He pressed her to his chest and directed her head to his shoulder.

"It's all right, Beryl. It is. Maybe it's a little fast, but that doesn't make it wrong. I love you. I want to marry you. I want you to be Mrs. Nate Caldwell. It'll be a great life."

A gasp rang out from Fable's throat. "Oh. My. God."

Nacaria clasped Fable's wrist and cut her a sharp look. In that exchange Fable understood. She understood what only Nacaria had figured out.

. . .

Artemis was dumbfounded. Zelda's explanation made perfect sense yet brought with it a truckload of questions and concerns. Demitra sat silently staring ahead. She had no idea what to make of the story Zelda had just parlayed. Salem was the one to speak first.

"Beryl is in the past, and she is pregnant? And until her baby is born it cannot travel through time?"

"Same reason why you didn't zap back with the others when you accidentally cast your spell. The unborn can't travel like that. They're tied to their world. I don't 'xactly know why, but they are."

"If Beryl cannot come home until her baby is born," Jerry asked, trying to clarify, "Can the baby come back with her then?"

Zelda waited a second, staring at Howard. He was listening to them all speaking but appeared to have very little comprehension as to what any of this meant. Then Zelda answered the question, "Yes, the baby could. But it won't."

"What happens to Beryl's baby?" Demitra asked. "Does it die?"

Zelda walked over to Howard and took hold of his hand. He glanced up at her as the understanding set in and a lonely tear began to fill his eye. "Beryl's baby is right here. Always has been. Howard is Beryl's son."

CHAPTER FIFTEEN

Howard's World Crashes Down

Howard sat on the sofa, hands dangling between his knees. He was staring up at Zelda as if he had lost all ability to form speech. Unable to break eye contact, he waited for the slightest flinch or playful glint which would explain her words away as some kind of ill-timed joke. Zelda held his gaze, understanding without having to read his mind. Howard Caldwell had spent his life in this house as the family friend. She watched him grow up. He had watched the Blanchard daughters grow up. He'd grown up with them. He'd watched them have children. He had seen those children grow up, now having children of their own. To discover at this time in life, one of those children he used to hold as a baby, watched go to prom, watched graduate high school, college, medical school...she'd been his mother the entire time. His mother. He could not bring himself to look at the Blanchards. He did not know how.

"Turn your head, Howard," Zelda told him. "Look at this family. They are your family, too. Always has been." Zelda reached over and blindly clasped Demitra's hand without breaking Howard's gaze. She pulled Demitra forward. "Demitra, meet Howard Blanchard. He's your grandson."

Demitra—mind racing, mind blown—was as astonished as Howard or anyone else in the room. She stumbled forward and knelt in front of her lifelong friend. As if looking at him for the first time she observed things she had never seen. The shape of his face. His jawline. His eyebrows. She began to cry. She didn't know why she was crying. It made no sense to cry other than now the man she had considered a friend all her life was something so much more.

"I never realized it. You have Larry's jaw line. And Larry's ears."

Howard's eyes started flooding as well. Never in his life had he been uncomfortable in Blanchard House or around any of the family. He was uncomfortable now. Insecure in their presence in a way he had never previously felt. Demitra sensed his uncertainty. With a mother's instinct she wrapped her arms around his neck and pulled him close to her. He buried his head into her hair and sobbed. She squeezed him tighter and cried herself. Finally, she pulled free and wiped his eyes and her own.

"Okay," she said, catching her breath. "Everyone, I believe you all know my grandson--who is two years older than me. Howard Blanchard... this is your family."

"I don't understand any of this," Howard finally managed to say. "Someone please help me understand."

Artemis had been watching speechless. A lifetime of memories with Howard were flooding her mind. She'd been in love with him once, and he with her. When that ended they'd been the best of friends. He was her Howard. He'd always been her Howard. Sweet, kind, dependable Howard. And now he was her nephew. Not merely a nephew, a grandnephew of all things! It was a lot to process.

She gathered her composure, and as shocking as it all was, she also found the humor in the situation. "I guess we now know the real reason Mother was so against our relationship when we were young."

"You got that right!" Zelda cried. "Me and Lympy stressed a whole lot about that when you two kids started dating."

Demitra was not in the mood for levity. Answers were all she was interested in. This monumental revelation had shaken the structure of the Blanchard family to its core. And she wanted to know why the secrecy had been necessary.

"Why?" Demitra began. "Why did you two keep this from us all these years? You and Mother, Hell—even Aunt Pastoria knew the truth for five decades! Why did you all allow this to go on and remain a secret?"

"Simple," Zelda said. "Cause if we said anything somebody might have done something to stop Beryl from goin' back in time."

"Would that have been so awful?" Cassandra asked. It had nothing to do with her, but it was all so very curious, and she could not help but imagine that stopping the time travel in the first place would have saved a great deal of torment.

Artemis didn't need Zelda to answer. She already understood. Shaking her head and smiling gently toward her new grandnephew she said, "If we had prevented Beryl from going backward in time, Howard would have never been born. He would just evaporate and all memory of him would be gone. This is extremely hard to wrap our minds around, but I wouldn't want to live in a world without Howard in it."

"He's got as much right to life as anybody," Zelda said. "Just cause it throws some chaos into the family doesn't mean we undo any of it. Howard is as much a Blanchard as Fable and Seth's youngens."

"Oh, my God," Howard sighed as he was dashed with the reality of his family rank, "I'm the same generation as Con, Rom, Hera, and Titan."

Demitra laughed out loud at the absurdity of it all. "Damn, you are!"

Howard rose from the sofa and began meandering around the living room aimlessly as it all settled in. He ran his fingertips along the mantle, glancing at the framed snapshots of past memories. He rubbed the smooth fabric of the white winged back chair by the fireplace, where Olympia usually sat in this room. He turned back around to address the family with the most ludicrous of all thoughts, "I am thirty-two years older than my mother."

Arielle chimed in with a grin, "Fable is your aunt!"

"Larry—my best friend—was my grandfather," Howard's eyes widened and watered.

Salem gulped and the words no one was saying, but everyone was thinking. "You've had sex with your great aunt!" Artemis and Howard both blushed and then burst into laughter.

"And Olympia Blanchard was your great grandmother," Demitra smiled proudly, head high as if she'd just announced he was born to royalty.

"And boy, she loved you somethin' fierce," Zelda grinned. "You ain't even got a clue what all she did for you while you was growin' up."

The thought made Howard feel warm. Oh, he suspected many times throughout his formative years, his father's old friend Olympia was intervening on his behalf. Once in high school when he'd been caught smoking in the bathroom and was going to be expelled, suddenly it was forgiven and forgotten by the principal. He also found it quite interesting that his father had been able to pay for college and set aside a sizable nest egg for Howard to start life with on a solicitor's salary representing only one client. Yes, Howard figured the hand of Olympia Blanchard had weaved through his life on many occasions, but he'd chalked it up to her merely being a good friend of his parents.

"I have a question," Jerry spoke up, breaking the flow of the moment.

"What darling?" Demitra replied.

"If Howard is a blood member of this family, why doesn't he have powers?"

"Excellent question," agreed Xander.

The thought rapidly swept over everyone. It was a consideration that had not crossed any of their minds yet. Did Howard have powers like all the other Blanchards?

"He does," Zelda answered. "Howard's got powers. Lympy bound him when he was born. It was important he grow'd up normal with his dad. Too much to explain and have risk undoin' his existence for him to have powers."

"He's been bound?" Artemis gasped. "Mother is gone. His powers are his birthright. He's a Blanchard. How do we unbind him?"

Zelda crossed over to the side window and pulled back the curtain sheer. The view looked across the meadow out to the apple grove. "The talisman bindin' him is buried under the second apple tree in the orchard. I know where it is. So does Pastoria. We figured at least one of the three of us would still be alive when everyone found out. I can unbind him any time he wants."

This information was almost more overwhelming than learning Beryl was his mother. For his entire life Howard stood on the sidelines, observing or hearing about the magical exploits of the family. He was the one waiting by the phone with baited breath in times of peril—waiting for a Blanchard to call him to say everything was all right. He was used to the sideline and always felt honored to be in their inner circle of confidence, but he'd never been an active participant in their exploits. He wasn't a Blanchard. Now... he was. Now... he had powers. It all frightened him. This was not who he knew himself to be.

"I'm a witch?" Howard asked shakily.

"You are a Blanchard Witch of Daihmler County," Zelda laughed. "Boy, that's a hell of a legacy!"

Everyone marinated on that for a moment. Howard Caldwell was a Blanchard. The great-great grandson of the incomparable Constantinople Blanchard. The great-grandson of Olympia Blanchard. It was quite a heritage.

Breaking the reflective moment Arielle asked Zelda, "What is his power?" "Ain't got a clue."

"Well, let's go unbury the talisman and find out!" Arielle exclaimed.

Howard stood up. "No," he said. "I'm not ready for this. I don't know if I ever will be. I need some time by myself."

Artemis approached him and grabbed his hand. "Let's you and I go for a walk. We will figure all this out together."

"Thank you, Artemis," he smiled nervously. "But I think I want to go home and be alone for a while. My whole world just turned upside down. All my life I've had an image of my mother. The woman who died giving birth to me. I see her. I have known her. Felt her watching over me my whole life. But none of that was true. My mother wasn't in Heaven looking out for me. My mother has been here, alive, all along and it was Beryl of all people. And she doesn't even know it. I have to process this."

Artemis understood. She walked him to the door and kissed him on the cheek. She told him she would call him the following day. Demitra wanted to run after him, but Artemis held her back. He had been hit with a lot. The Blanchards needed to give him time.

CHAPTER SIXTEEN

Wrenching Realizations

Everyone had taken a seat in the living room after Zelda explained to Beryl why she was unable to leave the past. Nacaria was doing her best to comfort her poor niece, but she was not sure how to even begin accomplishing such a feat.

"It's going to be alright," she said, caressing Beryl's back.

"No, it is not," Beryl whispered in tears. "I'm going to have a baby."

"I know, honey."

Beryl's teary eyes looked up at Nacaria in a desperate plea for guidance, "But what does that even mean?" Beryl asked. "I'm going to go back home in nine months with a baby?"

Nacaria glanced at Fable, Fable nodded, understanding that only the two of them grasped the truth of this current situation. Seth was raving about how exciting it would be when they all got back home and were all parents together. He was, as always, completely clueless. Fable kicked him hard in the ankle.

"Ouch!" he cried. "Why are you kicking me?"

Nate sat down on the arm of the sofa and took Beryl's hand. "I really don't know what all is going on here," he told her. "But Beryl, don't you see what this means. We are going to have a child. We will be married. We will make a wonderful life together. All this other insane stuff about you being from the future. I don't understand what game your friends are playing, but if you are truly having my baby—that is wonderful news."

Nacaria scooted off the couch to kneel down in front of her niece. She wanted to face her squarely on as she imparted the difficult reality. Placing her gentle, loving hands on Beryl's frightened face, she said "I need for you to hear what I have to say, Beryl. This is a jolt. A huge jolt to absorb. Yes, you are pregnant. Zelda is right and that is why I couldn't propel you back to where you belong. The good news is that in a few months after the baby is born—"

"Nine months!" Beryl corrected, understanding now that her stay in the past would be prolonged for some time. "Not a few. Nine!"

"All right," Nacaria said calmly. "You are correct. It will be nine months before I can take you home."

"But you'll have a beautiful baby to take with you!" Seth interrupted. He saw only the joy of the moment and none of its hidden sorrow. "This is a positive thing!"

Fable kicked him again. He shoved her shoulder, pushing her into the back into the couch cushion where she sat.

"Stop it you two!" Nacaria scolded. "And Seth, please stop talking."

"What is the matter?" Olympia asked Nacaria. She swiped some magazines to the side on the coffee table and sat down on its edge. Her long blonde hair, like Nacaria's own, fell into her face. Tossing it back behind her shoulder, Olympia placed one hand on Nacaria's shoulder and the other on Beryl's knee as she continued her thought, "I think there is more going on here than I actually understand. But if it helps, Pastoria and I have come to love Beryl. She is more than welcome to remain here however long she wants. Whether it is just for the duration of her pregnancy or even if she wants to marry Nate and live here from now on. She's welcome at Blanchard House however long she wants."

"Thank you, Mother—I mean Olympia," Nacaria smiled. "However, things are a bit more complicated than I think anyone but Fable and I understand."

"Explain it to me then," Beryl asked. "Once my baby is born, I can take it home with me—right?"

Beryl looked at her sister for reassurance but found none. Fable was shaking her head as a solitary tear rolled down her cheek. Beryl was afraid now. For Fable to be silent, let alone cry, meant things were dire indeed.

"I don't see what the big deal is here," Seth said.

Pastoria popped him on the top of the head, "Man, you are really irritating. I hope I never have any boys if I have kids."

"Tell me, Nacaria," Beryl pleaded.

Nacaria took a deep breath and caressed her niece's face. "The baby inside you is Howard."

Beryl had not for a moment anticipated that would be what Nacaria meant. Suddenly she began to shake her head and say "No" repeatedly. Fable grabbed her shoulders and tried to steady her older sister, but Beryl was becoming hysterical.

Nate leaned in to place a reassuring hand on her thigh, but it did nothing to assuage the hysteria.

"Caldwell," Fable said softly. "Didn't that tell you all you needed to know when you met him?"

Beryl looked into her sister's eyes and caught the sharp breath escaping her body involuntarily. She felt like such a fool. Not only had she not known what this man she'd come to care for so much did for a living, she also did not know his last name. It was strange to her to have never learned that tidbit. It never came up. It hadn't mattered. Nate and Beryl didn't need names. From the moment they met in the drugstore, the chemistry between them was enough to propel them forward into their relationship. Nate's kindness, his gentleness, his dedication to others eclipsed any need for trivial conversations about last names or job descriptions.

"Nate Caldwell," Beryl murmured. "Howard Caldwell."

"Who is Howard?" Olympia softly asked Nacaria.

"Howard Caldwell is Nate Caldwell's son. We all believed his mother died in childbirth. You actually become quite a mother figure to him."

"Me?" Olympia said in surprise. "Nate and I are great friends. However, I don't see myself marrying him and raising a baby."

"You don't marry him," Fable announced, reaching her wits end with her ridiculously self-involved grandmother. "You marry John Windham—among others." Fable shouldn't have said it and knew she shouldn't. But Fable's temper paired with young Olympia's attitude was more than she could take.

"I knew it!" Pastoria shouted, slapping her leg in disgust. "You are going to marry that son of a bitch Windham!"

"Not now, Pastoria!" Olympia screamed over her shoulder as she still looked onward to Beryl. "We have bigger fish to fry right now." Then suddenly her mind processed the rest of Fable's sentence. She twisted around to stare at her and asked, "*Among others*?"

Beryl looked into her aunt's eyes. Everything was blurry from her tears. "Howard?"

Nacaria nodded. "I think you have been his mother all along, honey. His mother doesn't die in childbirth. She never did. She returns to her own time."

"Howard Caldwell?" Beryl repeated. "That is who I give birth to?"

"Why can't she take him back with her?" Seth asked his mother. "Why can't Beryl take her baby back? She can just name him something else, and it won't confuse anybody, and we can all be together."

Nacaria shook her head—partly as an answer to her son and partly in growing frustration. She wished the younger generation, which also now included her own mother, understood more about how the Natural Order of things worked. "Because the same person cannot exist in their own timeline. One of them would simply cease to be."

"I don't understand?" Seth replied. "I know when Salem went back after David died, she sort of absorbed her old self. But that was because she was the same Salem of that time. But a baby Howard would not be the same person as an adult Howard."

"I am beginning to see what is going on here," Olympia announced. "This baby exists already in Beryl's natural timeline."

"Yes," Nacaria said. "This baby she is carrying is a dear friend of ours."

"But he's a grown man in his 50s!" Seth cried. "It won't be the same Howard."

"It is the same soul," Olympia clarified, finally comprehending a little of what Nacaria was saying. "If my self of tomorrow came back to today, she would absorb me, and I would disappear. But if a me of a different age came to me now, it would be a much slower process but the same result. Little by little, day by day one of us would begin to dissolve. Two souls cannot share the same space at the same time."

"Precisely," Nacaria replied. "Howard must stay here and grow up just the way he did. Otherwise, he will die."

Listening to this confusing conversation, the only thing poor Nate could think to contribute was, "Howard was my grandfather's name," as he rubbed Beryl's knee.

Pastoria stared at him. "That's nice Nate. Doesn't really seem the time to bring it up though."

"Beryl, this is all really crazy to me," Nate said. "But you and I care about each other. You will stay here. You will marry me. And we will raise our child together."

Beryl ran from the room and escaped upstairs. Fable tried to go after her, but Nacaria blocked the way, preventing her. Beryl needed time to acclimate to this revelation. Nacaria wanted her to have that. She, more than anyone else in the family, knew what it felt like to be ripped from your child. Her heart bled for Beryl. And for Demitra. Nacaria only hoped she was handling things correctly. She hoped she was looking after her sister's daughter in a way Demitra would appreciate.

Nacaria gave Pastoria, Olympia, Zelda, and Nate a history lesson—or future lesson as it was. Though she knew it was typically a mistake to give too much future information away, this situation involved all of them, and they had to be told. Nate had the hardest time accepting things until Fable and Seth took him outside and demonstrated their powers. Olympia also used her powers of telekinesis to convey that she and Pastoria were witches as well. When it was all said and done Nacaria took Zelda outside to the porch for a chat.

The absence of rocking chairs, a swing, or any decent place to sit forced the women to stand at the railing overlooking the flowerless yard. Though it was a nonsensical thought and completely impertinent to the current situation, Nacaria made a mental note to appreciate how comfortable the front porch at home was in her time.

Standing at the crisp white porch railing, Nacaria addressed Zelda privately, "I never thought it'd be you I would have to rely on, but my mother isn't going to be around when all of this takes place in the future. Aunt Pastoria will have long left Daihmler. I am going to need you to be the one who takes charge in the future, Zelda. You will have to aid my older sister, Artemis, through this. Everything is going to change, and everyone's lives will be affected by it. Can you vow to me that you will stand with this family and see us through?"

"Girl, I ain't gotta vow nothing. Your...momma, I guess...is like my own sister. I'll stand by the Blanchards 'till the day I die. I got you covered, Nacaria. I promise you."

Nacaria gave her a big hug. "You have no way of knowing this Zelda, but you are a true friend. You always have been. Thank you for everything you have done and will do through all the coming years. And it goes without saying that you must—"

"I know, I know. I am psychic, remember. I can't ever say a word about what I know to anybody until the time is right."

"Exactly. We must protect the timeline so that everyone gets born the way they are supposed to."

"So, will you do me a favor, since I'm doin' all this for you?" Zelda asked.

"Sure."

"Tell me, do I ever fall in love and have a family?"

Nacaria smiled. "Yes. Yes, you do."

"Well, whattaya know? Wasn't that sure I was able to love."

Nacaria laughed. "You have your own special way of loving, but you love pretty big."

"That son of yours is kinda stupid you know?"

Nacaria laughed again. "He's a boy. He does the best he can. It may surprise you to know you like him a great deal in the future. You watch football with him every Saturday and on Thanksgiving."

"Do we bet?'

"You do."

"Who wins?"

"You," Nacaria smiled. "You cheat and use your powers. He falls for it every time."

"I told you he ain't real bright."

CHAPTER SEVENTEEN

Setting a New Course

Beryl came downstairs the next morning. Her red eyes betrayed how little sleep she'd had the night before. Olympia was making breakfast for her sister and her new relatives when Beryl came into the tiny kitchen.

"Here, Beryl. Take my seat," Pastoria said, getting up from the tiny table.

"No, it's okay."

"Girl, you're with child. Sit down," Pastoria ordered.

Beryl sat down, and Olympia spooned out some scrambled eggs for her. Fable and Seth were standing at the short counter while Nacaria sat at the table beside her niece. Olympia took a seat with them.

"So, what's the plan?" Olympia innocently asked Nacaria.

Nacaria returned a disappointed frown, "You are usually the one we ask that question. It feels strange for me to be the authority around you."

"Sorry to disappoint you," Olympia shrugged.

"Actually, it is kind of nice," Nacaria admitted. "You have always been a bastion of wisdom. Quite honestly you have been a hard role model to live up to. I like discovering you are just as lost as everyone else when you are young."

Olympia grinned and observed Nacaria's flawless skin and features in the morning light. "Do I age as well as you do?"

Nacaria smiled. "You are always a beautiful woman. But to be truthful, I am prettier than you were at my age."

Olympia didn't laugh. Everyone else did. Even Beryl.

Nacaria got back to the serious matter at hand. She explained that she still had one more relative to locate and so she and the others would have to leave. Pastoria expressed concern as to how they would be able to get a message to the future once Beryl gave birth, until Nacaria pointed out that Howard's birthday was something every Blanchard knew and celebrated yearly. Nacaria would know exactly when to return for her niece.

Fable took a walk with Beryl after breakfast. She wanted a little alone time with her big sister before leaving. They walked through the apple orchard. It was strange to Fable to see the orchard so much smaller than during her own time. But it was also nice to see Blanchard property in the infancy of what she would later know it to be. She was just glad it didn't look like it had during Jebediah Blanchard's time. Fable had not enjoyed that period very much.

"I guess you are no longer the black sheep that messes up," Beryl said, forcing a strained laugh as she and her sister walked arm in arm. "You only had a wolf baby. I got pregnant with Howard."

Fable gave a hearty guffaw, "Yeah—that is pretty up there with mess ups." Fable's grin softened as the pity she felt for her sister came back into focus. "I am so sorry Beryl," Fable said. "You do not deserve this kind of torment."

Pausing to touch one of the small apples still in its infancy on the branch, Beryl replied, "It is strange for me to think about. I know I am going to have to leave my baby. My sweet, innocent little boy and I won't see him grow up. I am going to miss his first words, his first steps, everything. And I will go back home without him, yet he is going to be there. My baby. An adult, middle-aged man. A man I have known all of my life."

"I guess it'll be pretty weird for Howard, too. If he knows."

The thought hadn't occurred to Beryl. She was so focused on her own turmoil she failed to consider what this might do to poor Howard's feelings. "Do you think he does? Should we tell him? Or should I just keep this all secret from him? It's *Howard*. We love him. I love him even more now. I don't want to hurt him. Will you assess everything for me? Let me know what I should do or not do once I get back?"

Fable leaned her head onto Beryl's shoulder. "Of course, I will. I'll do anything for you, sis."

"And look out for him," Beryl added. "Even if he never knows you are his aunt. Please look out for him."

"I will."

"And don't let him and Artemis try to rekindle any old flames!"

"I won't," Fable smiled. "I got you, sis. And I've got your son."

...

Back at the house, Nacaria had the final potion in hand to return them all to their own time. Once home, she would concoct several new potions to take her through the various possible timelines until she found Yasmine. It was time to say goodbye to everyone. She, Fable, and Seth hugged Olympia, Pastoria, and Zelda goodbye.

"I'll see all of you in nine months," Nacaria said.

"Don't worry about Beryl," Olympia nodded. "She's one of us. We are a pretty groovy foursome. Pastoria, Zelda, and I will take good care of her."

"I know you will."

Seth hugged his cousin goodbye and told her to stay strong. Fable kissed her sister on the cheek but said nothing. She was too choked up to say goodbye. They had said what they'd needed to already anyway. Nacaria stepped forward and took her sister's daughter into her arms.

"I love you very much, Beryl Blanchard."

"I love you, too."

"Do your best to live a life while you are here," Nacaria recommended. "You waited a long time on love. Explore it with Nate now if he is willing. But remember, I *will* come back for you. This isn't your time. You *will* have to go back. But for right now, here in the past, there are no hospital emergencies, no family crises, or monsters to slay. Use this time to find out who you are and enjoy what you can while you can. You are on a path you are not yet aware you are on. This turn of events is a piece of that path. Get everything you can from it."

"I will try."

"I'll let your mother know what's happened. Everything will be all right at home. I will take care of it. We all love you."

Beryl smiled as Nacaria stepped away. Olympia and Pastoria stepped forward and linked arms with Beryl. They all smiled at the departing relatives. For a brief moment, Nacaria saw a bit of herself, Artemis, and Demitra in the other Blanchard trio before her. Nacaria clasped hands with Fable as Fable grasped Seth as she tossed the potion bottle onto the foyer floor. In a swirl of haze and vapor, the three future Blanchards disappeared.

...

Cassandra and Artemis were coming in the door with groceries when suddenly Nacaria, Fable, and Seth materialized in the foyer. Cassandra screamed and dropped the bag she was carrying. Laundry detergent exploded out of the bottle all over the floor. With the wave of a hand, she sent the liquid back into the bottle and righted it on the floor.

"You're back!" Artemis exclaimed, wrapping her arms around the three of them.

"It has been quite a journey," Nacaria sighed.

"We know," Cassandra replied.

"How much do you know?" Fable asked.

"We know about Beryl's pregnancy," Artemis informed them. "As well as who the baby is."

"Does he know?" Fable asked.

Artemis frowned grimly. "He does," she answered. "I spoke with him this morning. He is doing all right, considering. He needs some time to let it all soak in."

"Where is Yasmine?" Cassandra asked, noting that one of the missing was still unaccounted for.

"We still don't know," Seth told his sister. "We ran out of potion. Mom has to make more before we go searching for her. Any new info on where she might be?"

"No one knows," Cassandra said.

A sharp yelp came from the top of the stairs as Romulus, sensing his mother's presence in the house, leapt down the flight of stairs and into her arms. He began covering her face with licks. She clutched him close and kissed every inch of his head. Con was not as fast as his brother, but within moments he was hugging her legs and being swooped up into her arms with his furry twin.

Seth immediately ran upstairs to find his children. He had been separated from his son and daughter for what seemed like weeks and all he wanted was to hold his babies. He found Arielle with them in the nursery. She was feeding them lunch. Hera took one look at her father in the doorway and squealed in delight, running so fast toward him she almost knocked him down.

Once Fable had reunited with her boys, she went outside to find her mother. She wanted to fill her in on the exploits of the other realities she'd been to. Demitra listened to Fable recount her time in the distant past and then the more recent past. Fable let her know that Beryl was holding up as well as could be expected under the circumstances.

"My heart is crushed for her," Demitra said. "And Howard. This is all so tragic and devastating. This has to be the hardest thing Beryl will ever have to go through. Which makes sense I suppose, now."

"I don't follow?"

"Oh, that's right, you weren't here!" Demitra exclaimed. "Brace yourself for this; your sister is transforming. She is on a path that is going to alter her forever."

Fable looked very confused. "Beryl? Transforming? Into what, an android?"

"God."

. . .

Nacaria only had time for a short lunch with her husband before she had to leave. And truth be told that lunch consisted of ham sandwiches in the vault while he helped her put together five new potions. She had to find Yasmine, and she had no idea which Blanchard history timeline she might find her.

While the Obreiggons were in the basement making magical serum, Seth was pouring through old family photographs and journals trying to put together an outline of the most logical time frames his wife might be. The biggest problem was that Yasmine might exist in any one of them at any various point in time of that generation. Seth and Fable had basically existed in the same generation, just separated by a few years. That caused quite a problem for pinpointing his wife. She could be anywhere.

When his mother met him in the kitchen with her little drawstring bag of potions, he handed her the list. Written upon it were several possibilities. The first on the list was the time of Olympia's father Constantinople Blanchard. Second, Seth had listed Nancy's family—the Norwoods' time. Lastly, he wrote any date from Victor Blanchard's lifespan after the age they had just left him.

"Which should I hit first?" she asked.

"We," he corrected. "I'm going with you."

"No," Nacaria said, making a concerned face. "It is much too risky for two of us to go."

Seth rolled his eyes. "Mom, I think we've already pretty much blown the timeline to hell and back and really nothing has been altered. Apparently, Beryl was always meant to go back because she made Howard. Let us just trust that it's fate for you and me to do this. Yazzy is my wife. I am going to go find her."

"Okay." Nacaria wanted to argue but decided to let it go. She understood true love. There was nothing she would ever be able to come up with which would sway her son from doing this. And it was his wife after all. He had every right to try and rescue her.

Nacaria clasped his hand, looked at the list and decided they would stick in order of the years. First stop...the time when the Norwood family owned the Blanchard land. She focused her mind on Nancy Norwood's birth year and with a rush of dizziness and a cloud of mist, she and Seth disappeared.

CHAPTER EIGHTEEN

A Jaunt Through Time

A rickety rail fence stood several feet away from Nacaria and Seth when they appeared in the field of cotton. For the briefest second, Seth considered what would have happened had the exact spot he'd been standing in been the spot where the rail stood. Would it have broken? Would it have impaled him? Suddenly the real dangers of popping through time and trusting you'd land in a safe spot dawned on him. The nearby oak trees showed he and Nacaria that they landed in the right location. The oaks were not large—certainly not large enough to shade the future Blanchard house as they one day would. The fence separated the trees from the field where Seth and Nacaria stood by several yards.

"Why the fence?" Seth remarked.

"Well, Blanchard land wasn't always as large as it is in our time. That piece probably belongs to another farmer here." Nacaria looked around. "Did you know this used to be a cotton farm?"

"No," Seth replied. "What year do you suppose we're in?"

"Somewhere around 1830 I think."

"1831," called a voice from out of nowhere.

Seth and his mother turned around quickly to see who had spoken, but no one was there. They said nothing in response, only looking at each other in confusion. They waited for another sound. They heard one. A rather squeaky pitched chuckle that rang out from a few feet away, but still there was nothing in sight other than rows of cotton plants.

"What is happening?" Seth said, swallowing hard.

"Don't be scared none," the voice said. It was a woman's voice. "You folks good or bad?"

"Huh?"

"Guess you wouldn't right admit it if'n you were bad. Guess I'll have to reckon this out 'fore I show myself."

"Are you invisible?" Nacaria muttered, scanning the area around her.

"Fraid so," the voice answered. "Not all the time. Do it mostly to keep the sun from burnin' me when I'm pickin' the cotton. But when I seen you two bust on outta thin air, I figured I better stay hid till I figure you out. Y'all some kinda demons? Sure dress funny."

"No, we are not," Nacaria said, turning toward wherever she thought she heard the voice last. It was moving around. "We are witches actually. I know that sounds hard to believe and please do not be afraid. Witches are not what you've been led to think they are."

"Mom," Seth said, tapping Nacaria's shoulder. "She's able to turn invisible. I think it is pretty safe to assume she's a witch, too."

"Yeah, I be somethin' like that. Don't call myself nothin' so wicked. My people was gypsies back in the old country."

"Gypsies?" Seth gasped. "Wow. Is that where we come from?"

"We?" the voice repeated. "You some kinda kinfolk?"

"I think we are," Nacaria replied. "Are you a Norwood?"

"Yeah, I be one of the Norwoods. How you know that?"

"Because we are descended from a Nancy Norwood," Seth told her. "Do you know her? Does she live around here? She would be rather little I suppose."

"Don't know any Nancy livin' round here. But my sister-in-law is big right now. Heard her say she was gonna name it George if it was a boy or Nancy Ann if it was a girl. Think your Nancy is in her tummy?"

"That must be her," Seth whispered to Nacaria. "Well, I think we are very distantly related. We come from the future. That sounds crazy I know."

"No crazier than you just poofin' out of thin air here in my field. Or my being *clear.* I believe you. Let me right myself so you'ins can see me."

Nacaria and Seth watched as slowly an image began to take shape—shimmery at first as though everything behind her body shape was blurring. Then the little patch of landscape behind her became obstructed by the slowly-forming shape of a woman. She was hefty set, not exactly fat but sturdy. She had a burlap sack strung over her shoulder and they could now see that it was weighed down with balls of cotton with prickly seed particles inside them. She was dressed in dingy cloth that looked hand sewn. A bonnet covered the top of her head, but her ashy brown hair crept out of it in stringy strands. Her face was slightly weathered but remarkably pale for a woman who worked a cotton field. Her invisibility trick was paying off.

"Howdy," she smiled with a grin, which was missing a few teeth. "I'm Ora Mae."

Nacaria smiled brightly and replied. "I am Nacaria, and this is my son Seth." They all shook hands.

"Na-what?"

"Nacaria."

"Oh, I won't never be able to say that. I'm gone call you Blondie."

Nacaria laughed. "I like it."

"My, you got some mighty purty teeth." Ora Mae leaned forward, inspecting Nacaria's mouth. She then turned to examine Seth. "You do too, boy! Ain't ever know'd nobody to be old as you and keep all the teeth. What are you girl? 30? The boy looks about 18, maybe 20."

Nacaria beamed proudly. "I am actually 48. My son is 27."

Ora Mae didn't believe it. She told them she had never seen a 48-year-old with blonde hair, no wrinkles, and all her teeth. She also could not believe Seth was as old as he was.

"Y'all ain't farmers, are you?"

"No," Nacaria smiled. "We aren't. Although our home is located on this land in the future. Just right over there by those oaks."

"Well, I'll be," Ora Mae sighed. "You mean ta' tell me I ain't livin' in regular times? They's more years out there diff'rent than this?"

"I am afraid so," Nacaria smiled to the flabbergasted woman. "We have been traveling through many varying timelines. Yours is the oldest we've been to."

"Lan-sakes," Ora Mae gasped. "An' here I thought I was livin' as far out as it gets. So you 'ens live at the end years?"

Nacaria and Seth exchanged glances. They really didn't know. As far as they were concerned, their timeline was the furthest point of human history but considering the last few days of travel that may not actually be the case. Perhaps somewhere else, further along, descendants of Hera and Titan were walking around these same lands. It was much too much to think about for the moment.

"Well, what brings you folks here?" Ora Mae asked.

"We are looking for my wife," Seth explained. "It's an unbelievably long story.

Let's just say she was accidentally sent into our family's past. Only we have no idea where in the past she is."

"We are fairly certain she would be on this land," Nacaria added. "She would have been sent only to times when our family bloodline owned this land."

Ora Mae situated the sack on her back to the other shoulder and looked out over their surroundings. "We got this field and one other back on the other side of them woods there. Our house is in the middle of them woods. My brothers are in the other field right now. I could go see if she's there or at the house."

"She would have come here weeks ago," Seth clarified.

"Oh well she ain't here then," Ora Mae said. "This place ain't real big. We'd sure of seen her. My sister-in-law stays at the house since she's too big with the baby to work. My brothers ain't run across nobody and neither has me. I guess she didn't come here."

"Well, thank you for talking with us," Nacaria nodded and smiled. "We will check another time."

"You folks wanna come back to the house and meet the kin?" Ora Mae offered. "I'm sure they'd be powerful glad to see ya."

"I wish we could," Seth smiled. "But I am very worried about my wife. I want to find her as soon as I can."

"Well, I gotta respect that," Ora Mae grinned, the black edges of the few teeth she had left highlighted by the sunlight. "Not too many fellas hold much stock in their women. You go get your gal."

...

Nacaria and Seth next found themselves standing in the middle of a rainstorm. Luckily, Seth cleared it up using his powers, but they were still rather drenched. The cotton field was not there anymore. In its place looked to be rows of vegetables. The wooden rail fence was gone, and the oaks were a little larger. Near the garden stood a white painted house with flowers in the window boxes and a crisp front porch. The house was not large—a front door with two windows on either side and a second floor also boasting two small windows. The house was plank built with a gray tin roof. But it looked a great deal more inviting than the house Blaze Blanchard had lived in a few fields away.

"Well, that rainstorm sure cleared up fast," came a voice from the now open doorway. A man stepped onto the porch and looked out at the sky. "Never seen one disappear so fast."

The man caught sight of the soaking wet Blanchards and called out a friendly hello to them. Seth smiled and trudged forward through the muddy path. As he got closer, he felt something stir inside him. Something about the young man's eyes.

"I don't believe it!" Seth exclaimed. "You're Victor Blanchard, aren't you?"

The young man strained his eyes for a moment to see his visitor's face under the now-bright shining sun. "Don't reckon I know you, Mister."

"I knew you a long time ago," Seth said, taking a chance. "Is your sister Blaze still alive by chance?"

The man peered suspiciously at the two strangers, but after a moment he arrived at the conclusion they might be okay. "My sister is ailing pretty bad these days. Me and my wife take care of her."

Suddenly a small boy bounded out of the house holding a fishing pole. "I'm going to the stream, Papa! Tell Mama I'll catch us some supper!"

The man called out after him, "Con, you stay by the big rocks and don't wander down stream. Be home before dark or Mama won't be able to clean and cook them."

Seth turned to his mother and mouthed, "Con."

Oh, my word, Nacaria told her son with her mind. *That little boy is my grandfather.* Her fascination was turned to nervous surprise when quite unexpectedly, little Con stopped in his tracks. He slowly turned around to stare at Nacaria. It was almost as if he heard what she had told Seth. He stood several seconds staring at her before he flashed a quick smile and went back on his way.

"You folks come into the house," Vic Blanchard told them. "I'll take you up to see my sister. You say you know her?"

"Knew her," Seth corrected. "It was a very long time ago."

"You and me look to be 'bout the same age," Victor observed. "Were you and me friends when we were younger?"

"We were," Seth grinned. "But I doubt you remember me."

The house was rather nicely furnished considering the time. It was a vast improvement from what Seth had observed from years ago when Blaze lived on the property raising her baby brother alone. Victor Blanchard appeared to be doing rather well in life for his era. Entering the house, Seth saw a lovely young woman sitting at a table scribbling something into a book. When she saw they had visitors, she quickly closed the leather-bound book and nervously placed it in a drawer.

"I wasn't aware we had callers, Vic," she said, attempting to smile welcomingly.

"This is my wife, Griselda," Victor introduced. "These folks say they are old friends of Blaze's. I'm gonna take them up to see her."

Griselda seemed apprehensive. Nacaria noticed that she lifted her hands up in a strange way. Almost defensively. The action reminded Nacaria of the way Salem swept her hands whenever she froze people. It was not the exact same motion, but similar. It looked more as if Griselda were waving a circle at each of them. Yet nothing seemed to happen—only Griselda's demeanor suddenly changed. She seemed less apprehensive and almost excited.

"Please do," she said, gesturing to the short straight staircase rising up to the next floor. "Blaze never sees anyone but us. I'm sure she'd love company."

Victor allowed Nacaria and Seth to ascend the stairs before him. As they climbed the rather steep stair treads, she thought she heard Griselda whisper "It's all right, they are like us" to her husband before Victor followed them. At the top of the stairs stood a slender little hall with no pictures or furniture. Frankly, there was no room for either. The space was so narrow that pictures would have been knocked off by a passersby's shoulders. There were four small rooms, two on each side of the hallway. Victor opened the door to the back room on the left and went inside. He invited Nacaria and Seth to enter.

As Nacaria went inside she saw that the room was illuminated only by one window. Sunshine sufficiently lit the room and fell onto the bed a few feet away. A quilt of scraps sewn together rather beautifully covered the legs of an old woman. The closer Nacaria looked she wasn't quite sure how old the old woman was. It could have very easily been like Ora Mae and the woman in bed might be a mere 50 years old after a hard life had aged her. Her hair was mostly gray except for a few faint strands that glowed an orangey color in the light. The woman sat upright, reading from a worn Bible. She looked up at Nacaria in confusion. A mild look of recognition crossed her weary face, but it was only as Seth came in behind her that the woman in bed became ricketedly animated and excited.

"Seth!" she called out in a cracked voice. "Is that you, Seth Blanchard?"

"Blaze," he smiled joyfully. "Blaze Blanchard!"

"You came back. You came back!" Blaze was happier than she had been in a long time and that was rather evident. "I always hoped you'd come back one day."

Victor walked inside. His face now held an ear-to-ear grin. "I don't believe it. Outside, for a second it crossed my mind. But to tell the truth I have only let myself half believe the stories my sister used to tell me. You are real after all! Seth Blanchard—who used to feed me and bathe me and play with me at night. My great-great-grandson."

Seth was overjoyed to see these two people again. It had only been a few days for him, but it truly did feel as if years had passed between visits. Seth reached out and shook Vic's hand but then stopped and pulled him into a hug. "Vic, you helped me so much back then. I missed my children so terribly and having that special time with you made it easier." He turned to the woman in bed, "And Blaze. Blaze Blanchard, my personal hero. Hero to every future Blanchard everywhere. How are you my dear friend?"

Blaze patted a space on the bed beside her for Seth to sit down. "Oh Seth, Old Blaze ain't too well these days. Fixin' to die. Can feel it in my bones. Sure am proud to see you one last time 'fore I go meet the maker."

Seth kissed her worn, ancient hands. "Blaze, do you remember my mother? This is Nacaria."

"I do, a little. Oh my, she sure is right pretty."

Victor turned to Nacaria. "My great-granddaughter. I am enormously proud to meet you."

"The honor belongs to me," Nacaria replied. "Thank you. Thank you for—giving us all life I suppose."

Victor took Nacaria by the hand and suggested they leave Blaze and Seth alone to visit. He led Nacaria back downstairs and explained to his wife who she was. Griselda gave Nacaria a warm embrace.

"I cannot believe it," Griselda said. "I knew you were a witch once you came inside. I have a way of figuring people out. It is an ability of mine. But I never dreamed you were family."

"Not just family Gris," Victor beamed. "Our very own great-granddaughter. Boy is Con going to be surprised when he gets back from fishing."

Griselda walked over to a wall shelf and removed three cups and saucers which she placed on the table. A hot pot of coffee was ready on the iron stove top, and she poured the three of them a cup as they sat down to get acquainted. Nacaria was pleasantly surprised to find that the coffee was delicious.

Taking a second sip she asked Griselda, "So, you are a witch as well?"

"I am," Griselda answered. "I was actually writing in my spell book when you two came in here."

Nacaria was amazed to hear other witches existed so early in Daihmler's history. "Is there a large witching community here?" she asked.

"Aw, no," Griselda replied. "Far as we know, we are the only ones 'round these parts."

Nacaria was curious how Victor and Griselda had managed to meet. Two witches coming together in this time period in rural Alabama was not something she figured was highly likely.

"I was passing through here one day with my family, and I saw Vic pass our wagon on the road," Griselda recounted. "Immediately I felt him and how he was like we were. We stopped and talked to him for a spate of time. He invited us back to his place to meet his sister. Blaze put us up for the night and...well, it didn't take real long before Vic and I realized we should make a family together."

"Where is the rest of your family now?" Nacaria asked.

"We stayed a few days here on the farm," Griselda went on. "I figure my folks saw the spark 'twixed me and Vic. My folks moved on to New Orleans but agreed to let me stay here. It was hard for my Daddy to leave me, but it's not all that easy to find people like us. I think we all knew my place was to stay here and marry this man. I've never regretted it."

Nacaria was intrigued by the story. Intrigued by everything she was experiencing. What an unbelievably fascinating adventure she was having. Already she had met her own mother at an age younger than herself, Pastoria, Zelda, then Ora Mae, and now her great-grandparents and her little grandfather. It was an amazing experience, and she wished she could share it with her sisters.

Griselda topped off Nacaria's coffee and sat back down. Blushing a little, she addressed her guest, "I gotta ask, do women really show this much skin in the future?"

"You wouldn't believe what women can do in the future," Nacaria laughed.

"We don't have it all that easy here," Griselda confided. "Lotta my neighbors have some awful husbands. Treat them pretty terrible. I got lucky with my man. Vic here treats me better than any woman I know gets treated."

"That's really wonderful," Nacaria smiled, raising her cup as if to toast. "And as it should be."

Victor shrugged bashfully and replied, "I guess being raised by my sister and seeing what all she went through to keep me fed and clothed, I got a mighty respect for women."

"Your son learns that from you," Nacaria told them. "In fact, it is Constantinople Blanchard that teaches his daughters to never give up their family name. Because of him, I am still a Blanchard even though I am married. All Blanchard women keep the Blanchard name as a sign of respect. I just never realized that respect was all due to a woman named Blaze."

"I'm real glad to hear all this," Vic said. "Tell me, Nacaria. What brings you to this place in time?"

"We are searching for Seth's wife. My daughter-in-law is lost somewhere in our family history. Her name is Yasmine. I don't suppose she has passed this way, has she?"

"I'm sorry," Griselda frowned. "We have never met her. She hasn't come here."

Once Seth and Blaze had finished their visit and he had come back downstairs, Nacaria told him it was time for them to depart and keep looking for Yasmine. Vic protested and begged them to stay overnight.

"We really shouldn't," Seth said. "You can understand how worried I am about my wife. She isn't a witch. No powers to protect herself, so she is vulnerable wherever she is."

"I respect that my friend," Vic replied. "But it's getting dark out now. If you folks leave again, it is probably gonna be night wherever you land. Maybe you should get a fresh start when the sun's up."

Nacaria shrugged to her son, "He may be right, Seth. It's not like we have a car, or lights, or any way to find our way around. Maybe we should stay the night."

Seth was not totally sold on the idea, but he could not argue the logic. He agreed to stay the night, much to the delight of his great-great-grandparents. It wasn't long before little Con came running in with five freshly-caught fish. Seth helped Griselda clean and cut them—he had learned how to clean fish from his time with Blaze. The small clan of Blanchards dined together on the floor of Blaze's room that night. They all had so many questions for one another, and the things they learned about each other's world and experience enriched them all greatly.

"So, this lady is my what?" Little Con asked after listening for a while.

"She's your future granddaughter," Vic said.

Con looked at Nacaria, staring intently into her eyes. Finally, he spoke, but only to her and only to her mind. *I can see everything through your eyes. And everyone. Olympia, Pastoria, Salem. The future house. Your grandchildren. I don't know what to make of any of it. But I see them all.*

You leave a glorious heritage Con. Thank you.

Nacaria slept with Griselda that night and Vic slept with Con in his room. Seth insisted on staying in Blaze's room on a quilted pallet beside her bed. Nacaria could hear them laughing and talking late into the night. Griselda elbowed her gently and smiled to her in the moonlight streaming through the window above the bed. The two women enjoyed hearing them. As briefly as their time had been, Blaze and Seth had left indelible marks on one another's lives. Two friends, each existing on a spectrum of time with centuries between them. But they cared about each other, and it was beautiful to witness.

Griselda prepared a hearty breakfast of cornpone, a little bacon, and scrambled eggs before she, Con, and Vic would say goodbye to their kinfolk. Seth went upstairs to say a second final goodbye to Blaze. It was time for him and Nacaria to go. He had to find Yasmine.

...

Victor, Griselda, and Con stood entranced at the sight before them as Nacaria withdrew a potion and shattered it on the wooden floor of the little house. She and Seth evaporated into the ether of time as the early Blanchards waved goodbye.

And there it sat. Blanchard House. Not the version they were accustomed to but the one most closely resembling young Olympia's time. Everything looked so fresh and new, like it had only been built a short time ago. The two of them stood on the lawn by the oak trees, neither quite knowing what they should do next.

"Let's just go on in," suggested Seth. "He knows who we are now. I don't think we will have a problem."

Nacaria held her son's hand as they walked to the front door and gave a sharp knock. No one answered. She turned the knob slowly and let herself inside. As she and Seth peered into the foyer, they were surprised to see the starkness of the house. Sparsely little furniture filled the living room. The décor was simple. Rather early American. Plain.

"Is anyone home?" Seth asked.

Without any warning, Seth was inexplicably hurled backward through the front door. He landed with a painful thud on his back several feet away from the porch. Before Nacaria had time to scream, she found herself lifting from the ground and sailing backward to where Seth lay. Instinctively Seth jumped to his feet and caught his mother in the air as she hurdled down to the ground. They looked back to the house whereupon they saw a beautiful brunette woman coming forward onto the porch. The fingers of her outstretched right hand were bending toward her palms as her left hand raised toward the nearest and largest oak tree beside them. A cracking sound exploded above their heads as leaves, bark and various tree debris rained down upon them. Rapidly, thick branches broke into long straightish rods stabbing into the ground around them, forming a kind of cage imprisoning Seth and Nacaria. Seth attempted unlodging the branches from their place in the ground, but they were too deep. He looked at his mother then back to the woman.

"You have made the utmost mistake coming here!" she roared. "You have brought your fight to Blanchard land and that is to be your undoing."

"Wait!" Nacaria screamed. "I don't think you have the right people. We mean you no harm!"

The woman appeared unmoved by the plea. Wind swept up the sides of her long dress, pushing it behind her like a train as her black hair blew off her shoulders. She crept closer, reaching her hands back as if to assault them again with some unknown arsenal.

"Stop!" Seth cried out. "We are family. I think. Please listen to us."

"I am not as easily fooled as your other victims," the woman glared. "You are now about to die."

Seth grabbed his mother in his arms to protect her and braced for whatever was headed their way. But nothing came. Seth peered up over his mother's shoulder to see what was stopping the woman. A man stood beside her now. He held his hand on her shoulder and was whispering something to her. Suddenly she flung her hand outward again. Seth flinched, expecting imminent death. But to his surprise, the tree branches forming the cell around him and Nacaria unstuck from the ground and flew away, smashing onto the side yard.

The man stepped forward. He was dark headed with a thinly trimmed beard and mustache that made him appear almost like an old-world magician. He was even wearing a black suit. Nacaria initially felt frightened of him, but the way he smiled at her disarmed her fears. He knew her. And now she knew him.

"Nacaria and Seth Blanchard," he said bowing comically. "My beautiful granddaughter. You see, I did remember you."

"Constantinople Blanchard!" Nacaria cried, rushing toward him. He embraced her lovingly and beckoned Seth forward to shake his hand. "Welcome, son. I do apologize for Angharad's forcefulness. But we sometimes fall under attack from brutal forces."

"Angharad?" Seth asked.

"My lovely wife. Your great-grandmother."

Seth leaned into his mother, "Why did we never know her name before?"

"I have no idea," Nacaria whispered back. "Mother never spoke much of her. She just called her 'my mother".

You know I hear everything you say and think. Constantinople said with his mind. Nacaria blushed and nodded. Angharad came down from the porch. She still eyed them with suspicion, but she decided to trust her husband.

"Stanton told me of your visit in his childhood. Of course, neither of us ever expected to see you during the present. You'll forgive my attack."

It was not a request. There was something rather stern about Angharad Blanchard. Nacaria was not sure she liked her. *Perhaps this is why Mother never spoke of her.*

I still hear you. Her grandfather smiled again. *But she cannot. She is a cold thing isn't she. But she possesses her warm moments.*

Constantinople led his guests indoors and offered them refreshments. He reminisced briefly about the night Nacaria and Seth spent the evening with him and his parents and his Aunt Blaze. When he reflected on those memories, his demeanor seemed to change back to that of the little boy they had known only an hour ago. Angharad did not seem as nostalgic.

"I assume from your arrival here that you are still searching for your wife?" Constantinople asked Seth.

"Yes. I'd hoped she was possibly here."

"I'm afraid she isn't."

"This is not a very good time for a visit," Angharad declared. "Since your mate is not with us, perhaps you should move along."

"Now, my love, let's not be rude to our descendants."

"I have no children, Stanton. I am no one's mother."

"You will be given the time, apparently. At least one I'd hazard to guess," Constantinople smirked. He returned his attention to his guests. "We are frequently busy with witching matters, and there has not been time for children thus far."

Stanton? Nacaria grinned. Her grandfather gave her a playful wink and mentally replied, *She prefers the middle portion of my name. She is from Welsh descent. Very educated. Very powerful in the Celtic arts.*

Charming, Nacaria replied sarcastically.

"How did the two of you meet?" she asked out loud.

"I don't see where that is pertinent," Angharad answered.

Nacaria gulped nervously. She felt like a child being chastised over a poor report card. "I'm only interested in our family history. Do you have any family of your own, Anghared?"

"Familiar bonds are often tedious nuisances."

Constantinople smiled at the forwardness of his icy wife. For some reason he seemed amused by her frozenness. He answered Nacaria's earlier question, "We met at the Consort. The Consort is a new organization I helped found—"

"We are well acquainted with the Consort," Nacaria said abruptly.

I married her because she has immense power, as you have witnessed. A great ally in battle. And not unpleasant to look at. What she lacks in love she compensates for in strength. She will make formidable children with me.

Seth was about to ask a question when suddenly a screeching sound rang from outside. It was mind splitting. He covered his ears with his hands. Angharad jumped forward ready for action. Constantinople joined her. The screeching stopped the moment Angharad shook a certain glass jar on the coffee table. A liquid sloshed around inside it.

"The alarm means they are on Blanchard land," Constantinople warned Nacaria and Seth.

"Who?" Seth asked.

"We are currently in battle with an evil species not unlike vampires, only far deadlier."

It came to him instantly, all those stories at his grandmother's knee. Seth knew exactly what they were referring to. He could not believe he was about to see it for himself. "The Rain People," Seth stated automatically.

Angharad confronted him with a suspicious malice in her eye. "How do you know about the Rain People?"

"My grandmother told us stories," Seth answered.

Constantinople moved closer to the door, waving Nacaria and Seth to remain behind him and his wife. He opened the front door and marched outside, his wife beside him. Nacaria clung to her son. With no active power for battle, she felt somewhat helpless and endangered.

On the lawn by the start of the driveway stood a line of eight figures. They were people, but different. A thunder cloud rolled overhead. Seth looked up and saw that the sky was darkening. A light rain was beginning to fall. The line of eight intruders marched slowly closer. As they neared the fence Seth could see that although the rain had begun to fall much harder, none of the attackers were getting wet. The droplets appeared to simply fall into them and absorb away. Their flesh looked pale, and their hair was rather stringy and dark. As Seth focused harder upon them, his focus was suddenly broken as one of them rushed forward. It was a woman. She rushed in the direction of the porch.

Angharad waved her hands once again and sent the piling of branches she had used to attack Nacaria and Seth earlier toward the woman. The encasement around the woman had no effect. Seth and Nacaria watched as her body morphed and liquidated slightly until she had passed through the barrier. The others were moving closer now as well at a faster rate.

"I warned you, Blanchard!" one of the male figures encroaching bellowed. "You cannot impede my kind."

A long puddle of water had formed from the now torrential rain coming down. The water had settled into the track marks of the dirt driveway. Seth and his mother watched in sheer terror as the male figure threatening Constantinople stepped his foot onto the trench of water and in the flash of an instant he merged with the water and instantly appeared at the end of the trench mark. He had traveled the water trail ten feet in the blink of an eye.

"We will never allow you to ruin this country the way you ruined your own," Constantinople shouted. "Your homeland is a desert of death and accursedness. You should not have sailed to America. The witches of this land will stop you all."

The grim figure was not daunted by the warning. "You haven't the power. We will drain you dry and leave you a withered husk as we devour your lands and your people."

The woman approaching the porch cackled as she made it to the first step.

Constantinople reached out and with a swipe of his hand he withdrew every drop of moisture from her body. The departing water hovered midair before her, just out of her reach. Waving her hands desperately she tried to make contact with the vital liquid, but to no avail. Within seconds she began to dry—to crust—then she swirled into dust before their eyes, crumbling to the bottom step. Constantinople continued holding the moisture mid-air.

He called behind him, "I need a container. If I drop this fluid, it could reanimate her. We have to dry them out!"

To his grandfather's complete astonishment, Seth stepped forward. Raising his hand out toward the collected water, Seth summoned the wind from across the fields to come forward. Every nearby breeze merged into one strong current of air, sweeping the water clear of the house and yard, slinging it to the woods behind the house. Seth then looked to the sky and concentrated harder than he had ever concentrated—trying anxiously to pay no attention to the horde of Rain People now running at breakneck speed toward the house.

The rain abruptly stopped. That one feat seemed to slow the Rain People down as if the rainfall had been energizing them. The clouds parted making it possible for the sun to send beams back down to the ground in spots. A shriek rang out from a few yards away where Seth saw one of the attackers shrivel up like ancient parchment and fall to dust on the lawn.

"You have the power of the skies!" Angharad cried with an impressed voice and a newfound respect for her unwanted visitors. "Heighten the heat, brighten the light. Clear the sky of obstruction! Burn these devils out!"

Seth focused harder and harder. Nacaria placed her hand on his arm and called out an incantation. "Sun of life...heat, burn, magnify tenfold across these acres. Scorch this land. Bring us drought."

Seth began to tremble lightly. He felt as if his power was increasing to levels he had never felt them rise before. Nacaria held her grip on his arm. The sun felt hotter, as if the bright star itself were growing. Or perhaps the ozone protection of the atmosphere was parting. Seth had no idea, but his brow was covered in sweat, his back was soaking wet. The leaves of the oak trees were drying and turning to crispy brown. The few flowers growing wildly at the corners of the fence dried up in seconds. Seth saw the trenches of water evaporate instantly into rising vapor. He felt sunburned skin on his hand, arms, and face. The shrieks of the Rain People were deafening, even more so than Angharad's alarm had been. Constantinople Blanchard stood in extreme pride watching the attackers wither away and disintegrate into particles on the lawn of Blanchard House.

"You can stop now, son," he instructed Seth. "Stop before you permanently scorch my land beyond rejuvenation."

Seth released his hold on the weather and collapsed to the ground in exhaustion. Nacaria, along with Angharad, helped him indoors and laid him on the sofa. Angharad retrieved an ice compress for his head and neck.

"You will recover," she told him as she placed it. "Thank you, great-grandson." The words, though simple, conveyed much to Seth and Nacaria. Had they just won Angharad Blanchard's hard-to-come-by respect?

"Did I just end the Rain People myself?" Seth asked arrogantly. "Was Grandmother wrong about who really saved the world?"

Constantinople gave a hearty laugh. "No, my son. You did a magnificent job today. But those were only a few. Their numbers reach hundreds. However, all across the world we witches are finding them and stomping them out. Still, I remain impressed. And you should feel enormously proud. You two achieved something here today very few of our kind can boast. It was quite an honor to witness."

"I would love to have your power," Angharad added, with an almost sinisterly greedy tone.

"Your own power is nothing to be ashamed of," Nacaria laughed. "I wish I had any kind of active power."

Her grandfather kissed her hand and smiled. "You, my dear, have something more valuable. You are a battery and a sorceress of incantations. Without your assistance today, we might all be deceased right now."

"I sincerely hope you find your woman," Angharad said. "And now we will bid you goodbye as you go along your way."

Seth and Nacaria exchanged startled glances. Neither had ever been told so forwardly that they had overstayed their welcome. Constantinople was grinning once again. His wife's callousness really did provide him with amusement. He placed his comforting hand on Nacaria's shoulder and turned her ever so subtly so that he was staring directly into and through her eyes. He held the gaze a little longer than she found comfortable, yet she trusted him and knew there must be a purpose to his action. When he pulled away, she knew what he had done.

"Just as when we last met, I have looked into your eyes, my dear Nacaria, and I have seen them all. Olympia, Artemis, Demitra, Salem, Fable, all of them."

"What did you find?" Nacaria asked him gently.

"You will find Yasmine a good 72 years from now. She is with your mother, my future daughter Olympia."

"No that isn't possible," Seth argued. "If she were in that particular time, my aunts and our friend Zelda would have remembered that. None of them ever encountered Yaz during their past."

Constantinople Blanchard eyed his naive great grandson and grinned mysteriously. "Do not doubt me, son. I know more than you will ever experience. I have looked through your mother's eyes and into the past of my daughter's. I know what I speak."

"I trust you," Nacaria winked as she lifted the potion vile into the air.

"Wait," her grandfather interrupted. "Something more I have seen. I have a namesake. He and his brother are the divided beast. But not all is as it seems. They each carry the other's gift inside them. They will be remarkable men one day."

Nacaria had no clue as to what to make of that. She simply nodded, smiled, and dropped the potion.

Once more, Nacaria and Seth hurdled forward through time. When they stopped, they found themselves standing face to face, inches from the staring eyes of an Olympia Blanchard they knew. They were all standing in the Blanchard House foyer. Undoubtedly Olympia had been on her way outside when suddenly Nacaria and Seth zapped in front of her. She jumped back, startled, and then looked hard at their faces.

"I'd know my own daughter anywhere!" Olympia grabbed Nacaria tightly and pulled her close. "My baby. My sweet angel. You have been gone an entire year. A year since they dragged you out of this house and put you on trial. I can't believe you are here." She pulled back a few inches and really looked again at Nacaria. "But you are not my Nacaria. You are a little older than you should be." She turned around and witnessed the shadow on the wall of the staircase. She knew for certain now that this was not her Nacaria. "You have come for Yasmine, haven't you?"

"Yes," Nacaria stammered. "Yes, Mother we have. But I am so happy to see you."

Olympia beamed proudly. "And I you, my love. And I am pleased to see that your sentence does not last a lifetime as is evidenced by your very presence and relative youth." Olympia turned to Seth. "You must be Seth. I have heard a great deal about you."

"Where is she, Hecate?" Seth asked. "I haven't seen Yaz in far too long. Where is she?"

Olympia looked dismayed. "She isn't here now."

Olympia guided them inside and settled them down in the living room. Nacaria moved slowly, eyeing the shadow in the foyer which was now approaching her slowly, inch by inch, wall by wall until it hovered in the living room by the fireplace.

Nacaria walked to the mantle and stared, entranced, at the shadow of herself hovering there. She reached her fingers out and lightly stroked the wallpaper. The shadow flinched a little, confused and unsure of what it was seeing.

"Hi," Nacaria told herself. "I know your pain. Your fears. Your torment. You will make it out. You are a survivor."

The cathartic moment might have been beautiful to witness in any other situation, but Seth was losing patience. He knew this was probably hard on his mom and he knew that he should be elated to see his cherished grandmother alive again. Any other time it would have been all he could focus on. But not until he found Yasmine. His wife was the only person on his mind.

"What do you mean she isn't here now!" exclaimed Seth. "We have literally been everywhere to find her. We were told by your own father she was here."

"Remarkable," Olympia gasped. "You have seen my father? Really?""

"We don't have time for that!" Seth roared.

Nacaria took charge. "Mother, where is Yasmine now?"

"Sinclair took her away," Olympia informed them. "We had to get her out of here for a number of reasons, but most importantly to save her life."

Seth sprang to attention in his chair. "Save her life?"

Olympia gave a slight nod and explained her meaning. "Her soul is beginning to blur with young Yasmine. I feared this might happen, so Sinclair and I decided it would be best to put some distance between she and her younger self. He took her to a hotel. That has slowed the process, but it hasn't completely stopped it. They have shared the same world too long. Your Yaz has begun to suffer from headaches and inexplicable weakness. You must take her away immediately. I am not sure how many more days she can last. Or young Yasmine. She is upstairs in bed. I'm telling others it is the flu, but it is not."

"Where is the hotel?" Seth asked.

Sinclair could not help but smile at the sight of his fully grown granddaughter sitting criss crossed on the bed eating from a bucket of Kentucky Fried Chicken. She told him they had changed the taste and way it was cooked in the future and all she wanted, next to the Happy Meal they'd had a week ago, was to eat the original Original Recipe. It was the one thing which had successfully perked her up from her malaise. Day by day, Yasmine was losing strength as the battle between the two incarnations of her one soul were vying for dominance.

A knock came at the door. Yasmine gave him a confused look.

"It might be Olympia," Sinclair said. "Although, if that is the case, I would assume she would phone and have me drive out to get her. She refuses to drive."

"Maybe it's my family."

Cautiously, Sinclair opened the hotel room door. Two strangers charged in past him with Olympia standing in the hallway behind them. The man rushing past, however, stopped himself the moment he pushed by and returned his attention to Sinclair. He smiled a huge smile and inexplicably hugged him.

"Young man," Sinclair growled.

"Granddaddy!" Seth cried out. "I know you have no idea who I am. It's me, Seth! God how I have missed you." Seth released his grandfather as quickly as he had seized him. Then he barked, "Now, where is Yaz?"

"In the bedroom. Through that door. Hurry. She's fading."

Seth burst through the doorway. There he found his beautiful wife, the love of his life, his best friend and biggest antagonizer. Seth saw his love Yasmine sitting on the bed watching an old rerun of Welcome Back Kotter. Or perhaps it wasn't a rerun. He didn't care. He scooped her up in his strong arms and held her as closely as he could without smothering her.

"Seth! Seth! I knew you'd come for me."

"I will always come for you, Yaz," Seth kissed her passionately. "You are my life."

"Oh Seth, did you see her? Grandmother? And that's Grandfather out there!"

Seth laughed at her little girl excitement. "I saw them." He sighed in relief. She was safe. She was in his arms. Perhaps the only real thing he loved in the world, or at least this much.

"Take me home, Seth," she sobbed. "I'm not feeling very well. Let me say goodbye to them and then take me home to my babies. How is everyone? Did you find Fable and Beryl?"

It only took a few minutes to catch her up but after he had Yasmine was nearly speechless—but being Yasmine, she was only *nearly*.

"Howard is Beryl's son?" Yasmine screamed. "He's always been her son?"

"Always," said Seth.

"And she's some kind of god?"

"That part we don't understand yet. But she is supposed to be. Or becoming one."

Olympia came into the bedroom with Sinclair and Nacaria in tow. Though Yasmine was thrilled to see Seth and ecstatic to be returning home to her babies, it hit her the moment her grandparents came through the door that this would be the last time she would ever see them. She understood how fortunate this magnificent blessing of more time with them was, but she wanted still more. Freezing in her mind the images of this moment—when they were alive and together—Yasmine knew she would cling to this memory over the coming years whenever her heart missed them. Olympia approached, hands outstretched to clasp Yasmine's and told her it was time for goodbye. Yasmine's glossy eyes slowly met her grandmother's. Olympia understood how painful it was to the child to let go now. She had needed this time back in the past, but it was now the time to return to her own life and time before both Yasmines suffered the consequence.

"I have cherished these days with you, Yasmine. To see you as the woman you'll become fills me with pride."

"And me as well," Sinclair added. "My sweet little girl. All grown up. And married to Seth! But I can tell that he worships you, my sweet. That makes your old granddad very happy." He gave Seth a loving wink before placing his hands on the back of both their heads. "I love you two rascals very much. Always have. Always will."

Yasmine gave her grandfather a final kiss and wiped tears from her eyes as she faced Olympia. "I don't know what to say to you."

"Then say nothing," Olympia smiled. "We've already said what we felt. Go safely to your family. Love your children with ferocity. Look after all of my great grandchildren for me. Tell them each how much their Olympia loves them from beyond."

Olympia kissed Yasmine, then Nacaria. Nacaria hugged her tightly one last time before letting go forever. Olympia hugged Seth and directed him to his wife and mother, stepping back to give them room. Nacaria withdrew a potion from her satchel and focused on their own place in time. With one final smile toward Olympia and Sinclair, the trio evaporated into the air.

...

Traffic honked loudly through the window in front of them. A man was crossing the street against oncoming traffic and the cars whizzing by sounded their disapproval. Nacaria, Seth, and Yasmine looked around at their surroundings. A very stunned child stood behind them holding an ice cream cone. He dropped it to the floor in shock at what he had just seen.

"Brewbaker's Ice Cream shop in Tuscaloosa," Seth said to them. "I guess this is where the hotel used to sit."

"Well, at least we are home," Nacaria sighed in relief.

"I'll get an Uber," Seth said. Then he realized he did not have a phone on him because who would he have called back in the past? He added, "I'll see if I can use their phone and call Arielle."

Arielle sprinted for the door the moment Seth called. She was so glad she had taken a chance and answered the ice cream shop's call. She was there in twenty minutes pulling Yasmine, her brother, and her stepmother into one huge, Obreiggon-sized hug.

CHAPTER NINETEEN

Howard's Quandary

In the days following Yasmine and the others' return, life began to fall back into something resembling normalcy at Blanchard House. Nacaria, Xander, and Cassandra went back to their estate, Oleander, in Charleston. Artemis continued occupying herself with matters at the restaurant. Demitra immersed herself in a few cold cases the police department handed her which had stalled in their investigations, including the robbery case she'd previously declined. Jerry was busy as ever at his own job, but at night he had taken to whisking Demitra away for dinner out in order to lessen her time at home where Beryl's absence was hard to ignore.

Howard remained distant since discovering the Blanchards were in fact his very own family. Arielle was running the office without him as day after day he had failed to show up to work. But on day four she was taken by surprise when he came through the office door.

"Hello stranger!" she said excitedly, hopping up from her desk.

Making a disapproving face, Howard replied, "I see you've gotten comfortable during my little rest."

Arielle was in a very loose cotton tank top and her pants, if you could call them pants, were wide-legged, cotton pajama bottoms with yellow ducks on them. She was wearing no shoes at all, but Howard spied the tail-end of a furry unicorn slipper sticking out from behind the desk. She wore no makeup and had her red hair clipped to the top of her head. It did not appear she had even brushed it that morning.

"Well, yeah. By day two, I just figured if you weren't showing up this week, I'd be comfortable. Clients only come in by appointment, and I saw my clients already. I had to cancel all yours. And I don't have to look pretty to input data and answer phones."

"I understand," he nodded. "But tomorrow let's try to put some effort in again. I will be here from now on."

Arielle walked over to him and looked her boss in the eyes. "You all right? You've had quite an adjustment to make."

"I'm fine. Nothing to adjust to. I am still who I was last week. I am Howard Caldwell, representative of the Blanchard estate and several other prominent Alabama families. Nothing has changed."

He walked toward his office, stopping to pour himself a cup of coffee at the little kitchenette in the corner. Arielle followed him. "*Everything* has changed, Howard! You are a Blanchard! Doesn't that mean something to you?"

"Of course, it does," he replied. "But I have spent 50 years being plain Howard Caldwell. I think it's best I just keep being him."

"You have to face the truth. You can't ignore it," Arielle remarked.

Howard whirled around gruffly, something she had never seen him do. "I can do whatever I want. My life is the same one I had before. I am the Blanchards' friend and representative and that is all. I don't want to talk about this again, Arielle."

"Yes, sir."

"See if you can get the appointments back for tomorrow that you canceled. I have a lot of work to do. I don't want to be disturbed."

Howard went into his office and shut the door. He never shut the door unless he was in a meeting. Arielle was worried for him. Ignoring his wishes, she pulled out her cell from her desk drawer and called the one person that might be able to reach Howard's better sense.

Howard was deep into land value reports for his client, the mayor, when his door swung open without a knock. He glared up—ready to yell at his defiant assistant—when he saw Yasmine standing in his doorway.

"Yaz!" He stood up and rushed over to her, sweeping her up into a warm, loving embrace. "I was worried sick about you. I was so relieved when Artemis texted me you were safe at home."

"You didn't text her back. Or me," Yasmine acknowledged. "It hurt my feelings."

Howard looked ashamed as he went back behind his desk and sat back down. "I didn't want to speak to anyone. Sorry. Why are you here anyway?"

"Arielle called me and told me you'd come in and you were in a funk."

In a grouchy tone, he replied, "That isn't very employee-of-the-month of her."

"Well, she knows you are one of the most important people in the world to me. I have come to get you out of the funk."

"Yasmine, thank you. But please don't. Let it go. I just want to be by myself and catch up on work."

Yasmine plopped down on his desk, landing atop his land report. "Seeing as how I am your biggest client, and possibly your best friend, I reserve the right to ignore all your wishes because I know what's best for you."

She took hold of his hand and dragged him out the door. He was reluctant to go with her, but Howard had never been able to deny Yasmine Sinclair Blanchard anything. She drove him to Capital Park and forced him to walk with her to the ruins of the old capitol building. The ruins were an orange mortared brick, tall in places, crumbled in others. It was behind one of these tall walls where she led him to a surprise. As they turned the corner, Howard saw two men dash away with empty sacks and plastic bins. On the ground behind the ruin, a large quilt was spread out over the grassy lawn. A picnic basket full of cheeseburgers and onion rings sat beside chilled bottles of Dr. Pepper. A projection movie screen, the size of a large television, sat on the stone steps and a movie had just begun to roll through its opening credits.

"The Life Aquatic?"

Yasmine smiled. "Your favorite!"

"You hate Wes Anderson movies," Howard said, giving her a raised eyebrow.

"Yes, I do. I really, really do. But I love you and because I love you, I will lay here with you and eat all day and watch that terrible movie with you."

Howard smiled. No one on earth knew how to make someone feel better than Yasmine. They watched the movie in silence—her other gift to him. She did not talk all the way through it as was her custom. The burgers were delicious, and the Dr. Peppers kept coming, brought out from some hidden vehicle parked out of sight by the two men who'd set everything up for her. They even brought a plate of Moon Pies for dessert—Howard's secret indulgence.

Once the final credits rolled, Yasmine sat upright and looked at Howard. "Okay. Now that you are feeling better, let's talk this out."

Howard shook his head. "I don't feel like talking, Yasmine."

"Oh, I never meant to imply you were going to get to say anything," she said. "You are going to listen while I do the talking. I can't understand what you are going through, but there are parts I can relate to. I thought my brother Olley to be this glorious thing in my mind—my sweet, dead brother. So often throughout my life

I thought of him, and my parents. Then when he came back as Patric and tried to kill everybody, I had to retune my way of thinking about him."

"I don't see where that relates."

Yasmine went on. "It totally relates. I think this has far less to do with the Blanchards than it does that you have lost the lifelong narrative you've held of your mother."

Howard didn't reply, but he did not have to. Yasmine could tell from his expression that she hit a nerve.

"In your mind," she went on, "Your mother was this perfect being you never got the opportunity to know. She died for you. You have glorified her to a saintly degree because of that. And because your father loved her so much, he could never be with any other woman after her. He mourned her all of his life."

Howard's chin lowered slightly, a nod to the truth Yasmine was spilling.

"Howard—it's all still true. Your mother did sacrifice for you. She left you at childbirth so that you could continue to live. Your narrative still rings true, the only difference is that you now know you know her. Beryl is that saint. It's okay that you don't know how to think of her after this. I'm sure when she gets back she won't know how to either. It's also okay if you never think of her as a part of you. She can just keep on being Beryl in your mind. There's nothing wrong with that. And you don't have to figure any of it out today, or tomorrow, or even next year. Some things figure themselves out as time moves along."

Howard was listening. He was saying nothing, but he was listening.

"As for the witch stuff," Yasmine continued, "I know what it's like to be a part of an extraordinary family when you are only ordinary. You do, too. You have been a part of this family dynamic all of my life. But now you have something I don't have. You have discovered you are not just a fringe member. You are not an honorary Blanchard. You are a full-fledged part of that clan. You have powers if you decide you want them. If you don't, then leave them where they are buried. That's your choice."

Howard grabbed a chilled Dr. Pepper and twisted off the top. Downing a bit of it he looked directly at Yaz and said, "But to join this family now, at this age—when they are so close to each other and so—"

"And they are close to you, too, Howard," Yasmine reminded him. "Every holiday, every cookout, every death, birth, birthday, every Friday night dinner. You may not see it, but you have always been a member of that family. You are not walking in as a stranger. You are the Howard we have all loved all these years. And we have loved you for you, not because we had to, but because of who you are. You became family without need of blood. So now that it turns out you have the blood as well, it alters nothing. You have been a Blanchard all your life anyway. Only now there is evidence you really are one."

Howard leaned over and rubbed her head with his hand until her hair was mussed. She smiled at him. He smiled back. "Thank you, Yasmine. For all this. You have made me feel better."

...

For dinner that night, Yasmine cooked a huge and delicious pot roast, juicy and tender with enough brown gravy to appease Fable and Seth and all the kids. The side dishes were already set on the long Blanchard family dining room table as she marched the roast in. Artemis, Demitra, Jerry, Fable, Seth, Arielle, and Salem sat sprinkled around the table with the children; Con, Hera, and Titan were situated between two adults at all times. The family had long learned not to let the little cousins sit together or no one would eat. Romulus curled up at his mother's feet awaiting his plate she would set before him. Demitra was cutting up Con's meat while Fable tended to Rom's. Yasmine parceled out Hera's portion while Seth buttered the kids' rolls. Another lesson they learned the hard way, do not let children have the butter dish. There were two empty chairs among them. Beryl's absence was something everyone worked overtime to ignore, but it was a devastating blow to the energy of the family. As Yasmine handed her daughter the plate, a voice rang out from the foyer.

"Sorry I'm late!" Howard said, coming into the dining room and taking his regular seat. "I got held up on a client call. Alright! Pot roast! My favorite."

"Howard?" Artemis said in surprise. "You're here."

Howard gave her a sly wink and replied, "It's Friday night dinner, isn't it? And I am a part of this family after all."

Demitra's face widened into a great big smile. Rising up from her chair and walking over to Howard's, she kissed the top of his balding head. "Yes, you are. You always have been. Friday dinner wouldn't have been the same without our Howard."

CHAPTER TWENTY

Business and Accidental Magic

Once dinner was over and the adults had cleared the table and washed the dishes, Salem asked Howard and Yasmine if they would join her in the office. The three made their way to the family study. This room was rarely used except for important meetings. Located by the front door, everyone passed it every day, but only occasionally did anyone venture inside. It had primarily been used by Sinclair during his lifetime to run his corporation. Olympia used it for her charity works after his death until her own. Now it sat lifeless except for the two times a month Artemis went inside to pay the household bills. Salem closed the door behind them.

"Is something wrong, Salem?" Yasmine asked.

"No, not at all," Salem said. "I wanted to ask you for a favor."

"Ask away," Yasmine replied.

Salem put her serious face on as she began. "As you know when Travis retired two years ago, he put me in charge of the advertising firm. Well, he has an offer to sell the firm for a substantial amount of money. I have spoken to the potential buyer, and he expressed interest in my partnering with him. He is from New York and can bring a lot of exciting changes to the firm. However, he knows nothing about our clientele or our past or current campaigns. He will purchase the entire company, and I will work for him in a vice-presidential capacity, or I can buy in and own half the company myself as we try to build it into something huge together. Travis said he would just give me 50% and sell the other 50. But I do not want to do that. I would like to purchase it outright."

"How much do you need?" Yasmine asked.

Salem paused. "It's a lot, Yaz. It would be a big loan. I would need about a million dollars."

Salem waited for Yasmine to balk but she didn't. She sat as calm as could be, as if

Salem had simply asked to borrow her sweater for the evening. Howard suppressed the smile his face wanted to betray. Salem was so nervous, yet Yasmine did not find the request burdensome at all.

Salem made stern eyes at her sister-in-law. "Yaz, it *is* a lot of money. But I feel sure that I can pay it back with interest in a range of 10-15 years."

Yasmine came to attention suddenly as if only now realizing something. "Loan? Oh, you are asking me to *borrow money*?"

"That's the general idea," Howard chuckled.

"It's too much," Salem said with a short shake of her head. "It is. I get it. It's still a fantastic opportunity just to work for him."

"No!" Yasmine cried. "I don't mean that. I thought you were telling us what you needed. I didn't realize you thought it'd be a loan."

"Yes," Salem said. "A loan. Will you loan me the funds to make the deal?"

"Of course not!" Yasmine said defiantly. "I'm not loaning you anything. It's family money. Take what you need. It sounds like a terrific chance for you."

Salem was stymied. "What? No, Yaz, I just want to borrow."

Yasmine laughed and for a moment Salem saw the face of the innocent, naive little girl she used to play with. "That's ridiculous," Yasmine told her. "That money is just as much yours as it is mine. It belongs to everyone."

"Actually, Yaz," Howard clarified. "It's yours. Olympia left it to you since it was all originally Sinclair Industries money."

Yasmine had forgotten about that. "Well, that's just legalities. It is still family money. So just have Howard draw what you need for the purchase and that's that."

Salem did not know how to respond. She didn't want it gifted to her. "No, Yaz, I fully intend to pay you back."

"Why?" Yasmine asked in her innocent way. "You are my cousin. My sister-in-law. My *sister,* actually. We grew up together. It's just a technicality that Grandmother left it to me alone. It's all our money. Yours, mine, Fable's, Demitra's, Howard's. We are all family. It's family money. Whatever you need, it's yours. No loan."

"Yaz!" Salem cried.

"No loans," Yasmine declared. "Take it or leave it and work for some New York bigshot without any power or say so of your own. If you want the money, take the money. It is yours free and clear. But no sister of mine is paying interest and making monthly payments to her own family."

Salem was astounded. Her eyes overflowed with tears. "Thank you, Yazzy. Seriously, you don't know how much this means to me."

"You're welcome. We don't have to talk about it anymore. Howard will handle it all."

CHAPTER TWENTY ONE

Lemonade on a Sunday Afternoon

Artemis came outside to the front porch carrying a tray of lemonade and several glasses. She sat the tray down on a small table and poured herself and her sister a glass. From one of the rockers, Demitra took the lemonade and sipped as she watched Fable sitting in the yard with the boys. Romulus was laying on his back swaying back and forth while his mother rubbed his stomach. His left leg was shaking happily as she scratched his rounded chest. Con was oblivious to the two of them, using them more as an obstacle course as he drove his electric truck in circles around his brother and mother. Demitra shook her head and gave a sigh.

"You know I hid that charging cord the last time Con used that thing because he kept driving through the flower beds. But Jerry found it and recharged the damn thing for him."

Artemis kicked her feet up onto the porch rail and grinned as she crossed her feet, "Your husband truly loves those boys. It's really a beautiful thing."

Demitra nodded in agreement. "You know I was so sad when Larry died--the second time--that my grandsons would never know a grandfather's love. Boy Jerry sure showed me."

"He's a great man."

"It's his love for those boys that really helped cinched my falling in love with him." She stared off in the distance for a second. Artemis could tell by the direction of her gaze she was looking out to the old family cemetery. "Never imagined I'd love again. Now here I am."

"You really do love Jerry, don't you Dee?"

"I do. Oh, not the way I loved Larry. But it isn't really fair to Love to expect it to appear the same way when it comes again. I love Jerry in a way that is only his. It may be different, but it is real. I am a happy woman in this life."

The sisters watched as now Con was driving across the lawn while Rom raced beside him, occasionally jumping the electric truck. Every jump tickled his brother as if it were the first time. Romulus loved making his brother laugh and would do this all day if every jump garnered the same result. Fable got up from the grass and came back to the porch for her own glass of lemonade.

"I missed those guys so much while I was gone."

Artemis stroked Fable's hair and admitted, "I am a little jealous that you got to meet some of our old ancestors. Of course Nacaria is the one that got to meet everyone. Did she tell you what our grandfather told her about the boys?"

Fable nodded. "He saw them. Saw them over all that space and time just by looking into Aunt Nacaria's eyes. It's crazy to think that he knew his namesake's existence and his wolf brother. What did he call them? *Two halves of the same whole.*"

"Sounds like our grandmother was a real prize!" Demitra snorted as she rocked forward to sit her glass on the porch rail. "No wonder Mother never spoke about her. Nacaria and Seth said she was a real bitch."

"Uh, your own mother was a real bitch," Fable guffawed. "At least when she was young. I was shocked. I have never seen a more vain and self-absorbed woman in my life."

Artemis let out a howl, "I would have loved to have seen that!" Leaning up from her reclined stance she slapped her hand down onto Demitra's arm and exclaimed, "You remember how she was when we were little! Always telling us to behave like ladies. Scolding us if we were rude or snippy with each other." Artemis turned to Fable next, "And did you say she had marijuana?"

Fable pressed her hands over her mouth and nose as if she were trying to rub the escaping laughter away. "She did! A big box of it. At least it was hers or Pastoria's. Never really could figure it out. There is a lot about Olympia Blanchard we didn't know. Made me feel way more forgiving of my own personality and flaws."

The screen door opened as Yasmine and Seth came out with Hera and little Titan. They set the kids free to roam with their cousins. While Titan was content to sit plopped down on the grass snatching at the green blades, Hera jumped into the passenger side of Con's truck. Con steered them off down the path through the back meadow. Rom dashed behind them. Everyone knew he would look after them, he always did.

Seth settled down onto the porch swing, arranging pillows behind his back. He spread his legs out for his wife to nestle in against him as he lightly pushed the swing with his one dangling foot. The Blanchards relaxed in silence for a while, allowing the warm breeze to wash over them. Times of peace came infrequently for this family so when one came, they made sure to enjoy it.

Wondering why the house was so empty, Arielle and Salem found the others sitting outside enjoying the lovely day. Salem suggested a game of badminton, but Seth and Yasmine said they were far too relaxed to get out of the swing. Arielle suggested to her sister that they play a leisurely game of bocce instead. The sisters tiptoed around Titan as they went down the porch steps. He was now on hands and knees taking rocks out of the flower bed and lining them up in rows on the bottom step. Someone should have acknowledged how advanced a mechanical feat that was for a child so young, but no one was really paying attention. Occasionally, Demitra cautioned him to not put the rocks in his mouth, but other than that Titan did as he pleased.

Jerry came outside a little while later, announcing he'd fixed the leaky sink in the bathroom on the third floor. No one else really knew it was even dripping but they were glad to have a man around the house who noticed those things--Seth never did. Seeing that the family was enjoying the outdoors, Jerry went back into the house for a few minutes before returning with a platter of steaks and some sliced potato wedges. He fired up the grill by the pool and started making dinner. Artemis and Demitra exchanged a smile to one another, quietly recognizing the tranquility of the day. This didn't happen much around Blanchard House.

Of course, nothing lasts forever. The roar of Zelda's car rang out down the driveway and with her came the frenetic Zelda energy she always brought, ending the peacefulness.

As she stomped up the steps and plopped herself down into the third rocker, she began her rant. "Just did a readin' for DiDi Walker. Did y'all know she's a workin' down at the rubber plant in Hinkley? That darn husband a hers already went through all that money they won in that settlement with the delivery van that ran him over. Now that poor girl's workin fingers to the bone."

"That's terrible," Demitra replied. "Wasn't she Horace Berkly's daughter? I thought he left her well off."

"Naw," Zelda said, shaking her head. "'Member, after her momma died, he run off with that private nurse he'd hired. That nurse got all his money when he passed. Poor ole DiDi didn't get nothin' but that rat hole house that was fallin' apart even way back then."

The sounds of Seth and Yasmine snoring together on the swing began to compete with Zelda's blaring, just at the precise time Jerry texted Demitra from the pool that dinner was ready. She and Artemis went inside to fetch plates and silverware to take out to the pool while Salem and Arielle rushed in to grab drinks for everyone. Fable stood on the bottom porch step and sent out a call. Within a few moments a large buck with heavy antlers trotted out of the woods to her.

"Would you do me a huge favor and find the little ones and direct them to the pool? It's dinner time."

The deer bowed his heavy head and sprinted off. Soon everyone, even the sleeping duo in the swing, were seated around the large poolside table having a delicious summer meal together.

"For a minute I was afraid I'd never see this place again," Fable observed as she sliced into the perfectly cooked meat. "Y'all the food in the past is so bland. I am so glad to be back where meals taste good."

"Blaze was a pretty good cook," Seth said. "I mean, with what she had. She was a remarkable lady."

Salem frowned a little before saying, "I feel so terrible about sending you all hurtling backwards. I hope you all know how sorry I am."

Yasmine squeezed her shoulder as she said through a mouthful of baked potato, "I actually wouldn't trade my trip for the world. I got to see Granddaddy again. And my time with Grandmother was the best gift I've ever been given."

"Still," Seth groused, "You do need to get some control over your thought processes Salem. We don't want something like that to happen again. That little dude inside you wields some heavy magic."

Salem knew he was right but that was so much easier said than done. How could she be expected to police *thought.* A person couldn't help what thoughts crossed their mind. But she'd been thinking about it lately and had come to the conclusion that the thought itself wasn't the catalyst, it was her speaking the thought which turned it into a spell. She was now trying to be extra careful. Twice she'd caught herself about to make a statement which could have possibly been interpreted as a wish or a spell. Quickly she would caution herself, *do not say you wish this man would drive faster*. Or she'd warn, *Do not speak that you want this pregnancy swelling to end.* The results could have been devastating. It was very hard to censor thoughts while everyone else in the world has the freedom to speak their opinions or desires. It was something she'd have to get used to for a while, at least till little Olympus was born.

"I wonder what Beryl is doing right now?" Fable said aloud, not realizing she'd spoken her thoughts openly.

Demitra smiled at her youngest and replied, "I think about her too. All the time."

Zelda let out a rambunctious sound and slapped the table, "Lordy, I forget I can tell y'all stuff 'bout her now. Y'all ain't gotta worry none about Beryl. She's having a blast! There was this one time we took her to luncheon at Mildred Platter's house. Y'all never knew Mildred. She died when you girls was little. But God ain't never put a meaner bitch on this earth. She was so uppity. Had these two maids--blacks. Every housewife with any kind of middle-class husband had herself a black maid back then. Well, Mildred just had to have two. Well, we was at this luncheon she threw to organize some kind of library fund. Don't recall 'xactly what it was for, but we all had to go. Anyway, Beryl gets up and starts helping the maids clear up the dishes and wash them. Boy I thought Mildred would fall out on the floor. White women just didn't do that back then. But Beryl weren't used to be'in waited on. She made friends with one of the maids and took her out to lunch one day. Boy that caused a stir. 'Bout got kicked out of the cafe they was eatin' in. but your Daddy John Windham was in there that day too, having a business meeting. He saw the ruckus and went over to the manager and told him he really didn't wanna mess with Olympia Blanchard's cousin not unless he wanted to piss off The Windham law firm or Nate Caldwell. 'Tween the two of them they handled the business of just about ever'body important in town. That manager let Beryl and that woman finish their meal and then didn't even charge 'em."

"That's so cool!" Yasmine cried. "Beryl did that!"

"Beryl was quite a force in them days. There was lots of inequality goin' on and Beryl never let any of it get by her."

"What else did she do?" Fable asked.

"Well, she helped Lympy and me and Pastoria out of some jams. I got my arm nearly snatched off by a wendigo we was fightin' in Cullman, Alabama and she healed me up while Pastoria and Lympy sliced his head off with their Daddy's old sword."

Demitra was shell shocked. Her Beryl was actually involved in some of her mother's old adventures? All her life she'd heard Olympia go on and on about her youth and now to know that Beryl fought alongside her through some of those events. It was mind blowing. "Beryl stopped a Wendigo?"

"Naw," Zelda corrected. "Beryl saved me while your momma stopped the Wendigo."

Yasmine turned to Seth in confusion, "What's a Wendigo?"

Seth shrugged. She looked at Jerry, who asked, "Why in the world would you turn to me for an answer. I have no idea what anything is."

"It's a werewolf," Arielle answered. "I think."

Artemis chimed in, "A Wendigo is like a werewolf but one who has no human side at all. Very vicious things."

"Beryl's gonna have quite a few stories for y'all when she gets back. She was pretty badass." Zelda informed them.

"Beryl?" Fable gasped.

"Yup," Zelda went on. "You know that acid can y'all got in the arsenal down in the vault?"

"The one I used on Patric's wolves?" Yasmine asked.

Zelda nodded. "That's the one. Beryl made that. Put it together cause she didn't have no active powers in combat. Made it to help fight some zombies in Wetumpka. Just sprayed 'em down to bits."

The family listened to a few more stories as they finished their meal. It helped ease the pain of missing Beryl to hear about Beryl continuing to live her life, even if it was in a different time. When dinner was over, the kids went back to playing in the yard while the adults cleared up the dishes. All in all, it had been a charming Sunday, one they all needed after the drama and confusion of late. If only things could remain so peaceful.

CHAPTER TWENTY TWO

Mondays

Monday morning traffic was frightful. It seemed that year after year Daihmler grew more and more yet the road system wasn't adjusting to meet the demand. Salem remembered a time when it took her only fifteen minutes to get to town. Now it took almost thirty. Of course, stopping at Starbucks for a latte didn't expedite her drive.

Salem finally arrived at Howard's office. She was picking up the bank draft before driving back to Atlanta immediately after to sign the papers with her new partner Miles Thorsby. As she walked in, she said hello to her little sister and handed her a Starbucks Nitro she had grabbed for her on the way over.

"Still enjoying the job?" Salem asked her.

"Howard's great. I see why Yaz liked working here. It's low key, but interesting. And I get to watch General Hospital everyday while Howard's at lunch."

Salem giggled and went into Howard's office. He had everything ready for her as she sat down. "This is a big day for you Salem," he said. "After all your years of building a name in your field, you are finally going to own your own company. What are the big picture plans for Dandridge Advertising?"

"Well, first off we are changing the name to Thorsby, Lane and Associates."

"Lane?"

"My married name," Salem reminded him. "In Atlanta no one knows who Salem Blanchard is. I go by Salem Lane professionally."

"You sure you still want to do that?" Howard asked. "Now's the time to make changes if you plan to. After all you're not married to David Lane anymore. What happens if you ever get married again? I doubt your husband would like it much if you kept your first marriage name."

Married again? She just couldn't see that ever happening. She'd had the perfect marriage. The perfect husband. It didn't seem like anything that would ever be an issue for her. Salem was content to have her child on her own and live her life with her family and her business. Love was not in the cards anymore and she had made her peace with that. Of course, life had taught her to never say never. She understood Howard's point.

"If I ever marry, I'd hope I'd marry someone that understands that I didn't stop loving my husband simply because he died. There are no Lanes left. I am it. Hell, even this baby here in my stomach isn't a Lane. I would like some piece of my old life to live on. I'll keep using Lane at work and Blanchard everywhere else."

"So much in a name," Howard said, half to himself. "I've been Howard Caldwell so long—Demitra wants me to hyphenate and add Blanchard. As if the world is running out of Blanchards anytime soon."

"The Blanchard name carries some clout around here."

"So does the name Caldwell," Howard smiled. "Besides, it's not like I can explain the sudden change. You all may know I'm a Blanchard—and I may know I'm a Blanchard—but the way I am a Blanchard is not exactly explainable to non-witching people."

Salem laughed. "I guess you can't really go around Daihmler telling people you are Beryl Blanchard's son, now can you. You are thirty years older than she is. I see your point."

Salem grabbed her bank draft and left Howard alone to finish the legalities to the withdrawal of funds from Sinclair industries. She stopped by Arielle's desk to say goodbye to her sister before heading back to Atlanta.

"I really miss seeing you every day," Arielle said.

"Me too. It's so lonely in Atlanta without you. But maybe soon I will be back here permanently. One of the ideas I must discuss with my new partner is possibly moving our offices to Tuscaloosa. The baby is coming, and I really think I'm going to want my family around me when little Olympus is born."

Arielle squealed in delight. "That would be so perfect. And Lord knows Blanchard House is big enough. And my nephew can grow up with his cousins the way you did!"

"That's my plan," Salem smiled. She turned her gaze back toward Howard's closed office door. "Howard seems to be doing better don't you think?"

"He is," Arielle agreed. "Whatever Yaz said to him worked. It has to be so hard on him. I remember how difficult it was for me when I learned Blackie was my real mother. I loved Aunt Blackie, but it took me some time to see her in a new way. Now, we are very close. I'm actually having dinner with her midweek."

"Tell her hello for me," Salem said. "And I'm glad Howard is accepting things now. But between you and me, I can't help but wonder what his life would have been like had he known from childhood he was a Blanchard? And can you imagine what he would be like if he hadn't had his powers bound at birth? His life might have turned out completely different."

CHAPTER TWENTY THREE

Here we Go Again

Howard's workload was stacked pretty high on his desk. The days he'd missed caused a backlog for him, not to mention the Sinclair business he had handled during Yasmine's absence which he needed to finalize so she could resume her leadership in the company. Salem's brief interruption to collect the check threw him off task for a minute, but he was now back in the thick of returning calls and approving transactions. While scanning over an investment proposal for Sinclair Industries, he reached for the phone to call the corporation's main office to speak with the Controller. With his eyes focused on the document his hand blindly reached for the phone and couldn't find it. He glanced at his desk and there was no phone. He then felt his fingertips rubbing against each other. His hand was empty. Where was the document he'd only just been holding? And where was the desk? The light overhead? His chair?

Howard did not understand what was happening. He had been quietly at his desk and now suddenly he wasn't. He wasn't anywhere he could recognize. The hovel of broken brick, shattered windows, and debris everywhere told him he was in a derelict building. He stepped out of the door—which did resemble his office a little, even the reception area. But this place was a disaster. Burned out, no roof, splintered timbers, rubble, and broken brick all around made it seem as if it had been hit years before by a bomb. He stepped out onto the street. It looked a little like the business district of Daihmler. But everything was a wreck. He couldn't be sure.

Did a nuclear bomb go off or something while I was in my office? How did it not kill me too? Where is Arielle? His car was nowhere to be seen out front, although occasionally a random automobile did speed by. He did not recognize the make or model of any of them. He journeyed down the street and turned at the corner. Shops were all boarded up. The few people he did see were scurrying hurriedly as if afraid to be outside. The sun was high, and the sky was clear. No signs of a mushroom cloud or warfare. He pulled out his phone to call an Uber, but his phone was not in his pocket. His only choice was to walk home. It was only a mile away. He had jogged it before back when exercise was more a bigger part of his routine.

Howard's apartment was not there. The entire building was gone. He didn't understand. And then it hit him. *The Blanchards did something. This is too weird. Somebody cast a spell again.* Then he remembered Salem had just left his office. It had been her unborn baby who wrought the havoc before. Maybe Salem accidentally did something again. But what?

It took him nearly three hours to walk through town and down the winding back roads toward Blanchard House. As he passed one small shack of a residence, an old woman beckoned him from the doorway.

"What are you doing, Sir?" she called to him. "Are you looking to be killed? Come inside. Come inside and stay with me until the sun comes up."

Howard looked at the woman as if she were crazy. She certainly looked the part. Disheveled hair, rags for clothes. She was drawn and emaciated looking. She made him nervous. Something was off. Her behavior, the landscape all around. Something was definitely wrong. There was only one place, one family, he knew might have the answers. He continued walking toward the direction of Blanchard House.

He heard the woman shout at him from behind his back, "You damn fool! The sun is setting! They're coming out soon. You're gonna die tonight if you don't come back."

For a moment he considered taking shelter inside her house. Maybe she had answers. But somehow, he trusted the Blanchards more than this insane, haggard person. He knew Blanchard House was only a short walk from where he was.

When he saw the house, he grew terrified. Throughout his life Blanchard House had been a bastion of splendor. Beautiful flowers adorning the clean crisp white painted walls. The orchard, the grapevines, Olympia's rose beds. He saw none of that now. The house was putrid. Black scuff marks maligned the outer walls of the house. Timbers were missing in places, and the windows appeared to be bricked up. Every single window. Furthermore, the new addition to the house was not there. Neither was the kitchen addition around back which Olympia's first husband had built ages ago. The house was much smaller than what Howard had always known it to be. And it was falling into ruin.

Howard made his way up to the front porch. He tried to not look at the ground—that awful, desolate ground scattered with decayed corpses and clusters of dusty bones. No grass grew anywhere as far as he could see. And the place where those lovely old oaks had once stood were now marred by the broken, splintered trunks where it appeared the trees themselves had been torn from their feet.

He tried to open the door, but it was bolted shut. He did not know whether he should leave or knock, but coming here had been his only idea, so he knocked.

"Who is it?" called a frightened voice inside. It sounded like a girl but not anyone he had ever heard before.

"Howard," he called back.

The door swung open, and Howard found himself pulled quickly inside, then arms wrapped around him as if he had just returned from war.

"Dad! Dad! Thank Heaven you made it home. We had no idea what happened to you. We were on the supply run, and then suddenly you were just gone."

The girl was lovely, if not a little touched in the head for thinking he was her father. She had honey blonde hair that curled slightly in tresses at her shoulders. Her bright, blue eyes looked almost like a baby doll's. Had they been brown he might have thought, *Bambi*.

"Come in, Dad. You barely made it. The sun will be all the way down in a few minutes."

"Tess!" another voice rang out. It belonged to another girl. As she entered the living room, Howard saw that this one had dark brown hair—almost the color of cocoa. Otherwise, she looked exactly like the blonde who had let him inside. They must have been twins. "Tess, is that Dad?"

"Yes, Trix; it's Dad."

The brunette approached him. "Where did you go? Did you stumble upon a hiding place and make a kill? We looked everywhere for you. Echo is still driving around. I hope he makes it back in time."

"Echo?"

"Yes, Echo. Your son—our brother. What's wrong with you?"

Howard glanced at these two strangers before him and admitted, "I honestly have no idea."

Before Howard could figure out how to explain or what questions to ask, the sound of a vehicle sliding across the littered yard rang out. A door slammed followed by furious footfalls resounding over the rotting wood of the porch.

Loud banging came at the door. It was in succession, three raps, two raps, one rap, three raps.

"It's Echo!" Trix shouted as she ran to unbolt the door. The moment she did, a young man wormed inside while she tried to shut out something behind him. She was not successful, and a grotesque being burst through. It stood in the foyer heaving as though trying to catch a breath that would not come. His face was twisted like that of someone newly dead and beginning to decay. But it was not dead, and Howard knew the moment he saw it that this thing meant to kill them.

There were wailing sounds coming from outside and from the short glimpse Howard got from the brief second the door was open he saw that there were more creatures like this one in the yard. Echo scooted inside, dodging the deformed and bizarre creature that followed him. Howard watched in awe as suddenly Trix outstretched her hand and began vibrating it back and forth. All at once Howard saw what appeared to be liquid metal flying in tiny amounts toward her hand. He followed the trail of one stream and saw that a set of pewter candlesticks which had been sitting on the foyer table were liquifying before his eyes and being pulled toward the girl by whatever force she was exerting from her hand. Suddenly the liquified metal hardened into a long sharp blade in her hand. Without a moment's pause, the girl named Trix slashed the neck of the monster, sending his head flying off and rolling to a thud at the corner of the bottom stair. The creature's body collapsed lifeless onto the floor. Trix breathed heavily from the adrenaline surge. She looked at the knife in her hand.

"Great, another athame," Tess snorted. "Why do we keep sacrificing our precious heirlooms to make athames? Why not make a sword or a scythe or even a nice hatchet? We have enough little knives, Beatrix!"

"Sorry," Trix shrugged. "It's my go-to in a jam."

Howard looked at the body on the floor and then listened to the shrieking behind the walls outside. Scratching sounds came from the wood outside. The house practically vibrated from all sides.

"What is going on in this world?" he asked. "What was that thing? Who are you? Why do you people live in Olympia Blanchard's house?"

The trio of youngsters looked at him curiously.

The boy cocked his head to the side and with an expression of complete confusion, asked, "Uh, What's wrong with Dad?"

The one called Tess looked into Howard's eyes as if she were trying to X-ray him somehow. She looked puzzled. "I have no idea. But he came back different. He even looks different." Tess noted. "Oh no! Do you think he was bitten?"

"Nothing has bitten me!" Howard shouted. "Why do you call me Dad? I have no children. And where is Artemis or Demitra, or Seth or Fable?"

"Who?" Echo replied.

"The Blanchards! The people this house belongs to. Olympia Blanchard's family!"

"This house belongs to us," Tess told him. "We are Olympia Blanchard's family, although what a weird way to say it. Olympia Blanchard died 60 years ago when our grandmother disappeared."

"What?" Howard asked.

Examining him again with her suspicious eyes, Tess asked, "You aren't our father, are you?"

"I'm not really sure."

. . .

Howard found it difficult to concentrate as the four of them sat down to talk. The horrible noises from outside were too distracting. The boy, Echo, assured him the creatures could not get inside. The house was well fortified with reinforcements, both physical and magical. Tess, who seemed to be the oldest—at least she acted like it—started the explanations. She told Howard that Olympia Blanchard was a very minor figure in the Blanchard family history. They had practically forgotten her name until he had mentioned it. She died in a great battle with a vampire six decades ago. She had two sisters, Pastoria and Beryl, although there were rumors that Beryl was more distantly related. Beryl had a husband named Nate. He was also killed by vampires a year after their marriage. But not before he and Beryl had produced a son, their father Howard Blanchard. After Beryl vanished into thin air, Howard was raised by his aunt Pastoria. However, Pastoria died in another battle with the vampires some years ago. Howard Blanchard married a woman named Barbara, the mother to triplets Tess, Trix, and Echo. The two of them did what they could to stop the war with the vampires but by then the Witches Council had been decimated. Now what few witches were left were fending for themselves in a world gone to chaos.

"Where is Barbara?" Howard asked. "I'd like to talk to her."

"Mama died last year," Echo said. "A vampire tore her to shreds while we were infiltrating one of their nests. It was our mistake. We thought that during the day they would be in a sort of a tranquilized state. But that was when we learned that the real vampires are not like those things out there—those things are poor drained souls trying desperately to find blood before their bodies erode and decay. The real vampires don't need rest."

Trix chimed in, "Yeah, those bastards are just as powerful in daytime as nighttime. They just have to remain far from the sunlight. The nest we hit was three stories below ground."

Echo finished the history lesson, "Mom died fighting them off while the three of us got to the top outside. Dad wasn't there. He had broken his leg in a fight and was at home healing. We had gone out without him. He always blames himself for her death."

Looking closely at the amnesiac before them, Trix said to Howard, "You really aren't our father, are you?"

"No," he said.

"Who are you and where is he?"

Howard did not want to answer, but these poor kids—they looked to be maybe 18 or 19 at most—he could not lie to them. Not these strong warriors who had already been through more misery than any man ever could imagine there to be. He told them the truth.

"I come from another time. I guess maybe it's an alternative reality than this. I don't honestly know. I don't know anything. All I know is I am Howard, son of Beryl Blanchard. But I did not grow up with my mother. I guess that is where this world shifted. In my world, Olympia Blanchard thrived and had a huge family. I knew her very well. Beryl was not her sister. Beryl was her granddaughter."

"Granddaughter?" Tess gasped. "They were basically the same age. Beryl Blanchard was Olympia and Pastoria's sister."

Howard shook his head. "No, she wasn't. She was the daughter of Olympia's daughter Demitra. Beryl had been accidentally thrown back in time. That's how she happened to be in Olympia and Pastoria's lives when they were all roughly the same age."

"I have never heard of a Demitra Blanchard," Trix stated suspiciously.

Howard shrugged. "I guess you wouldn't have. Clearly in your world Olympia never married. She didn't have children."

"But in your world she did?" Echo asked.

Howard continued explaining, "In my world none of what is happening here is going on. There are no vampires ravaging the earth. The world is a beautiful place full of love and prosperity. The Blanchard family is enormous, and I just found out I am one of them. But there, in my world, I have no children. I never married. And I don't know anyone named Barbara."

It was all so hard to wrap his mind around. And from the looks of the triplets, they were as lost as he. Howard hung his head a moment and placed his hands to his cheeks. A world where Olympia died young. A world that never had Artemis or Demitra? No Nacaria, no Salem, no Seth, no Fable. It boggled the mind. His entire family was wiped out.

Tess interrupted his thoughts with a question which was both logical, yet not all that important in the moment. "Sir, if Beryl Blanchard was actually Olympia Blanchard's granddaughter...how did she not just erase when Olympia died? I mean, if Olympia didn't live long enough to have children, how could she have a granddaughter?"

Howard was as surprised as the rest of them when a chuckle rang from his throat. Her question was a good one--philosophically complicated--and he was just as much a novice at understanding any of this as he had always been back home with his Blanchards. But now he was the expert on Blanchard lore, and the very concept made him laugh.

"I have no idea," he admitted. "I have grown up with the Blanchards my whole life but until just a few days ago I had no idea I was one of them. I don't know how any of this works. Maybe since Beryl jumped back to a timeline that existed before her birth, she was then a part of a new timeline. So when Olympia died, Beryl was still a part of it regardless of Olympia's fate. Or maybe she did get erased. You said yourself Beryl disappeared."

"Well, wouldn't our father have as well if that were the case?" Trix asked.

Howard shrugged again, "Don't know. I do know that I was born in that timeline and obviously so was your father. He and I existed in the plain of reality we were always supposed to. Maybe that's why your father didn't disappear."

"But he's missing now," Echo commented. "And you are here. What happened to our father? Did he switch places with you? Is he now in your world?"

Howard's heart fell. It dawned on him the enormity of this situation and what it now meant for these three young people's lives. He didn't want to tell them the truth, but he knew he had to.

"No. He didn't go to my world." Howard frowned. "I don't know how to explain because it is all very new to me as well."

"Please try." Tess pleaded.

Howard did his best. He told the children all about Salem's original spell which sent the Blanchard cousins flying off into different directions of time. He told them about how he had only just learned Beryl was his mother.

"What happened to your Beryl?" Echo asked.

"In my time, she is still there--in our 1960's, pregnant with me. Eventually she is supposed to return to her own time, after I am born."

Tess thought a moment and replied, "Is that why our father's mother just disappeared one day? She went back to her own time?"

Howard stood up and walked towards one of the bricked-up windows. He wasn't sure why. People always get up and walk to a window when deep in thought, it seemed a natural thing to do until he realized the windows were covered. "I assume that's where she goes. I haven't actually lived that part of life yet--when Beryl returns--so I don't really know myself."

"But what happened to our dad!" Echo demanded, losing patience. "I don't give a shit about this Olympia person. I don't care what happened to our grandmother. All I want to know is where my father went!"

Howard grimaced as he gave them the only explanation he could determine. "My Blanchards say that one person cannot share their own timeline with themselves at the same age. I think when whatever spell went haywire and sent me here, your father ceased to exist because he and I are the same person."

"What are you saying?" Trix screamed. "Are you saying our father is dead?"

"No, not dead." Howard tried to clarify. "He simply stopped existing because I am also Howard Blanchard. Two men, the same age, sharing the same soul. There was only room for one. I have no other explanation."

It sounded harsh to say so bluntly, but there was no other way to say it. Howard knew it was a shocking blow to the other Howard's children. He felt responsible even though he knew he was not. But his mere presence in their world had eradicated their father's. There was no easy way to convey that information.

Echo was terribly upset. He threw a punch at the wall, denting the wood. He whirled around to face Howard again. The anger in the boy's eyes frightened Howard a little, but there was also a glimpse of a kind of loyalty...or perhaps reverence. As enraged as Echo may have been, Howard could tell from the look in his eye that the boy would never strike him. He looked too much like his father.

"Our father is erased then!" Echo shouted. "Is that what you are saying? All because someone sent you here by accident. So now we have no father?"

Howard teared up at the pain caused to these children. "I'm so sorry kids. I think your Howard is gone forever."

CHAPTER TWENTY FOUR

The Survivors

The emotional state of the triplets was not something Howard could get an accurate read on. They appeared to be accepting their father's erasure rather stoically. There were no signs of hysteria or devastation. He had a hard time figuring it out. Perhaps living amid the turmoil of their day-to-day life made mourning a luxury which survivalists could not afford.

Howard slept on the sofa that evening while the others went upstairs to bed. They offered him their father's bed but that did not seem like a good idea to Howard. He declined and rested on the dingy, dirty sofa. Of course, there was little rest—not with the horrific sounds seeping in from outside. Those terribly hungry creatures out there scratching and clawing at the walls all night in an attempt to find an entrance inside to feast.

Howard spent the better part of the night looking around the ruined lower rooms of the house. Laying on the couch, he could only stare ahead at the bricked-up hearth of the fireplace. The mantle was stacked with medical supplies—bandages, tape, disinfectant—where once sweet family snapshots sat framed in silver. Olympia's chair by the fireplace was gone. When he went into the kitchen for a glass of water, he couldn't help but glance around the space that in his time was the dining room he spent every Friday night having dinner with the Blanchards.

When morning came Howard was awakened by the blonde girl, Tess. With a gentle tap to his shoulder, she pulled him from the deep sleep he had finally managed to fall into just before sunrise.

"You need to get up," she said softly. "We must make a food run today, and we can use your assistance."

"Food run?" Howard repeated, swinging his legs to the floor and rubbing his eyes.

Entering the kitchen, he saw Echo was plating up two cans of baked beans while

Trix was pouring water from a bucket into chipped glasses. Howard did not find "breakfast" appealing, but he was hungry enough to ignore the nauseating offering. Besides, he did not want to insult the kids. This was all they had to offer—and they were willing to share.

"So how does a food run go exactly?" he asked, taking a bite of the stale, cold beans.

"There are some out of the way grocery stores that still have a little food," Echo explained. "The people left are really considerate about not taking everything. Of course, we have to drive out of town a ways. Tess used to work at this little food mart in high school out past Lake Tuscaloosa. Not a lot of people know about it. It still has some stuff left and it gets replenished when possible."

"There are men who take semi-trucks out across the state and bring back what they find and store there for everyone else." Tess elaborated. "We've had to build a makeshift infrastructure to keep everyone alive. We all do our part."

"And there's a gas station there that has an abandoned tanker," Trix added. "We can siphon out what we need. Not a lot of vehicle use anymore, except to drive out for supplies, so gas lasts a while."

Howard was impressed. These three people were kids basically, not even old enough to vote, yet they'd had to grow up hard and fast. Listening to them describe the way life worked here and the things they did to survive made him feel a sense of appreciation for the Howard Blanchard he had usurped.

After breakfast Howard and the triplets ventured outdoors to begin their journey. The beans, still resonating in his unsettled gut, almost came up the moment the door of the house opened, and Howard smelled the outside. He had almost forgotten how repulsive the outside was with its putrid rotting corpses and lack of vegetative life. But now one or two new bodies lay strewn on the ground—the remnants of the starving creatures of the night before that had not made it successfully into the house to eat those living. The sun was killing them, and their grotesquely twisted features, open sores, and wounds made Howard ill.

Echo started the truck, which had oddly enough not been damaged. Howard commented on this fact and was educated by Tess that the creatures are driven by the smell of blood. Damaging vehicles was not something that really occurred to their base animalistic mindset. Their only motivation was life and unless life was inside the truck, they would bypass the truck altogether. Tess brought out several empty buckets and placed them in the back of the truck while Echo and Howard retrieved a few buckets filled with apples from the house. As he carried the buckets, Howard wondered why these had not been on the breakfast menu.

Howard climbed into the cab with Echo as the girls jumped into the truck bed. Echo started off down the highway. Howard had not seen the depths of devastation which had been done to the town he had loved and lived in his entire life. Daihmler, as he knew it, was gone. Eradicated. It was mind blowing to realize an entire way of life could be so easily dissolved and fall into ruin. Everywhere they went was littered with decay and the devastation that followed. Bodies in all stages of decomposition lay on the ground along the way. In college, Howard had been something of a war buff, studying the world wars, Vietnam, Korea. Daihmler looked like the battlefields if no one ever cleared the bodies. And not all of the bodies were those of the monsters. Too many humans, ripped to shreds, lay rotting in the morning sun. Whatever those fiends were which roamed at night, they did on occasion find nourishment.

The roads were almost completely cleared of traffic. Howard noticed only two automobiles pass them as they drove out to the lake. Along the roadside many cars lay smashed, or abandoned, but very few moved through the streets. Outside of Daihmler, the city of Tuscaloosa was just as ravaged. More so in fact, probably due to a higher population. Echo drove the truck over the bridge crossing The Black Warrior River. Howard looked down to see a few floating barges with steel shipping crates. The barges looked to have people on them.

"Are those..."

"Yeah," Echo said. "Pretty smart, too. Float those barges out and just drift down river. Those animals can't get you in the water. It's pretty safe unless you drift to the shore. Folks live in those crates. You'll see some houseboats on the lake when we get out there."

As the lake came into sight half an hour later, Howard observed men standing at long folding tables along the roadside, with buckets lined up on the tabletops. Behind them other men were trudging back and forth from the lake's shore. Echo pulled the truck to the road's shoulder and stepped out.

"Hey, Blanchard!" a man called out to him from behind one of the tables. "You placin' an order?"

Echo stepped over to the table. Howard hung his head out of the window to listen. "Whatcha got today, Joey?"

The man peered into a few of the buckets and replied, "Got some croppy. Got a shit ton of catfish. Got a little bass."

Echo looked back to the truck bed where Tess called out, "Catfish!"

Echo turned back to the man, "What are you trading for today?"

Joey cupped his hand to Echo's ear and said something Howard couldn't hear. The man was blushing as he said it, and Echo gave a mild chuckle, nodded his head, and jumped back in the truck.

"What was that all about?" Howard asked.

Echo explained as he restarted the truck and continued down the road. "He and his men fish the lake. Lots of fish in there these days. They trade fish for other things. He told me his wife needs some tampons and Midol if we can find it. Plus, his usual...he wants some beans, rice, and apples."

"You can get all that for him?"

"Going to try," Echo said. "We can eat that fish for a few days. The apples are easy. We have apple trees on the property at home. We keep them picked and ready to trade when we go out. We used to have grapes and berries too, but the ground is so toxic now from whatever those things leak out of their bodies when they roam around. We fenced off the apple trees a few years ago so the ground around them is still okay."

Beasley's Market was tucked away behind a back road, out of sight from the main highway. This was the primary reason any food still lingered on the shelves. Few people knew of this place before the world went crazy and even fewer of those had managed to remain alive. The small community store was boarded up by survivors trying to keep it from being ransacked by the monsters. The code to the padlock was something only those in-the-know knew. Echo unlocked the chain and opened the doors for entry.

As Howard walked inside the store, he was surprised to see how much light there was until he looked up to see the skylights in the ceiling. The shelves were bare, but not empty. He watched Tess and Trix enter with cloth sacks and begin stocking the items they would need for the next couple of weeks. Can goods mostly. Beans, corn, spinach. There was no meat to be had anymore. The fresh meat would have long been taken or rotted by now and the stock of canned meat was most likely one of the first things scavenged when this place was discovered. Howard found a box of Hostess chocolate cupcakes and grabbed it excitedly.

"No," Trix called out from the medicine aisle. "Look at the expiration date. Those things went bad years ago."

Howard began checking dates on some of the can goods. Most of these were expired as well, but the kids were still taking them. Maybe they knew something he didn't. He thought about it and wondered if perhaps the expiration date on vegetables was more of a marketing tool than a real warning. If the public at large knew their can of lima beans really would last 10 years, they may not toss out old cans and go buy more. That made him take a second look at the cupcakes. Maybe it was worth a try? He decided to not risk it.

Tess grabbed the items the fisherman requested while Echo went outside to the abandoned tanker and siphoned off a little gas into a canister. Howard was about to walk over to him to see if he needed help when Trix tapped Howard's shoulder.

"Grab two buckets of apples from the truck and follow me."

Howard did as she requested and followed the brunette twin around the back of Beasley's Market. A metal shed—the kind you'd normally use in a backyard to store lawn mowers or garden tools in—stood behind the store. This had been placed here recently and was not an original store fixture. Trix dialed the combination to its padlock and swung open the metal door.

As the sunlight illuminated the storage shed, Howard saw buckets of unshelled peas, butter beans, unshucked ears of corn, tomatoes, cucumbers, and a few small baskets of strawberries and blueberries. There was also a large plastic cooler in the back. Trix opened the cooler and smiled.

"Deer meat!"

Howard was amazed. Inside the dingy white cooler, cooled down by a mixture of ice and melted slush were sealed plastic bags of meat scraps.

"Hard to choose," Trix said mostly to herself. "We haven't had meat in ages. But those peas and that corn will last us longer."

"Can't you grab it all?" Howard asked.

Trix shot him a dirty look as if he'd said something offensive. "You give what you take. We have two buckets of apples to leave. We can only take two buckets. If we want meat, it's one bucket for one package."

"How do you know all this?"

"We have been living by these rules for a long time. The living must look out for each other now. We can't be greedy. Everyone lives by a certain code. You give something, you take something."

Trix chose to take a bucket of peas and one bucket of spinach. She told Howard the meat would probably make them sick anyway since it had been so long since they'd had any. Fish was about the only meat they had eaten in a year or more. Howard took the buckets she traded the apples for to the truck.

Howard observed other sheds on the side of Beasley's store which he had not noticed until he was carrying the peas and spinach to the truck. He asked Tess what was housed inside those structures. She explained to him that one held books to be traded. One had clothing for men, one for women, one for children. Howard was impressed at how organized this world was when it had to be. The few remaining people had truly developed a system to help one another out.

Echo stopped by the lake to pick up his bucket of fish and leave his payment to the fisherman. The fisherman, Joey, was relieved the Blanchards had found his wife the things she needed. He had one additional request for the group before they left.

"You able to swing by the complex?" Joey asked them. "Got some fish for 'em if you can get by there."

"Happy to," Tess smiled. "It's on our way, and we still have plenty of light left."

Joey loaded three pails of fish into the truck bed and shut the tailgate. Tess and Trix secured them as Echo started the truck and headed back towards Daihmler. Howard was not sure what was going on and did not have to wait for an answer. Echo provided it as they drove back into the remains of Tuscaloosa.

"There's one apartment complex left. We have friends there. My best friend Amelia is there actually. Only person left alive that I grew up with besides Tess and Trix."

Echo turned onto a desolate street that looked as war-torn and ravaged as every other street. Yet sticking out from the piles of rubble and burned-out buildings, was a five-story apartment building. It was glaringly visible amid the nothingness remaining around it. As the truck pulled closer to it, Howard could see the impressive fortifications around the building. Surrounding the entire structure lay overturned transfer truck trailers, end to end, all forming a wall of metal to protect the apartment building from ground walkers. Mounted to the top of the barricade stood an endless number of spears, swords, saw blades, jagged metal rods, and pointy wooden stakes stretching the entire circumference of the wall. All were set at varying heights ensuring nothing could climb over without impaling itself. Only a couple of bodies lay stabbed through atop the trailers, proving it was a rare event for one of those monsters to make it up top. At the foot of the trailer fortress were bear traps strewn all around providing the first layer of protection. Some traps held decaying bodies in the teeth of the traps. Swarms of insects flitted around them.

"Are those vampires?" Howard asked as the disgusting odor emanating from them reached the truck.

"No. They are what is left once a human is drained completely but not killed. Probably got trapped last night."

There was one entrance into the apartment complex, once the group managed to side-step the bear traps. Camouflaged behind a thick sheet of tin, made to look like it was part of one of the truck trailers, was a barred door welded between two of the trailer beds. A sentry walked the top of the wall behind the spears. He had seen Echo approaching. He climbed down to the barricade door and let them inside.

"Hey Mitch," Echo greeted. "Got some fish for you. Joey sent it."

"Awesome man!" Mitch exclaimed, taking the buckets from them. "You wanna head in and see Amelia while you're here?"

"That'd be great."

The bottom floor of the complex was covered in iron bars. Another guard unbolted the only door and allowed the group to enter the building. Amelia, Tess explained, lived on the third floor with her sister Miranda. She led Howard and the others up the three flights of stairs.

In the darkened hallway, only lit by sunlight streaming through narrow windows, Echo led them to the sisters' apartment. Amelia greeted them at the door and welcomed them inside. The apartment was devoid of the personal touches Howard half expected. It was clear that life in this realm was bent more on the practical; the days of comfort were long gone. Amelia was a lovely young woman, 17 or 18 years old. She had curly, reddish-brown hair and a bright smile.

"I didn't expect you today!" she beamed as she hugged her friends. She looked quizzically at Howard—it was obvious she noticed a change. "Hi, Mr. Blanchard. You look different somehow since I saw you last. Have you been ill?"

Howard felt a little embarrassed by the question. What in the world did their Howard Blanchard look like? If in a world of starvation, constant fighting for survival, and never-ending stress how could Howard Caldwell possibly be the one who looked ill?

"It's a really long story," Tess said, covering for Howard. Before she could explain further, Amelia's sister Miranda came in from a room down the hall. Miranda was a little more plain looking than her younger sister. Bookish, Howard thought. Howard estimated her to be close to Fable's age. She shared Amelia's reddish-brown hair, but it was cut short at the neck and hung straight.

"Mr. Blanchard!" Miranda cried, giving Howard a hug. "We haven't seen you in weeks. Are you alright? You don't look well. We may have some medicine downstairs in the dispensary if you are sick."

Howard turned to Trix. "What in the world does your father look like? How can I look so bad in comparison?"

Trix shrugged and tugged nervously at her eyelash. "Dad was pretty fit. You're a little pudgy to be honest."

Amelia and Miranda were confused until Echo filled them in on what had transpired over the last two days. As Howard listened to the boy's explanation, he was pleased to hear Echo clarify that none of what happened had been Howard's fault. It did pain him, however, to hear the boy's voice crack in parts as he fought the urge to cry. Amelia expressed her sympathies to the triplets but tried to tiptoe around saying the wrong thing so as to not embarrass Howard further.

"And you must be going through so much yourself, Sir," Amelia said, expressing concern for Howard's feelings.

"Thank you, young lady. Honestly, I am a little surprised that you aren't more surprised by all this. I mean, a man from another reality...it's a bit much to wrap one's head around."

Miranda gave an involuntary giggle, "Well, Sir, we live in a world overrun by monsters and our best friends are three witches. So, nothing really comes as much of a shock anymore."

"Touché," Howard replied.

They all took a seat on the meager offerings of the sparse room, and Tess joined Miranda in the kitchen to pour up some fruit juice. As Howard took the juice, he choked on the first sip as his tongue realized this was not actual juice from a bottle. This was something homemade, sugarless, from whatever fruits were on hand to crush into water.

"What happens to you now?" Miranda asked Howard. "You're stuck here I suppose?"

"That's a kick in the head!" Amelia remarked.

Howard gave an uncomfortable laugh. "I don't really know what will happen. I expect the people back home are going to figure out what happened and find a way to pull me back. But I really can't be sure."

After a few polite moments of small talk, Amelia stood up and tugged Echo's arm to follow her out into the hall. Closing the door behind them, she lowered her voice and placed her hands on her friend's face.

"Truth only," she began. "Tell me what you are feeling."

Echo hung his head, letting go of a small bit of the tension he'd been holding within. "I guess my dad is dead. This is too much. Too crazy. That man in there is my dad. At least he looks like and acts a little like him. But the man I have known my whole life isn't here. This is different from when Momma died. That was awful but it happens. This...this I can't process."

Amelia stroked his wispy hair and pushed his overly long black bangs out of his eyes. "That's okay. You don't have to right now."

Echo looked into her eyes and spoke, but it came out more as a question than a reply. "Maybe when he goes back to where he came from? That might be when it hits me that Dad's gone."

Amelia pulled him into a hug. He laid his head on her shoulder. He had needed this. Needed his best friend. Their love was not a romantic love, and it wasn't the same kind of thing as he had with his sisters. This was a special relationship, and only Amelia truly knew how to get Echo to take his guard down.

Back inside the apartment, Miranda felt the same kind of concern for the girls. Tess and Trix were staying strong—stronger than was necessary to be. They had a right to mourn their father, yet Miranda could see that whatever tenuous bond existed between them and the lookalike stranger who'd replaced their father, it was keeping them from truly accepting the loss.

Howard was feeling immense guilt over what happened, and Miranda could sense that as well. As they all sat making inane small talk as they gave Echo and Amelia time outside, Miranda felt the need to break up the tension and say the unsaid for her friends.

"You guys are experiencing a terrible situation right now. One of the weirdest situations I've ever heard of, too, I might add. If any of you need to talk it out with a friend, I hope you know I'm always here." She laughed abruptly out of the blue. "Where else could I be? I am always here."

Tess gave a polite chuckle back. "That's life now, I guess. Where else would we ever be?"

Trix, the blunter of the twins, spoke out. "I don't know how I feel. I appreciate your offer to talk but don't see where there is much to talk about. This guy showed up and squashed our father out of existence." Howard cringed and turned embarrassingly red just as Trix added, "It's not his fault though in any way, so I can't be angry at him. He didn't ask to be here."

"Thank you for that," Howard said meekly.

"And it's just the way it is," Trix continued. "When Mama died, we had to accept and move on. There isn't time anymore to waste on thinking about the how's and why's. We have to survive and try to get this world restarted."

Echo returned with Amelia and told Howard and his sisters it was time to go. The sun would be setting soon, and the thirsty monsters would be coming back out on the prowl. The little group said their goodbyes and walked back down the three flights of stairs to the barricade around the complex. Echo drove them back to Blanchard House.

. . .

By the time the truck made it back to Blanchard House, it was midafternoon. The sun would be setting in a couple of hours. Howard helped the others unload the truck with the provisions they'd gathered that day. Howard made himself useful by cleaning the fish on the porch for Tess to fry. It was the only food they had for dinner. The rest which they had collected that day would have to be doled out slowly, two meals a day, for two weeks.

Over dinner, Howard expressed to the trio how remarkable he found their lives to be. The precision by which they lived, the honor code with the other existing survivors. He was impressed. He found himself staring very closely at both Tess and Trix as he spoke. Finally, Trix brought it to his attention.

"Why do you keep staring at us?"

Howard blushed slightly and said, "Sorry. It's just that I never had children. Seeing you three—knowing all my DNA exists in you—makes me wish I had made different choices. I would have loved watching the three of you grow up."

The kids succeeded in convincing Howard to use their father's room that night. He felt immensely uncomfortable doing so but didn't relish the idea of sleeping another night on that filthy soiled sofa. As he climbed the stairs to his doppelganger's quarters, he heard the scratching sounds again. The moans. The incessant unending attempts of those fiends outside trying to get in.

CHAPTER TWENTY FIVE

Another Catastrophe

The Blanchards were not prepared for another blow to their serenity. They only had a few days of peace from the last catastrophe, now they were facing another one. When Arielle came home with the news that Howard was missing, everyone took it very seriously. It had taken her most of the day to notice. After Salem left with the bank draft to return to Atlanta, Arielle continued her work innocently believing Howard was in the next office. It was only after the workday was done and she had walked into Howard's office to say goodbye that she noticed he was gone. There was no other way out of his office without going past her and she was certain he had not sneaked by without her noticing. She knew something was wrong. His absence could mean only one thing, he had vanished just as Beryl and the others previously had.

Demitra was beside herself. "He can't be gone! Not now." She looked to her sister for assurances. "You don't think something has happened in the past to Beryl or the baby, do you? Has Howard been erased somehow?"

Artemis calmed her sister and tried to soothe her worry. "It seems unlikely that any of us would even have a recollection of Howard had something happened to Beryl or the pregnancy. If we still remember Howard, then Beryl must still be in the past with mother and her baby is safe."

"What happened then?" Jerry asked. "Did his powers kick in now that he knows about them?"

"That's a good point!" Demitra exclaimed. "Maybe so."

"Doubtful," Artemis replied. "Mother bound his powers and until we unbury them and set them free, Howard is still a powerless witch. This seems all too familiar." Artemis questioned Arielle further.

"You said Salem had been in the office."

"That's right."

Yasmine chimed in. "I gave her some money to buy into her firm, and she was seeing Howard to pick up the cashier's check."

"You didn't tell me you did that," Seth smiled as he patted his wife's arm. "That was very sweet of you, my love."

"Thank you."

"Salem has been needing to rise up from her current position with that company," Seth went on. "For you to give her the funds to buy in was really generous."

Yasmine blushed. "She deserves it." Seth kissed his wife on the cheek.

"Stop cooing you two and focus," Artemis demanded. "Arielle, what did you and Salem talk about?"

"I don't know," Arielle said, trying to recall. "Just about her firm and how she might move back to Daihmler after the baby comes. Nothing major."

"Was any mention made of Howard?" Artemis asked.

Arielle thought about it a second and as if a light bulb went off in her mind she said, "Yes! Actually, Salem said something about wondering what Howard's life would be like if he'd known he was a Blanchard from the start."

"I see," Artemis said, pondering a thought in her mind.

"That's not like it was last time though," Seth pointed out. "Salem was just supposing. Her baby sent us back to places that were factual. *Imagining what life might be like if something happened that didn't happen* isn't factual."

Artemis looked at her nephew. "I am not so sure, Seth."

Artemis excused herself. She needed space to think about the matter. She walked out to the front porch and sat down in the rocker. She ticked off the circumstances of the last spell gone haywire and how the powers Salem's baby possessed could have manifested the events. Until Olympus was born and demonstrated his abilities, no one could really know what his abilities were. However, judging from the magnitude of what happened before there was no doubt her son was powerful. Artemis understood now that his powers dwelled in the sphere of bending time or time travel. Considering Xander's ability to zap to any location he thought about, it seemed logical that Olympus' powers worked similarly—only time was not a barrier for the baby. But if what Arielle said was accurate, Salem was not talking about a real past, only a suggestion of a "what if". Still, Artemis pondered, if Olympus did possess the ability to travel time, wasn't it at least possible he might also possess the ability to jump to another reality? An alternate reality? This was all unheard of in the witching world. Artemis had no examples in her life of such magic, but the Blanchards were an old and powerful clan. Salem was also half Obreiggon—another old and powerful family. And who knows who the sperm donor was that Salem used at the Fertility Clinic. Everyone assumed it was just a regular male donor picked from a catalogue, but what if that male was a magical being? It was a thought no one considered before. Though highly unlikely, there was still no denying that baby Olympus was already proving to be quite a witch, even from the womb.

Artemis wished her mother was here. She would know what to do. For a moment she considered returning to the secret Hecate vault again, but she didn't want to become too dependent upon using that room. She'd been lucky last time, but the things in that room were dangerous. What she needed was a wise witch to bounce things off of—and she knew just the lady. She went inside the house and shut herself away in the study to make a call.

Up until a few years ago, Ursula Craven had reigned as Queen of the Witches Consort for many years. Though there was now a king on the throne, so to speak, it was Ursula she knew and trusted.

Artemis explained to her friend what had been going on. Ursula was astounded at the entirety of the latest Blanchard exploits. The idea that Beryl was currently living in another time and carrying a child which would remain there was mind-blowing to Ursula. She wanted all the details, but there wasn't time for that now. Artemis quickly brought her back to the crisis at hand and asked her opinion on the matter. After hearing Ursula out, Artemis rejoined the others in the living room.

"It is possible," Artemis informed the family, still gathered in the living room. "According to Ursula Craven, her father's records do show that on the rarest of occasions a witch has been born with the ability to warp time enough to cross it—in both directions."

"Do you mean Olympus will have the power to travel to the future?" Fable asked.

"The past, the future, possibly even different dimensions," Artemis explained. "His mother has the power to halt time. His grandfather has the ability to transport himself across great distances in the blink of an eye. Time is clearly an Obreiggon forte, at least in the strain running through Salem. It's possible."

Demitra was confused. "But according to Arielle's conversation with Salem, nothing was mentioned of the future. It was simply a *what if*."

Artemis countered that idea. "Yes, but it was a *what if* about Howard's future had he known everything from the beginning. I think it is possible that Salem's baby's power once again inadvertently took her words as a spell. Salem sent Howard to a future where he grew up knowing he was a Blanchard."

Seth was as confused as ever. "I am completely lost. What you are talking about is alternate realities. Alternate timelines. Those don't exist. Time is one straight line."

"Is it?" Fable countered. "How do we actually know that?"

"Because no one has ever seen an alternate universe!" Seth argued.

"Maybe no one we know," Fable supposed. "But that doesn't mean someone hasn't. If this is true, then I think we just proved other realities can exist."

The prospect was horrifying. Demitra was afraid. The past was vast and encompassing but still held a linear map which could be followed. But a supposed future scenario was just too much territory to ever be able to track. Howard could be literally anywhere.

"This is awful," Demitra frowned. "Howard has no powers to protect himself. And he could be in a million different realities."

"Yes, but it might be very simple for Salem to send us to the same place, on purpose this time." Artemis replied, hoping to assuage her sister's fears.

"How do we get back?" Seth asked. "Last time Mother had potions."

"I don't think potions can work with something this complicated," Artemis said. "Salem is going to have to go with us this time. It's the only way to be sure we can return."

Seth waved his hand to grab everyone's attention. "That won't work. It won't work for the same reason why Mother, Fable, and I couldn't bring Beryl back with us. Beryl can't come back until Howard is born. An unborn baby can't travel out of the time it's a part of."

Artemis returned an almost prideful smile as she clasped her hands together and shook them forward at Seth. "Normally, yes, you would be correct, but I have a feeling your unborn nephew isn't as constrained to the rules of time as the rest of us. And as long as he resides inside of Salem, neither is she."

"But Salem is due any day now," Fable reminded them. "She can't make such a trip. What if she goes into labor?"

"More importantly," Artemis noted. "What if Salem gives birth *before* we can go find Howard? If her child is born, his power is no longer accessible by Salem.

We would have to wait years before the baby was old enough to understand how to wield such a force to rescue Howard. We have no choice but to go now!"

Arielle pulled out her phone. "I'll call her. I'll make her come right back ASAP."

Two hours later Salem was back in Daihmler, and the family were attempting to figure out who should accompany her on the mission to save Howard. Everyone felt as if they had a vested interest in the endeavor and all were arguing about who should in fact go.

"Howard is my grandson," Demitra insisted. "Crazy as that sounds since he is older than I am, but he is in fact my flesh and blood. I am going to go."

"Salem is my sister and she's pregnant," Seth said. "So, I am definitely going."

"She's my sister, too!" Arielle reminded everyone. "Plus, Howard and I spend every day together. I want to go."

"If Seth goes, I'm going too," Yasmine announced. "I am not going to be separated from him again."

Artemis clapped her hands together to shut everyone up and turn the attention to herself. "I am Hecate. I am the head of this family. I will decide who is going."

"Why can't we all go?" Fable asked.

"Because we need backup in case something goes wrong," Artemis answered. "Of course, if something does go wrong, I have no idea what any of us can do without Salem, but still, it is too complicated for everyone to accompany her."

"Then who goes?" Arielle asked.

"Seth and Arielle will go with Salem," Artemis declared.

"Sister, I hate to contradict you, but I am also going!" Demitra declared.

Artemis faced her down, "No you are not. You do not have an active power if there is trouble. Seth can summon the elements and Arielle's telekinesis is one of our most powerful resources. Only they are going."

"Aunt Artemis," Yasmine pleaded. "Let me go. I do not want to be apart from Seth again. I have a bad feeling."

"Then you need to remain here so that if anything goes haywire your children have their mother. And Yasmine you have no powers whatsoever, I wouldn't let you go even if there were no one else."

Yasmine was not happy with the response. She plopped down on the sofa like an angry spoiled child, with arms folded and a pouty face.

Everyone appointed to the rescue team readied themselves for travel. Artemis instructed Salem and the others to be quick and careful. She also reminded Salem to control any words that came out of her mouth so that they would not be faced with yet another miscast spell. As Salem linked hands with her brother and sister, Artemis gave her one final reminder that they were going to a future where Howard grew up a witch, not the actual future of their current present. With that, the trio of siblings began to vanish into oblivion as Salem tapped into her baby's power.

But in that one split second before they disappeared, Yasmine jumped from the couch and slapped her hand onto her husband's shoulder, vanishing with them, leaving her aunts horrified as she disappeared.

CHAPTER TWENTY SIX

The Plague

The Blanchard triplets—Tess, Trix, and Echo—faced a mixed bag of emotions. From how things appeared, their father was gone. Not dead, erased. Yet their father was with them. Same face, same mannerisms, same DNA. The same man, yet not their father. The situation called for tears, but no tears came. It is hard to cry for the loss of someone who is still standing in front of you.

The triplets were playing cards in the tiny kitchen, long accustomed to the horrendous sounds emanating from outside the walls of the house from a lifetime living with them. Howard Caldwell was too disturbed to join in or for sleep. He could not relax at all. The only thing calming his nerves was to walk the house, checking doors and boarded windows, ensuring everything was still stable and secure. He covered every inch of the interior of Blanchard House, walking in the footsteps of where Howard Blanchard once walked. The house was so different here. Olympia and her brood had filled their house with life. Howard Blanchard's house, part of a world where Olympia had not lived relatively long, was more like a dismal fortress than a home. Weapons leaned against walls at odd angles. Rusty colored stains, that might have been old, dried blood, smudged across the occasional wall. No light could enter, as every window, upstairs and down, was bricked or boarded with clumpy plastered pressed into the cracks. This was a citadel not a home. Everything was functional.

Howard found his predecessor's bedroom the gloomiest of all. In his time this would have been Artemis' bedroom. Colorful quilts stitched by hand would have covered the bed or lay decoratively folded over the back of a cushy chair. This room looked nothing like that now. Weaponry and maps littered every surface. The frilly lace curtains over the bricked windows were stained with blackish residue. The same lace pattern remained on portions of the unmade worn bed covers. Howard could imagine this room had once been pretty. Probably decorated by the other Howard's wife, Barbara. Oddly enough, there were no pictures of her anywhere. No photographs of anyone, anywhere. In Howard's world, the second-floor hallway walls were covered with family photographs. Olympia's treasures. Not a one lined the walls now. This was a world where only four Blanchards had survived. It was a shocking contrast.

Howard unfolded one of the maps out of curiosity. It displayed the streets of Daihmler and the surrounding farmlands. Black ink scribbled across almost the entire surface. Notations of known vampire nests. Red inked X's were placed over locations where, Howard assumed, the Blanchard warriors had destroyed vampires.

He was jolted from his observations by a sudden scream followed by raised voices downstairs. Some kind of commotion was going on below. He rushed down to see if the children were under attack by one of those fiends who may have found a way in. As he jumped the bottom two stair steps and bounded into the living room, he saw Tess, Trix, and Echo flanked in battle position. Opposing them stood Yasmine, Seth, Salem, and Arielle.

"Howard!" Arielle cried.

"You know this guy?" Echo asked Seth as he nodded his head towards Howard.

"Yeah, man," Seth answered. "He's our family."

"He is inexplicably ours as well," Trix snarled, never breaking her readied stance to attack.

"Yaz!" Salem screeched, able to now take stock of the situation. "What are you doing here?'

"I hitchhiked," Yasmine smiled. "I told y'all I am not leaving Seth's side again." Yasmine ran to Howard and gave him a hug. He hugged her back smiling.

"So, I was right," Howard began. "I figured Salem's little rugrat sent me here."

"I am so sorry Howard!" Salem cried. "I had no idea."

"Don't sweat it. Not your fault. Or little unborn Olympus there either. He doesn't know what he's doing."

The triplets were not amused by this little reunion. The appearance of these strangers inside their reinforced home had nearly scared them out of their wits.

"Who the hell are these people?" Trix demanded. "And how did you get inside our house?"

Yasmine glanced around at the dilapidated conditions marring the house she had loved all her life. "This is our house actually—at least it was supposed to be. What happened here?"

"And what is making all that noise outside?" Seth asked.

"Answer us first!" Echo said. "Who are you?"

Salem waddled over to him, her hand on her belly. As she approached, Echo and his sisters broke their formal guarded stances. In her extreme condition she did not look too intimidating. "Hi, my name is Salem Blanchard. This is my brother Seth, his wife Yasmine, and our sister Arielle."

Echo nodded cautiously, "My name's Nathan, but everybody calls me Echo. These are my sisters Trix and Tess. We are Blanchards, too."

"You are?" Yasmine gasped. "What year is it here?"

Trix and Echo looked at each other and shrugged.

"Years don't really mean much around here anymore," Tess explained. "Every day is just the same. Sometimes it's hot outside, sometimes it's cold."

"Mom died a year ago I guess," Echo said, mostly to his sisters. "It was hot then too so I'm guessing it was a year. Wasn't it like 2015 or something when we last had Christmas? How many years was that?"

"This is the same time period as ours," Salem realized. "Just in a world where Howard grew up a witch."

"Can we break this standoff?" Seth suggested. "We aren't here to hurt you guys. We just came for Howard."

The triplets relaxed, as did the others and everyone stood around the room rather informally, taking in the situation.

"What happened here?" Seth asked.

Howard cleared his throat and did his best to explain. "In this dimension, or whatever you want to call it, Olympia died after Beryl showed up. Beryl had me when she was supposed to though, so I grew up a Blanchard. Well, not me actually—their father. But this is a world where Olympia never had a family."

Yasmine was confused. "Then how are you here?"

Howard gave a half nervous laugh. "That's the million-dollar question. I can only guess it's because Beryl's presence to the past timeline imbedded her and me into it. Despite what happened afterward to Olympia."

Yasmine was amazed, so much so she had to sit down. She stepped back and dropped to the sofa, only the moment she did she observed its filthy condition and jumped back up to her feet, wiping invisible cooties off her dress. "Wow," she said. "So, this is a world where you were the only Blanchard. Crazy."

"But what is happening outside?" Seth asked again. "What is all that noise?"

"Vampires have taken over," answered Howard.

"Well of course they have," Yasmine sarcastically replied. "How?"

"I don't know," Howard said.

"I do," Seth announced as a fantastic look crossed over his face. He grabbed Salem's arm and shook it. "What could have changed so drastically in this world? Olympia Blanchard wasn't here. Remember the stories she used to tell us about the early days when she and Zelda and Pastoria fought all kinds of crazy things? They battled and defeated a vampire once."

"Oh my God," Salem gasped. "That vampire cell we found at Dredmore Asylum. The chart said he'd been captured by Olympia, Pastoria, and Zelda."

Seth was nodding furiously now. "Maybe if Olympia wasn't alive to stop that vampire..."

"The entire world died," Arielle gasped.

Tess faced their unwelcome guests and huffed, "We have no idea what any of you are talking about."

Salem gave an apologetic smile Tess' way, "We are just trying to figure out what could have turned our world into yours," she explained. "It seems our grandmother made quite a difference in her lifetime."

Tess shrugged, "I can't see where it matters very much. The fact is this world is overrun by monsters. Those things outside are not the vampires. They are byproducts of the vampires. The true vampires are hard to find."

"And virtually unstoppable," Echo added. "Now that pretty much the whole witching community has been wiped out."

"Sorry to tell you this," Trix smiled. "But you folks came to a fucked-up place. And now you're stuck here."

"Actually, we aren't," Salem contradicted. "I have the power to take us back home. So, if you will excuse us, we will be on our way. Sorry to have inconvenienced you. We will collect our cousin Howard and go."

Trix charged forward in anger. "What are you telling us? You are just going to leave? This man is our father! Well, maybe not the father we know, but his coming here took our father away. If you leave, you better figure out a way to bring our father back!"

And there lay the crux of the situation for Howard Caldwell. Salem was there to rescue him now from this very brief trek into a scary version of what his life might have been like. He could return home now. But how could he? How could he so flippantly leave after devastating these three kids' lives? He pulled Salem, Arielle, Seth, and Yasmine into the foyer to confer privately. He felt something should be done regarding the triplets. His guilt over having caused the demise of their father was not something he could forget. To return home and abandon the wreckage he would leave behind was not something he could live with. The gravity of the situation had not dawned fully on the others. They regarded this realm as just another timeline to leave. Howard explained to them while Tess, Trix, and Echo waited in the living room.

"Do you mean my spell killed their dad?" Salem gulped, trying not to become emotional.

"It wasn't your fault, Sweety," Howard consoled her. "But yes, in a way."

"Because one person cannot share the same time space with their exact same self," Salem replied, remembering the cosmic rule her grandmother once explained to her. "I think I understand now what happened to me."

Once, a few years ago, Salem tried to stop the deaths of her husband and son by sending herself back in time. Her belief that she would be able to prevent them from getting into the car accident which took their lives ended up becoming a major life lesson as to the limits of witchcraft. Salem failed to save them and ended up trapping herself in a never-ending cycle of living the same day over and over. Olympia came to her rescue then and explained why her attempt was futile. Salem had gone back to her *own* time—a time she was currently living in. She had been unable to prevent the deaths because the Salem who had prevailed, had no knowledge of the accident.

"The reason I couldn't save David and Michael was because the two me's could not exist together in the same space. I realize now that the Salem that survived was the Salem from before. The me that went back to undo it was the one that got erased."

"Just like the other Howard was," Seth noted.

"Wait, though," Yasmine said. "I *did it*. The past I went to had me in it. I even talked to myself."

"Yes, but that Yasmine was six years old," Seth explained. "That's not the same thing as you going to a time you presently exist in at the same age. If you went back to yesterday, you or your yesterday self would disappear and leave the other one. But that is why Granddad took you to that hotel, because even being aged so many years apart your soul and little Yasmine's soul were beginning to battle for survival."

"I am so confused," Yasmine said.

"It's not important," Salem said. "The point is that our Howard took the place of their Howard. Their Howard is dissolved now. He's gone forever."

"What do we do?" Arielle asked, looking back over her shoulder at the triplets. Echo, Tess, and Trix were waiting in what used to be the Blanchard living room. They looked so downtrodden, so defeated. The three of them had been through more horror than anyone could understand. And they had lost so much in their young lives. Arielle felt some kind of pang for them that she did not understand.

"We can't leave them here," Howard asserted. "They can't manage to survive this world much longer. I have seen only a glimpse of what is happening out there, and it is brutal. This world is over. Destroyed. It is only a matter of time before those three die here."

"Are you saying what I think you are?" Arielle asked.

"We bring them home with us," Howard declared.

"Wait," Seth sighed. "That's crazy. Look at them. They are warriors. They are used to chaos and armageddon. How would they adapt?"

"They'd probably love it," Yasmine said. "They would discover what peace is."

Howard was emphatic in his conviction. "They are my children," he said. "I may not have raised them or been the same man they knew, but biologically speaking they are my offspring. I won't leave them here."

"Then it's settled," Salem said. "We take them with us."

CHAPTER TWENTY SEVEN

Rescue Mission

The noise outside Blanchard House had grown louder over the hours. One could only assume more of the grotesque ex-human monsters created by the vampires were amassing. This appeared to be a routine occurrence which was not seeming to alarm Tess or her siblings. But for the Blanchards who resided in a safer world, it was a terrifying situation. Salem and Arielle huddled together in the middle of the room as far away from the door and bricked windows as possible. Yasmine clung to her husband for protection by the stairs as she listened to the clawing and banging going on outside the walls of the house.

Howard was in the living room with his "children" trying to explain the situation to them, as well as his answer to it. His solution was a lot for them to comprehend, much less accept, and there was not much time left to consider it. Still, he described what their lives could be like back in his world as opposed to the daily struggle to survive the reality they currently faced.

"But our father?" Tess sobbed.

Howard lifted her calloused hand into his own and said, "I'm sorry, honey—he isn't coming back. But I will be your father. In a very real way, I already am. You three are part of me. My flesh and blood—even if we are strangers."

"This is all we know," Echo said. "This world."

Howard glanced around the disheveled room raising his brow. He gestured toward the sealed windows locking out the dangers of their world. The pounding on the outer walls. The wailing sounds coming from the creatures outside.

"Death. Bloodshed. Endless fighting. Never being able to relax for an instant. On guard at all times," he described. "Come home with me and find beauty, peace, and family. Oh, there is a ton of family. Come with me kids. I am your father now. I won't leave you here."

"Howard!" Yasmine cried from the foyer. "You don't mean you'd stay here?"

Howard looked back behind him to his friend. "I will not leave these kids here."

"You have no powers," Seth pointed out. "How can you even help them?"

"I'm not leaving them," Howard repeated. "If they stay, I stay."

Trix looked at Tess, as did Echo. During the course of this very long and bewildering stay Howard had already figured out Tess was their authority. She was the one the other two looked to for guidance. Tess hesitated before answering, expressing concerns.

"Why should the Blanchards in your world welcome us there? They do not know us at all. What would we do? At least here we have this house, and we know how to scavenge for food."

Howard chuckled. He didn't mean to be insensitive. It was just funny to him that anyone would have a hard time deciding to leave this place. "With me you won't have to scavenge for anything. I will help you acclimate. And the Blanchards will welcome you with open arms. Family is sacred to them. Anyone with a drop of Blanchard blood in their veins is their priority. Believe me. It's a better life awaiting you there."

"I wanna go, Tess," Trix said, adding quickly, "If you think we should. I don't want to live this way anymore. What happens when we are old and can't fight anymore? Mom was the strongest witch we have ever known and even she couldn't survive this life. I am tired. I am willing to try anything that isn't this."

Tess considered her sister's plea and gave her answer. "We will go. Is that alright with you, Echo?"

Echo wore a pained expression. Something was on his mind. "I want to go. But..."

His sisters eyed one another and nodded in recognition. They understood their brother's reluctance. Tess turned to Howard. "Amelia."

Howard nodded in total understanding.

"Who is Amelia?" Yasmine asked.

"Echo's girl. She lives with her sister Miranda in the last remaining building downtown. I met her today."

"Other people are alive here?" Salem asked.

"Not many," Tess replied. "But some live here and there in pockets. Amelia is part of a small community living in an old apartment building."

"How many people live there?" Arielle asked.

"I'd say about a dozen live in that building," Tess answered. "It's well fortified. We saw to that. We have tried to get Amelia and Miranda to move in with us for protection, but they choose to stay near the community they've always known."

"I can't leave Amelia here," Echo said.

"You love her?" Howard asked.

"It's not really like that," Echo said. "She's not *my girl.* We were friends as kids and have been ever since. She's about the only person left I knew from before things went crazy. I won't leave her here."

Salem spoke up. "Then let's convince her to come with us."

"Come with us to your world?" Trix repeated, dumbstruck at the offer. "You'd allow that?"

"Of course," Salem said. "You are family and if they are important to you, let's bring them with us."

Echo was blown away by the generosity. "Thank you."

"We need to do this soon," Salem warned. "My baby is due any day now and once he is born, I will not have access to his power."

"It is much too dangerous to travel at night," Tess informed them. "We have to wait for the sun to rise. Those things outside will have to go back to their nests."

...

Blanchard House of this reality did not have the bedrooms of Olympia Blanchard's family. Echo gave up his bed for Salem and Arielle, sleeping on the couch downstairs. Tess bunked with her sister so that Yasmine and Seth could take her bed. Howard reluctantly took his doppelganger's room. He was not comfortable with the idea, but the triplets seemed to want him to. Perhaps they had a deep need to see their father come out of his room one last time. Or maybe in some way they were baptizing Howard with the essence of their dad. It was all very awkward for Howard, but he did not refuse them.

No one got much sleep that night as they waited for the dawn to come. Once the sun rose into the sky, Tess Blanchard cooked a meager breakfast—if you could call canned Vienna sausages and creamed corn breakfast. The group left the confines of Blanchard House and stepped outside. Salem and her siblings' reaction to the landscape around them was reminiscent of Howard's when he had discovered the place. There was nothing of beauty here. The Blanchard family land was nothing now but one large war-torn battlefield. The putrid rotting corpses of the vampires' creatures left a stench in the air that was nothing like the aroma of their grandmother's rose bushes which Artemis still kept up faithfully back at home.

Echo's truck was large enough to hold everyone. Salem, being in fragile condition, rode up front with he and Howard while the others sat in the truck bed taking in the devastation all around as they drove into Daihmler. As they drove past familiar places, Yasmine filled the minds of Trix, Tess, and Echo with what her Daihmler looked like as opposed to theirs. It all sounded like Heaven to them. Flower shops, restaurants, clothing stores, grocery stores, schools. They had been very young when those things went away, and the devastation had begun.

The truck drove past the little house where the old woman had beckoned Howard yesterday to come inside for safety. She was standing in her doorway, looking out to see what living person was left who could be driving up the road. As the truck went by, she caught a glimpse of Howard's face in the window and smiled. She was pleased he had survived since she last saw him.

A little further down the road, Seth could hear his wife describing the broken-down structure on their left as the Hinkle Tackle Shop in her time. Seth turned to observe the remnants of the place where his Uncle Larry had taken him many times as a boy. Larry always bought worms there before he would walk Seth down the little path behind it to the stream.

Passing in front of where Hinkle once stood, Seth caught sight of another living person. Another woman. She was ambling along the broken and weedy sidewalk. Behind her she dragged a rusty dented child's wagon. The back wheel was wobbling as if it could fall off at any moment. The wagon appeared to have a few cans in it—probably food she had found in some abandoned nearby house. There was a bucket in the wagon also, lightly sloshing water. She must have been down to the stream. There was something familiar about the woman. Seth turned back to look once more before Echo drove out of range. He recognized her haggard face. Vanessa. Vanessa Collins, the preacher's daughter he was seeing before he figured out he loved Yasmine. She looked so frail now. Broken. Beaten down by this world and the plague upon it. How much longer would she survive? Seth felt pity for her. He hoped she would be okay. He said nothing to his wife. There was no need in pointing her out. Hopefully soon he and Yaz, and the rest of the Blanchards would be home again—home in a world where Vanessa Collins, and everyone else on Earth, was not doomed.

The truck turned onto main street. Echo slowed down. Main Street was littered with debris. Broken bricks from buildings long fallen spilled into the jagged, cracked remains of the pavement. Abandoned vehicles left in the street had to be dodged carefully. Echo maneuvered the street with a learned skill he had obviously mastered from repetition. In some places there were so many obstructions to the road that the truck had to slow to barely a roll. It would not do to rupture a tire or crash into something. Working vehicles were too precious a resource now.

The town of Daihmler looked like something you might expect to see in a third world country. Homes in ruins. Smoke drifting out of holes in rooftops. Every so often, they would spy a lonely individual roaming the roads. Some looked to be carrying provisions, but some appeared to be roaming. Maybe they roamed from boredom. Maybe they had gone mad. None of them paid any attention to Echo's truck passing them.

"I'd think some of these people would try to rush the truck and steal it," Salem mentioned to Echo as he continued driving.

"They have no need," he replied. "No one ventures far from their barricade. Nothing is better anywhere else."

"Besides," Tess added. "They have to reserve strength in case one of those monsters gets through to them. Energy and endurance are much too precious to waste fighting ourselves. We live by a certain code. We look out for each other. We have to."

Echo turned onto another desolate street but at its end Salem could see the apartment building. Like Howard had the day before, Salem and the others were aghast at the visage of a ruined society. Nothing was left except this one fortified structure. But how long could even it last in a world gone insane? Looking ahead at the man-made fort of overturned trucks and trailers with their mounted spears and blades, the disgusting sight of the withering bodies skewered atop them told them all they needed to know about the perils of this world.

"Are those vampires?" Yasmine asked Trix as the disgusting odor emanating from the bodies reached the truck bed.

"No. They are what is left once a human is drained completely but not killed. Probably got trapped last night."

"They look like they've been here a long time," Arielle observed.

"The sun killed them," Trix explained. "They are the real danger we have to protect against. The vampires don't bother us much anymore. They have their supply."

"I don't understand," Arielle asked.

Trix did her best to describe how things came to be as they were. "Early on the vampires captured humans. Thousands of humans. The news was full of missing person reports. Eventually we all came to realize it was the vampires attacking and stealing people they thought fit their requirements."

"Requirements?" Seth repeated.

"For nourishment," Tess clarified. "Blood. Their food supply."

"Oh my God," Yasmine gasped. "Those poor people. What happened to them?"

"No one knows," Echo said, getting out of the truck and joining in on the history lesson. "It's thought that there is a capital city somewhere. Or hell, maybe several, where the humans are fed well and kept alive to be drained every day—like we used to get milk from cows. That blood is distributed among the vampire population."

"That is ghastly," Howard said.

Echo nodded and replied, "Those creatures you saw outside the house, Dad—Howard—those guys are the humans they didn't take. Bitten and drained but left to wander around. It is those things that decimated everything. The vampires have their blood supply, and they breed them to ensure more generations of cattle. The rest of us are just left to fend for ourselves against these hungry masses they left behind."

"Kind of like zombies," Salem noted.

"Sunlight kills them," Tess chimed in, assisting Salem out of the truck. "It doesn't kill a vampire. Not instantly, anyway. The vampires can come out on overcast days or lurk in shadows during daylight hours. It takes several minutes for the sun to boil their blood and kill them. Plenty of time for them to strike and get to shaded safety."

"We have to get your friends out of here," Howard said.

Just as they had the day before, the men patrolling the top of the barricade signaled to the door guard to allow Echo, Tess, Trix, and the man perceived as Howard Blanchard inside. However, this time they took pause at the four newcomers with them.

"Are these folks with you, Blanchard?"

"Yes, they're okay," Echo answered.

"Ain't lookin to move in here, are they? We are full up."

"No," Tess explained. "They are with us, just to visit Amelia and Miranda."

The man at the gate informed Echo, "Amelia is sitting with Mrs. Reardon."

The bars covering the bottom floor of the complex looked to be well protected as far as Seth could estimate. The Blanchards had to adjust their eyes. There was no electricity. The only light came from the barred windows. Blanchard House did have electricity, which caused Seth to wonder how. He didn't ask though, assuming they must have used magic or a generator. The climb up three flights of stairs took a while because Salem had to move slowly. As they moved, Echo explained how everyone in the building took turns with Mrs. Reardon, an elderly woman dying of cancer.

Salem noticed through one of the windows in the stairwell that there was an enclosed square courtyard centered in the complex. It was brimming over with vegetation which was being tended to by a few people. The residents grew their own food, reducing their need for outside supplies. Finally, they reached the third floor, and Echo took them to Mrs. Reardon's apartment, which was not terribly far from Amelia and Miranda's place. Echo went inside to talk with his friend privately. The others waited in the hall.

"Artemis is going to be very surprised when we come home with a truckload of people," Arielle whispered to Yasmine.

"Well, we can't just leave them here in this awful place. They are family after all—I guess. Are they?"

Arielle pondered a moment, trying to wrap her mind around the insanity of it all and replied, "Yeah. In a weird way. Since they are part of Howard and Howard is Beryl's son—Wow! I just realized that it makes Tess, Trix, and Echo Fable's nieces and nephew!"

"Grandnieces and nephew!" Yasmine giggled.

Echo returned after quite some time with the news that Amelia had agreed to go—on the condition that her sister Miranda would. Tess said she would go to the apartment and have a word with Miranda. The others accompanied her while Echo waited with Amelia until her relief came to take over watching Mrs. Reardon.

Miranda and Amelia's apartment also being on the third floor pleased Salem. Making that three-story climb had not been easy and she did not want to ascend another flight. The sparseness of the sisters' apartment was as startling to the new arrivals as it had been for Howard the day before. The functionality of it made sense in this crazy world, but its lack of any homey touches told Salem that these women had not grown up living here. This was a relatively new home for them, perhaps for everyone living in the building. All refugees from some other life coming to live unitedly in hopes to remain alive.

Miranda Perkins met her two friends and their guests with a smile. She sat and listened as Tess ran down the current circumstances and its available options. Miranda was rendered speechless by the generosity of the offer. The idea of being able to flee this ravaged society and go to a world resembling the one she'd not seen since she was a little girl was very appealing. Of course, she had questions. Was the travel through space and time safe? Would she and Amelia be a burden to this new Blanchard family none of them had ever met? But Howard assured her that it was his personal intention to help his new children and their two friends acclimate to that exotic new world and he would be with them every step of the way

As Miranda spoke with Howard, Seth, Arielle, Yasmine, and Salem took stock of the woman they were offering sanctuary to in their world. Miranda appeared to be a kind person, attractive but mousy. The thing the women noticed most about her was the stylishness of her haircut. In fact, she looked almost too stylish for a woman living through armageddon until Salem spotted the salon chair in the next room.

Miranda must have noticed her looking because she turned her attention away from Tess and said, "My mother was a hairstylist long ago before hell broke loose. She taught my sister and me. Amelia cuts everyone's hair in the building. I prefer looking after the little ones."

"Little ones?" Salem asked, rubbing her belly.

Miranda smiled. "We have a few children here. I teach them and look after them while their parents work."

"Work?" Yasmine repeated.

Miranda smiled, "Oh my yes. There is much to do here. There are people who work the gardens. People who reinforce the fortifications. People who scavenge for supplies. I watch their children. Me and one other woman. Looks like you'll be having your own baby pretty soon."

Tess took hold of Miranda's hand and gave it a friendly squeeze. "I know you must have misgivings about leaving the people here in a lurch, but will you go with us? Echo won't leave here without Amelia, and we hope you'll come with us as well."

Miranda looked morosely out the window, staring out over the fallen city and the scars time had left on what was once a beautiful place to live. "I'd love to get out of this hell. But are you guys sure you would be okay with us tagging along? My sister and I have nothing to offer, nothing to bring to the table. We will be burdens."

Salem leaned in and patted Miranda's hand. "You are people, and it is a witch's duty to protect the earth and the people on it whenever we can. You will not be burdens, and you will be safe."

"Can we take everyone else?" Miranda asked.

Salem frowned. "I don't think so. I am not strong enough to manage that feat. I'm really not sure I can manage all of us, but I'm going to try. But we must hurry. We have to go as soon as possible. My baby is ready to be born any minute. We have to get out of here before he comes."

It was about an hour later when Amelia was relieved from duty and came into the apartment with Echo. Everyone saw her for the first time. Amelia was lovely. Very much like her sister, only younger and with curly, reddish-brown hair. Amelia met everyone and thanked them all for the opportunity they were offering her and Miranda.

The group of nine quietly and unceremoniously left the apartment complex compound and loaded up in Echo's truck. It was decided that no goodbyes should be made to the other residents. The last thing they needed was to have to deny others the freedom Miranda and Amelia had been offered.

As they drove back towards the Blanchards' refuge, Salem began to feel a little funny. She told Echo they needed to hurry. She could feel the baby stirring. She wasn't in labor, but labor might come soon, and she needed to get everyone back to Blanchard House so they could return home.

"Does your power to take us out of here only work in the house?" Tess asked. "We could pull over and go now."

"I can wait till we get back to the house," Salem said. "I really don't want to go into labor in the middle of downtown Daihmler when we zap back. I would rather be home with my aunts. I can make it. Just drive us fast."

Echo got them home by midafternoon. Driving was once again slower than anyone would have preferred due to the amount of debris along the roadways. A storm was brewing overhead as the ominous sky began to darken. Echo pulled up to the house. Everyone hopped out of the back of the truck while he assisted Salem out. He escorted her across the littered yard and around the bodies of decaying creatures.

"Let's hurry inside," she urged him. "I don't feel well."

Seth joined Echo and the two of them practically carried Salem indoors with the others in tow. Once inside and standing in the foyer, Salem wasted no time. She reached out to clasp two hands, instructing everyone to grab someone else until they were all touching someone in the chain. Salem focused her mind, visualizing home while she honed into her unborn baby's great power. She could feel the force growing inside her being, swelling into her every internal square inch. She was just about to emit that final push which would lift them from this hell and propel them home when something struck her from behind. The force of the impact knocked her to the floor directly onto her stomach! Seth and Tess fell with her, struck by the same blow.

The three of them scrambled from under the front door which now lay on their backs. Before anyone had time to get their bearings, they saw the origin of the force. Heaving in the doorway stood a man, fiercely purveying the group. His red eyes seemed to be glowing above his menacing face. He had pale skin and long, dark, wild hair. Situated on either side of his maniacal grin were two long, sharp, glistening teeth. Miranda pulled her sister Amelia out of the fray, scrambling to the living room where the two sisters cowered against the wall.

"I sensed there were witches not of this world. And now I have found them."

"Who are you?" Echo shouted as he instinctively stepped forward, spreading his arms behind him to bravely shield his own sisters and new relatives.

"I have known about you and your family for a while now," the vampire snarled. "You were not a threat to us. Yet now I find your coven has multiplied."

"They aren't staying!" Echo exclaimed. "None of us are. We are not a threat to you. Just let us leave and we will cause you no trouble."

The vampire threw his head back and let out a bone-chilling cackle. "I could feel it in the air. There is a witch here with the power to take my kind to a new world. New blood. New life. New conquests. And when we have drained it dry, she can take us to yet another. Long have we waited for that kind of power to come forth. Endless realms to dominate."

Salem cowered on the floor. Beneath her, a pool of liquid—her water had broken. The baby was coming! She looked to her brother in terror. "Seth! The baby!"

Seth rushed towards his sister, but the vampire swiped him back, sending him crashing through the rail of the staircase. He did not get up. Yasmine screamed and jumped onto the stairs through the gap in the broken rail and cradled her husband in her arms.

"The unborn child," the vampire sneered, returning his attention to Salem. "Is that the source of your power?" He approached Salem and lifted her to her feet. She stood before the monster, clutching her stomach as she fought a contraction.

"If I turn you now," the vampire continued, "Your child will never be born. But you, my dear, will be one of us, and you will always possess that spectacular resource."

"Get away from her!" Arielle cried. She darted forward and placed herself between the vampire and Salem.

"You are very brave," the vampire laughed. "And very dead."

He reached out and clutched Arielle by the throat. He was just about to rip her head from her shoulders when she gave a nod to someone over his shoulder. With her throat still in his grasp, he looked back. The pregnant witch stood with her forearms raised facing each other. Arielle braced for it as Salem slammed her forearms together. The vampire reacted swiftly the instant he saw the two sides of the foyer floor and the left and right wall pitch toward him in a hinging motion, smashing together in the very place he had been standing. He leapt away in time but dropped Arielle in the process. Howard lurched forward, grabbing Arielle by the foot, and snatching her to safety away from the vampire.

The two of them scurried to the stairs where Seth was now regaining consciousness in Yasmine's arms. As Salem fought the pain coming from her abdomen, she knew the baby was coming soon. Howard and Arielle rushed to her side. Howard directed her to breathe deeply. Trix and Tess stepped forward, placing themselves between Salem and the vampire. The vampire looked upon the sisters and saw that they were smiling. They continued to smile as they then parted to reveal Howard standing with not only Salem, but two Salem's. Both equally pregnant and equally in labor. Their brother was gone. Or was he?

"I guess that's why they call him Echo," Yasmine whispered to Seth from the stairs.

It was indeed why he had garnered that particular nickname. Echo Blanchard's power had shown itself to be quite useful—the ability to take the form of any other living thing in his vicinity—and he had just turned himself into Salem. The vampire stared intently. He sniffed the air. But even his superior senses could not differentiate between the real Salem or the false one.

There was only a split second to act when the vampire was distracted by Salem and her doppelganger. Seth closed his eyes to focus his mind. Outside, every cloud in the nearby sky parted. He tapped into his newfound ability to intensify the sun as he had in the past with the Rain People.

He reached his hand out from the stairs in Salem's direction. "Salem! Ari!" he shouted. "Come here. Like we did with Patric!"

His sisters understood. Salem grabbed his hand and reached for Arielle's. The three of them had harnessed their forces once before. The Obreiggon siblings surging their powers into each other like an electrical current, magnifying it tenfold. Then once it felt at its pinnacle, Salem let go of her brother and sister and slammed her arms together once more.

Instantly the entire house exploded around them, sending shards of wood, tile, shingle and furniture sailing outward on all four sides with a force none of them had ever experienced. With the exception of the floor beneath them, there was nothing left of Blanchard House. Nothing. Everyone around starred in collective shock as pieces of Blanchard House littered the grounds on every side where it once stood.

The sunlight poured down around them all. It should have been cause for celebration, but the victory was short lived. Blanchard House's destruction revealed a startling sight. Standing in the yard, glaring viciously ahead, stood more vampires—real vampires like the one they had been trying to kill. The male vampire before them laughed.

"Sunlight," he said. "Yes, it is painful, even deadly after a while. But it takes a while. And you are not the first witches we have turned."

In the yard, a female vampire stepped forward. Lifting her hands to the sky she restored the clouds, even darker clouds, shielding her kind from the painful rays just as quickly as Seth had parted them.

She laughed Seth's way, "Your power isn't uncommon."

Salem's demonstration of her abilities had revealed her. The vampire now knew which Salem was real and which was Echo. The monster charged toward the genuine pregnant witch. Without considering her vulnerability, Yasmine dashed forward clutching a piece of the broken stair railing in her grip. Thrusting it before her she stabbed the vampire in the stomach. He flinched and staggered backward but did not fall. He withdrew the wood and tossed it to the ground.

"Missed my heart," he laughed.

Suddenly he grabbed Yasmine by the arm and with one quick motion slung her over his head. Seth watched in unbridled horror while his wife hurdled through the air as though she weighed nothing more than a Frisbee. Yasmine let out a cry as she sailed out of range of the house, landing with a bone-breaking crash into the yard at the feet of the other vampires. They seized upon her. Seth charged forward but the head vampire thrust his hand into Seth's throat, sending him tumbling backward onto his back gasping for air as his windpipe broke. He strained for air that would not come. Still he crawled toward the yard, digging his hands and fingernails into the wood grain of the floor to pull himself forward to save his wife. The vampire kicked him in the face, breaking Seth's nose and rendering him motionless. Salem screamed as her brother lay helpless on the floor.

Arielle watched as the vampires finished feeding upon Yasmine. Yasmine's body lay blood-soaked and motionless in the yard. Arielle screamed. Trix came charging forward, a sword in hand. She swiped at the vampire, chopping off his hand. He recoiled and thrust his other out to grab at the weapon, but Trix was too skilled. With a quick side dodge and a heel spin, Trix Blanchard proved to be quite the warrior as she sliced off his left arm at the elbow. The vampire was stunned at the action.

Howard darted forward and grabbed Seth's legs, dragging him back out of the fray. He grabbed Arielle's wrist as well, dragging her to himself and Seth. Howard then did the same to Salem. Echo, now returned to his own form, jumped forward to pull Trix to safety as the vampire raged and whirled in circles in an attempt to gain his bearings as to what he still had the power to do. He was bellowing in pain or infuriation. Echo motioned for Amelia and Miranda to run to him as he and the others huddled together. Amelia looked into her big sister's eyes for guidance.

"Hurry!" Tess shouted. "We have to go now!"

Miranda nodded her head in reassurance to Amelia, took hold of her hand, and darted toward Echo, half pulling her reluctant sister along behind her. The vampire leapt forward toward the running sisters, with only his powerful teeth as a weapon. He latched onto Amelia's heel and bit through her Achilles tendon. She screamed in agony and collapsed onto the floor, letting go of Miranda's hand as she landed with a thud.

Miranda cried out for her sister even as Echo grabbed her arm and jerked her to safety behind him. He looked to Amelia and tried to formulate a plan to reach her. The vampire still had hold of her. Echo grabbed the sword Trix had dropped earlier and jumped forward, slicing off the vampire's head. He grabbed Amelia by the arms and hit the floor, pulling her across the planks with the vampire's head still attached to her ankle.

"We have to go!" Salem shrieked. "The baby is coming!"

Seth tried to choke out words of protest, but they would not come. His windpipe was demolished and blood from his broken nose was pouring into his throat. He felt a reassuring pat on the back and glanced upward to see Tess moving forward. Suddenly she was gone. Vanished. Howard twisted all around to see where she had gone, but she was nowhere to be seen. Suddenly the vampires outside began charging forward across the yard toward the Blanchards. The little Blanchard clan huddled together in terror. Echo was almost back to them now with Amelia in tow as the vampires were now only yards away.

As the sound of the vampires' charging feet resounded atop the wood decking of the floor where the porch had once stood, heading for the threshold of the house, Tess's voice suddenly rang out. "Trix! Use the truck to reach us!"

Trix looked out and saw her sister materializing beside Yasmine's torn and battered body. Using every ounce of her strength to maximize the process, Trix reached out toward the direction of Echo's parked truck. Using her power to manipulate metal, she forced the metal parts of the truck to dissolve in seconds and reshape into one long pole—one end reaching to Tess' outstretched hand, the other end reaching to Trix's.

"Now Salem! Now!" Echo shouted as Howard flung forward to close the gap between him and the group, grabbing Echo by the arm with his right hand and reaching back to grip Arielle's with his left. Arielle grabbed Miranda. Miranda grabbed Salem. Salem grabbed Trix. Trix grabbed Seth.

Doing her best to suppress the increasing stabs of pain of childbirth, Salem focused her mind to her unborn son's immense power to wield them all home and to safety. The vampires charged into the house. Salem's power shot forth, and as her family began to dissolve into nothingness and leave this hell behind them, she thought she heard someone scream.

CHAPTER TWENTY EIGHT

No Place Like Home

"Go back! Go back!" Echo screamed. "They grabbed her! They grabbed Amelia and pulled her out of my hand!"

"Oh, no!" Arielle shrieked.

"My sister!" Miranda exclaimed as Arielle closed her arms around her in comfort. Miranda's face twisted in agony as the realization set in that her sister was gone forever. She crumbled to her knees beneath Arielle's embrace.

Demitra and Artemis ran toward the foyer. They had been sitting in the living room when they saw the group reappear out of nowhere. Seth's bloody body was convulsing. Artemis fell down beside him and lifted his head into her lap. Demitra looked down to the mangled body of Yasmine and cried out in horror.

"She's still alive!" Tess alerted everyone. "Yasmine isn't dead yet. That's why I brought her with us."

"What's going on?" Jerry shouted bounding down the stairs after hearing the commotion below. "Oh, dear God!"

"We need Beryl!" Arielle cried, joining the others. "We need Beryl to heal them. If Beryl isn't here, what do we do?"

"I'll call an ambulance!" Jerry said. "We need an ambulance."

The paramedics pulled into the driveway of Blanchard House within 15 minutes, sirens and lights blaring. Working quickly to stabilize Seth and Yasmine, they loaded them and Salem into two ambulances and sped off for Daihmler General Hospital. Artemis, Demitra, Fable, Arielle, and Jerry were right behind them in the car.

They faced a long wait in the hospital waiting room for someone to come tell Artemis and Demitra what was going on with Yasmine and Seth. Fable went with Salem into delivery. Arielle wanted to be the one in with her sister, but the aunts insisted she remain with them to explain what all happened in the other world.

Arielle told Artemis, Demitra, and Jerry everything. When she had finished, they were dumbfounded.

"Howard has children?" Demitra gasped.

"Well, *that* Howard did. Those are three of the four strangers we brought back with us," Arielle explained. "The other woman is one of their friends. I'm afraid her sister was supposed to come back too, but apparently the vampires got her before she could dematerialize with us."

"This is insane," Artemis said.

Demitra was still too focused on the other aspect. She required clarification. "Arielle, are these people actually Howard's children or just people from another universe?"

"I guess it's how you look at it," Arielle replied. "They share Howard's DNA. Just as if they had been born in our world. It is my understanding that they are every bit his children except for the fact that they just met a couple of days ago."

"But they *are* Blanchards?" Artemis asked. "They have Blanchard blood in their veins?"

Arielle nodded. "Yes. They are descended from Olympia Blanchard. Just like Con and Rom, Hera and Titan."

"So those two young women and that young man are my great grandchildren?" Demitra said.

"It appears so. Beryl is their grandmother."

"Astounding," Demitra sighed, trying to dissect the information.

"Tess, Trix, and Echo," Artemis repeated. "Well, we have to look after them and make them feel safe and welcome."

"The other one, too," Jerry added. "What was her name?"

"Miranda."

"Is she a witch too?" Jerry asked.

"No," Arielle said. "She's just a regular person like you are."

"A regular person who has no family left and is a stranger in a strange world," Artemis noted. "I guess we have a lot to figure out when we get back home. If only someone would come tell us about Yasmine and Seth."

"I have a concerning question," Jerry asked. "If Yasmine was attacked by a hoard of vampires and she lives..."

"I was trying to not think about that," Demitra replied.

"I have been unable to think of anything else," Artemis noted. "But we will cross that bridge when we come to it. For now, let us just pray the two of them survive the night."

Back at Blanchard House Tess, Trix, and Echo were overwhelmed by the condition of the house. They wandered the many rooms of the house, which was a mirror image to their own, except for some pretty important distinctions.

"Did you girls see that other wing!" Echo exclaimed, bounding back into the living room.

"And their kitchen is enormous," Tess commented. "They have a whole dining room where our kitchen was."

Trix's eyes enlarged as she looked around the well-appointed room—a clean room. Spotless in fact. There were no bricks on the windows, no scuff marks marring the walls, no brown rubbed markings from long, leaning boards or discarded weapons against doorframes. There were no blood stains on the couch. No one had ever lain there bleeding out after an attack. This version of their home was immaculate.

"They have real furniture," she exclaimed. "And art! And pictures on the wall. This is a home. I cannot believe the difference."

"I have a feeling we are going to like it here," Echo grinned. "But man, we sure brought a mess of heartache to get here, didn't we?"

Tess hung her head and answered, "We did. Poor Miranda. And poor you, too, Echo—we lost your Amelia."

The sentence shook Echo back to reality. His shock at the much fancier version of his childhood home had been a heavy distraction. "I can't believe she's gone. And if we had just left them there at the apartment, she would be alive."

Trix reached her hand out and lifted his chin. She gripped his chin and gave his head a good shake before mouthing the word, "No." Echo's teary eyes looked into her own. She gripped his chin harder and pulled him closer by it. Her widened eyes bored into his as she said the word aloud this time, "No."

Echo wiped the tears from his face, and he looked at her with cold, distant eyes. "Okay," he said. "Okay."

"None of the people we left behind were ever going to last long," Tess added in an attempt to console her brother. "Everyone we know is going to eventually be killed by either the vampires or their fiendish byproducts. We got out, and we got Miranda out. That is the only way we can look at it."

"But the Blanchards may have lost one of their own... that Yasmine lady," Echo said. "Tess, why did you grab her? You saw she was being bitten. What if one of those things turned her?"

Tess shrugged. She really didn't know why she had rescued Yasmine. Instinct perhaps. Hope, maybe. "I can't answer that. I only saw that she was reachable and so I went for it. It looked like the vampires were more interested in eating her than turning her. I just saw the opportunity to reach her and took it."

"Maybe they only fed," Trix hoped aloud. "Maybe they only fed."

About an hour had passed at the hospital as Demitra and Artemis waited for news. Fable joined them in the waiting room with the news that Salem had given birth to Olympus. He was a healthy eight pounds two ounces. Salem was recovering well in the maternity ward. As Arielle started to fill Fable in on the existence of the three new Blanchards, Charlie Bennet appeared in the doorway of the waiting room.

"Ahem," he said in their general direction.

Demitra, upon seeing her friend and occasional employer, rose from her chair and went over to him. "Charlie, what brings you out here so late tonight?"

"Are you serious, Dee?" he said with a raised brow. "I got a call at the station saying that two Blanchards were brought in tonight, one with a smashed face and broken windpipe and the other practically drained of blood needing an emergency transfusion. I raced here as fast as I could. Can you tell me why Yasmine has a dozen punctures all over her body? And why is Seth so banged up? What happened tonight?"

Demitra sighed and placed her hand on Charlie's shoulder. "I really don't think you actually want to know."

"I have to know. It is now an open case."

"It's not going to be easy to explain in your files," Demitra informed him.

"Witchy stuff?"

"Definitely."

"Do we have another monster lurking in Daihmler like that werewolf a few years back?" Charlie asked nervously.

"No," Demitra told him. "There are no monsters here. This happened...elsewhere."

"Shit Dee," he grimaced. "Your family has me in quite a spot."

"Can you make this go away?" she asked. "Make up something."

"I'll do what I can, but this shit is all over the place now. Every tongue in Daihmler is wagging. Hell, the mayor called! Gonna be a whole lotta people wanting to know who attacked them. I can come up with something, I guess. But Dee, if one of them dies, an autopsy report is gonna expose everything. Yasmine looks like she was bitten all over by vampires or something."

Demitra gave him a strained look and said, "Let's not go there. Let's just pray she lives."

Yasmine barely clung to life through most of the night, but by morning the blood infusions she received seemed to be working and her vitals returned. It would still be touch and go, but the Blanchards felt hope that she would pull through. Seth was going to be fine as well. Doctors repaired his throat and reset his nose. He would stay overnight.

It was long after midnight when Artemis and Demitra Ubered home. They had sent Arielle, Jerry, and Fable back hours before. The house was quiet when they came in, but Howard was still there, waiting for them in the dimly-lit living room.

"How are Yaz and Seth?"

"We think they'll be okay," Artemis said. "Yaz is pretty critical right now. We will know more tomorrow. Are you all right?"

Howard gave a slight nervous smile and answered, "I guess you were filled in."

"Yes," Demitra said, giving him a hug. "You did the right thing bringing them home."

Howard returned her hug and sighed. "I know I'm not really their father, but I feel like in a way I am. At least I feel responsible for them."

"They are your children now," Demitra smiled. "Just like you are our family now. All of this is crazy and complicated, and it will make no sense to anyone other than the members of this family, but they are Blanchards, and they belong here."

Howard shook his head in agreement and squeezed her hand. "Well, I promise to take them to my place tomorrow and get them out of your hair. I didn't know what to do tonight. I put them in the guest rooms."

Artemis patted her old friend's cheek, "That was the right thing to do. And you cannot expect the four of you to live in that tiny place of yours. They can stay here. We have plenty of room. In fact, you really should consider moving in as well. It is your birthright, and you can be close to them."

Howard shook his head. "I am not that ready for Blanchard life. Baby steps."

"The offer is always open," Artemis smiled. "But as for these kids, they need to be here. They should get to know this family."

"What about Miranda?" Howard said. "I can take her back with me."

"Let's just let things rest for the moment until we all gain our bearings," Artemis said. "If she lost her sister tonight, I think she might need to stay close to her three friends. We will look after her as well until she decides what she's going to do."

Howard sat down and placed his head in his hands. "It's a mess, that's for sure."

"A mess that wasn't your fault," Demitra comforted him. "And it is a family mess, not yours alone. We will all figure it out together. Like we always do."

CHAPTER TWENTY NINE

The New Blanchards

Artemis arranged for her restaurant manager to handle things for a couple of days while she got acquainted with the new arrivals at Blanchard House and helped them to acclimate. She was preparing a large breakfast for everyone as footsteps sounded softly on the kitchen stairs.

"Is that bacon?" Echo asked timidly as he entered the kitchen.

"It is," Artemis smiled. "Good morning."

He smiled uncertainly at the stranger cooking. He had only seen her in passing the night before. "May I have a piece? It's been years since I've tasted bacon."

Artemis' warm laugh filled the kitchen, "You can have as much as you like, son. I'm making it for all of you."

He smiled, took a plate from the counter, and grabbed a couple of pieces. Artemis patted his back and piled about five more on his plate, along with a couple of freshly baked biscuits and a large spoonful of scrambled eggs. She showed him the butter and jam and coffee waiting on the kitchen table.

As he took a seat to eat, he smiled back at her and said, "My name is Nathan Blanchard. But everybody calls me Echo."

"I like that... Echo," Artemis said. "I heard about how your power works. It is an impressive ability. Your nickname fits. I am your Aunt Artemis."

"Nice to meet you. This is a lot to get used to." Echo grinned as the taste of the crisp bacon exploded in his mouth. "Oh, man. I forgot what this was like."

His sisters came down, awakened by the aroma of breakfast. Artemis observed for the first time that the girls looked identical except for the color of their hair. They appeared just as unsure and timid as their brother had when they stepped down into the kitchen.

"You girls have gotta taste this!" Echo called to them. "Bacon! Real true to life bacon! And these biscuits. Man!"

"Is it alright if I get some?" the blonde twin asked Artemis.

"Of course, it is! It's all for you. You kids haven't had a decent meal in a long time from what it looks like. I'm going to enjoy feeding you."

Tess nodded gratefully. "Thank you very much. I'm Tess Blanchard, and this is my sister Beatrix."

"Trix," the walnut-haired one corrected. "Thank you for the food."

Artemis sat down with the three of them just as Demitra came down to do the same. She declined breakfast, only wanting coffee. She was much too eager to meet her new descendants and judging from the way they were eating, Demitra didn't want to take any of the food away from them for herself.

"My name is Demitra. I guess I'm sort of your great grandmother."

"Pretty young to be that," Echo grinned. "Never seen such a beautiful great grandmother before."

Demitra blushed. "You're a charmer, I see. Nevertheless, I am your great grandmother. I suppose that's the side effects of time travel."

Tess set aside her plate. There was still a little food on it, but judging by the pale expression on her face, her stomach had gone so long without such foods she needed to pace herself. Instead of eating she took the lead in the conversation.

"It is really kind of you to allow us to stay here last night. I'm afraid we may need to impose a few days longer until my brother and sister and I figure out what we are going to do."

"You will be living here from now on," Artemis told them. "There is no need to figure anything out. This is your home."

"Not quite," Echo said. "Oh, it's really close to what we come from, but this place is so much bigger. And it's magnificent! You actually have flowers outside! And grass. And furniture that's pretty, not just functional. Our house didn't look like this."

"Well, thank you," Artemis replied. "But I wasn't only referring to the house. We—Demitra, myself, all of us in the family—we are your home now. You kids do not have to be alone anymore. You do not have to fight to survive anymore. You are part of us now."

"That's a lot to take in," Trix said. "And of course, there's Miranda to consider."

Suddenly Echo's face became crestfallen. The joy of eating was now replaced by the memory of something else. "Amelia should be here, too. I can't believe she's gone." He looked pensively at the wall for a moment—lost in thought, or perhaps a nightmare. "What those things must have done to her..."

Tess quieted him with a gentle hug and rub to his back. He put his chin to her shoulder and closed his eyes. "I know. I know," she whispered to her brother. "Try to not think about that."

Echo, still leaning his head on his sister's shoulder, added, "And poor Miranda. She's lost everything now."

"She has us," Tess said.

Artemis entered their conversation and said, "I haven't actually met your friend yet, but know that she is welcome here as well. We have plenty of room. My mother saw to that. I hope the four of you will come to think of Blanchard House as your permanent home."

"I second that," Demitra smiled. "When my daughter, your grandmother, returns home in a few months, I want you here for her to get to know."

Suddenly Trix sat up right. The silverware on the table began to liquify and run towards her. Within seconds the flatware reformed in her grip as a long sharp knife. "No one move," she warned. "There is a wolf sitting on the landing of the kitchen stairs. It's staring at us."

Demitra quickly laid her hand atop Trix's to calm her. "No, that's Romulus! He is my grandson. Your cousin actually."

"That animal is your grandson!" Echo exclaimed. "How?"

Demitra smiled at the boy and waved to Romulus to come forward. Rom approached the table and placed his two paws on top, looking to his grandmother. Demitra kissed the top of his head and laid him a plate of bacon and eggs on the floor. The new Blanchards looked perplexed.

"There is a lot we all have to learn about each other," Demitra said. "And we will all have time later. For now, just please do not be afraid of Romulus. He is very sweet."

"That is quite an interesting power you have there, Trix," Artemis acknowledged. "What all can you kids do?"

"Well, I can change metal into any form," Trix replied. "Plus, I have amplified reflexes. I'm pretty fast."

"I can make myself invisible," Tess said. "I also get visions...sometimes. They aren't very reliable."

Demitra laughed and squeezed her hand. "You get that from me. My visions were very unreliable when I was your age too."

"We already know Echo's ability to change into other people," Artemis smiled.

"Not just people," Echo expounded. "I can do animals, objects, anything within a few feet of me. And once or twice I've been able to talk with animals."

Artemis and Demitra laughed out loud and high-fived each other as they simultaneously exclaimed, "They are Blanchards for sure."

The kids looked puzzled.

Demitra smiled at her new descendants and said, "Your aunt Fable communicates with animals, too. You three are definitely my great-grandchildren." She looked at her watch and frowned at the time. "I'd love to talk longer, but I need to shower and drive out to the hospital. Yasmine and Seth should be waking up soon."

"I'll meet you there in about an hour," Artemis said. "I want to chat some more with the triplets."

Once Demitra was out of sight, Artemis' face turned more serious in demeanor as she asked them, "Level with me, please. In your world, does a vampire victim who survives always turn into a vampire as well?"

Tess frowned. "I don't really know. All that happened to the world sort of happened without our awareness until everything was in turmoil. We have never known anyone who survived an attack. I'm afraid we can't be much help with Yasmine and what is going to happen to her. But generally speaking, victims who were drained turn into a different kind of monster."

"Different?"

"Hungry," Trix explained. "Weak. Dying little by little if they can't find blood to keep them going. But they aren't vampires. To become a vampire, one of them has to infuse you with their own blood."

"Did that happen to Yasmine?" Artemis asked.

Echo shrugged his shoulders. "There's no real way to know. I guess when she wakes up, you'll find out. Maybe the doctors got to her in time to save her from dying and turning into one of those zombie things. We really don't know how it works."

...

Yasmine was extremely weak when Demitra went in to see her. Seth insisted upon seeing his wife himself, although he was not able to speak quite yet. Yasmine was startled to see her husband's condition—wrappings around his throat and bandages and a brace across the bridge of his nose. Seth could only take her hand in his own and sit beside her bed. Demitra did the talking.

"How are you feeling, Yaz?'

"Okay, I guess. I feel strange. Weak and kind of nauseous."

"You need rest," her aunt advised.

"No," Yasmine replied. "Every time I close my eyes, I see those horrible faces coming down at me. Biting me, ripping me, drinking from me." She shuddered at the memory, and Seth gripped her hand reassuringly.

"We'll take you home as soon as you are strong enough." Demitra smiled. "You'll be all right."

"How did they save me?"

"It was Tess from what I understand," Demitra started. "She ran for you. Apparently, she has the ability to turn invisible. Then Trix used whatever it is she does to metal to forge a long pole to reach the two of you and you all disappeared together."

"So, everyone made it home safely?" Yasmine asked. "Howard too?"

"All except Miranda's sister. She was snatched by the vampires."

"Oh no," Yasmine whimpered. The thought of those fiends doing to Amelia what they had done to her brought a wave of panic into her gut. Seth sensed her feelings. He laid his head down on her hands and pressed the back of her hands to his cheek.

Yasmine looked down upon her husband with such love and gratitude that they were safe. His warm cheek made her cold hand tingle. She looked down at his head laying on her. He hadn't shaved. That blondish scruff scratched the skin of her hand a little. She didn't mind. She loved him so much. He was her everything. She loved his laugh, his touch, his kiss, the smell of the blood coursing through his veins. Such warm delicious blood. She watched the artery in the side of his throat pulse as his head laid upon her. So much life flowing through that artery. She could smell it. She could almost taste it. Then her tongue moved across the top row of her teeth. *What is that?* She wiggled her tongue across the two teeth on either side. They felt a little pointy.

CHAPTER THIRTY

Settling In

Blanchard House was bustling in the days after everyone returned home. Yasmine rarely left her room after she came back from the hospital. Seth found that she seemed withdrawn, maybe depressed. She didn't say much, and she spent very little time with her children. In fact, she seemed quite opposed to seeing them. She didn't mind Seth's company, however. Especially at night. The lethargy Yasmine felt during daylight hours seemed to turn more energetic once the sun went down. It even verged on the threshold of sexual excitement. In the days since she and Seth were released from the hospital, they had made love every night. Seeing his wife come back to life a bit, Seth held hope that he would find her returning to mothering the children by morning. But by morning her listlessness returned, and she took little interest in the children. Fable told him it was the shock of her attack. She had been through a lot. She likened it to a kind of postpartum depression and suggested to Seth that until Yaz felt more herself, it was probably best to keep her distance from Hera and Titan. Fable took over their care with help from Miranda.

Miranda was doing everything she could to be useful around the house—looking after the children, light house cleaning, whatever she could do to help out. Artemis tried to assure her that she needn't enslave herself to earn her keep, that she was welcome and not a burden. Regardless of what she was told, Miranda kept herself busy. Once the day was done and nothing seemed to be left to do, Miranda would sit on the porch steps and cry. It was easier to handle if the children needed her, or there was a spill to clean up. But in the deafening quiet of the countryside evenings, as she stared up at the stars, the burdens and sorrows she had sidestepped all day caught up with her. And she grieved.

Salem's hands were full with Olympus. It had been a long time since she'd had an infant to care for. The 2 a.m. feedings and endless diapers once long forgotten were now everyday life again, but she was loving every minute of it. She had just rocked Olympus to sleep when Artemis sneaked quietly into her room. Salem could tell something was on her aunt's mind. Artemis was always so direct unless a subject was really sticky. Salem walked to the mobile over the bed and lightly spun the arms causing the giraffes, monkeys, and zebras to dance.

"I don't want to disturb you," Artemis finally said, "but after you lay him down, can I speak to you in my room privately?"

Salem laid her son gently in his bassinet and made her way down the hall to her aunt's bedroom. Artemis was seated on her frilly pink settee and beckoned Salem to join her. She poured her niece a glass of sweet tea.

"What makes you so anxious?" Salem asked.

"I have a tricky conversation to have with you," Artemis started. "I love you so much. You are like my very own daughter, and that baby is like my own grandson. I hope you know that."

"Aunt Artemis," Salem said. "You raised me from a little girl. I know what I mean to you. Whatever you have to say, just say it. I promise to hear you out."

Artemis sighed and spat the troubling words out. "I want to bind Olympus' powers until he's old enough to understand how dangerous they are."

"Do you honestly think that's necessary?"

"I really do," Artemis nodded. "Just look at what all has happened. Beryl is trapped in the past. Howard is a Blanchard. We have three new descendants living under this roof and a refugee from another dimension. Don't get me wrong—I am glad to know them all and have them here, but Olympus has an immense ability that no child has the capability of controlling. I think he should be bound until he's old enough to carry such a responsibility."

Salem wanted to argue. This was her son. He was a witch, and a witch should have every right to their own powers. No one bound Hera or Titan or Con. It did not seem fair. But then the memories raced through Salem's mind. That awful, frightening day when she saw Beryl, Fable, Seth, and Yaz vanish in thin air. The thought that she might never see them again was something she never wanted to experience again. Then she thought of the triplets. Their life was arguably better now, but they'd still lost their father. And that was Salem's fault. And Olympus'. When she really weighed Artemis' request, Salem understood it was valid and she had no logical way to argue it. Artemis had a duty to protect not only the family, but the world.

"I will agree, for the time being," Salem acquiesced. "But only if he grows up knowing what the power is and is trained in theory on its use during his childhood. It shouldn't be sprung on him in adulthood without preparation."

"My exact thoughts."

Artemis gave Salem a kiss to the forehead and went downstairs. There was more on her plate that afternoon regarding the family. She had asked Howard to have a glass of wine with her after he left the office. He was going to be coming out to the house anyway as it had become his custom several nights a week to spend some time with his children individually. Tonight, he had plans to take Trix out for dinner.

He arrived at the house shortly after 6 p.m. and found Artemis waiting on the porch in Olympia's old rocking chair with wine poured and ready for him. He plopped down in the rocker beside her and took his glass.

"Hard day?" she asked.

"You wouldn't believe how difficult it is to concoct a record of a life out of thin air for four people who just showed up a week ago. Luckily, Sinclair had people on staff at Sinclair Industries with a background in forging documents. I even have a degree in early childhood development for Miranda in case she wants to apply to a daycare one day."

"You are very thorough," Artemis said. "How are things going getting to know the children?"

Howard grinned a little sideways smile and puffed out his chest ever so slightly. "Pretty well, I think. Tess is easy. She's open and trusting. She and I are a lot alike; I can tell. I never knew their mother, but I am guessing Trix is a bit more like she was. Trix is harder. She presents herself strong as steel, but underneath she is this scared little girl. I am getting there though. Tonight, I'm introducing her to sushi."

"And Echo?"

"That boy is really something. You know he's named after my dad? Nathan. My Dad would be proud of him. He has a good head on his shoulders, too. Been thinking about what I can do to help him get started in life. Got to give that some thought."

"Well, while you are pondering that," Artemis smiled. "I've been wondering about some things myself. For example, somewhere out there in the orchard is a bottle containing your powers."

Howard grimaced. "I was wondering how long it was going to take you to get around to that. Arielle won't stop bringing it up at work."

Artemis gave him a friendly nudge. "Not the least bit curious, are you?"

Howard's face betrayed the truth. "Well, yeah. Of course, I am. Who wouldn't be?"

Sipping her wine Artemis smiled at him and said, "There is a way to find out."

Howard set his glass aside, sloshing a little wine into the potted begonia beside it. Leaning forward, elbows on his knees, he stared out over the front yard. "Artemis, is it wrong of me to not want to know? To not want any part of it?"

Artemis was confused. She set her own glass down and placed her hand on his back. "Howard, I am afraid it's a little too late to stop being a part of this family. You've been around a lot of years, and we all love you too much to let you go."

Howard leaned back again and faced her with a chuckle, "Oh Artemis, I don't mean the family. I love this family. You all are all I've got. I mean the witch stuff. I kind of like boring old, plain Howard Caldwell. I realize I am not exciting or powerful. I don't do tricks or save the world. I push a pen and pencil around and keep the family money churning. That's about all the excitement I need."

"You don't want your powers, I take it."

"Not right now," he said. "Maybe never. I have lived this long being the way I am. I don't think I want to be anything more. Besides, I am a dad now. I have three kids to get to know. I will leave the adventures and the protection of the Natural Order to the rest of you. You've been doing this a long time."

Artemis leaned back into her rocker again and retook her wine in hand. It was Howard's choice. Whether she agreed with it or not was not her place to say. His world had been shaken from the rafters enough lately. She would not ask him to walk toward more upheaval. For the time being, Howard Blanchard's dormant powers would remain buried where Olympia Blanchard buried them.

"Get that mutt out of here!" Yasmine screeched from her bed so loudly that the entire third floor heard.

Seth, Arielle, and Fable came running. Yasmine was sitting upright in her bed, covers drawn towards her chest as Romulus paced the floor in front of the bed, growling up at her. His sharp teeth were snarling and his red eyes glowing as if he did not trust her.

"How dare you call my son a mutt!" Fable screamed. "That's your nephew!"

"Well, he's not acting very nephewly right now. He looks like he's setting up to attack me!" Yasmine cried. "Maybe we were all wrong about him, and he is actually turning into the way Patric was the older he gets."

"Yaz, that's a terrible thing to say," Seth scolded. "And you know he understands everything you say."

"I don't care!" Yasmine shrieked. "Just get him out of this room!"

Fable tugged her son's ear and instructed him to leave. She followed, slamming the door behind her as she went. Seth faced his wife with an incredulous look on his face.

"What the hell is wrong with you, Yasmine Blanchard?!"

"Nothing is wrong with me. I just want to rest."

"You have been resting for over a week. But every day you grow more and more tired. Then at night you get either horny or hostile and unpleasant. I have never heard you speak to Rom like that before. You love Rom."

"He clearly doesn't love me anymore," she pointed out. "Maybe it is time to put that creature down once and for all."

Seth sat down on the edge of the bed and stared at his wife. He was beginning to not recognize her. Something about her was gone. The Yasmine that went away to that other reality was not the one who had come back. He tried to find his wife in the eyes of the woman sitting in their bed, but it was becoming harder and harder to do that.

"I didn't want to say anything," he finally admitted. "I was hoping I was wrong. But Yaz, something has happened to you ever since those vampires attacked you. I'm a little worried their bite did something to you."

As he talked, she gently rubbed her tongue across the two sharp teeth in her mouth which she had figured out how to retract and protract days ago. No one else had seen them. Seth's neck looked so inviting. She wanted to taste him. Yet she knew inside she shouldn't. This feeling was wrong. And he was right, she had not returned the same and she knew it. But sometimes, at night, when she was not so tired like she was during the day, she just didn't care.

CHAPTER THIRTY ONE

Tears Will Fall

Xander, Nacaria, and Cassandra called Blanchard House first to make sure it was a good time to visit before Xander zapped them from Charleston to Daihmler. They wanted to see the new baby. Neither Xander nor Nacaria had the privilege to know Baby Michael, Salem's first child. After his death it was a source of much regret for them. The Obreiggons did not want to miss a moment of baby Olympus' life.

With all of the chaos of the last week, no one had thought to fill Nacaria in on the new Blanchards. She was a little overwhelmed by it all as she entered the house and met her new grandnieces and nephew.

"I guess we come as a shock when you thought you were just coming to see the baby," Tess noted, shaking her hand.

"Yes, you do," Nacaria agreed before adding, "I bet it's a bit unsettling to you three having to adjust to a new kind of life with people you really don't know."

"It is something I don't think anyone else can understand. But so far it has been really nice," Tess replied.

Nacaria leaned in and half whispered in her ear, "I spent twenty years of my life as nothing more than a shadow on these walls, unable to interact or participate. So, I understand a little about what it feels like to reconnect with people you do not actually know anymore. If you ever need to talk to someone who relates a little, just call on your Aunt Nacaria."

Salem was ecstatic to see her parents and sister. Nacaria and Xander took turns passing the baby back and forth. Xander swore Olympus looked like his father, Lotek Obreiggon. Nacaria found herself surprised by this statement. She was so accustomed to being immersed in Blanchard lore; she had half forgotten that Salem's child was also of Obreiggon descent.

Cassandra spent some time with the baby and then took a walk with Arielle, getting caught up on everything that happened since she returned to Oleander. After their walk, she went upstairs to see Yasmine and Seth.

"Hello?" Cassandra called as she tapped on the door to Seth and Yasmine's room.

Yasmine was asleep in the bed. At least it appeared she was asleep. Cassandra did not hear snoring sounds, nor did she see a rise or fall to her sister-in-law's chest as she breathed. In fact, she did not appear to be breathing at all. Something tingled inside Cassandra's senses as she crept closer to the bed. Yasmine showed no sign of life.

"Yaz," she said quietly, shaking her gently.

Yasmine did not respond. Cassandra placed her two fingers on Yasmine's neck. She could not feel a pulse. Cassandra didn't fall into full panic mode yet. Though she did have a nursing background, it was very possible her sister-in-law's vitals could be sluggish after having lost so much blood. Even transfusions would not have restored the amount she had lost. Cassandra hovered her hand over Yasmine's mouth and nostrils to try and feel exhaling. She felt nothing. Yasmine's lips were parted enough so that air could escape had she been breathing.

Cassandra was about to run out for help when she noticed something. As Cassandra moved away from the bed, the overhead light cast down upon Yasmine's face. Something glistened behind her lips. Carefully Cassandra took her finger and lifted Yasmine's upper lip. Fangs. Vampire fangs shone under the light.

. . .

Artemis was preparing dinner when Nacaria came down the back stairs. From the energy her baby sister was emitting, Artemis knew right away an argument was about to ensue. She didn't wait for Nacaria to initiate. Artemis met the hostility head on.

"Spit it out. You have your mad stomp going on. What is stuck in your craw this time, Nacaria?"

Nacaria wasted no time laying into her older sister. "I believe if a decision was going to be made to bind my grandson's powers I should have been at least consulted."

Artemis did not care to waste her time discussing the settled matter. "Why, Nacaria?" she asked. "Why did I need to run anything by you?"

"Because Salem is my daughter, and Olympus is my grandson!"

"And Salem is Olympus' mother," Artemis reminded Nacaria. "Therefore, when

I had the discussion with *the only person* pertinent to the situation, why would I then feel the need to get permission from you? Salem made the choice. It was mine and Salem's to make."

"And not mine, you mean?"

"Frankly, no," Artemis spat back. "I am the head of this family. I am the hecate of this coven. You are not even a member of this coven. You belong to the Obreiggons in Charleston now. This had nothing to do with you."

"I strongly disagree."

Artemis faced her sister, only inches from her face. "Was it a wrong decision?"

"What?"

"Exactly what I just asked," Artemis repeated. "Knowing the range of power that little baby wields and the damage it can cause, was binding his powers until he's older the wrong decision?"

Nacaria thought a moment and answered, "Well, no. Under the circumstances, it was probably the safest thing to do."

"So why did I have to consult you?"

Nacaria stumbled for an answer. Artemis did not wait for her to come up with one.

"There was no need in wasting precious time consulting you. It had to be done, and we did it. The only reason you are upset is because you feel left out once again. Just like you did when you first returned and saw that my relationship with your children is more parental than aunt-like. You felt shut out, Nacaria. But I was not trying to shut you out. I was simply tending to the family. That is my job. *My* job. Mother left me the responsibility, and it is a heavy one at times. Please do not pile more baggage on me when I have to perform it."

"ARTEMIS!"

Nacaria and Artemis both looked at each other in surprise. Then it came again. Seth was screaming from the third floor. Artemis and Nacaria bolted up the stairs and into Seth and Yasmine's bedroom. There they found Seth cradling his unconscious wife, holding her top lip up for them to see what she was becoming. Cassandra stood beside the bed with her hand on her brother's shoulder.

"Dear God, no!" Artemis cried, tears erupting from her eyes. She raced to the bed and snatched Yasmine's body out of Seth's arms and into her own.

"My sweet angel girl," Artemis wept, rocking her in her arms. "Not this child. Not this child."

"Daddy what's going on?" came a little voice from the doorway. It was Hera.

"Go back to your room, baby girl," Seth told her, wiping tears from his eyes.

"Is Momma sick?" Hera asked, fear in her voice.

Nacaria lifted her granddaughter in her arms and removed her from the room. Artemis held Yasmine to her chest and fell back into Seth's. The two of them held Yasmine and cried together. Within minutes Salem, Arielle, Demitra, and Fable were in the doorway. Behind them stood Miranda, Echo, Tess, and Trix. No one knew what to say, what to do. Jerry approached and peaked through the arms and shoulders at the scene in the bedroom. Lightly he tapped Tess, Trix, and Echo, directing them to come with him downstairs. He motioned for Cassandra to join. Jerry Miller understood. This was a moment for Yasmine's Blanchards. Those who had lived with her all her life. Miranda disappeared into the nursery.

"Leave the children with me," she told Nacaria. "Go to your son. I'll watch the little ones."

Nacaria left Hera, Titan, Con, and Rom with Miranda and went back into the room with her family. For a moment she stood watching from the doorway. Though she was a member of this family, times like these reminded her how long she had been away from them in years past.

The room was deathly silent. No one said a word. Seth was still holding his wife in his arms as Artemis cradled him in hers. Fable laid down on the bed, wrapping her arms around Yasmine's legs with her head on her abdomen. Salem curled up on the bed beside Artemis. She pressed her cheek to her aunt's and rested her chin on Artemis' shoulder as she gently caressed Yasmine's cheek. Tears streamed down Salem's face. Demitra sat beside Fable and stroked her daughter's hair while staring into the strange face that was once her beloved niece. Nacaria moved from the door to stand behind her son, gripping his shoulder in solidarity. Arielle, falling somewhere between those who had gone downstairs and those cradling Yasmine Blanchard in their love, stood against the wall. She had not grown up with Yasmine, but she had loved her sister-in-law for years. She could not bring herself to step out of the room.

Finally, after a while, Fable asked the questions most everyone else was thinking. "Is she dead? Or is she a vampire? What is happening to her?"

Demitra closed her eyes and let her psychic ability penetrate her niece's being. It only took seconds to find the answers. "Yasmine is transitioning. When the sun goes down, she will wake up. But it won't be our Yaz. I think that person is gone now."

"She's a vampire?" Arielle asked from the wall.

"I'm afraid so," Demitra said mournfully. "Our sweet innocent little girl. This is what they've done to her."

The family embrace tightened. No one felt like letting go. Arielle moved to the bed, taking a place at Yasmine's feet. Fable reached her hand out and clasped Arielle's neck—a family chain of solidarity.

"What do we do?" Fable eventually asked Artemis. "It's Yazzy! We can't destroy her."

"No one is destroying my wife!" Seth roared, sweeping Yasmine completely into his arms, breaking the link anyone else had to her. He hunched over her with his back to the rest of the family, his body a shield to his wife's lifeless form.

Tears had stuck a few strands of Artemis' long black locks to her cheek. She pushed her hair back and looked to Seth. "Seth, she's gone," Artemis whispered. "This isn't Yasmine."

"None of you are going to hurt her!" Seth screamed. He lifted his wife's body into his muscular arms and started for the door.

"Where are you going?" Nacaria asked him.

"I don't know. But I'm going to take her where she will be safe. I can reach her. I can bring her back."

"There's no bringing her back, Seth," Artemis said, rushing to him. "This isn't reversible."

Seth whirled around, still holding Yasmine protectively. "What's your idea then? Kill my wife? The only woman I have ever loved—will ever love! This is our Yazzy. Little cute Yazzy." He kissed Yasmine's cheek. "Remember how afraid she was that night when Granddaddy brought her here? She'd lost her entire family." He looked at Fable next. "Remember when we'd play hide and seek and let her stay hidden for an hour while we ate ice cream? She never even got mad at us. She laughed about it with us. Salem? Remember how you and Beryl used to play dress up with her and put her in all kinds of outlandish outfits? You would paint up her face with the aunts' makeup, and she'd end up looking like a clown by the end of the night. It's Yaz. No one is hurting Yaz!"

Artemis placed her hand on Seth's arm. "No. No one is going to harm Yasmine. I promise you that. But we must restrain her before she wakes up, Seth."

"No, you're going to kill her."

"Look at me Seth," Artemis commanded. "I have never lied to you. I will not lie now. I promise you—No, I take vows with you. I will not allow anyone to destroy

Yasmine until we are certain she cannot be saved."

Seth believed her. He had not needed her to vow. He would have believed her anyway.

Artemis addressed everyone in the room, "Tonight we will assess the situation. We will see what danger she poses. But the sun is setting soon. We must restrain her for the night. Tomorrow we will determine what must be done."

CHAPTER THIRTY TWO

One Last Kiss

Yasmine was taken to the magic room and bound with every chain the Blanchards could find on the family property. Jerry and Echo searched the various storage rooms and outbuildings on the property until they had found the heaviest, most unbreakable restraints. They bound Yasmine to a chair, wrapping her to fit in several passes, then wrapping over her in crisscrossed lengths stretching under the chair and back around. As added precaution, Salem froze Yasmine's legs, arms, and torso leaving only her head free to move and think. It was the first time Salem had ever tried such a feat and was glad to see it worked. Yasmine sat in the chair against the fourth-floor window at the far end of the room. Seth and Artemis took positions on the other side of the room in two chairs—sentries watching. The only door to the room was guarded on both sides. Xander secured the inside and locked door while Arielle stood sentinel outside at the top of the stairs down from the tower. As the sun set through the many windows of the tower room, Seth and Artemis waited for Yasmine to awaken so that they could evaluate her condition.

As darkness descended outside, Yasmine's face twitched a bit, like a sleeper waking from a night's rest. As she attempted to move her arms to stretch, the inability to do so caused her to jerk her eyes openly quickly. She immediately took in the predicament. She sneered at her husband.

"I see you've taken the necessary precautions."

"Yaz, honey, we have to talk about this," Seth urged. "I have to know what is going on in your mind."

"My mind is awake like never before," Yasmine grinned. The two sharp fangs protruding from her mouth disfigured the simple prettiness her face once possessed. "I can hear every leaf rustling outside these windows. I hear the squirrels climbing the trunks of the oaks. I know there is a mouse living behind the wall of the kitchen pantry. I am alive."

"That's not true, Yaz. You're not alive," Seth said. "Please tell me how far this goes. Is there any way to get you back?"

"Back to what?" she laughed. "Back to watching all of you hold all the power while I cooked and cleaned and supported you?" Suddenly she stopped herself. The reddish hue to her eyes changed a little. A tiny glint of the Yasmine they knew returned. "Oh, Seth I didn't mean that! I don't know what's happening to me."

A sudden hope filled Seth. His Yaz was back—at least for the moment. Surely that meant she was still able to be saved...restored. Surely.

"Describe what you feel Yasmine," Artemis instructed.

"I can feel the power surging through me, Seth. All I need is one little taste of blood. My head is pounding. My body is aching. Blood will make that stop. I can feel it. Please Seth, let me taste you. I'm so hungry."

"He can't do that, Yasmine," Artemis said. "Please try to fight this if you can."

Yasmine shrieked in pain, "There's no fighting it. I need blood!"

Artemis approached her. The strained look upon her niece's face told Artemis that Yasmine was struggling to move her body but was unable to budge. Salem's spell was holding.

"Yasmine, we love you. We are trying to figure out what to do to save you. To get you back to the way you were. Help us. Only you know what's going on inside yourself."

Yasmine looked up into her aunt's eyes, the makings of tears looked as if they were trying to come, but they didn't. "It is too late, Aunt Artemis. I'm changing too much too fast. It's like there's a beast inside me and every second I'm slipping away. Or worse, maybe I'm starting to enjoy becoming it."

"Tell us what you're feeling."

"I want to drink," Yasmine said. "I'm starving. And I want to kill. I want to hear my victim screaming. I want to feel what it feels like when they try to fight me and know they can't. I want to smell their fear while they claw against me for life as I strike them down and drain them dry. I want to feel the rush of their blood coursing through me. I know that once I do, every joy they ever felt, every moment of ecstasy, every pain and heartbreak will surge through me like the different flavors of a delicious meal. I need to eat. *I am so hungry*!"

Artemis stood looking down at the thing her niece was becoming. She did not know what to do. She looked back at Seth. His head was in his hands. He was defeated. Powerless to save his beloved.

Then, for a brief flash, Yasmine seemed like herself again. "You have to kill me," she pleaded to her aunt. "Kill me while I still have a soul that hates what I'm becoming."

Seth rushed forward and crawled over to her. Placing his arms on her legs he looked at the many chains binding the woman he had always loved. His heart was shattered. His red face, raw from wiping tears, stared into her eyes.

"I can't kill you, Yaz. I love you more than I've ever loved anything in this world. Please stay with me. Fight this thing inside you."

"I can't," she whimpered. "Seth kiss me. Kiss me one last time and then end my suffering."

Seth leaned up and placed his hands on her cheeks. He did not know how to say goodbye. How to kiss one final kiss to someone who had defined his life. He pressed his lips to hers and kissed his wife for the last time. As he felt the stabbing pain in his bottom lip, he remembered he was not kissing his wife. He was kissing a vampire. She bit into his lip. Seth fell back in shock and stared into her eyes, eyes that were no longer Yasmine's but those of a fiend lurking beneath the exterior.

"Seth!" Xander screamed dashing forward to his son. "Seth, she bit you!"

"You taste divine," Yasmine smiled. "I want more than a mere drop or two. Give me more!"

"You bit him!' Artemis howled. "What have you done?"

"Relax, witch!" Yasmine laughed. "I just had a little sample. He is still human. To turn him I would have to infuse him with my own blood. I only wanted something to tide me over. And to give me a little strength."

The few drops of blood Yasmine acquired from her husband's lips were enough to embolden her strength. Suddenly Salem's spell was broken. Yasmine began to shake and twist and strain against the restraints. Xander dragged Seth backward to the wall as Yasmine began to pull at the chains around her wrists. The iron links of the chains stretched under her pressure until a link snapped, freeing her from the confines. Braced for her to strike, Artemis was thrown off guard when she didn't. A sudden look of terror crossed Yasmine's inhuman face. For the briefest moment her eyes returned to those of their beloved Yasmine.

"Hera!" she exclaimed. "Hera is calling for me. She wants her momma. Don't let her come up here, Artemis! Don't let her see me like this. Don't let my children see what their mother has become! Kill me! Please!"

Artemis faced Seth and Xander. Wiping her tears from her eyes she gave them a knowing nod. Seth understood what it implied. She was going to end Yasmine's existence. There was no other choice. It was what had to be done.

Seth shook his head and began shouting, "No!"

Artemis focused her mind on her power. She envisioned her grandfather's sword coming to her. Within seconds, one of the windowpanes of the tower shattered as Constantinople Blanchard's sword came bursting through and into Artemis' grasp. She whirled around to face her niece, drawing the sword behind her, ready to slice at Yasmine's neck.

"We love you, Yasmine," Artemis cried. "We love you so very much. We will always love you. It is with this love, I set your soul free."

Seth saw Artemis swing the sword forward toward his wife's throat. Instinctively he shrieked, "Daddy save her! For me!"

Xander did not understand why he did what he did. Perhaps he owed his son something for the years of neglect and estrangement. Perhaps his own heart was breaking for the lovers because he too knew what it was like to face life without the one you hold most dear. He might never know why he sprang to action at the cry of his only son, but he did. In the flash of a second, as the sword came down upon Yasmine, Xander Obreiggon zapped to her, grabbed her arm, and zapped away. The sword crashed down on the back of the empty chair. Yasmine was gone. Xander was gone. And Seth and Artemis stared in bewilderment at the blank space before them.

CHAPTER THIRTY THREE

Repercussions

Artemis was furious with her brother-in-law when he returned later that evening. Nacaria jumped to Xander's defense, but Artemis was nonetheless enraged by his actions. Seth was beside himself with grief. Sitting on the living room sofa all he could do was lean in against Fable's shoulder as she held him in her arms.

"You had no right to interfere!" Artemis roared.

"I know I overstepped," Xander replied. "But my son—"

Artemis charged forward. "Your son," she roared. "Was in grief and not of rational mind. His words were an instinctual impulse, not well thought out. Yasmine was ready. She wanted to die. In fact, she begged me to end her. You heard. You were there."

"I know, I know," Xander said. "But Seth wasn't ready. He needs more time."

"Time is something we don't have!" Artemis shouted. "Now there is a vampire loose somewhere, and it's our own Yasmine! Who knows who she might harm or kill? What if she begins a plague like the one Howard and his children just fled from? It was our duty to stop that from happening."

"I didn't think that far ahead," Xander said.

Artemis could not except his careless explanation. "As the leader of your own coven, perhaps you should have. Do you lack the forethought to anticipate such a future fallout from a decision like the one you made?"

Nacaria spoke up, "I don't think it is fair to call Xander's leadership into question."

"I think it is," Artemis cried. "His judgement just put a great many humans in danger."

"And what about us?" Echo asked. "Will we all be in danger again now? Will Seth's wife come back here to finish the job the vampires from our reality started?"

"Stay out of this Echo," Fable warned. "I don't mean to be rude to you, especially after all you've been through, but you can't possibly comprehend what we are feeling right now about losing Yaz."

"My brother doesn't feel what you guys do," Trix noted. "But we do know what it is like when the world falls to shit and its people live in constant fear and danger. I don't think he's out of line to be worried the same thing will happen here now."

"Trix is one hundred percent correct," Artemis stated. "Xander put the entire world in danger tonight."

Nacaria stepped to the center of the room and raised her hands up to calm the family. "I think we all need to take a beat and calm down. We haven't even asked Xander where he took Yasmine. Maybe we are prematurely worrying."

Xander looked around at the Blanchard faces staring at him and gave them more information. "I took Yasmine to an island I know. There are no inhabitants on that island. There is enough wildlife to feed her for a while until Seth is ready to let her go."

"There," Nacaria said. "You see, Artemis. No harm no foul."

"That's where you are wrong, baby sister," Artemis corrected. "We had a moment of clarity in the magic room. One final coherent moment of goodbye to the girl we have all loved all these years. That moment was erased by Xander's impulsive act of idiocy. Now when we find Yasmine again, it will not be our Yasmine. It will be the monster inside her. Her soul is gone now. And so is her chance for peace."

"I disagree," Nacaria said. "I think that may make it easier for us to kill her if all traces of Yasmine are gone when we find her again."

Artemis was angrier than she had ever been in her life. No one was going to convince her that anything about what Xander did that night had a silver lining. She paced the living room floor in anger. Trying to formulate a plan. Suddenly she reached for her grandfather's sword from the coffee table.

"Xander, I want you to transport me immediately to where you took Yasmine. Salem, if you would be willing to accompany us, I would appreciate the help. You can freeze Yasmine, and I will end her. We will not continue another day with this problem lurking out there."

"I'm going, too," Seth whimpered.

"No, you aren't," Salem told him. "It is dangerous now. Your children need you alive. And you have already said all that needed saying to her. What we find will not be Yasmine. Let your last memory of her be your last memory of her."

Xander clasped hands with his daughter and sister-in-law and they evaporated in a flash. When Artemis and Salem opened their eyes, they were standing on the shoreline of a dark, windy island. The rocky coastline was experiencing high tide and water loudly splashed all against the banks. There was no light except the one coming from the moon overhead and the stars. Artemis found a few stray pieces of driftwood. Envisioning lighted torches, she brought fire to the wood and handed her companions each a light. The three set off in search of the vampire.

The vegetation on the island was minimal. The island was mostly desolate. They walked for nearly two hours without a trace of Yasmine. Every so often they stumbled across the body of a rabbit or an unrecognizable animal. But never anything more. Yasmine was clearly good at hiding.

The sun came up after another couple of hours, allowing the trio to discard their torches. They retraced their steps beginning once again at the shore. With the tide moving out the trio found the shoreline was covered with some sort of crunchy substance. Upon closer inspection, Salem saw that it was actually thousands of empty clam shells, washed up to the shore from the ocean. The sound the waters made drifting over them was almost melodic.

The light of the morning was bringing no additional clues as to Yasmine's whereabouts. She was nowhere to be found. The absence of caves or rock ledges made it questionable as to how she might be able to hide from them. But on the other side of the island, they found something.

"Look," Salem said, first taking notice.

"Footprints," Artemis noted.

"Several sets," Salem added. "These are smallish, looks like the size of Yasmine's feet. The others are larger. Men maybe?"

Xander scanned the flat landscape of the island. Its low vegetation and almost non-existent treescape provided the ability to see rather far into the distance. "Someone has been here," he said. "But they are gone now. But who? Who would know about this place?"

"How do you know about this place?" Artemis asked him.

"This island belonged to Atheidrelle's family. We used to sail here from time to time. This is near Charleston."

"Atheidrelle's family?" Artemis gasped.

"Daddy, do they still own this island?" Salem asked.

"I'm not sure," Xander said. "I don't think anyone's thought about this place in years."

"Well, someone has," Artemis said, pointing back to the footprints. "Someone has been here. And perhaps that someone took Yasmine away with them."

"Why?" Xander asked.

Artemis was about to say something, about to scold him once again for his decision and the dangers it now presented, but her line of sight caught something in the distance Xander had missed. Smoke. The faint trail of smoke was drifting above the reeds and marshy stretches beyond the beach. The three of them ran toward it.

There, tied to the trunk of a burned-out tree, was a body strapped to the trunk by sooty iron chains. The misshapen remains looked to be about the same height as Yasmine would have been. Salem cried out in horror, burying her face into her father's chest.

Artemis sighed and said a quick prayer at the feet of the smoldering corpse. Standing up she cleared her face of its tears and said, "Someone handled the situation for us. Poor Yasmine. My way would have been quicker and less gruesome. Because of you, Xander, Yasmine suffered an agonizing end. Don't ever interfere in my family business again."

"I'm sorry Artemis," Xander said. "I meant to—"

"I think it's best now that you take us home. Then I think you, Nacaria, and Cassandra should probably be on your way back to Oleander. This visit has come to an end."

CHAPTER THIRTY FOUR

Moving On

Over the next few months, a dark cloud loomed over the hearts of everyone at Blanchard House, none so more than Seth. Gone was his zest for life. His joy. His heart. His depression only deepened with the passage of time. With Yasmine gone, Seth was lost inside himself and no one could reach him. He did not leave his room often. His daily gym visits were a thing of the past. Even his children held no special influence to spark meaning back into him. He interacted with them occasionally when proximity of passing in the kitchen or Hera wandering into his room put them together. But the interaction was perfunctory, not engaging. Salem moved back to Daihmler, opening offices in Tuscaloosa, but even her daily presence had no influence on Seth. His only desire was to shut himself away in the room he shared with his wife and forget a world existed outside their door.

Seth's malaise had only one benefit, it provided Miranda a distraction from her grief over Amelia and gave her a purpose. Miranda fell unceremoniously into the role of caregiver for the children. Every morning she dressed Hera and Titan, made certain they were fed, and played with them often throughout the day. Hera needed her mother while Miranda needed to feel useful and distract herself from her own grief. Their mutual longing for something missing bonded them together. At night Miranda would brush Hera's hair while she read to her. Miranda laid down with Titan at naptime and bedtime. She attended to all of his nightly feedings unless Artemis got to him first. Miranda's attentions did not stop with only Seth's children; she became a pseudo tutor for Con as well. Most afternoons Hera and Con could be found atop a blanket spread in the grass behind the house with Miranda using a set of flash cards to introduce things like math and the alphabet. She took Hera and Con to weekly Gymboree classes she'd signed them up for. Salem usually took Olympus with her to work at the new firm, but it was Miranda who volunteered to take the baby to all his pediatric checkups. And Romulus had become Miranda's constant companion until Fable would come home from work.

Fable's veterinary practice took up most of her day and her boys filled the evenings. Occasionally she tried her hand at dating again, but with dismal success. Several times a month she and Arielle hit the bar scene, but the moment men discovered Fable was a single mother, they generally disappeared back into the crowd.

Artemis was hard at work at The Cobblestone and had hired Tess as a waitress and Trix as a bartender. Echo was taken under Howard's wing and was now working full time in the office as his apprentice. Arielle now had the both of them to look after. Yasmine's holdings in Sinclair Industries fell to Howard to fully manage. Seth showed no interest in the responsibility and had signed power of attorney over to Howard. This made Arielle and Echo's assistance all the more important to help oversee the other client accounts.

Demitra and Jerry got to know their new adult great grandchildren rather well over the months and when not spending time with them, they took a few trips with Jerry's parents when work would permit. Life resumed a kind of normalcy for the family of witches. It was a false normalcy disguising an avoidance to face the difficulty of living life without Beryl and Yasmine. Beryl became a subject they rarely talked about although in truth, everyone was anticipating her return. The closer Howard Caldwell's birthday neared the more anxious the Blanchards became.

It was on a Sunday in March, about a month before his birthday, when the Blanchards got a surprise visitor on their doorstep. The house was practically empty. Fable and Miranda had taken the children to the zoo in Birmingham. Arielle hitched along, having them drop her by Quinlan Castle so she could visit with her mother. Seth was, as usual, locked away in the solitude of his bedroom. Salem was napping with the baby. Howard had the triplets out for Sunday lunch and Jerry was busy in the chicken house, replacing some boards and shingles Friday's thunderstorm had damaged. Only Artemis and Demitra were downstairs labeling a few potions they had made for some ladies in town who were having some romantic difficulties. When the knock came at the front door, Artemis answered, expecting to find one of the ladies had come to collect her concoction. The last person she expected to find was Pastoria Blanchard and her grandson Ocean standing there.

"Aunt Pastoria," Artemis gasped as the old woman waved an aged piece of paper in her hand and barged past.

Ocean followed, giving his older cousin a hug while whispering, "She insisted I drive her up here. She won't tell me what this is all about. She just said we had to come immediately."

Before she had the opportunity to shut the front door, Artemis saw Zelda's car pulling up in the driveway. As Zelda hurried into the house she declared, "Pastoria called me when she pulled into town and told me to get over here."

Artemis followed her aunt into the living room where she had already taken a seat on the couch next to Demitra. Demitra was eyeing Pastoria concernedly. Pastoria looked frail, tired—not at all in good health. It had been a while since the girls had seen their mother's sister. She had aged a great deal in the two years since they had last laid eyes upon her.

Demitra asked the obvious question. "Are you all right? You do not look well. And what's in your hand?"

"I'm not well," Pastoria told her nieces. "I'm 88 years old and time is catching up to me fast. But my health is not the reason I have come home. I have a letter to read you. It is from Beryl."

"Beryl!" Demitra exclaimed.

"Yes," Pastoria said. "She wrote it many years ago when she and I were almost the same age. She told me to hold onto it until the night before Howard's birthday."

"That's still a month away," Artemis pointed out.

"Yes, but…" Pastoria stopped speaking. She coughed a little into a handkerchief and tried to continue but couldn't. She nudged her grandson to speak for her.

"Grandmother is pretty sick. Cancer. She found out last week." Ocean looked as if he were about to cry. "Stage 4. Lungs. Not much they can do."

Demitra gripped the young man's hand in solidarity. "What can we do for her?"

"No one can do anything," Ocean replied. "If Beryl were here, maybe. But grandmother says she'll be dead by then. She said she had to deliver something before it was too late."

Artemis understood now. "So, you two have come early. Before Howard's birthday."

"Yeah."

Pastoria coughed again into her linen as she handed Demitra the letter. Demitra read it aloud.

Dear Mother,

The days are drawing nearer to having the baby. It has been a bittersweet experience knowing I will miss all the important years of Howard's life. Carrying my baby these last months has been hard but strangely joyful. I know that with his arrival comes my end here, but I understand now that my purpose is greater than my despair. I made my peace with it all months ago.

I have genuinely enjoyed my time here. I have come to know Olympia and Pastoria, and even zany old Zelda so well these last months. In a strange way I have felt at home. Nate and I got married! He really, truly loves me. And I love him. At last, I know real and lasting romantic love. We have been very happy under the circumstances. I suppose knowing the end date to your life forces one to find the happiness in every moment.

You can never know how much I have missed you all. For a long time, I looked forward to getting back to your time and seeing you all again. Resuming my old life was something to look forward to. Yet as I remained here longer, this became my life in a manner of speaking. The idea of leaving Nate, Olympia, Pastoria, and Zelda deeply saddens me.

But as it turns out I think I was mistaken to assume my life would go back to how it was before. I have changed. I am still changing. Profoundly changing, Mother. Something is happening to me which I do not fully understand. It is physical as well as spiritual.

Do you remember how I was mysteriously invulnerable to Atheidrelle's attack a few years ago? It has been happening again, this time with frequency. A couple of months ago I was crossing the intersection in town after having lunch with my husband. (I love saying that...my husband). I suppose I didn't look properly before I stepped off the curb. A man in a pickup truck crashed into me. The front of his truck wrapped around my legs, indenting the truck but leaving me unscathed. I am apparently invulnerable now.

My healing abilities have magnified as well. I visited a hospital wing a couple of weeks ago, to heal a certain sick child. The strangest thing happened while I was there. While healing her I had the feeling I could simultaneously heal the little boy in the bed next to her. I found myself connecting to them both at the same time as my powers began to restore them to health. But then I suddenly became aware of another child behind the wall in the next room. I felt as if I could loop that child into my healing thread as well. Then I sensed that child's roommate. I suddenly found myself healing the entire children's ward all in one effort. I am not sure what is happening, but my powers are expanding and evolving rapidly.

Mother, I know things now. I do not speak about them to Nate or my sisters. (That's what I call Olympia and Pastoria these days). I should not impart future events into their minds if I can avoid it. But Mom, I know Howard has children. Somehow, I know he has children even though in my other reality he was a bachelor and childless. And Mom, I can feel that Yasmine is gone. Did she die? Somehow, I can feel that her soul has vanished.

There is more. It is something I am saddened to write, but also exhilarated to experience. I will not be returning home when Howard is born. I can feel it. Feel it. The same way that I know about Howard's children and Yasmine's death, I know I will not be returning to your timeline. I cannot explain it. There is a glowing goldenness lurking beneath me. Like a light piercing through all realities and filling my soul day by day. I can see it. I can feel it. I feel so powerful. Changed. I have such peace. I have no idea what is happening to me, or where I am going once the baby is born, but in my soul of souls I have the knowledge that it will not be my old reality I return to. I am not coming back.

Tell Nacaria there is no need to come for me. It would not make any difference. I am headed to somewhere there are no words to describe. Know that I love you. I love Fable. Tell Howard how much I have loved him. I am proud of the man he grows up to be. It has been my great privilege to learn I was his mother. Take care of everyone at home. I love you all.

Forever yours,
Beryl Blanchard Caldwell
(I just wanted to write that. I have had such a good marriage)

Demitra looked to Artemis. "She isn't coming back."

Artemis grabbed her sister's hand in support as well as sorrow. "Your daughter is becoming a God. She is moving on to bigger things we will never fathom."

"We've lost her," Demitra sobbed. "I will never see my little girl again."

Artemis thought for a moment then smiled brightly. "Not necessarily."

CHAPTER THIRTY FIVE

Goodbye

Artemis and Nacaria had not spoken for a long time. Ever since that night when Xander interfered with Yasmine's death, Artemis hadn't had contact with her youngest sister. When she telephoned Nacaria in Charleston, it was a surprise to Nacaria. At first Nacaria seemed cold, still harboring resentment for the way her eldest sister had admonished Xander. But once she heard the reason for the call all animosity melted away. Artemis told Nacaria that Demitra needed her and Nacaria was not going to let her sisters down.

Xander teleported himself and Nacaria to Blanchard House a few minutes after the call came in. Nacaria found her sisters waiting in the kitchen. She came in, with Xander in tow, and nonchalantly poured herself and her husband a cup of coffee. Artemis gave Xander a nod. He nodded back. And like that it was understood all was forgiven and need not be mentioned again.

"So, I understand we are taking a little trip," Nacaria winked to Demitra. "I have already prepared the potions. I just need to grab a few grains of Mother's bone dust from the vault, and I will be able to transport Demitra and myself back."

"I can't believe it," Demitra tearfully said. "Thank you. The thought that I would never be able to see my daughter again...thank you for doing this."

Nacaria smiled, her own tears beginning to well up. "I'd do anything for you, sister." She exchanged glances with Artemis. "I'd do anything for both of my sisters."

The three Blanchard sisters embraced. Nothing was powerful enough to divide them permanently. No squabble, no hurt, no force on earth. They had lived through far too much together to ever be truly parted.

"Are you certain you don't want to go too, Artemis?" Nacaria asked. "I can get all three of us there."

Artemis shook her head. "Though I would love to see Beryl one last time, this trip is for Demitra. This is about a mother and her child. I will stay here. Beryl already knows how much she means to me. I have a feeling Beryl is beginning to know everything there is to know about everything. This trip is for Demitra to say goodbye and find peace."

When Nacaria and Demitra materialized, they found themselves standing in the lawn behind the house in the exact location where the kitchen they had just left would eventually be built. Around them they observed the area was roped off with stakes and twine. Standing a few feet away wearing extremely startled expressions on their faces, were young Olympia Blanchard and a man.

"Well, that was unexpected," Olympia proclaimed as she addressed her arrivals. "Nacaria! You've returned! And brought a friend I see."

Demitra was flabbergasted. There stood her mother—her very own mother Olympia Blanchard—standing four feet from her. She was young, younger than Demitra. Younger even than Demitra's youngest child. She had no idea what to say.

Nacaria, being a little more experienced with this situation, made the introductions. "Olympia, I'd like you to meet my sister Demitra."

Olympia's face brightened as she took Demitra into her arms. "Well, holy shit!" Olympia cried. "I have another daughter to meet! I have heard so much about you from Beryl."

"I'm sorry—" Demitra stuttered. "This is quite a lot to take in. Wow! Mother. You were stunning."

"Yes, I am a great beauty," Olympia said boastfully. "Everyone thinks so. Ladies, I'd like you to meet John Windham. I believe he is your father from what I've gathered."

John Windham was tall and slender. He wore a light gray suit and had a look of utter bewilderment across his long thin face. His dark hair was clearly where Demitra and Artemis got theirs. He smiled at the sisters, then bowed for some reason, followed by an apologetic chuckle.

"Forgive me ladies," he said. "Olympia's world is something I know about but try to steer clear of. She has told me a little about you two, and I believe there is a third sister as well. You will bear with me if I seem uneasy. This is a little surreal for my tastes."

"Yes," Olympia laughed. "I have agreed to keep the supernatural world as far away from our marriage as I can. John and I are to be married in a few months."

"Hence the kitchen," Demitra pointed out.

"How's that?" John asked.

"These stakes and lines," Demitra noted. "You're getting ready to build the family kitchen, complete with a secret vault underneath for all the Blanchard family magics to be stored where you don't have to see them."

John looked a little surprised by her knowledge on the matter. "Why yes, actually. The construction crew will break ground next week. How did you—"

"They are your daughters John," Olympia reminded him with a tone which indicated he was possibly the stupidest person in the group. "I'm sure they've heard the story before."

Both Demitra and Nacaria were trying to remain nonchalant. Not an easy task, considering neither of them had ever seen their father before—not in a way where they ever remembered him. This man standing before them was their very own father. It was an occasion they never expected to walk into. They savored every second of it. They found themselves mentally recording every trait he possessed. The tone of his voice. His mannerisms. His awkwardness in the sight of witchcraft. His demeanor with their mother. These would be the only memories they would ever own of John Windham.

John did not seem to be as enthralled with learning about his future daughters as they were in him. Though he was not rude, he was brief. Expected in his office in half an hour, he made his excuses for departure and bid the strangers an awkward farewell. He kissed his intended on the lips and left to begin his day. Olympia turned to her adult daughters and grinned proudly.

"He's very handsome, isn't he?"

"He really is," Nacaria answered.

"We make very beautiful children together I can see," Olympia grinned. "I can't wait to get to that part!"

Demitra blushed. She had never heard her mother speak so brazenly before.

"Did I embarrass you?" Olympia sniggered. "You'll be happy to know your mom is a virgin when she marries. If you get technical about it. We have done some stuff."

"Oh my God, I really don't want this in my mind," Demitra snapped. "Can we see Beryl now?"

"Oh, Beryl doesn't live here anymore," Olympia informed them. "She moved in with Nate once they were married. She's a regular little housewife now."

"Beryl?" Demitra gasped. The idea of Dr. Beryl Blanchard as a housewife was the most foreign concept. Demitra could not envision her eldest daughter—so full of independence and ambition—being content with such a life.

"Oh, my yes," Olympia chuckled. "She gets up every morning, cooks her man breakfast, sends him off to work, cleans the house, does the laundry, irons his shirts. But she pops over here for lunch most days so just hang out awhile and she'll be on over."

On their way inside Demitra whispered to Nacaria, "I cannot picture my daughter, Miss Independent Doctor, as a 1960s housewife."

"She's a Mrs. now. I guess she always wanted to see what it feels like to be another kind of woman. Now she has had the chance. Frankly, I'm happy for her."

"I am too," Demitra said. "Only it just doesn't sound like my Beryl."

Nacaria did not disagree but added, "I think she's experimenting with being her own Beryl now. While she can."

Around half past noon, while Demitra and Nacaria were sitting at the small round table in the kitchen (which would eventually become the Blanchard dining room), they heard the front door open and shut. Demitra nearly jumped out of her skin when she heard that sweet familiar voice ring out from the hall.

"Girls, I'm home!" Beryl Caldwell called as she bounded into the kitchen. "I am starving too! It's like the closer little Howard here gets to his due date, the hungrier—"

Beryl stopped in her tracks as she turned the corner to the kitchen. Locking eyes with her mother, she burst into tears from the doorway. Without saying anything, she merely opened her arms. It took only a second for Demitra to react. The woman standing in the doorway was not what she had anticipated. Her normally thin, trim, professional daughter now had a hugely round stomach poking out over lemon yellow capri pants and a swirly pink and orange maternity blouse. She wore a psychedelic scarf tied around her head with the ends dangling over her right shoulder. Beryl authentically looked like someone from the 1960s and nothing like Demitra had expected.

"Beryl!" Demitra finally cried, jumping from her chair and taking her daughter into her arms. The mother pressed her child's head onto her shoulders and the two wept for a long time without saying a word.

Nacaria glanced over to the stove where Olympia was watching the same scene play out. She was mid-flip in a pork chop when she set the spatula down to dry her eyes on a dish towel. Nacaria rose and walked around Demitra and Beryl to give Olympia a gentle side hug herself.

"Touching to see them like this isn't it?" Nacaria said.

Olympia wiped more tears from her porcelain cheeks. "It really is. I couldn't stand my mother! Seeing them…are we like that when you all are born?"

Nacaria laughed and hugged her twenty-something mother again. This time Demitra pulled out of her hug with Beryl and went over to young Olympia as well. "Yes," Demitra smiled. "We are exactly like this. You and your daughters are the best of friends, all of your lives."

"That's so sweet," Olympia replied, smudging her eye make-up with the dish towel again. "My mother was such a bitch."

"I've met your mother," Nacaria laughed. "She really was."

Demitra rejoined her daughter and the two of them sat down, holding both hands across from each other. For a time, mother and daughter used no words, their eyes said everything.

Finally, Beryl broke the silence. "Olympia, I had no idea when I came over… I thought it would just be you and me and Pastoria. Zelda called me this morning to say she has a reading and won't make lunch today."

"I was pretty surprised too when these ladies appeared out of thin air while John and I were going over the kitchen plans in the backyard. Glad they didn't show up ten minutes before that or they'd have seen quite a show."

"Is Mother kind of a tramp in her youth?" Demitra whispered to Beryl with a smile.

Beryl winked. "Turns out, she was young once too!"

"Oh, how I have missed you," Demitra cried.

"I've missed you too Mom, but didn't you get my letter?"

"Of course, I got your letter. That's why I'm here! I can't just never see my little girl again. I had to come back and see you one last time," Demitra said.

Olympia went back to frying her porkchops as she talked over her shoulder rather nonchalantly about the enormous changes happening. "We can't figure out for the life of us what is going on with Beryl. My sister is at the library right now trying to figure it all out. Doubt she'll find any books with this kind of thing in them, but she went to look up India and Zen Buddhist teachings. We figure Beryl is in some state of enlightenment we've never heard of."

Demitra whispered to her daughter, "I know what's happening to you. Take a walk with me after lunch."

Lunch lasted three hours. Pastoria got home in the middle of it and the five Blanchard women whiled away the time in laughter, sisterhood, and reflection. It was a moment in time neither Demitra nor Nacaria would ever trade for anything. Demitra learned so much about her daughter's time in the past—as well as a little of what Olympia's life was like in the 60s. As the stories began rolling out, Nacaria and Demitra learned a little more about some of those exciting adventures Olympia, Pastoria, and Zelda had in their youth. Fighting a few supernatural creatures still roaming the earth and not yet totally stamped out by the Witches Council. What Demitra had not known was that Beryl tagged along on a few of those escapades, her much-needed healing power coming in handy to save innocent victims and even Olympia and Pastoria on occasion from battle wounds which would have otherwise been fatal.

After lunch, Nacaria helped clean up the dishes with Olympia while Demitra led Beryl outside for a walk around the property. Demitra marveled at what things once looked like before she was born, but primarily her focus was her daughter.

"Tell me about my grandchildren," Beryl asked excitedly. "I will never meet them I don't suppose. Tell me what they are like. Who is their mother? Did Howard marry in this new reality?"

"We never met his wife," Demitra explained. "Her name was Barbara. That's all we know. She had been dead a year or two already when Howard met them. But your grandchildren, Beryl…they are truly extraordinary. So powerful."

"Are they nice people?"

"They are," Demitra beamed. "Tess is the wise one, like you. Trix is tough as nails, but kind. Echo—Echo is so handsome. And he has the power to heal, like you have, though it isn't honed yet. They bring me a great deal of joy."

"I'm glad."

"What happened to Yaz?" Beryl asked, her face changing into one of deep sadness. "I feel her soul is gone. It feels like death."

"She is dead," Demitra frowned. "She was attacked in the other reality and turned into a vampire. When she came home, we didn't know she was changing until it was too late."

"You guys had to kill her?"

"We tried. But something interfered. It really doesn't matter now. Someone killed her, we know. We aren't sure who, but it really doesn't matter so much I suppose. She's gone forever."

"How is Seth?"

"Devastated. He will never be the same."

"I am sorry I won't be back," Beryl said. "I feel such guilt over that. It sounds like the family is hurting. My absence is going to add to that."

"It isn't your fault, my love," Demitra stopped walking and placed her hands on her daughter's shoulders, directing her to look into her eyes. "You are fated for greater things. It is your destiny." Demitra turned from Beryl and looked out to the magnificent sky above them and all that falls under it. "In fact Beryl, more and more I am realizing it has been destiny all along for all of this to come to pass."

Beryl did not understand what she meant.

"Salem's little boy set a course into motion which has undone all we ever thought things would be. There must be a reason for that. Some greater reason we are not meant to understand. God understands. You, Beryl, will also soon understand. Stitches in time have been sewn, largely by you. What fabric it will create none of us know for sure, but I have come now to trust that there is a reason."

Beryl could feel that her mother was correct. Some greater will was at work, and Beryl felt it was also at work inside her. "Do you know what is happening to me, Mother? I am not afraid. Not afraid at all. I trust everything I feel. But my curiosity does get the better of me sometimes. What is happening to me?"

Demitra took a deep breath and looked her daughter squarely in the eyes and said, "Beryl, you are becoming God. Literally."

Beryl's eyes widened. "Me? I don't understand?"

Demitra smiled. "I think your mind—no, your soul—is beginning to understand incrementally as it is able to. You are becoming something none of the rest of us can fathom. There are no words for what you are destined to be."

"Why me?" Beryl asked. "What have I ever done that deserved such a fate?"

Demitra laughed. "Darling, when I look back upon your life, your grace, your character, your compassion...I can think of no one else I've ever met that should receive such a destiny. They call it The God Strain. There have been others like you throughout time. And now your time has come. It's the only reason I can give you up without my heart ripping to shreds."

Beryl laid her head on her mother's shoulder as they continued to look skyward at a presence neither of them could see, or even knew was there. It just felt as if it were—lurking somewhere up there in the heavens. Demitra wiped a tear and said, "Every day for the rest of my life I will mourn the loss of you. But when I look up at the universe, I will take comfort knowing that you are somewhere out there making it all go round in whatever special ways you will. You'll be in everything I see every day. A bloom. A raindrop. An ant crawling. A newborn crying. My daughter. One of God's chosen. A God herself."

...

Nacaria and Demitra did not leave that day. They remained until Beryl's due date. Demitra got to know her son-in-law. Nacaria spent more time with her mother and aunt. They both even helped Olympia plan her wedding to their father. And then came the special day, the day they knew Howard would be born.

As the contractions began, Beryl clung to Nate Caldwell, her husband. He stood by her bedside the entire six hours of her labor. Demitra gave them their space, agreeing to come in only at the end. She understood that though Beryl belonged to her once, Beryl belonged to Nate now...and Olympia and Pastoria and Zelda. Nate Caldwell would live the rest of his life raising his son alone, loving the one woman he would lose that night. Theirs was a true love. Storybook, with a tragic ending. Demitra gave it the respect it deserved and kept out of their way.

"I will always love you Beryl, my sweet," Nate sobbed as he said his final goodbyes to his wife. Her pains were growing more intense. The baby was crowning. It would all be over soon. "I will never regret a moment of our short life together. It was the best gift life ever gave me."

Beryl looked into her husband's eyes. She waited for the agony of the last contraction to pass so that she could speak to him. "I have no idea what happens next for me, Nate. But baby, I need you to know that nothing that has ever happened in my life measures up to one moment I have spent loving you." She took another breath and squeezed it out in successions as the next contraction hit. Once it subsided, she added, "Please let our son know his mother loved him. He can never know until he's grown who I was, but you can tell him of the love I have for him."

"He will know, Beryl," Nate vowed. "I promise you he will know you loved him."

"I may be missing out on his childhood," Beryl added. "But I have the privilege of having known him as a man. Oh, Nate what a good man our son turns out to be."

Demitra approached her daughter's bed. It suddenly struck her as ironic that she had given birth to Beryl in this same bed, in this same room at Blanchard House, thirty years from now. "My sweet angel girl," Demitra smiled, stroking Beryl's sweaty forehead as her other hand clutched her daughter's. "It has been my esteemed privilege to be your mother. I have never loved anything as much as I have loved you, my first born."

"You'll watch over Howard and my grandchildren?"

"You know I will."

"I love you, Momma. Thank you for everything you ever did for me. Thank you for being the kind of mother I wish I had the opportunity to be. I became everything I am because of you..." she paused and looked over at the doorway. "And you three fools," she laughed.

Demitra looked behind her and saw young Olympia, Pastoria, and Zelda filling the doorway. Beryl motioned them closer. She took hold of all three of their hands.

"You have been my sisters these last months. My very best friends. Thank you." And to Olympia alone she said, "And later on, you're about the most wonderful thing any of us ever knows. Thank you for who you will become in my life." She grabbed their hands and her mother's and smiled. "We are the Blanchard Witches of Daihmler County. I love you all."

Suddenly she grew rigid as the final contractions came upon her. Zelda scooted everyone out of the way and got in position to take the baby. Beryl screamed in pain. Nate moved closer to her and held her hands as she pushed. Her reddened face shook, and her breath caught as she gave that one final push to set baby Howard free to the world. Zelda pulled the baby out and held its mucus covered body up for Beryl to see, the umbilical cord still dangling. Beryl's face grew joyous. Angelic almost, as she laid eyes upon her son.

Those eyes brightened. And brightened. The shine from them turned a kind of yellow, then golden, then to almost a piercing blinding white. The others in the room shielded their own as Beryl's entire being began a continual escalation of glow which was much too much for a mortal eye. A sudden flash bounded from within her. The light she emanated passed through them all and everything else in the room. Without knowing why, Nate and the women turned their heads away—the moment far too Holy for them to witness. The explosion of light burst outward, illuminating the room until nothing in it was perceivable. Then, as quickly as the light burst, it was gone. And so was Beryl. The bed was empty. Beryl Blanchard had moved on.

Nate fell onto the bed grasping the sheets, sobbing for his wife. Demitra stood shell shocked at what she had just seen. Olympia instinctively knew what to do. She took hold of the baby from Zelda's trembling hands and handed him to Demitra Blanchard. Demitra broke from her shock and looked down at her crying grandson. The smile returned to her face as she looked into the eyes of that tiny being and knew he was a small piece of herself.

She lifted him to her face and gave his forehead its first earthly kiss. "I love you, Howard Caldwell. Welcome to the world. I will be seeing you again in a few years."

CHAPTER THIRTY SIX

The Matriarch

Howard did not hear the door to his office open when Demitra Blanchard came in. He glanced up from his computer to see her tear-stained face drawing closer to him. He stood to greet her only to find that she had wrapped her arms around his back and pulled him in to perhaps the tightest embrace he'd ever had.

"I love you," she said. "I love you so much. You are part of me and always will be. I don't care who is older than who. You are my grandson, and you are my heart and soul."

Howard had no idea how to respond. He hugged her back nervously and said, "And I love you too, Demitra. Are you okay?"

She released him and sat on the edge of his desk, smiling. "I have just come back from watching you be born. And it was probably the most beautiful moment of my life."

Howard plopped down in his comfy desk chair, amazed at what he had just heard. "You were where?"

She leaned forward. "Oh, Howard, I have so much to tell you. So much Beryl told me to tell you. She loved you so much. I cannot begin to explain how much. But she isn't coming back. Her destiny has already taken her on to other things we will not ever understand. But I will tell you everything she said."

"Beryl isn't coming back?" Howard replied. He looked so disheartened. As if he might cry.

Demitra shook her head. "I'm so sorry. She can't. They took her. Whoever runs the show out there, they wanted her now. Your birth was the starting point to whatever lies ahead for her."

"I see," Howard frowned, not knowing how to process the disappointment.

Demitra took hold of his hand and with her other she lightly touched his forehead. "I was there though, Howard. I was there the moment you came into this world. And

I gave you your very first kiss, right here on your head. You will always have me. I am sorry your mother was taken. But I am here. I will always be here for you. Always."

The Cobblestone restaurant was hopping when Demitra, Howard, and Echo pulled up. As they handed the car off to the valet and traversed the stairs up to the restaurant, they could see the back of Trix Blanchard through the windows of the bar. Artemis had said she was turning into quite the bartender. Demitra understood why as they approached the doors to enter. Through the glass, had one been paying close attention, three glasses were being filled with ice, liquor, and a mixer without any hands assisting while Trix was busy flirting with the customer at the bar in front of her. One by one the finished cocktails floated unseen by anyone not outside the window, over to her where she lifted them from behind the counter and placed them on the bar to their prospective owners.

"That's a little dangerous," Howard pointed out to his companions as they walked in. "What if someone catches her doing that?"

"You think Trix gives a damn?" Echo scoffed. "She always does exactly what she wants to do. Just let it go."

The manager of the restaurant sat the three generations of Blanchards at a table and told them their server would be with them momentarily. Tess was their server. She finished delivering food to the hungry patrons behind them and approached their table.

"Hi!" Tess smiled. "How is my wonderful family today? Hungry? We have a swordfish that looks amazing."

"Is it fresh?" Echo asked.

Tess gave him the eye and said, "We live in the middle of Alabama. The nearest ocean is hours away. So no, I doubt it's very fresh. But it is delicious."

"Can you take a break and eat with us?" Demitra asked. "I happen to know the owner quite well. I think she'd be okay with it."

"Uh, you can broach that subject if you want to, but I wouldn't advise it. Aunt Artemis just fired one of the cooks and is back there doing it herself. I am not about to ask her anything today. But I get off in an hour anyway. I'll join you for dessert."

Trix had the same schedule and promised to pop over to the table when her shift was completed. While Demitra, Howard, and Echo ate dinner, Demitra kept noticing Howard spying on the bar.

"Relax," Demitra said. "No one can see her using her powers. It's fine."

"I'm not worried about her using her *powers*," Howard scoffed. "But look at the way she's carrying on with the male customers. She's practically poking her chest out at them."

"It is official Howard," Demitra laughed. "You are a dad."

Echo laughed and patted Howard on the back. "Look at this way Dad, my sisters and I didn't have much of a chance to date back in our world. Trix is just having a good time and enjoying herself in a way she never got to."

"It's too much, if you ask me," Howard said. "She's acting like..."

"Fable," Demitra smiled. "Remember how wild Fable was at that age? I see a lot of Fable in Trix. She'll figure it out. Fable turned out fine."

Echo gave his great grandmother the eye and asked, "Didn't she fall in love with a werewolf who almost killed all of you?"

"Well, there were some mistakes here and there," Demitra chuckled.

The girls joined them at the table once their shifts were over. Trix bragged about all the tips she had made that night and Tess teased her over the way she'd made them. Howard gave a little speech about presenting oneself in respectable ways so as to not create a false impression and end up with a poor reputation. The girls gave him the "Dad respect" and listened but made eye rolls to one another.

Demitra told them all about her experience with Beryl and the things Beryl knew about their existence. She told them the message Beryl had for them all and how much their grandmother truly loved each and every one of them. Though the kids had never once met Beryl Blanchard, the idea of her and her regard for them gave them a sense of pride and happiness.

"It is important to me that you know about her," Demitra told them. "But I also know she is, and now will always be, a stranger to you. Even to Howard here a little. He has known Beryl all her life, but he has never seen her since learning she is his mother. Now that she is gone, I hope you will all lean on me when you need her. You are all part of me. I will always be here for the four of you, for the rest of my life."

"You realize, Dee, I am probably going to die before you," Howard chuckled.

"If you keep eating the way you eat you definitely will," Demitra retorted.

"You're a great great-grandmother," Tess smiled at Demitra. "In fact, I'm going to start calling you GG. Nobody else will understand, but we will."

"GG," Demitra smiled. "I like it."

"I do too," Echo chimed in, lifting her hand. "Our GG."

...

Back at Blanchard House, the children were all tucked away in bed for the night as Miranda made her way down the hall to grab herself a bite to eat downstairs. She saw light under Seth's door. She gave a soft knock. He grumbled something.

"Seth," she began. "The kids are asleep now. I was going down to make myself a sandwich. Can I make you something and bring it up to you?"

"No," he muttered from behind the door. He paused and added a grouse, "Thank you."

Miranda went downstairs where she found that Fable had the same idea. Fable was mid bite of a double-decker sandwich when Miranda stepped down.

"Join me?"

"I think I will," Miranda said. "I am tired. I think Titan is teething again. He has been very fussy all day."

"Once those teeth start coming in, they keep coming," Fable smiled.

"Oh, Con and Hera are talking about school again," Miranda said. "I think they really want to go to school with other children. Have you thought about enrolling them?"

"I have thought about it," Fable said. "I think Con should go to school. I was worried it might make Rom jealous, but Con has to grow up as normally as possible. I'll get him enrolled before fall semester starts. But you'll have to speak to Seth about Hera."

Miranda gave a sad frown. "I can't really talk to Seth about much. He doesn't ever come out of that room. Besides, even though I have been here several months, I still don't really know Seth. He is pretty much a recluse. Can you handle Hera's enrollment?"

Fable gave it some thought as she took two more bites and said, "I'll enroll her myself. But I will list you as guardian. That child must have a parental figure with school. I am so sorry the kids have sort of fallen onto your shoulders—"

"Oh, I love it!" Miranda exclaimed. "At first it made me feel useful. Like I was contributing back for all you guys have given me. But now... now I really love those kids. Not just Seth's, all of them. I like looking after them."

"And you have been a lifesaver around here for it," Fable said. "I'll enroll Hera and list you as her designated parent. I am afraid Seth is not going to come out of this funk for quite a while. If ever."

"Is this healthy for him?" Miranda asked.

Fable patted the stool beside her at the counter and as Miranda sat down, she gave her a bit of a history lesson. "Yasmine grew up here. She was like a sister to us all. She and Seth had an incredibly special relationship all their lives. We never really understood it until they finally admitted they were in love. From then on, it was crazy real. They fought like siblings, loved like Romeo and Juliet, and were each other's absolute best friend and hero. Love such as they had doesn't happen much. Seth is not ever going to get over losing her. I don't even try to reach him now. And he and I were always close. But this loss, it's too big to climb over. He's soaking in it, and I think he will need to soak in it for a long time. We just need to give him the space he needs to work it all out. Until then, those kids need a parent. And you are doing a pretty great job being that for them. Thank you."

CHAPTER THIRTY SEVEN

We Are the Blanchard Family

Artemis debated on whether or not it was a wise idea to have a big family cookout. In the months since Yasmine died and Beryl left, the Blanchards teetered on a fine line between moving forward with life and remaining latched to the past by continuing to mourn their losses. Amid all of it, Demitra was experiencing a kind of renewal. Losing her eldest child had not darkened her excitement for the new life ahead with Howard and the new additions to the family. Demitra's great-grandchildren had never experienced a Blanchard family event and she argued Artemis into submission.

Xander, Nacaria, and Cassandra came down from Charleston, and Arielle invited Blackie to drive down from Birmingham. Jerry invited his parents, Cally and Vestus. The Millers had finally been told about Demitra's family and if truth be told they rather enjoyed their visits to see their supernatural in-laws. Cally had developed a special kinship with Romulus, who rarely left her side on visits.

Jerry knew instantly that his parents had arrived, along with their dog Tipton, because Romulus sprang from the doorway, down the road chasing their car, howling the entire time until Cally stepped out to pet his back. Though Tipton was merely a dog, Romulus did enjoy running over the fields with him in ways none of his cousins or his brother could.

Fable watched from the yard as the two canines traversed fields she used to play in as a child herself. It made her happy to watch. Salem passed Olympus off to Cassandra who rarely ever got time with her nephew. Everyone helped everyone unpack their cars and lay out all of the various contributions people had prepared for the meal and brought from home.

Artemis, Demitra, and Nacaria stood together on the side porch watching their enormous family gather together on the side lawn where the picnic tables were set up. Xander went into the house through the back door and crept up the kitchen stairs to his son's room. He didn't bother knocking. He barged right in. Seth was sitting on the bed, staring into nothingness as his father sat down beside him.

"Son, it's time for you to come down now. It's time for you to rejoin this family. You've locked yourself away long enough."

"Leave me alone," Seth said, pulling away and turning himself onto his side where he could face the wall.

"Son, listen to me," Xander said. "I know what it's like to lose the one you love. Your heart breaks into pieces, and you feel like you might die from the pain. Then when you don't die from it, well, that's almost worse because you have no escape."

"Yeah, but you ended up getting to be with your love. I never will."

"You're right Seth," Xander said. "I did. Yet it took me twenty years. For twenty years I felt the way you do now. But Seth, there is another reason you need to get out of this room and rejoin life. You have children, son."

"You did too."

Xander felt a pang of guilt and deep shame. "Yes, I did. And I chose to pretend I didn't. I chose to live inside myself and drown in my pain. I did exactly what you are doing now, Seth. And how did that make you feel growing up?"

Seth shifted a few inches. Xander took it as a sign he had struck a nerve.

"How did that make you feel, son?" Xander repeated. "Did you feel valued? Did you grow up knowing your father loved you? I did love you, you know. But did you ever feel that I did? Or did you grow up wondering why you were not enough to coax your dad out of his living death and come to you? Remember what that felt like, Seth. Remember how it felt believing you were not enough for me, enough to jolt me into being in your life. That's how your little girl and your little boy feel now."

Seth rolled onto his back, a tear starting in his eye.

"Isn't Hera about the same age Salem was then?" Xander went on. "Isn't Titan about the age you were—give or take a year? History does like to repeat itself doesn't it, son. Please do not make the mistakes I made. Your children need their father. So did my children. I made the wrong choice. It took years to undo the damage. And judging by the way you are acting today, I didn't undo the damage. My son is following my example. Please, Seth. Be better than me! Be your children's hero."

Xander left the room. Seth was still on his back, staring into space and time. Xander Obreiggon hoped he had reached him. Hoped he had stopped him from continuing to do something he'd hate himself the rest of his life for.

Outside, Cally and Vestus were meeting Echo, Tess, and Trix for the first time. Miranda was busy arranging the plates and silverware when Arielle grabbed her by the arm and dragged her over to the Millers.

"And this is Miranda. She's an honorary Blanchard like myself and you guys. She's always lurking in the background because she thinks she's in our way. But we could not do anything without Miranda. She is such a help with all the kids."

"So, you are the woman our great grandson raves about!" Vestus exclaimed. "Every time we talk to Con he goes on and on about Miranda and how much fun she is. It's a pleasure to meet you, my dear."

Miranda smiled. It made her feel as if she belonged knowing Con had told his great grandparents about her.

Nacaria was holding Titan on her hip and attempting to get him to show her his loose tooth when out of the corner of her eye she saw her son step out of the back door. She elbowed Xander next to her and gestured in the direction. Xander smiled and crossed the yard toward his son. Artemis saw Seth emerge from the house and gave a wink to Salem.

Two cars were coming down the road, one at top speed as it always did. Zelda was late and she knew it. The old woman popped out of her car and to everyone's surprise, her hair was mossy green. As she walked across the yard in her flowy orange dress, everyone stopped whatever they were doing and stood looking at her aghast.

"Zelda!" Fable cried. "What the hell happened to your hair?"

"My stupid daughter Sarah did this to me this morning. I can't get it out."

"With that hair and that dress, you look like an Ompa Lumpa," Seth laughed as he swept his daughter up into his arms. Little Hera was laughing at Zelda as she wrapped her arms around her Daddy's neck. Something she hadn't done in ages.

"I can fix it, Zelda," Miranda promised. "After lunch I'll run into town and grab some color at one of the beauty supply stores. I can get that green out."

"Well, I'll thank you to try!" Zelda cried. "I done felt like a blame fool all day! Had a readin' this mornin' and my client wouldn't stop laugh'in. So, I told her she had chlamydia. She don't, but it serves her right."

The second car was pulling in now, Blackie's car. Arielle ran out to greet her mother, as did Nacaria. Nacaria had not seen her best friend in months, although they did frequently text one another. Blackie D'Angelo was just as beautiful as the last time anyone had seen her. Flowing black hair, smooth white skin, aged in the correct places to demonstrate she was middle aged, but still a great beauty.

Arielle escorted her to the yard and began to make the introductions. Trix, Tess, and Echo stood motionless. They said not a word, only looked to one another, then back to Blackie. Finally, the silence was broken when Tess raised her hand to touch Blackie's cheek.

"Momma!"

"My God," Trix gasped. "It is. Momma, you're alive!"

Trix fell onto Blackie, sobbing, gripping her tight. Blackie looked to Arielle in confusion, then over to Nacaria.

"Oh, dear Heaven," Nacaria said, placing her hand over her mouth. "Barbara. Barbara Blanchard was Blackie D'Angelo."

CHAPTER THIRTY EIGHT

The House of Duquesne

It was soberly dark on the marsh as the moonlight shone over the grassy swamplands. The House of Duquesne stood tall like a demon staring out over the land. The lighted windows like eyes, the stony parapets like a drawn mouth positioned to scream. Thaddeuss D'Angelo walked the stone corridors of the massive house. He stepped onto the wide stone staircase of the main hall and climbed each thick wedged step to the large landing above. The gallery of paintings which depicted the members of his family, each more sinister looking than the next, stood tall and overpowering around him. He walked to the portrait of his sister and stood before it.

"We have a chance now. A chance that has presented itself quite from nowhere. The God Strain has come to us, my dear Atheidrelle. Of all people, it has been our own sister Blackie we have to thank. There are D'Angelos now who bear that great power. All we must do is bring them here and all of the plans we thought were lost will flourish again. Leave everything to me. This house will live again. I will bring the Blanchard D'Angelos to The House of Duquesne. I will restore you to life. And together my sister, we will rule the world."

ABOUT THE AUTHOR

Micah House lives in Birmingham, Alabama with his husband and son. He is a former columnist and has published two short stories, *Thursie* and *The Three Mrs. Rogers*. His first novel, *The Blanchard Witches of Daihmler County*, was the first in the Blanchard Witches series. This novel, *Stitches in Times*, is the third book in the ongoing series.

BOOK 4 SYNOPSIS

THE BLANCHARD WITCHES

THE HOUSE OF DUQUESNE

Artemis Blanchard is doing her best to make the newest members of the family feel a part of the fold, but new dangers are presenting themselves in every direction. Atheidrelle Obreiggon may be dead, but the Blanchards are not safe from her family's evil. Her brother Thaddeuss D'Angelo is uncharacteristically interested Blackie's children. He wants the power of The God Strain, and he will do anything to acquire it. The Blanchards will have to fight the battle of their lives on enemy territory as they descend upon the D'Angelo family stronghold. Welcome to *The House of Duquesne*. Here unfathomable secrets will be exposed as the balance between good and evil will come to a head beneath its roof.

Milton Keynes UK
Ingram Content Group UK Ltd.
UKHW020639310723
426074UK00019B/1438